EVERYTHING IS ORI

Paul Serge Forest

EVERYTHING IS ORI

Translated from the French by
David Warriner

QC FICTION

Revision: Peter McCambridge
Proofreading: Ann Marie Boulanger, Elizabeth West
Book design: Folio infographie
Cover & logo: Maison 1608 by Solisco
Fiction editor: Peter McCambridge

Originally published under the title *Tout est ori*
by VLB éditeur, 2021 (Montréal, Québec)

ISBN 978-1-77186-317-9 pbk
ISBN 978-1-77186-318-6 epub
ISBN 978-1-77186-319-3 pdf

Legal Deposit, 2nd quarter 2023
Bibliothèque et Archives nationales du Québec
Library and Archives Canada

Published by QC Fiction, an imprint of Baraka Books
Printed and bound in Québec

TRADE DISTRIBUTION & RETURNS
Canada - UTP Distribution: UTPdistribution.com
United States & World - Independent Publishers Group: IPGbook.com

We acknowledge the financial support for translation and promotion of the Société de développement des entreprises culturelles (SODEC), the Government of Québec tax credit for book publishing administered by SODEC and the Government of Canada.

Société de développement des entreprises culturelles
Québec

Financé par le gouvernement du Canada
Funded by the Government of Canada | Canada

1

Laurie Lelarge reacts

It was sometime between Pentecost and Trinity Sunday, somewhere between the rivers named after Pentecost and the Trinity. Every year, once or twice during the week it lasted, Rogatien Lelarge found his awareness of this spatiotemporal coincidence refreshed, saw it was enough of an eye-opener to make him smile just like that, and kept it to himself. The two holidays weren't far apart on the liturgical calendar, like the two rivers on Highway 138. The names things were given, he had come to think, were like the inside jokes of our ancestors, passed down to tell us their truths. Confiding, conspiring. You either got 'em, or you didn't.

If Rogatien had let his granddaughter Laurie grow a bit older before he kicked the bucket, he could have told her all about religious holidays and rivers. He could have told her there's no better season to be alive in this place when you're in the business of molluscs and crustaceans: you've shifted all the big hauls you landed in May, the wind is fresh, the profits are sizable, and the beer is good. There's nothing to do but sit back and relax on the veranda, and wait for summer.

In the village of Baie-Trinité, there was only one building bigger than Rogatien's house: Rogatien's processing plant. The house flaunted its long facade to the Saint Lawrence, at the precise point where the river shows it means business and begins to offer vistas of endless blue. It was hewn from stone and had four gable dormers in its sloping roof. A covered wooden veranda formed a belt around it that wouldn't quite buckle. Out front was a cold stretch of beach where you were almost always sure to be alone. That year, the government would decide to make it a listed heritage building, a month after Rogatien's death, just to piss everyone off. For once, at least, it was the Ministry of Culture, and not those fuckers at Fisheries and Oceans.

But for now, the whole Lelarge family was out on the veranda drinking Molson Ex or Orange Crush. It was their traditional seafood party number three, the one with, usually, the slimmest pickings of crab, but not that year. There was plenty to go around. The Lelarges, after some debate and a vote, had set up the propane burner on the veranda to make sure the kids didn't mess around with it, even though, a minority argued, it might be a fire hazard. Rogatien was feeding Player's to the cancer lurking in his left lung. Suzanne, his daughter, was smoking Du Mauriers. Réginald, his youngest son, known to everyone as Saturn outside the family fold, would rather have had the burner farther away so he could smoke his weed on the sly. Robert, the firstborn son, smoked from time to time, but not so much since his second daughter had been born. His face was cold and his hair, gelled.

They were all going on about the fishing that spring (good), the season the Habs were having (what do you expect when your best player is Martin Rucinsky?), the girls' grades at school (excellent), the fall of the Nasdaq (Robert ended up taking a bit of a beating; the others thought it was a crazy idea to invest in the internet), and before the talk turned to the company's future (uncertain), Rogatien got up to put a pot of clams on to boil with Saturn. The wind was fresh. The buds were holding back their blossoms. A billow of salty steam escaped when they lifted the lid to put the shells on the burner. The light still belonged to winter. It was spreading itself thinly over the fine sand of the shore, mere metres away from the veranda.

Earlier, the young sisters Florence and Laurie had been warbling cheerily at live crabs in an attempt to goad them into a battle of skill and agility. It had not gone as well as it had at seafood party number two. Now keeping a lower profile, Florence was reading a book about reptiles. Laurie was getting pretty much all the others to shell her shrimp. At one point, there was a flash of consternation in her eyes, all of a sudden, as if she had touched on some transcendent reality that had thus far escaped her. She looked France, her mother, straight in the eye and asked quite the question.

"Mama, why do we call this seafood? It's food for people, not the sea."

"That's just what it's called, Laurie. It's an expression," France replied, knowing full well this wasn't going to cut the mustard.

"Laurie! Laurie!" her uncle Saturn cried. "I'll tell you."

But just as he was about to tell her, he realized his long, black frizz of heavy-metal hair was dangling in the clam water, and instead he cursed.

"Réginald! The kids!" Suzanne piped up in her signature tone, a patented blend of gentle and firm. "No, Laurie, seafood means molluscs, or crustaceans."

Laurie, a five-year-old redhead quiet and studious by nature but whose slightest spark of curiosity would ignite a fire of persistence, gave Suzanne a hazy look. In the pupil of her niece's eye, Suzanne saw the haze opacify, thicken, become lactescent, digressive almost. That boded well. Whatever came of it, she'd rather answer that question than last year's: "Why are you fat, Auntie Suzanne?"

The little one spoke up first: "What's a crustacean?"

Her older sister Florence, black hair, dark complexion, nine years old, looked up from her book about reptiles to answer in the way of the wacky zoologist they often watched on television. Her impression fell flat and drew a brief stare. She would have blushed, had it not been for her complexion.

"A crustacean is an arthropod. Like an insect. It's a bug that comes from the sea, one you can eat."

"But we eat fish from the sea too. And fish aren't bugs." Laurie wasn't about to let them swim off the hook.

"You're right, Laurie. Fish aren't bugs," Saturn clarified helpfully.

"Seafood is food for people. It's an offering from the sea," Suzanne added, always ready to bring a spiritual dimension to any question. "It's our reward for the sea's work."

It still wasn't clear to the little one, whose face was like a storm brewing.

"Seafood is food from the sea, for people, Laurie. That's all you need to know. Now off you go, it's time you played with those crabs again." Robert put his foot down, a father fast losing patience, before complaining, to no one in particular, that his Molson Ex was getting warm. It was better cold.

Later, he would latch on to wine as he went the way of the newly moneyed.

Laurie raised her two little fists. A curious sound—slurpy, yet silky—curtailed her wailing. She turned to see its source: Rogatien.

"What are you doing, Grandpa?"

"I'm savouring the seeds in my shrimp," regaled her grandfather.

When the time came to suck shrimp eggs, the Lelarges were divided into two camps: Rogatien and Réginald would indulge shamelessly in the salty delight of such a plentiful burst, while Suzanne and Robert couldn't stomach the thought of it—although, when push came to shove, it was really just a matter of twisting Suzanne's arm.

"The seeds?" Laurie fizzed, taking a step toward her grandfather.

"Yes, look here, the shrimp's belly is full of seeds!"

"Wow! Like a fruit. Like the seeds in an apple. Do mussels have seeds too?"

"No. Shrimp are the fruit of the sea because they have seeds. Mussels are the fruit of the sea because they grow in the seaweed."

"What about lobsters?"

"Let me ask you a question, all right?"

"Okay," Laurie nodded, not taking her eyes off the gutted shrimp.

"Have you ever eaten seaweed?"

"Yuck! No!"

"Seaweed is the vegetable of the sea, but we don't eat it. Seafood, that's the fruit of the sea, and it's good to eat. It's yummy, and a little bit sweet."

France found all this quite endearing. Florence preferred to read about reptiles. Saturn went to fetch the clams that were already a touch overdone. Suzanne lit another Du Maurier with a dramatic flourish. Robert let them get on with it. Laurie would soon run out of food for thought.

"And what about fish? Fish are tasty too."

"Yes, but there aren't any families that get together to have a fish party."

Rogatien paused to take a drag of his Player's. And pretended not to blow the smoke in Laurie's face.

"Grandpa?"

"Yes?"

"Can I have a taste of the shrimp seeds too?"

Robert would have told her the eggs were unfit for human consumption if she had asked him the same question in his own home, but he wasn't. Beside him, France was on the brink of tears. Oblivious to the beauty of the moment, Robert grimaced as he swallowed the warm dregs of his Molson Ex. Réginald plonked the pot of clams down on the patio table and announced they were ready.

"Don't do it, Laurie," Florence warned, too late.

This instant would reveal something deep inside Laurie, but not only that. Certainties as to the edibility of things, taken for granted by the Lelarges, suddenly began to falter. Parallel conversations stopped in their tracks. All that could be heard was the growl of lobster trawlers returning to the wharf nearby. Too caught up in this moment of truth, everyone watched Laurie bring the open carapace to her mouth, suck hard, wipe a hand across her lips, chew a bit, then swallow.

"Well, Laurie?" Rogatien broached; no one else could have.

Laurie didn't say a thing. She started to go round in circles. People were waiting for a response, be it a smile or a bout of vomiting. Saturn and Florence were the first to realize something was amiss. Afterwards, the others would say it was as if they were in a trance, waiting for a clear verdict. Saturn dropped his clam on the veranda. It shattered and he uttered a flabbergasted "Woah!" followed by a fearful "Ho-ly!" and a terrified "Fuck!" Florence sprang up and seized her little sister by the shoulders. She gave her a shake or three and asked if she was all right. No. She was not all right. Laurie coughed a bit and everyone turned pale, but not half as much as her. Rogatien gave her a pointless slap on the back. France began to scream "Laurie!" over and over. "Laurie!" "Laurie!" Robert went down on his knees in front of his daughter. He saw the scary little scarlet spots breaking out around her mouth. Then Laurie's neck flushed crimson before it was peppered in white blotches.

"Laurie! Laurie! Open your mouth!" said Robert, in the calm but firm voice it is customary to adopt in an emergency, before adding: "Open your mouth if you can hear me!"

Laurie complied. Her blued tongue quivered. Like a bloated capelin on the foreshore, Rogatien would add whenever he told fishermen the story in what few months he had left to live.

Looming over Laurie's tongue was a red lump as big as a cherry; it was her uvula.

"Go call an ambulance, Réginald, and fast," Robert ordered.

Réginald failed to respond.

"Saturn! I'm talking to you! Go call an ambulance. And Dad, go see if you can find Fortin!"

It was the first time anyone in the family had called him Saturn. As for Rogatien, he usually knew where he could find Fortin, the village doctor and semi-professional ornithologist. And so, he went off in his pickup truck with the horn he used to call the moose; he was going to use it to rouse the doctor. Florence and France were panicking in each other's arms. Florence was looking, and France wasn't. Laurie's breathing started to whistle like a kettle. Suzanne warbled a mournful throat-song to open the successive doors of the afterlife for a new angel, but would later insist she had been convinced from beginning to end that the little one would pull through.

When they arrived with a shot of adrenalin for Laurie, the paramedics couldn't help but wonder, as they laid eyes on Saturn, whether she was the only one in need of it.

Like any delicacy, seafood has more than one way of killing you, but the Lelarges had never really given that much thought. Until then, they'd always blamed the vomiting on the booze the night before.

2

Business

That fall, the doctor had to show Rogatien an X-ray of his cancer before he would finally believe it. He was just getting ready to go on his annual trip. Matane, Gaspé, Moncton, Halifax, Boston, Montreal, Quebec City: the agenda hadn't changed in nearly forty years. He would get back in time for the holidays and then head off again to winter in Florida, where he owned four classy apartment buildings around a shuffleboard court and a house some distance away, on the oceanfront. He was no stranger to the whims of a travelling salesman. No one knew—or dared to imagine—how he filled the evenings on his autumnal tour. When anyone asked why he was going away, he simply said it was for work, to which he referred with loving pride as "business." But that year, he wouldn't be going anywhere.

He started coughing around Thanksgiving. He had wanted to set off around All Saints' Day, despite having lost around sixty pounds since the summer and despite the constant chills he was having (and no, they weren't just a few little shivers). Suzanne had tried to talk him into going to see Doctor Fortin or going out to some public place or other where he might run into him "on the off chance," but, for as long as she had been grown-up, the relationship between Rogatien and his daughter had hinged on a reciprocal disobedience. It had fallen on Suzanne to persuade France to persuade Robert, who was supposed to be driving his father to the airport in Baie-Comeau. When he saw him step out of his house, a skeleton in a hat with a little suitcase, he didn't think twice about doing what his sister and his wife had asked, and drove him straight to the hospital.

"You see, Mr. Lelarge, everywhere there are these little lines..." the young doctor pointed out. "That's healthy lung."

"Hmm," went Rogatien in front of the light box, through his tubes.

"Here, the black bit, that's the part of your left lung that's collapsed."

"And that big grey lump, I presume that's my death in the flesh?"

That threw the doctor for a second or two.

"Well, that's the bulk of your cancer," she said. "But you can see there are bits all over your lungs as well..."

Rogatien was still traumatized after Laurie's reaction during seafood party number three, as was everyone in the family, for that matter. He remembered saying in those two hours of uncertainty, when her throat was all puffed up, that being the eldest it was his time to die, not the kids', for Chrissake. And he had not been the only one to come to that conclusion, which was now catching up with him. With barely three litres of breath left in him, he told Laurie not to take a bite of the club sandwich—it was chicken, but still—that sat unfinished in his hospital room. To Florence, he said go to business school; to Robert, you'll be happy with the will; to Suzanne, get married—but, with a tender smile, there was no rush; to Réginald, something no one ever found out.

Rogatien died very quickly, happy, in the end, with the sequence of events. Suzanne insisted on bathing the emaciated corpse herself. She refused to go to the church funeral, preferring to stay home to shave her head and sing from her belly. A clear memory of those few days would stay with Florence her whole life long; for Laurie, only a flash would survive: Suzanne standing at the cold buffet table, bald, in a horrendous dress.

A subarctic winter descended on Baie-Trinité in the wake of Rogatien's death. In Baie-Trinité, it seems, winter makes a meal of colour. When it's really cold, the sun comes out, the overabundant snow and the ice on the river spread it everywhere, and everything turns white like the inside of a light bulb. Otherwise, the sky is overcast and the sun doesn't have the strength to break through. Light is rare. The ice stays white, but the river and the conifers turn black and everything with any sparkle in other seasons can only express itself in greyscale. As a young adult, Laurie would take two photographs of Baie-Trinité in the winter, one on colour film and the other on black and white. Both images turned out absolutely identical.

People weren't afraid to say, it worked out pretty well that Rogatien died at the beginning of the winter. The fishermen wouldn't be back before the end of March. Robert was scared they'd play hardball now the old man's authority had turned to ashes along with the rest of him.

All his life Rogatien had been a direct man and so the assumption was that his will would follow suit, but as they left the notary's office Robert, Réginald, and Suzanne figured their father must have paid by the word, it was that short. None of them would forget the preamble: "Since there has to be a boss..." A handful of words, and that was settled. There had to be a boss. During his lifetime Rogatien had often said, evasively, his estate would be settled naturally and fairly. He always said "naturally" before he said "fairly" whenever he talked about it. Since there had to be a boss, then, the eldest, Robert, inherited fifty-one percent of Lelarge Fisheries. Suzanne got the house in Florida and the real estate division Lelarge of Florida, Rogatien's personal effects, and twenty-four and a half percent of the Fisheries. Réginald, the youngest, found himself the owner of a further twenty-four and a half percent and the house in Baie-Trinité, but on the condition he went into rehab. The will didn't say the rehab had to work.

Accountants in Quebec City worked out that the three Lelarge siblings could get somewhere between twelve and fifteen million for all that. The processing plant alone must have been worth five million. A third of the population of Baie-Trinité worked there from mid-March to the end of November. In the winter, most of them claimed unemployment and went off ski-dooing in the woods. Things got very quiet in the village.

It wasn't like them, but the Lelarges didn't speak much for a few weeks. They knew that they would see one another again, that they would have more numbered seafood parties, that nothing had been broken. But they needed a season. It was mainly Émilien who consoled them. Émilien was the manager of the Baie-Trinité credit union. He had often wondered if those three knew that place only existed to lend their money to the village.

After the breaking of the seal, they each went their own way in a dusting of snow.

Saturn went off to rehab, which he insisted on calling his "me-hab." Between hot tubs and full-body mud masks, between support groups that had you sit in a circle and spill your guts and workshops that had you stand on a chair and fall into the others' arms, he gained confidence and slowly detoxed. That all went down in the Eastern Townships. There were quite a few drug addicts from respectable families there, and a handful of chefs from swanky restaurants who had gone to cure their alcohol addiction. He came out sober, his hair just as long, and more of a businessman than ever. Then he had the unfortunate idea of going to celebrate in Jamaica.

Suzanne, not that she was known for her sense of rhythm, went to India for two months to play the tabla drums with a guru as cliché as they come. She brought back a tam-tam Laurie was told not to touch, on the pretext that it was for making the gods dance. Florence, meanwhile, was beginning to approach her aunt's eccentricities the way her parents did: with an open mind that could easily swing shut.

Robert tried to explain to his two daughters what was happening.

"What's a see-ee-oh?" Laurie frowned.

"A CEO is a boss. That means I'm the boss of Lelarge Fisheries now."

"So that means you get to keep the giant crabs?" Florence deduced.

"Er ... yes ... if I like."

"But you know I'm allergic!" her sister complained.

"It means that we're the ones who are going to pay the fishermen now, like Grandpa did before," Florence clarified, always prepared to seize a teaching opportunity.

"It's not really like that," Robert nuanced. "It's the company that pays the fishermen."

The concept of a legal entity laboriously made its way into the girls' minds. Robert, who was less and less inclined to keep a lid on his fantasies of limitless growth, could already picture them as heiresses to a global seafood empire. They were going to have to learn English, good manners, and how to stand up for themselves.

When he broached the subject with her, France suggested that they take a business trip as a family. She was growing warier of the whims of a travelling salesman.

At spring break, they took off for Matane, Gaspé, Moncton, Halifax, Boston, and Quebec City. Everywhere, Robert announced the advent of an online platform for negotiating the renewal of supply contracts. He gave all the bigwigs his personal cellphone number: 418-555-0149 and his email: robert.lelarge.ceo@lelargefisheries.ca. He would have preferred @lelarge.ca, but the domain name had already been snapped up by a pickle tycoon. In the Massachusetts snow, Laurie got to play with Howie, the son of the vice president of procurement for the Red Lobster restaurant chain. She was picking up English like it was contagious, making snow forts and planting carrots in snowmen. France and Robert couldn't believe it. Skating on the frozen lake, Florence had her first kiss from Howie's big brother, Cameron. He was as blond as the beach in Baie-Trinité, and just as rough around the edges.

3

Bars and measures

Between the church and the plant, Baie-Trinité had an elementary school where the Lelarges had long laid down the law. The school was named Saint Mary the Immaculate. It had burned to the ground some two or three years earlier.

France Brault had become the school principal when Florence was nearly four years old. She was pregnant with Laurie at the time. She didn't have a lot to manage: three classes of ten students, one teacher for each class—and a fourth guy, a wearer of many hats who taught English (his first language), music (he sang off-key, but he did all right on the xylophone and knew his way around bars and measures, so to speak), and gym class (all that took was a lot of patience and a little sadism). France also had to oversee maintenance for the building, wooden from top to bottom, with a bell tower: an old, oversized schoolhouse, overrun with growths to which the school board preferred to turn a blind eye.

France fretted about her children's education before they were even born. Quebec City born and bred as she was, the lack of a decent school in Baie-Trinité was something that had worried her since the day she moved there. The nearest private elementary school was in Chicoutimi, a five-hour drive away. Boarding schools didn't take children under ten and that was far too heart-wrenching a solution anyway. She had been relieved to get the job as principal of St. Mary's. In the beginning, she demanded accountability daily, mouth pursed with insistence, smart little frames perched on her nose, hair in a no-nonsense bun. Her ever-expanding belly threatened to burst her black turtleneck at the seams. Laurie was a big baby.

Janie, Jacqueline, and Magella, the three teachers, knew all too well that France had come there to keep an eye on her kids and that they wouldn't have it easy when her eldest started school. Whenever they went out for a smoke together, Magella would curse, Jacqueline would egg her on, and Janie, the youngest by far, would listen approvingly. Magella would go on and on about young Florence—with her dark complexion, raven hair, and that redhead little sister of hers—saying her mother must have had a fling. They had taken their concerns to the union, but that didn't do much good. As for James, the teacher who wore many hats, he didn't give a crap. He was a good friend of Saturn's.

Florence had started kindergarten with Jacqueline and everything had gone all right in the end. She was a polite and conscientious little girl, who already knew how to read. She would share toys, even when it was her turn to choose first and she picked the Playmobil castle. She would call out her classmates who disobeyed the teacher's rules with a rigour that sometimes had to be tempered. More than anything else, she knew her place. In grade three, she was given permission to create a website for the school, so that she wouldn't get too bored in class. France had put someone who worked in communications for the Fisheries on it. Florence, having proclaimed herself multimedia content editor, wrote several pieces for the site as well as posting her classmates' written homework assignments.

A short time later, Laurie started kindergarten and showed all the qualities of her sister, with a bright red head of hair to top it all off. Her voracious curiosity took some channelling, but there was a little library for that, replenished just before she got there thanks to an anonymous donation. Any lingering misgivings the teachers had about the Lelarge girls soon went away: they were adorable and well-mannered, and it didn't show in the slightest that their parents were millionaires. France thought of the three teachers as friends. She would sometimes go clam-digging with them. She was now only working the two days a week that were in her contract.

Then one fine Saturday Laurie became allergic to seafood and the shit hit the fan good and proper.

The staff at the school had to devote an entire professional development day to a first-aid course. The instructor went on and on about anaphylactic shock and how to use an EpiPen. There was a needle and a dummy for them to practise on. They all lined up to pump a shot into its rubber thigh. In case of emergency, the instructor said, the needle was long and strong enough to go through a pair of jeans. Even James winced. When the course was done, France stepped in to explain the school board's new policy on food allergies. Seafood was being banned all over the place. Anyone eating it at home had to wash their clothes in hot water before wearing them in class. All students and staff were required to wash their hands when they got to school—it would have been awkward to ask only those close to the plant workers to do so.

In the weeks that followed, France walked Laurie every day to the door of her kindergarten classroom, where she gave her a kiss on the forehead, in front of everyone. She would then roam around the school all morning, her eyes peeled for any breaches of her food allergy policy.

"Miss Janie," Laurie said to her teacher one day before recess, "I'm allergic to seafood. If I eat any, someone has to jab me with the EpiPen, or else I'll die like the other day."

"But you're not dead, Laurie!"

"I came back, but everything went white, or clear, or I don't know. But Jesus wasn't there."

Miss Janie, touched, replied with tenderness.

"Hmm, Laurie, it seems serious, what you're saying. Does it make you afraid?"

"No, no."

"There's no need to be afraid, Laurie. We're taking care of your allergy."

Laurie gave her a funny, almost stifled, kind of smile.

The next day was when Miss Janie saw the first graffiti, scrawled in red felt pen on the wall: "Maxime smelz [sic]." She grabbed a gallon of white paint to cover up the words and didn't make a stink about it until she found two more examples the following week: "Karine is cross eyed" and "Keven is poor." When Miss Janie wanted to forbid her from using felt-tip markers, Laurie explained that her friends couldn't understand what she was writing because they didn't know how to read. She wasn't wrong.

Three days later, Florence wrote on her blog about the porcupine problem at school: they would always dump their excrement at the foot of the walls and their non-stop gnawing was making it hard for the students to concentrate, as well as weakening the foundations. She wasn't wrong either.

Miss Janie, a girl from the village who was fresh out of university, had a word with Jacqueline and asked her not to tell anyone about it. Jacqueline took it upon herself to put everything right. The union didn't want to get involved, so Jacqueline found herself in France's office, without Janie.

"What you're telling me, never happened," France denied, with obsession.

"But Florence is the only one who can make changes to the website."

"No."

"And Laurie is the only kid in kindergarten who can write!"

"It was another student who did that, most likely little Maxime..."

"You're suggesting that Maxime himself wrote that he smells?" Jacqueline didn't dare think.

"If you knew what I know about Janie, you'd see everything she's told you differently," France fudged.

The family took a little trip at spring break, which didn't fix a thing. Florence and Laurie were nothing but trouble when they got back. They said naughty words in James's English classes. *Fuck* this. *Fuck* that. Miss Janie and Miss Jacqueline stopped washing their hands and were given a written warning. A union rep and a school board superintendent made the trip from Baie-Comeau to have a word with France. Trussing up her bun, France explained that the girls' grandfather had just died, that it was a difficult time for the family. She was wearing square-rimmed glasses back then—that was the fashion in the city—and everything she said was just as sharp. The glasses hardened her jaw. Her voice threatened to break. The next day she got an email from the school board superintendent. It suggested that she take some time off: not that she was wrong, not that there was anything to reproach her, but it would be better that way. France's sole response was to send a photo of Miss Janie taken in a bar in Baie-Comeau. One of the young teacher's nipples had spilled out of her cleavage, her eyes wore a blank stare, and she had a twenty-dollar bill halfway up her nose. The faces of Saturn and James, who were standing beside her in the photo, had been blurred. No one learned much for the remainder of that year at St. Mary's.

Summer came back around and the vacation with the girls gave France more than one occasion to regret her ploy. One teary night of lucidity, she told Robert everything, and he came down like a tonne of bricks on his children. There was no more swimming, no TV, no video games, and no computer time for the rest of the summer. Not so much as a walk in the woods. Books were the only thing they were allowed. And the hammock would not be strung up again. In August, Robert had to fire Miss Janie's boyfriend: he had been caught on CCTV filling his pockets with periwinkles. To settle the problem of the girls once and for all, Robert went to see Madame Noëlla, formerly Sister Marie-Ange, to entice her out of retirement, armed with an envelope to make his case. Miss Janie didn't have the seniority to be rehired that year, it seemed.

Three days in to grade one, Laurie, happy to be back in class after a summer of reading and already terrified by the thought of displeasing Madame Noëlla, opened her desk: it was filled with water and cooked fall shrimp. Three big lobsters were crawling over the shrimp, slowly devouring them. The good sister was writing the alphabet on the board. She had not ruled out the prospect of corporal punishment. In complete silence, Laurie pushed her chair back a little, pulled her EpiPen out of its little case, and injected herself. The adrenalin went to her head so quickly she didn't even feel the needle. Her pupils dilated and all she could see was white light. Her heart began to beat so fast it was in her throat. She started to sweat buckets and puked a great jet of orange juice and oatmeal. Madame Noëlla turned around. Laurie still had the needle of the EpiPen planted in her thigh.

At the hospital in Baie-Comeau, the pediatrician played her a VHS cassette entitled *The EpiPen: What You Need to Know*. Laurie came to the realization herself that it had perhaps been a little premature that time.

A classmate had played a rotten trick on her, the police officers found. But the memory of that vomiting was strong, and while pretending she was absorbed in a book, Laurie would often read too much into the paranoid versions of events that France and Robert were hashing out in the next room.

It was starting to get a bit cold and the three or four deciduous trees enclaved by the mass of conifers around the bay were yellowing, but in their woollen pullovers and rubber boots, Florence and Laurie could still make sandcastles on the beach. A cat in the habit of prowling for crab sidled up to them.

"Whose cat is that? Is it Miss Janie's?" Laurie recognized.

"Yes. It's the only calico cat in Baie-Trinité."

"What do you think will happen if I jab it with my EpiPen?"

"I dunno ... can cats be allergic?" her big sister failed to prevent.

"I think they're allergic to dogs ... and maybe to other cats sometimes," Laurie reasoned with a glint of perversion in her eye.

Such was the expression of her budding love for paradox.

"Maybe it'll start to like dogs. Here, kitty, kitty!"

Florence began to whistle to call it over. She managed to lure it with the shell a crab had shed. Then she scooped it up and held its neck tight in the crook of her elbow while Laurie prepared the syringe. Laurie targeted the fleshy part of the thigh. Electrified by the injection, the cat tore off at an unreal pace, like a comet with a mostly brown tail, disappearing into a clump of eelgrass.

Not long after, a sly stroke of arrhythmia finished it off, then the next tide came in and served it up to a shroud of urchins and starfish, but all of that would have been news to Laurie and Florence.

Janie and that boyfriend of hers cashed their unemployment cheques for another month or two, then they moved to the suburbs of Quebec City. Their bridges were burned in Baie-Trinité.

First intermission

the clam

No one calls these things bivalves. For some, they're steamers, and for others, they're softshells. When all's said and done, they're just clams, that's what they call them in New England. In Latin, they go by *Mya arenaria*, and with a name like that, you might think they were a thing of beauty from the Eastern Bloc, a women's tennis champion perhaps. On the outside, they're dressed in white, just like at Wimbledon. On the inside, they're molluscs, with everything that entails.

In these parts, there was a vulgar meaning to the word clam, not the same as the one that went with the word for mussel. On the North Shore, a *clam* was any glob of mucus, coughed up or spit out, in contexts where the word phlegm wasn't quite strong enough. Horking up a good load from their oropharynges before spitting in the schoolyard, the little boys had a way of warning Laurie: "Whoa, check out that clam." Laurie pretended to be disgusted, but would turn around all the same, out of a curiosity for fluids, to eyeball the thickness of the stuff. In the first few months, she played up her seafood allergy, but soon came to see the meanings were different. Likewise, Rogatien, not one to complain, found the word made a handy container for his cancer: "Some of these fricking clams I get," he would observe in confidence, "I could swear there's little bits of lung in there."

You don't fish for clams, you harvest them. On the foreshore, at low tide. Anyone with an eye for it can't miss the little holes in the wet sand. That's the way clams breathe. All you have to do is take a spade, shovel a bit of sand away, and there they are. You can fill a bucket fast.

To make things easy, clams on the North Shore are a pure white. Elsewhere, they might be a purply-grey. On the matter of a woman's derriere, Gainsbourg sang that it was a thing of beauty on the outside, but everyone knew what it did on the inside. When it comes to clams, no one knows. It's hard to imagine spending your life inside a shell with no eyes, then end up eaten by a starfish.

The life of a clam hinges on filtration: it draws in and expels water all day long, taking pains to keep in its digestive system any animalcules (essentially plankton) passing in the current.

That ability filters down to cause one heck of a clamour when harvest time comes around. Before Laurie got lumbered with her allergy, the Lelarges would go clamming together as a family, as soon as some of the snow had melted on the beach. It was a bit of fun, and it was a tradition. "Put your rubber boots on, Laurie, we're going clamming," France would beckon. That meant winter was on its way out. Laurie found it highly amusing to spot the little breathing holes on the foreshore. She would point them out, Robert would dig, and because he was too stiff to bend down, it was Laurie who would pick up the clam. She had always done it, but not before the age of five did she find herself on the receiving end of the mollusc's defensive reflex. She had just picked one up and still had it in her hands when it schlepped out its siphon, a tube as long as itself, and expelled a powerful jet of transparent liquid. "It just did a pee-pee!" Laurie screamed and started crying.

"I want to go wash it off," she insisted.

"Laurie! Quit whining! It's not pee-pee, it's water," Robert tempered.

"No, I saw it, it came out of its prick," Laurie protested, between two heavy sobs.

"What kind of word is that, Laurie?"

"I want to go wash it off."

"The water didn't go through your snowsuit."

"I want to take off my snowsuit!"

More often than not, the Lelarges ate their clams steamed. The sinewy siphon retracts as it cooks. After the first harvest, France would make her annual chowder with the cooking water from the clams, their meat, some salted pork belly, onions, potatoes, a touch of celery, and a whole lot of milk.

After taking two baths, little Laurie came down to the kitchen. France was scooping the meat out of the shells.

"That clam I picked, Mama, was it a boy?"

"Yes, Laurie."

"He had a prick."

"What did your father say about that word? You're right. He had a penis."

"How do clams make babies? And what about that, there? Is that the clam's vulva?" Laurie really wanted to know, pointing at a fleshy part of the mollusc.

"No. It's not its vulva. And I think they do like humans do, the daddy clam puts his penis inside the mama clam."

"Does she have to open her shell, then?"

"I don't know, Laurie. Can't you have a look in Grandpa Rogatien's books to find out?"

You shouldn't drink water: fish fuck in it, or so the saying goes. In truth, the female clams lay their eggs in June and the males fertilize them when they pass by, ejaculating into the current. The eggs become larvae, then they grow a shell and latch on to the seabed in shallow waters. But once you mistake a siphon for a penis, you might imagine all kinds of strange things.

Lelarge Fisheries sold clams in bulk as well as two- and five-pound bags.

4

From Gagarin's point of view

They knew one another. They knew one another in the sense that their paths went farther back than they let on, and that those origins, the history swept under the rug in their dealings, morally defined each in the other's eyes.

In their youth, Robert Lelarge and Frédéric Goyette had both played on the line for their respective high school football teams. Lelarge was the centre for Bay Secondary in Baie-Comeau and Goyette played defensive tackle for Manikoutai High in Sept-Îles. They faced off against one another on the line of scrimmage at the regional final. Stories like these are always hard to tell without taking sides, but reportedly the referee was summoned by the authorities to have his eyes examined after the game; he refused and was never seen again on the fields of the North Shore, nor anywhere else. Short-sighted he may have been, but the ref was not deaf, and he had doled out three penalties for taunting the opponent, despite no foul of the sort having been flagged all season. It also had to be said that those two, Lelarge and Goyette, knew one another in the sense that they had each separated the other's shoulder before. Then there was the state of the field: bordering on the unplayable. The wind had blown the sand out of the long-jump pit and onto the grass. The rest of the story was as tough to get to the bottom of as an old wound. You could only look at the scar and imagine the rest.

Once in the first half and maybe once in the second, Lelarge apparently grabbed hold of Goyette's face mask to stop him in his tracks. The ref didn't call the fifteen-yard penalty. The fourth time it happened, Lelarge apparently yanked on the mask before using it to fling his opponent to the ground. The ref kept his flag in his pocket. With nine seconds left to go, Sept-Îles were leading twenty-two to seventeen and Baie-Comeau were on the offensive, deep in Sept-Îles territory. Robert Lelarge took the ball. They needed a touchdown. The quarterback, a tall, blond future mayor of Baie-Comeau, moved into place behind him. Up ahead, on the line of scrimmage, was Goyette.

"Going after my face mask again, are you, Lelarge?"

"Shut your fucking trap," Robert roared.

"Your sister Suzanne showed me her snatch on the beach the other day. Smelled like rotten scallops," Goyette purred, pleased to see his research into the family paying dividends.

"Red. Forty-three. Black. Twenty-two. F. Ka-boom. Hut! Hut! Hut!" the quarterback interrupted.

Lelarge put the ball in the quarterback's hands. Then he looked up to block Goyette, who threw a fistful of sand right in his face. Goyette tackled him hard. A linebacker nicknamed The Cat pounced on the opening to charge at the future mayor. Sept-Îles won the game, as far as anyone knows.

Robert Lelarge's path was paved: he would go on to do his bachelor's in business administration at Laval University, meet an easily impressionable girl from Quebec City, and return to work for his father as vice president of something or other at the Fisheries. All of which might have been forgotten and left to dissolve in the glutinous mess of teenage humiliations.

Frédéric Goyette had a thin head of woolly brown hair and broad shoulders. Easily six foot four. He couldn't always shave his heavy beard and there was a strangeness to his face that he owed to a subtle asymmetry in his eyelid openings. It was easy to flounder in his gaze. Attempts to read his expressions almost always capsized in misinterpretation. After that football final, he took off to study guitar at the Conservatory in Rimouski, then signed up for a jazz guitar course at a university in Montreal. His avowed goal was to become first the Django, then the Pat Metheny of Quebec. He and his band came close to playing the opening act for UZEB, and those days had left him with the volatile memory of an ambition that knew no limits. But then, no one was into electric jazz anymore.

Frédéric used every last cent he had to scoot off to Scandinavia. He was in withdrawal from lots of things. In Tromsø, he met a girl from just down the road in Godbout by chance, and the vastness of the big, wide world by design. He had never loved like that before, not a girl, not a panorama: so surely, so profoundly, and at a pace his body took on like a slow swelling. The girl's name was Myriam. She ended up moving in with him, into his tiny apartment on Joliette Street in Montreal.

Not long after that, as they were slouched in front of a B-movie on TV, that same lassitude closed in on them.

"Fred?"

"What?"

Myriam's big blue eyes turned his way. He hadn't noticed she was crying.

"I miss the sea."

She was talking about the Saint Lawrence, where it turns to salt water.

"Yeah. Me too, I think. It's been a while ... the smell..." Goyette mused.

"... the seagulls ... are we breaking up?"

"No."

Frédéric enrolled in a biology program. After his degree, he was hired by the Canadian Food Inspection Agency. He bought a little house with Myriam, in Baie-Comeau, on Champlain Street. They kitted it out top to bottom at IKEA and put up a pole to fly the Quebec flag out front. By the time the Lelarge Fisheries board decided to invest in a new water treatment system, Frédéric had just been made regional director of inspections and, by extension, the local manager for the Canadian Shellfish Sanitation Program.

Robert had plenty of reasons to hate Frédéric Goyette: he looked like a fisherman but wasn't one, he played the guitar, he was a civil servant, he wasn't like him, he had once thrown sand in his eyes, and at any time he could outlaw the harvesting of shellfish around Baie-Trinité or bring production at the processing plant to a halt.

To those who called him a pen-pusher, Frédéric pointed three things out: paralytic shellfish poisoning, amnesic shellfish poisoning, and diarrhetic shellfish poisoning. As filters, shellfish accumulate everything shallow waters may contain. And nope, it ain't always pretty. Those toxins with unequivocal names could also be found in the digestive glands of lobsters and crabs, but if you asked Robert Lelarge, only a dumbass would eat that crap.

And Goyette had plenty of reasons to hate Robert too. He'd been born with a silver spoon in his mouth and did business the same way he played football: playing dirty when the ref wasn't looking. That said, he found Saturn and Suzanne pretty easy-going, and that cooled his jets.

Frédéric Goyette liked the very beginning of spring, when the season of reports and meetings ended and the time for inspections started, along with the fishing. He would pull on his blue jacket, start to neglect his beard again, sometimes clamber aboard the coast guard icebreaker and, the rest of the time, drive around in the pickup he used for work. His Volvo would stay in the parking lot at the Agency's offices in Baie-Comeau. His truck had an orange flashing light on top that he had never used. He went at a civil servant's speed, the drivers in his wake resorting to all kinds of dicey passing manoeuvres. Summer and winter alike, there was always a flask of espresso by his side.

The Esbjörn Svensson Trio's albums were often blasting at full volume when Goyette twisted and turned his way up and down Highway 138. He knew it by heart, the treacherous road that clung to the coast all the way to Franquelin before retreating inland around Godbout. Svensson's music seemed to be cut from the same emotional cloth as the 138. Now and then, there were big, booming stretches that burst into many a melody just as he was getting close to Baie-Trinité and everything turned to blue. He was sure that no one besides him listened to that stuff driving along the 138, and that was what he liked about the 138 and the North Shore too: you could make of them what you wanted.

When he rolled into Baie-Trinité, he would park his truck at the entrance to the wharf and, even though everyone recognized him, he spoke to no one and returned no smiles. Robert's daughters would giggle their way up to him whenever they were free. For a long time, he had known they found him handsome and it was a very guilty pleasure for him to see how they had blossomed from one year to the next. He would walk over to the plant and, before he got there, someone would always have let Robert, Saturn, or Suzanne know he was coming. He would have rather it had not been Robert. It was almost always Robert.

Robert had never been able to talk his father Rogatien into installing a shellfish purification system. His first decision, once his father's body had cooled, had been to get one put in by a process engineer Saturn had met in rehab. The system would allow Lelarge Fisheries to market whole Iceland scallops, complete with shell and coral: a high-end product with huge profit margins. They would also be able to boost clam production twentyfold—since the purification would open up areas deemed "lightly contaminated" by Goyette—and, why not, get back into mussel farming. It was a no-brainer for Robert, who had always wondered why his father had been dead set against the damned system.

Drawing up the plans and doing the market study, raising the capital, and allowing the time for the engineer to relapse had taken five years. The pools, filtration system, and recirculator had been installed over the winter. The bins had arrived in March. To purify shellfish, all you had to do was allow them to end their lives in clean seawater. That way, they excrete all the toxins from their natural environment and fill themselves with water that meets federal regulations for turbidity, temperature, salinity, and oxygen content. The last hurdle, before a hundred or so harvesters could supply the plant with lightly contaminated molluscs, was for Goyette to come sign off on the federal standards and issue a permit.

Frédéric went into the plant with Robert, who insisted on showing him around as if he'd never seen the place before. The new system occupied a whole corner of the building, over three floors. It could process twenty tonnes of shellfish a day, far fewer if they were scallops, because scallops, strong swimmers that they are, try to escape and need bigger bins. Everything was fine.

"Everything is fine. You'll just have to wait three weeks for the sample analysis."

"Excellent, Goyette," Robert replied, with the everlasting touch of sarcasm he saved for speaking to the man.

He liked to repeat his last name because it was less attractive than his own.

"Anyway, best of luck with your expansion. This for export, is it?" Goyette tried his luck.

"As if I would tell you!" Robert rebuffed.

"All right. I'll find out in due course. I'll call to give you the go-ahead when I get the results."

"Perfect, Goyette. I'll be waiting."

"Just one thing..."

There was a silence, just like at the end of the Columbo movies.

"I'll give you those permits," Goyette the inspector went on, "but on my way here I saw some harvesters, out past Pointe-à-Poulin. You know it's too contaminated out there."

"Nothing to do with me. Must be some locals. In any case, Pointe-à-Poulin's closed because of pollution, not because of toxins."

"You said something like that to me a couple of years ago, before we found those rotten scallops..."

The mere mention of rotten scallops always made Robert see red. He could feel the anger rising up from his chest to his teeth.

"But that's all done and dusted. Look at this machine of mine, it's a Cadillac!" he trumpeted, with a wave of the hand to his giant stainless steel ziggurat.

"Just to let you know we'll be keeping an eye on your bivalve mollusc production as it grows, such is our duty, eh?" Frédéric red-taped.

"Very well, Goyette. Say hi to the Queen for me!"

Most of their encounters ended that way, with Robert inviting him to give the Queen his regards. Every time, Goyette would turn around and go on his shit-stirring way.

5

The Moroccans

It took some moral and financial shit shovelling to build Suzanne's hobbit house. Everyone knew that, as soon as she got back from vacationing in Turkey, she wouldn't let go of her monumental plans, even though the bedrock of the hillsides here was nowhere near as soft as it was over there. There was only one contractor from the other side of the river willing to tackle the job. He had a freakish Dali-esque moustache and drove a red pickup sporting a pompous coat of arms on the wings, complete with a scroll bearing the slogan "Gotta blast it all." The architect seemed more down to earth. The whole thing took two years to build. Rather than see Suzanne sell her shares to an outsider, Robert pulled strings to have the company take out a mortgage for her, knowing full well it was a beyond stupid thing to do, since no one would ever want to buy a hobbit house in Baie-Trinité, except maybe the government someday to turn it into an interpretative centre about rocks or something. The budget exploded because of the dynamite.

The place was built on two levels. The main floor had a lounge that extended onto a terrace with a view over the bay. Upstairs, sixteen rooms as big as closets were devoted to just as many divinities, spirits, and shamans. All that brought many a curse to Robert's lips, but not in front of his daughters.

Saturn maintained Rogatien's ancestral home to the Ministry of Culture's standards and dreamed, when he got drunk with a Montreal chef he met in rehab, of turning it into the world's greatest seafood restaurant. Still, he preferred to live in his place, a gigantic hunting cabin that reeked of beer and seafood pizza, on Cléophas Lake with his buddies. The gigantic hydroponic setup in the basement stank the place up at first, but then Saturn figured out the ventilation. It was his own personal factory, catering to his needs and those of his friends and friends with benefits: it takes a lot of that stuff to distill into oil.

Even though board meetings with secretaries and minute-taking were theoretically held in the conference room at the plant, the big decisions were made around Robert's table at home. You could see the wharf right from the dining room and keep an eye on the boats unloading. Robert preferred to work alone and was already setting up a home base for himself on the top floor. He and France had bought their house a few days after their wedding. The parish priest, who had only just married them, had a fatal Ski-Doo accident and a locum priest was brought in to replace him. The diocese suggested that they buy the presbytery, without even putting it on the market, young and influential Catholics that they were. It was a three-storey house, poorly soundproofed, made of nothing but wood, which posed such an extreme fire risk they had it fitted out with sprinklers when the girls were born.

That Sunday, they had decided to bring some migrant workers in from an agency in Montreal to harvest the clams and mussels that would be going into the new purification system. It was either that or rehire employees they'd fired for stealing from the company.

"With the wages we pay them," Robert fumed, "they can afford to pay for their whelks. I can't believe Dad used to put up with it."

"He must have figured the stuff was theirs for the taking too, in a way," Saturn philosophized. "Anyway, we won't have that problem with the Moroccans: they don't eat seafood."

"Uncle Réginald, it's Jews who don't eat seafood. Moroccans are Muslim," Florence sighed from the room next door.

She had learned that in high school.

"I think she's right," Suzanne hastened to concede.

"Florence, mind your own beeswax," France disciplined from another, distant, room.

"If they eat any without paying, we'll send them back to Montreal. They're a dime a dozen where they come from," Robert ruled.

Suzanne looked at him with a sudden slackness in her lower jaw.

"...I mean, at the agency," Robert tagged on, insisting he wasn't racist and had never intended to imply otherwise: he had friends who were Muslims.

They hastily erected some dormitories. And made sure everything was just halal enough. The Moroccans arrived by bus on the first of April. Once kitted out with buckets, shovels, and rubber boots, all one hundred and five harvesters ventured onto the lightly contaminated mudflats around Baie-Trinité. At first people in the village thought it was a practical joke, but "the Moroccans" (in truth, there were a few Kabyle Algerians as well) were there to stay. Robert got a journalist from the local weekly rag to come write a piece about the workers' willingness to integrate, and this time she wasn't to mention, as she was in the habit of doing when she wrote about Lelarge Fisheries, that it was an advertorial. When they crossed paths with Laurie or Florence, the Moroccans would say "Hello, Miss," even though Robert had strictly forbidden them from speaking to his daughters.

Robert had never liked fishermen: their odour, their patois, that undecipherable innuendo between the teeth of an enigmatic smile. The only thing he didn't feel up to doing for the company, and so the only thing he hadn't insisted on taking care of himself, was dealing with them on a daily basis. He had left all that to Suzanne. He knew they would find that unsettling. He told Suzanne a price, and Suzanne ended up getting it. The fishermen had wheedled a way to profit from the death of the man they called "the boss" but the company hadn't lost a thing. To meet their demands, all they'd had to do was increase direct sales to Red Lobster. Soon, fishermen started competing for the privilege of selling to the Lelarges: with them, they were sure to offload their catches for a good price. Cap-Chat Seafood, on the other side of the river, went bust. The little processing plant in Gallix, too. New crews began to dock at the Baie-Trinité wharf. They came from as far away as Cloridorme.

Harvesting clams isn't a noble occupation like fishing. It's a gig for retirees with needy offspring, compulsive gamblers in remission; a lame way to make a few bucks; a little something under the table when everything else under there is invariably a tad sketchy too. Those who panhandled in town often wound up picking shellfish in Baie-Trinité. Before they installed the purification system, the Lelarges bought their clams the way scrap metal merchants came by their scrap metal. The wharf was the drop-off point. They would cover the cost of a commercial harvesting permit for anyone who brought in three hundred kilos.

The arrival of the Moroccans, who were paid a wage and given room and board to work in areas that were off limits to ordinary pickers because of light contamination, raised more than a few hackles. Everyone in Baie-Trinité knew someone who relied on mussels or clams to make ends meet. Word soon got around at Cécile's greasy spoon, Ti-Claude's bar, and the Fisheries plant, but Suzanne only cottoned on that trouble might be brewing when the two Serges gave her a piece of their mind.

Suzanne was down at the wharf when the two Serges showed up together. It was not a good omen. The first, Serge Cabana, was manoeuvring his lobster trawler and the second, Serge Berthelot, had brought in an impressive haul of whelks. Cabana, a hulk of a man, used to scare Laurie when she was little. People in the village would say he was the only lobster fisher who always had a whopper on his boat. Laurie would see him coming in his 3XL plaid jacket, with his unsteady gait on terra firma and his salt-and-pepper beard, and go hide before she laid eyes on his wind-worn face, the root cause of her fear. His nickname was Hercules. The other Serge, a skinny guy, inveterate smoker, and fisher of invertebrates, owed his moniker to the answer he gave when asked his name: the *e* was closer to an *a*; the *g* got caught in his throat and sounded more like an *h* voiced on the out-breath. *Sar'h* became the written form for this throat-clearing the sea folk had a knack for.

Sar'h and Hercules were among the few fishermen the employees at the plant knew. Most of the seafarers lived further down the coast, or out on the Gaspé Peninsula. Hercules and Sar'h lived smack dab in the middle of Baie-Trinité. Sar'h even had a brother, Louis Berthelot, who worked at the Fisheries. When the other fishermen tied up at the wharf, they would ask Suzanne or one of the dockers how the two Serges were doing and insist on getting the same prices as them.

"Hercules! Sar'h! It's not often we see you together! Big day out at sea! Fancy a little coffee? We've got a new cappuccino machine. Apparently for more than one you're supposed to say *cappuccini*. Weird, eh?"

Suzanne walked over toward them. She always wore ample dresses and, if the weather was on the cool side, a faded jean jacket under a sheepskin vest. Her big breasts would swing when she walked quickly. She had hooked more than one fisherman like that.

"Don't bother, Suzie!" Sar'h barked, between two puffs of Player's.

"We've got something serious to say to you," Hercules warned.

His voice sounded as if it were coming from a vast, echoing cathedral-like place inside him.

Suzanne watched as the two Serges lent the dockers a hand. Before they even sat down at the picnic table she had pulled over by the wharf, they insisted on immediate payment for their dues. Suzanne, even though she could smell a rat, was surprised by the hostility in their tone. She went in to print two cheques: fifteen thousand dollars for Hercules, two thousand for Sar'h. She lit a Du Maurier; Sar'h, a Player's with the butt of the last one; Hercules, not a thing. Sitting down, they told her about Lawrence Roy, a guy from Rivière-Pentecôte. Suzanne admitted she only knew him by name. He was in the habit of selling clams to the Lelarges, not a lot, but enough for him to go to the strip club. Anyway, Lawrence had just hung himself with the metal handle of his clam bucket in his brother's shed—for such a nice neck of the woods, the North Shore sure sees a lot of suicides. He did such a good job that, when his wife found him in a pool of blood, his bald head had rolled ten feet away from his body. Suzanne started to cry, a flood of unstoppable tears. Sar'h glanced at Hercules, who was telling the story, to say, go easy. But instead Hercules mustered the full force of his voice to bring the house down and make sure the message got through:

"When the boss snuffed it, we thought things would go to shit with Robert in charge. But so far, with you, things ain't been too bad. Unless you start treating us like flunkies, like you're doing with those fucking Moroccans, then all of a sudden, you know, the fishing might not be as good."

Sar'h placed a hand on Suzanne's shoulder when they got up to leave because she was crying; Hercules gave him grief for it on the way back to the wharf. The sun was setting over the land and turning the sky over the water pink. Soon, cobalt blue, the water would slip away into the night. Suzanne went back to her cave to tell Ganesh and Rogatien's everlasting spirit all about it.

Second intermission

the crab

When you're twelve years old, there are some words you just know are vulgar. Most often, they have something to do with an all-too-real bodily function you've yet to discover. These words are abstractly—and thus absolutely—vulgar. There's no definition for them, aside from crudeness. One of these words might just slip out at the dinner table and raise a few eyebrows. And so innocence slips away. Every new word learned carries a promise of grinding teeth. Vocabulary is eyed with suspicion. It might preclude the hazarding of a *phallus,* or a *sodomy*, into the conversation, but the dictionary can't cover all the bases.

That's how you come to see how every word can conceal its erotic potential in the paunch of an *a* or the appendage of a *p*, and how some numbers can do as much with their curves. Later on, the same goes for everything else in life. Laurie discovered this, thanks in part to that spidery and not particularly appetizing-looking crustacean, the crab. Lelarge Fisheries put two kinds of crab in cans.

The common crab, or rock crab, as the Americans call it, is built like a tank. Small, stocky, and incredibly strong. It won't hesitate, when trapped, to amputate one of its six stumpy little legs to get away. Its claws curve in on its big, ovoid carapace. In nature, like some holidaymakers, it buries itself in the sand up to its eyeballs. It only emerges from its hideout to claw at a scrap of dead bird or fall prey to a very much alive bird and end up dropped and smashed on a rock for food: it can be broken.

It takes no extra effort to catch these critters because they swarm all over lobster pots. They're the arthropod equivalent of weeds. It had never occurred to anyone to eat one until restaurateurs in Boston, then Montreal, expressed interest to Robert in 1999. Its earthy flavour, they said, reminded them of the crab they had tasted in Vietnam or Galicia. At first, Robert gave them a really good price, but demand quickly shot up. And since the fishermen had always thought of the common crab as a nuisance, the profit margins were enormous.

The other kind of crab—the one the Lelarges meant when they said "crab"—had the airs and graces of an international supermodel, all legs and claws. Fittingly, it's found around the world too, in subarctic conditions, all the way to the Sea of Japan. That's the snow crab. It's easier to catch in the spring, when it ventures into shallower waters to reproduce and comes within the clutches of inshore vessels. It's easily baited with mackerel, but the law complicates the catch:

fishing the females is forbidden. These crabs must be sorted by hand, every hand at the mercy of the males and their pincers. With some specimens measuring up to ninety centimetres across, it would be wise to call these crabs "Sir." Crabs grow by shedding, and it's at the end of a moult that a female reaches sexual maturity. When he senses the time is right, Sir will clamber onto her and insist on helping her out of her juvenile shell so he can ejaculate on her eggs now they're out in the open.

Snow crab meat is sweet, salty, smooth, stringy, and outrageously expensive. City chefs make it a delicacy, but no one could ever persuade the Lelarges there was a better way to eat crab than in a club sandwich. You just had to replace the chicken with crab meat, butter the toast with garlic butter, and not make the mistake of forgetting the bacon. In the more informal setting of their seafood parties, they would eat it plain with the help of a pocket knife. Rogatien used to put salt on there for his old taste buds.

In the wild, it's the snow crab that eats the common crab, never the other way around—unless the snow crab's already dead, that is. Staying clear of the *Cancer* genus is another thing the snow crab has going for it. It falls under *Chionoecetes*, which is Greek for "snow dweller." Its full name is *Chionoecetes opilio*: shepherd of the snow dwellers. Not all scientific names are quite so poetic.

One day, Florence and Laurie read that the Latin word for crab was *cancer*. This was quite the eye-opener for them. A crab had made off with their grandfather. Hitherto plagued by misplaced guilt surrounding her dead grandfather and her star sign, Laurie now understood the link between the crab and her horoscope.

It might have been best if they hadn't taken their research to extremes, as usual, but they also discovered that one of the symbols used to represent the star sign Cancer resembled the number sixty-nine. This was where their reasoning, until then on solid ground, went awry: the Cancer constellation, which included Laurie's lucky star and the one under which Rogatien was supposed to be resting in the sky, did resemble the shape of a six and a nine.

That summer, Florence was twelve years old and Laurie was eight. They wandered away from the campfire one night to lie down farther along the beach. After half an hour, Robert lost patience.

"Girls! What are you doing over there, lying in the sand? You'll catch a cold."

"No, no," a meditative Laurie replied.

"We're stargazing," Florence explained, eyes all asparkle.

"We're looking for the big sixty-nine in the sky," her little sister enthused.

Robert had drunk a whole bottle of Opus One. It took some time for him to react. When he did, his tone was all the more severe.

"Who told you about that?"

"The internet," Laurie had the misfortune to reply, in spite of Florence's elbow-jabbing.

The next day, two little girls were treated to a long conversation that was short on straight answers. The computer was moved somewhere in the presbytery that was easier to keep an eye on.

6

The EpiPen years

They had to plan a little trip to Quebec City to get a diagnosis for Laurie. The Lelarges' predicament called for specific tests, all using fresh samples. And so France brought along everything the doctor ordered: clams, crab, shrimp, urchins, mussels, lobster, Arctic surfclams, whelks, razor clams, scallops. Enough to set their minds at rest, and for one heck of a lunch. France promised Laurie she would give her the tour of the plant she'd been hoping for ever since Robert became the see-ee-oh, if the test results came back negative. Florence was keen to go with them, but mostly so she could go on the rides at the amusement park in the mall.

The doctor injected Laurie with the pulverized and repeatedly diluted samples. Five jabs in the right arm, five in the left. He said the skin would swell up. Just in case the swelling was widespread, he insisted on doing it in the intensive care unit. The walls were white and, in the big room where everything was beeping, Laurie could see kids her own age dying. Laurie's arms swelled up only very slightly, to everyone's surprise. A mild allergy to shrimp, the pediatric immunologist and allergist concluded six hours later. If she ate any, Laurie risked coming out in a rash. Unless she munched on a big bag of them, she wasn't going to die. She was free to look, smell, touch, or catch whatever she pleased.

On the drive home from Quebec City, her head turned to the river as it began to hint at its full vastness by Cap-à-l'Aigle, Laurie took some deep, liberating breaths. She told France she didn't even want to stop at the house when they got back to Baie-Trinité; she wanted to go straight to the plant.

"You'll still have to be careful, Laurie," France snapped.

Laurie knew that meant no. And she immediately understood what that no involved. They would be getting new EpiPens at home, in the car, at school, on the boat. She would no longer go fishing for mussels. She could forget about ever playing with crabs. She would not be free of the little case she always had to carry; best-case scenario, they might suggest replacing the one with teddy bears on it with something for big girls.

After Cap-à-l'Aigle, the 138 splits away from the water with a gentle curve. That was where Laurie's silent tears started to flow. France didn't say a word. Florence, sitting beside Laurie in the backseat of the Porsche Cayenne, was watching her sister cry, waiting for her mother to do something. Laurie was embarrassed to be crying. She pressed her face to the window as tight as could be, but couldn't help burdening the silence with sobs and sniffs. As they approached Port-au-Persil, Florence reached for Laurie's thigh with the tips of her fingers. In the rearview mirror, they could see France's dry, anxious eyes behind her red-framed glasses.

Laurie's childhood—her perceptiveness on the drive home from Quebec City was perhaps so terribly profound that it was realizing this all at once that made her cry so hard—would be filled with such moments. France started cooking seafood again for the family. For Laurie she would concoct peculiar substitutes, often a real mish-mash. For instance, when Robert, France, and Florence would be tickling their taste buds with scallops wrapped in bacon, Laurie would be licking her lips for the bacon and trying to find a way to get rid of the puck of boiled potato it enveloped. She would often check with Florence if she was remembering right:

"The doctor in Quebec City, he said I was just allergic to shrimp, not to other seafood. Isn't that right?" she spelled out.

"Yes, Laurie. That's what he said."

"So why do we have to put my dishes in my own cupboard?"

France had had Laurie's name engraved in elaborate lettering on the door of a kitchen cupboard. When the two girls were putting away the dishes, that was where they had to put anything stamped with an L.

"I don't know, Laurie. Ask Mom."

"Every time I ask her, she says we still have to be careful."

Whenever he met with the grocery bigwigs at Provigo or Metro, Robert never left without asking them where their daughters would be going to high school. He had even been in touch with cousins in Quebec City and Montreal; he knew they would put the girls up. But France had said no. She refused to let Laurie go; some daddy's girl, she was sure of it, would end up force-feeding her sushi. She didn't want Florence to go either: it would have been unfair to give her, and her alone, a better education. In any case, they could play the country girl card to get into university and spin a yarn about being a fisherman's daughter. Everyone loves a good fishing tale.

One morning, Florence went off on a yellow-orange school bus to Bay Secondary in Baie-Comeau and came home that night with breasts. That same day, Laurie went into grade four. Without her sister around, she felt more allergic. She sneezed a lot. To everyone at school, even Madame Noëlla, it was quite obvious she was losing her fizz. There was something burned-out about the red in her hair and her eyes were often downcast.

France hadn't noticed a thing.

Laurie had made a myth of, and for, herself. A legend all her own. A secret that would grow so big, it would dissolve any allergy. If she was allergic to seafood, it was simply because she herself was a child of the sea and had to avoid cannibalism. Between her legs and inside her mouth, it was soft and sticky like the inside of a shell. From afar, only the black circle of the pupils in her pale eyes and her red eyebrows could be seen. She had a lobster's eyes. As for the shell, she wasn't sure. She sensed she could feel it beneath her skin when she wanted to touch her breasts. Yes, she was the Crown Princess of the Seafood People. If by chance she happened to suffer another anaphylactic shock, she wouldn't die. She had a Prince Charming to give her the kiss of life: her EpiPen.

She started collecting shells out of necessity, in case she needed them. Her favourite was the whelk's spiral. As far as houses went, she thought it was very chic. She hid her collection in a Mille Bornes card game box, an old English version they didn't play anymore. The box never budged from the maple shelves in the huge games room on the middle floor, sandwiched between hundreds of other boxes. She'd tossed the game itself in the water. Someone in the Magdalen Islands found the Driving Ace card washed up on the beach.

Up on the top floor, Robert had finished setting up his personal office. He had brought high-speed internet to Baie-Trinité before it was even wired in to Baie-Comeau, and this had bestowed him with the fleeting aura of a benefactor. He was forgiven for the Moroccans coming. On Robert's computer keyboard, the number pad was much more well worn than the letter keys, and when he talked on the phone he spoke loudly and mostly in figures. The sounds of business carried throughout the house.

France kept as busy as she could inspecting the school (as the principal) or the plant (as the boss's wife), fretting about things, and going online to plan romantic getaways that would never happen. She thought it was a good thing for Robert to be working from home: it would give her husband the chance to take a break once in a while and come downstairs to instill a value or two in his offspring. Robert took a result-oriented approach to fatherhood, and the Sunday family movie night was a high yield potential opportunity for paternity (or HYPOP, as he shortened it to in his head). When the movie was over, Robert would deliver a moral exegesis about it. None of them had anticipated that as the years went by the movies on TV would descend gradually into softcore. Once he realized that a kissing scene would inevitably now lead to the intrusion of a breast, Robert decided that going forward, they would rent a DVD from the family section at the video store instead.

"But we both have breasts, Dad," Florence pointed out, in vain.

The first family movie they rented was *My Girl.* When Robert realized the boy was going to die from an allergic reaction, he scrambled to turn off the TV, but the damage was done. On the couch, Florence turned pale; Laurie went all washed-out; France fainted. The TV was gone the next day. From then on, Sunday evenings would be board game nights.

Then Laurie had her own coming of age; the year she turned eleven, she spent the summer reading John Grisham on the beach and imagining her future law career while Florence disappeared. Laurie was already beginning to find the waters of the Saint Lawrence too cold for swimming. Now and then, she would sculpt something in the sand: the Eiffel Tower, the Taj Mahal. France kept an eye on her with binoculars. Reading stimulated her imagination, and imagination stimulated her reading. She didn't feel alone.

The next year, when she was twelve, was the summer of John Irving. Those sunny days, the only things that could interrupt her reading were the coming of nightfall or the frightening approach of Hercules, the fisherman. Now and then, she would look up toward the water and reach for binoculars to watch the Moroccans harvesting away in the lightly contaminated zone. She would then turn homeward to meet France's reciprocal binoculared gaze. When she couldn't see her, something shifted in her mind and, sure she was alone, she would masturbate discreetly without interrupting her reading. Her only desire was to become a character in a story like the ones she read.

That September, she started to take the bus to Bay Secondary with Florence, who wasn't happy about it.

The journey took an hour and a quarter, by the end of which she, so redheaded and coastal, glued to her EpiPens, and liable to blush so hard she might almost turn blue, would be like a lobster without a shell. But she enjoyed the long drive, especially at the beginning of fall and the end of spring: one bay followed another and the sunlight sparkled on the immense Saint Lawrence when she looked up from her book.

Since France and Robert liked to see her reading, but knew nothing of literature, she read whatever she wanted. At thirteen, fascinated though she was, she might have been a bit young for Houellebecq. There were stops in Pointe-des-Monts, Godbout, two in Franquelin, one in Pointe Mistassini, one in Saint-Pancrace, and one final stop at Potvin Lake. Some years—it was the youth protection agency that decided—there was a stop at the end of Auntie's Lake Road, where a family of recluses lived. All four kids came to the bus stop on one Ski-Doo in the winter. In all, there were about twenty of them on the bus. They each had a seat to themselves and Laurie sat on the side where she could see the river.

In winter, it was dark on the bus both ways. Laurie couldn't read, and nor could she lose herself in the landscape. A guy from the vocational college would sit beside Florence despite all the empty seats. He wore a Yankees cap and had 50 Cent blasting from his big headphones that doubled as earmuffs. He would open his binder and Florence would rest her head on his lap in the shadows. Florence would sit up again between thirty seconds and two minutes later, then unbutton her coat and pull her tights down in the darkness. Laurie could see the broad strokes and hear the rustling. When the guy got off the bus in Godbout, Laurie would turn and stare at Florence. Florence would give her a shady look in the light of the red blinking stop sign on the side of the bus. Laurie would return home sun-starved to the presbytery to eat her plate of stew or salmon pie, then resume reading while pretending to study.

Board game night had become, like Christmas Mass, a reluctantly upheld tradition. It was France who insisted on it the most. Laurie was in the second year of high school when one fine evening Robert got it into his head to dig out the game of Mille Bornes. He teased everyone, saying no one but him could be the Driving Ace (Florence, who was clamouring for a car of her own, didn't find that funny). He opened the box and out poured the shells. "Laurie!" France flipped her lid. But Robert's interest was held by one particular item in the collection, the shell of an Iceland scallop with a most unusual colour: a kind of coral pink, fading to violet, studded with almost microscopic dots that aroused a powerful sense of strangeness when you lingered on it. When he had come across it in the plant, Frédéric Goyette had sent it away to the federal lab in Halifax for testing and had come close to shutting everything down for a week. That must have been five years ago.

"What are you doing with this, Laurie?" Robert fumed, brandishing the shell.

"It's been ages, Dad. I can't remember."

Laurie was lying. She had spent entire evenings gazing at that shell since she was nine years old, trying to make sense of its atypical hue and, especially, its spots, which could only be an omen. It was Goyette who had given it to her. He had stumbled upon her on the beach one day when she was organizing her collection: here the pectinidae, there the gastropods, in the middle, the heterodonts. The tests in Halifax revealed nothing in particular. Without knowing why, Laurie was mesmerized, holding Goyette's shell in her little hand, rotating it, contemplating it from every angle, lying flat on her stomach in bed for hours, for too long, until she felt guilty about it. It gave her a bit of a buzz. The shell of this Iceland scallop opened a hollow of potential inside her, one she could feel swelling and gradually taking over. When she looked at it, without feeling she was becoming something other than herself, she could sense the promise of another, enthralling, way to be herself. The attraction was not dissimilar to that of pornography, which was why only books for adults could divert her interest.

"It was Goyette who gave it to you!" Robert accused.

"Yes, it was. He said he'd give it to me if I showed him my snatch."

Robert had to sit down. France gasped. Florence giggled. Laurie waited two days before hissy-fitting that she had been kidding about Goyette and his indecent proposal. This worked to Laurie's benefit: the last thing she wanted was to talk about the overwhelming feeling that shell aroused in her, something she had yet to understand. It ended up working out to Goyette's benefit too: Robert had already hired a hitman to kill him, making sure he put him through hell first.

7

Robert in the land of the rising Saturn sun

All in a fluster and as infrequently as possible, Robert Lelarge would make the journey to Montreal. He would grow suspicious just walking down Sainte-Catherine Street and keep checking his pockets to make sure his wallet was still there. In the car, it was worse: he'd had the hubcaps of his Corvette stolen in the underground parking garage at the Place Dupuis mall when he was a student and, ever since, the blare of car horns had been like red rags to a bull. Grunting like an animal, he would cut in front of other drivers and get cut off in turn. He would twiddle the dial on the radio, trying to tune in to something calming. That didn't take long in Baie-Trinité, but here there were far too many stations on the overcrowded FM band. Every inch of his skin could sense the bodywork about to crumple. *Bang!* It might happen at any second. He'd have to pull over on the non-existent hard shoulder in the Ville-Marie tunnel to fill out a fender-bender report with a Sikh or some newly moneyed so-and-so, or maybe explain himself to a guy in a leather jacket who seemed nice enough to earn his trust, only to pull a machete on him.

When he managed to park, it would be in a pool of slush or on some stinking, suffocating patch of overheated asphalt. He would get out of the Porsche Cayenne, activate the alarm system, and just get from point A to point B, veins in his face bulging, ready to jostle whatever was needed on his way through.

He pulled strings to make meetings with the bigwigs happen in Quebec City, where there weren't any nasty surprises. He could manage Boston at a pinch when there were Americans he had to meet, but New York City wasn't going to happen.

In the taxi whisking him from Narita Airport to the Shinjuku Park Hyatt, Robert felt like he was sleeping, but his eyes were open. Saturn, by his side, was snoring for real. In front of the hotel, the driver had to crescendo: "wake, Wake, WAke, WAKe, WAKE!" Saturn eventually grumbled something or other. He turned to his brother and saw nothing of Robert but drool and the whites of his eyes. It scared him shitless for a second. He knew it was just the daze of the culture shock, but it was still an uncomfortable reminder of the final look pasted on the faces of late friends when they overdosed.

He pulled himself together. The driver mustered the courage to extend a polite hand for payment and readied the other to check Robert for a pulse. Saturn gave him the twenty thousand yen and dragged his brother by the armpits into the hotel. A shivering Robert managed to put one shuffling foot in front of the other and walk from the elevator to his room, as Saturn encouraged him one "Come on" at a time. Struck by an epileptic bout of homesickness, all Robert could see was white.

But none of all this should have happened, or at least, not like that. For some months, Robert had been negotiating with some people in Japan, seated comfortably in his presbytery. Nothing major. Logistics, really. Just so he could shift the stock at a decent price if Red Lobster thought twice about its order, and to gain a foothold in the ultra-high-end frozen market. Just drawing up a little contract for some canned snow crab and Arctic surfclams. He was trying to shift a few tonnes of scallops too. Then, right before the fishing season, a radioactive tide hit Japan. Rumour had it they were hauling in luminous oysters near Mito, four to a shell. Like every human being who turns on the TV once in a while, Robert saw the images of the reactor, broadcast by NHK and surrounded by incomprehensible characters, figures, and exclamation marks. A Tokyo wholesaler called in the middle of the night to offer sixty million dollars for the company. A deluge of fear is harder to plug up than an isotope leak. Robert sensed that the impact on the Japanese seafood market would last a long time. Almost as long as it'd take to empty the Gulf of St. Lawrence. If he could find two or three big clients in Japan, the company would soon be worth two hundred million. Ichiro Utsumi, the president of the Isumi Conglomerate of Tones, Colours, Pigments, Molluscs, and Crustaceans, was prepared to buy seafood by the kilotonne, frozen or canned, starting that very year. He did insist, however, that Robert travel to Tokyo so they could speak face to face.

Until Laurie remarked that he had been pale for a few days, Robert hadn't breathed a word to anyone. He ended up spitting it out to his brother and sister too; it was just due diligence, if you asked him. At first, Saturn offered to go to Tokyo in his place; he'd always dreamed of seeing Japan.

"By all means, go to Japan if it's your dream. You're a multi-millionaire. Unfortunately for you and for me, I'm the one they want to see."

"Whoa there! I'm a multi-millionaire on paper. *On paper*," Saturn ambiguously specified.

"Well, you could always go and say you're me."

"Oh, yeah!"

Before Saturn cut his hair, Robert got him to practise for the role in front of his wife and sister. In the kitchen at the presbytery, Laurie watched the skit unfold with a sigh. It wasn't going to work. Suzanne said the brothers moved too differently—Saturn with more of a squish—and it would show in their aura. France thought their English was too dissimilar, Saturn's being more peppered with street slang.

"OK, OK! We'll go together," Robert eventually agreed. "But please, get a haircut anyway."

"You're not really in a position to negotiate. Either you go with me and my hair, or you go on your own. I can put a tie on, but that's all."

Saturn laughed out loud, and his head nodded all by itself. The roots beneath his wild frizz were looking greyer.

"Why don't you go with Dad, Mom?" Laurie asked.

Florence had just moved to Montreal for college, and this was Laurie's last hope of avoiding weeks alone with France.

"What am I going to do, all on my lonesome in Japan, while your dad's busy doing business? Plus, you can't so much as boil yourself an egg," France was quick to rebuff.

Laurie—poor her—was stuck with her mother.

At the hotel, the day after their arrival, Saturn went to wake up Robert the way he did when they were kids and went fishing, by putting ice cubes in his shorts. Robert blamed his grogginess on the brutal jet lag and all the fricking overcrowding in the city. Saturn figured it was just the Orient making him so disoriented. Somehow, the time difference had the opposite kind of effect on him and, apparently, he had already found a way to fuel up.

"Already powdered your nose?" Robert asked, opening his eyelids a couple of millimetres.

"No. I've had ten coffees."

The light of day and Saturn's suit (tight pants, short jacket, skinny tie, all black and white) opened Robert's eyes and gave him a bit of energy. Still, he hastened to specify one condition.

"I don't want to take the subway. I'd rather be inside a can of whelks."

"No need, it's right there."

Saturn pointed to the building that stood like a monolith on the other side of the window. As districts went, Shinjuku was very much vertical, but everything else paled in insignificance.

Robert dressed in black and white too. Together, they looked a bit like Jules and Vincent in *Pulp Fiction*, but the eldest had something more bureaucratic about him than John Travolta. They took some poorly ventilated underground passages that had Robert on the verge of hyperventilation. The skyscraper was called the Tokyo Opera City Tower, and the Tokyo Opera was indeed somewhere in there. The head office of the Isumi Conglomerate of Tones, Colours, Pigments, Molluscs, and Crustaceans occupied part of the forty-fifth floor.

A young woman greeted the Lelarge brothers with a handshake and an inclination of the torso gathered in a single gesture they attempted to return without butting heads. The young woman came around the other side of a wooden desk milled from a single block to guide them to the conference room. The walls were bare concrete. Over the desk, another block of the same wood fixed to the concrete bore the English name of the company, a third carried an inscription that must have said the same thing in Japanese, and one more sported a logo: a stylized ensemble of boat, waves, and stripes, which together suggested a crab. Workspaces were separated by wall panels of multicoloured frosted glass at various heights. Analysts busied themselves behind the screens. The men wore a white shirt buttoned to the neck; the women, a blue blouse with a white lacy frill or a discreet collar. Robert found the silence heavy. He thought he saw fear on the employees' faces, or a swiftness that was unknown to him.

Mr. Utsumi rose to greet them in the conference room. He had a neatly combed head of white hair, and a little goatee. He spoke softly in staccato English. Two men and a woman, all three in their forties, were with him. At the back of the room was a big window. The weather had been clearing since dawn and Mount Fuji was rising from the mist on the horizon. Mr. Utsumi spoke at length about it, then Robert and Réginald gave him some cans of crab and some Grade A Amber maple syrup. He asked them to tell him about Rogatien.

"At the beginning, it was all about shrimp," Saturn began.

Saturn had a knack for spinning a yarn. They listened open-mouthed: the Japanese in wonder, and Robert, because everything before his eyes was still white.

No, Robert was not acclimatizing well to Japan. Day by day, he was developing an obsession with the Isumi Conglomerate of Tones, Colours, Pigments, Molluscs, and Crustaceans. Such an unlikely business model, it struck him; he suspected a scam.

The first three days, nothing passed his lips but a little grassy green tea. In a thinly veiled attempt to get him drunk on sake, Saturn forced him to sit down in a tavern. Robert ordered a breaded pork chop; Saturn, poached octopus on a big bed of rice, as he explained how awash Asia was with tentacular businesses.

"Here, when you're in business, you're really in business. You're in the business of business," Saturn laboured on. "Look at Yamaha: they make snowmobiles, home cinemas, and violins, for fuck's sake. Hyundai ... Christ, Hyundai, in Korea, they can sell you a car, a crane, a life insurance policy, or a gun. And Hitachi ... Hitachi, fuck me! They make TVs, armoured tanks, and the best vibrator in the world. Or so I'm told!"

Robert was nodding off. He breathed a long sigh.

"You've done your homework," he yawned.

"It was Nanami who told me."

Nanami was the Conglomerate's vice president of procurement and, perhaps, Mr. Utsumi's daughter. After the fourth meeting, she had run into the two brothers in the lobby at the Park Hyatt, supposedly by chance, and had immediately asked if she could touch Saturn's hair. "It has a very interesting texture," she reasoned.

It took two weeks to fine-tune the deal. The Conglomerate's executive team and the Lelarge brothers met in the mornings. In the afternoons, Robert called Suzanne, who answered, even though it was the middle of the night for her. There were two or three conference calls with Serge Cabana and a few other influential fishermen. At night, Robert locked himself away in his hotel room. Tokyo's lights were a galaxy in his window. Robert's obsession grew deeper: he dreaded what he might find out about the Conglomerate's intentions as well as precisely how Saturn would fuck things up.

It had to be said, Saturn didn't sleep at night and in six days he had managed to attract quite the little entourage. A guy by the name of Ito was by far the most concerning of these hangers-on: a big guy who always wore a black Mao jacket and eighty-thousand-yen faded ripped jeans. You could see the tattoos on his legs through the holes in the denim.

On day nine, Saturn started waking up Robert several times a night by phoning him or bursting into his room. He would share the occasional brilliant flash about the negotiations, the odd Japanese baseball statistic, or some fragment of a general theory about the attractiveness of Japanese women. He swore phonetics had a lot to do with it. Certain Japanese vowels—very short, with something guttural about them—would pass for moans of pleasure in any other language.

A solid twenty million a year for the next ten years. Robert hadn't been expecting them to yelp with joy when he mentioned urchins. And if Lelarge Fisheries were to triple their existing production, the contract with the Isumi Conglomerate of Tones, Colours, Pigments, Molluscs, and Crustaceans alone would bring in fifty million a year, or more if the exchange rate with the yen was favourable. Robert had drafted an offer to purchase the defunct Gallix processing plant as well as North Shore Fisheries, a rival company from a time that already seemed so long ago.

Saturn ended up having the memorable sake bender he had dreamed of going on with his brother since the day they landed. They sat at the bar in a swanky drinking den. They yelled in Quebec French and didn't care. They ordered two bottles at fifty-five thousand yen apiece.

Ito showed up just before midnight. Saturn bellowed a friendly greeting. He told him about the contract, money and all; it made Robert uncomfortable, even though he was starting to feel the booze. Ito and Saturn went out into the alley. Robert could sense a tinge of radioactivity in the air. When they came back, they persuaded him to go with them to a French restaurant.

Around four in the morning, Robert agreed to take a drag of the joint Ito and Saturn had been smoking on and off since they'd got into the car. Ito parked near a row of fairly low-rise wooden buildings with stucco facades. They took their shoes off at the door and were given slippers to put on. They proceeded to a changing room and slipped into bathrobes. Ito was tattooed from his neck down to his ankles, except for a circle around his cock and balls. Robert was surprised to see his brother's pubis was completely hairless.

"This place is called a soapland. In Japanese, they say ソープランド," Saturn pronounced. "And this is the only reason I'm along for the ride with you to this particular empire."

They offered him a line of coke. Robert settled for a few more drags of the joint that wouldn't end and kept telling himself out loud, just once wouldn't hurt.

On the other side of the changing room was a vast room with deep Japanese bathtubs, framed in wood, in all four corners. The walls and floor were covered in brown and beige ceramic tiles. The air was thick with a fine mist. The humidity caught in your throat. Six girls came in through a door at the far end. They were naked. Robert's thoughts slowed to a crawl. It seemed to him that the two girls coming his way to lead him into one of the bathtubs were the prettiest. They motioned for him to sit on a U-shaped stool, designed to let the male genitals hang loose for them to wash in the most mechanical of ways. Robert was getting a bit hard. They had him get into the bath water. One of the girls had her hair tied up in an elaborate bun. She eased into the bath facing him, elbows on the edges of the tub, breasts out of the water. The other girl had hair down to her shoulders and more of a square jaw. She set about giving Robert a hand job under the water, and from that point on he felt himself close to ejaculating. A very distant sigh from Saturn didn't put him off. After the bath, the girls rubbed his body dry with a towel that felt a little rough. They covered each other, from top to toe, in an insoluble lubricating jelly. On the floor was a clear blow-up mattress, the kind you see in aboveground backyard swimming pools. Robert lay down. The girls began to rub their slippery breasts on his stomach, their arms on his scrotum, their mounds on his neck, and soon more combinations of the above. They worked as a team and their choreography left little room for improvisation.

Robert wasn't thinking about anything anymore. He had closed his eyes. All over his skin he could feel the abundance and generosity of the friction-free contact, as if his entire being was sliding inside something feminine. In the midst of this full-body slip-and-slide, his brain managed, while bypassing the process of thought, to distinguish a thigh here, a breast there, two coarse, hairy mounds. This was how he could tell where his body ended and the two girls' bodies began.

Suddenly, in less than a second, there was just one hairy mound. Robert opened his eyes. The remaining girl was already on her feet, her eyes filled with a fear she was trying to contain. She screamed something in Japanese. Ito came out of a neighbouring bedroom where he was just finishing up. Saturn, in his U-shaped seat, was getting his blow job and not saying a word.

"What's going on?"

Robert found the echo of his voice all out of proportion, spacious though the room was.

"It looks like one of the girls has disappeared," Ito replied, with concern, between two sentences snapped in Japanese at the five remaining girls, ready to make a run for it with their hands hiding their privates.

"Disappeared?" Saturn woke up.

"We'd better get the fuck out of here, guys," Ito concluded. "Someone is up to no good."

Third intermission

the shrimp

"What did the shrimp fisherman say to his greedy colleague?"

Most people at the employees' seafood party, at public meetings, or plush business award ceremonies at the Château Frontenac, knew the answer. But they kept their mouths shut so as not to deprive Rogatien of the primal pleasure of telling his joke.

"Don't be shellfish!" went the patriarch's refrain.

Robert sighed every time he heard his father working up to the punchline: "What did the shrimp fisherman..." After the old man's death, he had noticed that it was when remembering this terrible play on words, especially the slurred "shellfish," that his father's voice sounded the clearest in his mind. We don't choose what we remember. Most images and sounds encrusted in our memory were destined to be forgotten. Only some very little things saved them from their fate.

Before fizzling out in the firmament of hackneyed wordplay, the joke had served its purpose, and it wasn't just to make people laugh. Rogatien had had the presence of mind to deliver the punchline to the first seafarer who broached the idea with him of trawling for shrimp, back in the early sixties. It was the first time he'd heard of a trawl net. With that same spark in his mind, the patriarch had offered to buy from the fisherman all the tonnes of shrimp his nets promised to haul in. He founded a company, which started out as Lelarge Shrimp Incorporated. Casinos in Las Vegas were just starting to fill wine glasses with shredded iceberg, shrimp, mayonnaise, horseradish, and ketchup. The shrimp cocktail would go on to become the height of defrosted chic, and things would stay that way for three decades. Rogatien, well he would go on to get rich. The following year, he had a little army of shrimp fishermen trawling for him: the Shellvation Army, he should have thought to call them. Too bad. That would have given him a good laugh.

Back then, they just talked about catching "shrimp," because it was the only kind they knew. That was before the Asian shrimp made an appearance, bigger, not as tasty, never fresh, farmed in its own crap. In the seventies, the government people came along and started calling the shrimp by its scientific name, *Pandalus borealis*, in their reports. In Latin, the way the priests used to speak. Naturally, the early inhabitants of the Quebec suburbs had to fill their shiny new wine glasses, so they started eating shrimp, lots of shrimp, which had to be given a name. In Matane, someone came up with the idea of browbeating a teenager into wearing a questionable pink costume with sewn-on antennae, bringing in a brass band, and calling that a festival. Rogatien, and Robert in his wake, were all for "Northern Shrimp," but "Matane Shrimp" was the name people latched onto. At Ti-Claude's bar, a tourist once had the misfortune of using that term to refer to the shrimp in his cocktail. Saturn punched him in the face and—it was the powder in his nose talking—threatened to skewer the guy on a freshly broken Molson Ex bottle. A big one.

It's hard to imagine a Freudian shrimp. Oedipus is such a stranger to the species, you see. Shrimp are born in April, all of them male, just below the surface. There the larvae stay for a few months, before plunging deep, the male way, to the bottom where the adults live. At two years old, they can reproduce by inserting their spermatophores (little white balls of sperm) into the females' bellies. They do that with their feet.

In the St. Lawrence Estuary, if the males live to four years old, their testicles will empty and grow bigger. Some weeks later they'll become ovaries, filled with eggs. The water temperature determines the exact time they change sex. For the shrimp, this is all part of the life cycle. They keep growing from one moult to the next. They'll live through the sexual act again more than once, but as females. If female shrimp are bigger, it's simply because they're older. The eggs they yield are ripe for a gourmet's sucking. When the tongue bursts these minuscule seaweedy spheres on the palate and coats the mouth in a sheen of iodine, it's a good reminder that one is not born, but rather becomes, a woman.

Things would not be that easy for Laurie.

Florence went away to Montreal, first college, then business school. On the school bus, the guy from the vocational college, soon imitated by all the other boys, fingered and tongued a gesture to Laurie that she didn't understand, and they laughed at her because she didn't get it. And yet, she had read all of Houellebecq, moist enough to go blind. She wanted to dive into Proust and read Marie-Victorin's *Laurentian Flora* too, but in the evening she just didn't have it in her. It was as if her head was filling with hot, black mud. She could feel it, behind her eyes, piling up in the great open field.

At night, she could hear France snoring heavily. Robert, one floor above, would stay up late bellowing his numbers into the phone. Laurie was having trouble sleeping. She would get up at all hours and go to the bathroom, just to lock the door and look at her body in the long mirror. Her red mane was thickening by the day. The lactiferous potential of her breasts was becoming hard to deny. Her threadbare undies could no longer cover her buttocks or contain her hairs. She had reached her adult height: a good five foot seven. Her pale skin would have no moult to go through. All this was a harsh reminder of her mammalian condition. She was fifteen years old and was not from the sea.

It was the month of May. The boats were lining up to dock at the wharf. There were so many of them, they had to keep unloading until well into the night. Robert was sleeping at the plant. Laurie had found a way to stay clear of France. She was walking on the beach in bare feet, driven along by bouts of impatience. The night was cool and the hustle by the wharf did nothing to stir the calm of the sea. Laurie passed the Moroccans' dormitories and dipped her feet for a few seconds in the icy water. She stretched out in a clump of eelgrass where, in spite of a milky trail of moonlight on the river, she was invisible. With her binoculars she saw two guys around her age unloading big shrimp trawlers. She told herself it was possible. The crew on those boats liked to cook their catch at sea so they could stay offshore for longer. Laurie knew those two dockers. They were no strangers to teasing her on the bus and had recently dropped out of school a year early to work at the wharf. They wanted to save up and buy a boat.

"Hey, boys! Gimme a bag, will you?"

"Is it for your dad?" they asked, catching their breath.

"Yes!"

She hadn't imagined it would be so easy: in her plan, she was going to corrupt them with her breasts. They tossed her a paper grocery bag from a cut-price supermarket filled to the precious brim, which she clutched tight as she returned to her hideout. The juice from the shrimp soaked through the paper and started dripping down her fleece. The salty, all-embracing scent of the just-cooked crustaceans flirted with her nose, though yes, it did bring a little swelling to her throat.

She grasped the first shrimp, a male. She rubbed it on her cheeks and her tongue. She held it by the eyes, between her first three fingers, and the antennae came and curled into the palm of her hand. She didn't know they'd be that hard and pointy. She pulled off the head with a twist and tossed it over her shoulder. With her thumbnails, she dug into the shell and tore it all the way down the abdomen. She rubbed her hands to get rid of the dislocated feet stuck to them. She let the shell fall to the sand at her feet. She chewed a little. It was salty and suggestive, but she didn't dwell on the taste. All that mattered was to finish it, and fast. The second shrimp was a female. She inhaled the eggs with her mouth and her nose.

It was Suzanne who found her, fast asleep in a pile of shrimp shells, in her blue jogging suit. The grocery bag had caught in the eelgrass, evidence the morning breeze might otherwise have blown away. Suzanne was heading out for her sunrise meditation stroll. She said Laurie's name, and said it loud, with the awkward surprise of someone discovering a teenage girl in a compromising situation who knows she must keep the secret.

Laurie did it all again the very next day because while it might not have been deadly, it sure was delicious.

8

Never in the same river twice

Florence returned to Baie-Trinité every summer in a Mazda made in Hiroshima. She had tried to wangle a Mercedes out of her parents. Some of her friends at business school drove a Merc to class. She figured France and Robert had their reasons for not wanting her to become like them, but she kept her mouth shut. It was still a nice little Mazda.

She liked to wear light white linen dresses on her dark skin, even though it was never really very hot. They had freed up an office for her to use in the administration wing. Robert paid her a consultant's fee. The workers openly called her "the boss's daughter," and soon she had made quite a reputation for herself. They said they'd be in for a rough ride down the line if she was that much of a stickler after only two years of university. They called her "the precious little princess" behind her back.

Highway 138 might begin at the Ontario border, but it's after Quebec City, heading east, that it becomes the stuff of lore (staggering drunk down Sherbrooke Street not long after moving to Montreal, Florence saw a sign marking the 138—it made her laugh out loud). There's a traffic light at the end of the road out of Sainte-Anne-de-Beaupré. When it turned green, Florence knew what lay ahead. She would floor the accelerator pedal and shift no higher than second gear. The Mazda would dig its rubber claws into the pavement and shoot its way up the vertiginous climb over Cap Tourmente at five thousand revs per minute. Seven hundred metres higher, two minutes later, in another place entirely, Florence would plug her nose and pop her ears.

Yes, the 138, it's the stuff of lore, like a wild dance when the river beckons the road near the shore only to push it away again into the valleys, but always keeps a hold on it with one hand. (Mori Ishikawa thought it was more of an asymptote that curved toward the river, which he was sure was a sea, then an ocean.) But the 138 is larger than life the way a bullfight is: you're in it for the long haul; it takes at least four hours to get anywhere, and no one likes wasting their time. Things get complicated, too, with an interlude right in the middle: the Saguenay, where a ferry crosses the fjord because a bridge would unsettle the whales. A coroner from Baie-Comeau coined the term "ferry fever" for the irrational urge that drives otherwise prudent motorists to pass a swaying logging truck on a bend in spite of the fuel tanker bearing down on them in the oncoming lane, flashing its headlights. Dying is less painful than watching the ferry sail away when you get to Tadoussac just in time to see the barrier closing right in your face.

Just before Sault-au-Mouton, Florence, going a hundred and thirty-five kilometres an hour in her Mazda, passed and swore at Mori Ishikawa, doing ninety-two in his Lincoln. Both were passed in Pointe-à-Boisvert by a plumber in a Yankees cap. He was screaming along at one-seventy in a convulsing Civic. Ninety's the limit, but the provincial cops don't bust anyone going under one-twenty-three. Everyone knows where their radar traps are.

The summer was a sunny one and, with a little cover-up, you could stay out until late on the presbytery veranda, where the bugs weren't too bad. That was where the two sisters convened to catch up at the end of Florence's workday, while France was in the kitchen. They carried on until well into the night, each in their own rocking chair, giggling like two grannies. Florence would have a Molson Ex when the time came for a drink before dinner because they didn't have her kind of beer at the convenience store. Sometimes Robert poured her a Chablis. Laurie wasn't allowed to drink, even though she was going to be seventeen in a few days' time.

Down from the veranda where the young grannies were nattering, the village was buzzing with new vim and vigour. The Moroccans' barracks—there were three hundred of them that season—formed quite the enclave, what with their unofficial mosque and clandestine bar. Fishermen, workers, managers, everyone by the shore was swimming in cash. There were too many new pickups out there to count. The Harley dealer in Baie-Comeau was thinking about opening a satellite showroom. Saturn was overseeing the interior renovation work at Rogatien's ancestral home. He and the chef planned to open their restaurant in August: a bit late in the season, but just in time for the Michelin Guide critics' visit to Quebec.

Mori Ishikawa started combing the beach every day and everyone thought there was going to be a surge in tourism until it became evident that there would be no more Japanese and that this one was here to stay. Frédéric Goyette, the local manager for the Canadian Shellfish Sanitation Program, was the only one to have stuck to his routine. Florence went down to see him on the wharf, to say hello and tell him she was back from business school, she was doing an internship at the Fisheries, as well as to see the appeal of crossing a line flicker across his rugged face. Then to walk away with a sway of her hips. In her four years in Montreal, she had gained that kind of confidence too.

"Why did you do that?" Laurie was embarrassed to ask when her sister returned to the veranda.

"Haven't you ever noticed Frédéric thinks we're cute?"

"Er ... yes. I think so. But especially you," hesitated Laurie, who had never quite seen it that way.

"That's what's good about coming back in the summer. It's easier to see everything that's changed."

"Frédéric's always thought we're cute, you say. So what's really changed then, is you."

"You're right. When I come back, I don't realize what's changed. What really strikes me is what hasn't changed. I can see how things work. The village, the family, the business ... the way things have worked since I was a little kid, the stuff I couldn't understand until now. Every year, I grasp a little bit more."

"That's probably it," Laurie replied.

She was going to add that it was like allergies, they pass without you realizing, but as she was about to open her mouth, something rose in her throat to stop her.

"It's like working at the Fisheries. I grew up thinking everyone in the village worshipped Dad—"

"I'm not sure it's really you coming back that's helped you to see that. People *really* seem to like him a lot less since last year," Laurie interrupted in italics.

"Maybe, maybe," Florence hesitated, watching the clouds turn yellow. "In any case, you, you've changed, that's obvious."

"Really?"

"It's obvious. I'd say you're more ... more ready."

Laurie sighed, and it was a long one. Her eyes moistened.

"Ready for what, then? Tell me if you know what it is," she added, after a silence, "because that's what I'm wondering too."

"Well ... ready. Ready for the rest ... I don't know, do I?" Florence said, not knowing what to add but aware of having involuntarily stirred something in her sister, before diverting the tone to mockery: "Ready for lurve!"

"Oh, give it a rest! Can't two sisters on their own talk about something other than men?"

"I see what you're saying, but still! It's about time, don't you think?"

"I just want something to happen. That's all. Not necessarily a guy. I can't wait for something to happen to me, not someone. I figure I've got a lot to learn, see, and feel ... but I don't think I've changed that much all of a sudden."

"Not all of a sudden. No. I'm telling you. Look at the water. If you never take your eyes off it, you'll never notice the tide is rising. But if you walk away and come back an hour later, it's a different story."

Laurie had the impression it was Suzanne she was hearing, but she had spent enough time in her life looking at the water to understand. A long pre-Socratic silence ensued.

"Take your time," Florence said to her, like she always said. "But you can't always just wait for something to happen to you," she added for the first time. "For now, we're putting together a nice little birthday soirée for you."

"I can't think of anything sadder," Laurie overflowed.

Florence gazed at the horizon. In the pink sky, layers of blue were peeling away in the wind. She took a breath, then offered to go make Laurie a London Fog.

On the 138, not long after the road forks at Sacré-Cœur, Mori Ishikawa had been sure he was going to die. Driving on the right didn't come naturally to him, and in every curve he found himself close to a head-on collision.

In Baie-Trinité, he was combing the beach. That is to say, he was noting in a little book the amplitude of the tides; by order of contamination, the areas of the beach, their ups and downs; the names of the Moroccans he encountered; the comings and goings of the shrimp trawlers; the number of rocks visible at high tide. He always wore cargo pants, a fisherman's hat and, over a white shirt, a dark cardigan. In a shoulder bag, he had binoculars and a camera. He carried a black plastic case. The Moroccans were the first to hear him speaking a clear and forthright French, albeit with the odd stumble.

He had found the breeze salty and cold, but unusually light on iodine. He would later recall having doubted the estuary, the gulf, and what could come out of it. At low tide, he went far out and turned around to see the village. It wasn't just there that the coast curved in on itself and yet, for kilometres around, it was the only place where humans had chosen to live. On the cliffs, the forests of conifers were abundant with stillborn trees, dry and grey, still bearing parched needles.

The wind would strip them bare. It all gave Mori the impression of a ruggedness that had been haphazardly tamed, but tamed nonetheless. He was not on home ground here, but he felt all right.

He didn't provoke anything, not really.

By the wharf, he crossed paths one morning with a stocky, close-shaven man, grey at the temples, his otherwise black hair slicked back at the sides with a lot of gel. Scars of old, but fierce, acne pockmarked his face. The man was wearing a well-tailored short-sleeved shirt under a wrinkled nylon Lelarge Fisheries jacket. Dressed like that, this could only be Robert.

"Hello, are you Mr. Robert Lelarge?"

The dapper Japanese man's mere presence on the shore had been wearing on Robert for the last five days. He felt like an outlaw as memories of the soapland flooded his mind. Then a terrible angst made him go weak in the legs and jaw, squeezing his chest, gripping his urethra, and relaxing its sphincter. Things went white in his eyes, but he managed to hold his urine.

"Yes. What do you want from me?" he replied in a flustered falsetto.

Mori feared he had lacked politeness.

"Excuse me for approaching you so directly, Mr. Lelarge. I am Mori Ishikawa, commercial envoy for the Isumi Conglomerate of Tones, Colours, Pigments, Molluscs, and Crustaceans."

Robert was flash-frozen for a few seconds, organically perplexed, his eyes all but rolling back in their sockets. He would not, as he had been preparing to do, have to hold out his hands for the cuffs.

"Oh. Right. OK," he blurted, before redeeming himself with a faint "hello."

"Thank you for welcoming me to your very picturesque village."

Realizing that what he said next could be worth millions to him, or cost him just as much, Robert was compelled by a pressing urge to put all this off until later.

"Please come to my home for dinner tonight, Mr. Ishikawa. It will be a pleasure for my family to welcome you."

"I would be honoured."

Then Robert remembered something. His hands made an attempt to grasp the moment. But the moment slipped away like a mist.

"We're celebrating my youngest daughter's birthday, as it happens."

Mori looked at him with confusion. He promised to be there at six.

After that, things played out like a farce in two acts. Sar'h, the whelk fisherman, was the sole witness to the first. Around four-thirty that afternoon, he was on his boat, chugging his first cold one after unloading his catch. He saw a slight Japanese man wading into a cove, equipped with a mask, flippers, and makeshift snorkel. Sar'h was observing the scene from too far away to see whether it was a pair of Y-fronts or speedos he was wearing, but they were red and they were tight.

Mori stood there for a long time, with the river just over his ankles, shivering and squeezing his ribs with crossed arms, refusing to take the plunge. Sar'h said to himself the guy was nuts if he went in. He was going to call out, then thought better of it: his hoarse voice wouldn't carry that far. As it were, being where he was, the Japanese guy would have been just as nuts not to dive in. Mori ended up turning around, taking a few steps in reverse on the muddy bottom where his flippers were sinking in, and letting himself fall back-first when the water was halfway up his thighs. Sar'h saw the day-glo end of the snorkel go in among a little cluster of rocks, disappear, and emerge repeatedly, expelling little geysers. This went on for a good half-hour. Sar'h stayed put, with no desire to raise anchor, smoking, drinking, and cursing in amazement.

The weather was still nice out. France had laid a table on the veranda with a white cloth and her grandmother's silver. Laurie had been asked to choose the meal: General Tso tofu. France asked Florence if she knew how to make it. Florence would figure it out. She took the Bimmer France only used these days to go grocery shopping in Baie-Comeau. They would have tofu there. She stocked up on tea and Orangina because Laurie really liked the stuff. Robert gave her two hundred dollars for her to bring back some Pomerol and Pommard. Florence thought he might let Laurie have a small glass. Nope.

Back in the village, it occurred to France to buy some multicoloured cardboard cone hats, just like when Laurie was little. Laurie's skin was the price to pay for her red hair; it was easily marked and the little elastic loop left a red stripe under her chin. The three others drank beer while they left the wine to breathe. Laurie drank Orangina from a beer mug, through a pink straw, in small sips. She had smiled briefly when her sister handed her the pack of cans with an expression of empathy. Otherwise, she was watching the water, telling herself she could actually see the tide going out. She was breathing slowly, with too serious a face for her seventeen years and six o'clock on her wrist.

The doorbell rang. Robert wondered out loud who it could be, exactly as he used to on Christmas Eve when it was Santa Claus at the door, which is to say a touch staged and theatrical. Laurie suspected her parents might have made the mistake of inviting her classmates. She was done with high school and never wanted to see them again. Robert returned with the Santa in question, who was Japanese. France did a better job of containing her consternation than her two daughters. Even the wine stopped breathing.

"Miss Lelarge, I wish you a very happy seventeenth birthday," announced Mori Ishikawa.

He looked like he had been practising the scene. Proffering it with two hands and an ample bow of the torso, he placed a wooden crate containing eight large urchins on the table. The urchins, they had a fair idea, but the crate, no one knew where the heck he could have found that.

9

Putting Saturn on the map

It was the first time Mori Ishikawa had tasted General Tso tofu. He was taking small bites, which he alternated with micro-sips of Pommard, taking care to always put his utensils back in their place. He was answering in short sentences only when he was spoken to, sentences imprinted with a devout deference that rendered them enigmatic.

"I'm sure it's not as good as it is where you're from, Mr. Ishikawa," France ventured in the midst of a silence as vast as a prairie.

"Japanese cuisine is varied. This is not a traditional recipe of my region."

Mori settled for stringing two truths together. Laurie was now looking through the gaps in the boards at her feet.

"What do you eat, then, in your region?" Florence carried on mawkishly.

Since the beginning of the meal, it was toward her that Mori's gaze had most naturally turned. It was also to her that he had responded with the least tension.

"On special occasions, glazed eel. The rest of the time, lots of rice and seafood."

"Laurie is allergic," affirmed France, not letting a second pass, as if there were something bitter in her mouth she couldn't help but spit out.

Her brusqueness stretched into an amplifying silence. Instinctively Mori turned to see, through the screen door, the table where he had left the crate of urchins. It had disappeared.

They moved into the living room, to open the presents. Mori thanked the family for their hospitality, but he was mindful not to outstay his welcome. Still, he couldn't leave without enjoying an after-dinner drink, Robert invited, turning all eyes on himself. Following a complicated decision-making process, Mori found himself in the corner with a Southern Comfort. He had not loosened his tie.

Without saying a word, Mori watched Laurie receive her gifts. Robert and France gave their daughter the keys to an apartment in the upper town of Quebec City, where she was supposed to be going in August. Laurie had enrolled at Mérici College. She knew that none of that would come to be. Whenever France brought up the near future, she would say, with an overcast air, "Yeah, yeah, yeah." That would bring a pucker to France's cheeks. Laurie said thanks and pocketed the keys with practised detachment. Mori tried not to seem like he was decoding her look. Set in white against the white of her eye, he caught a fleeting glimpse of the dense, familiar fog he was seeking.

Then Florence gave her sister some big Ray-Bans made especially for her short sight. In another small package, wrapped with a lot of gold ribbon, Laurie found an Italian skin cream. Florence turned to Mori, who was too quiet. She cupped both hands over Laurie's ear and whispered that it worked miracles on cellulite. Another parcel with even more ribbon and a few faux pearls revealed a jar of balm, this one for rashes. At the sight of her in that moment, no one would have denied that Laurie needed it.

Mori left with much bending at the waist and congratulations to Robert for his family.

Laurie went straight to bed. All evening, she had been looking forward to one thing only: diving right back into Kundera.

Florence took it upon herself to right the wrongs. She followed Robert to his office, where she gave him a solid piece of her mind until he admitted it had been a bad idea to invite a trade representative to Laurie's birthday. He'd had no choice, he added, and that was where the conversation would end because the Tokyo Stock Exchange was closing soon.

France went into the garage to retrieve the crate of urchins she had stashed there and to find a hammer. Almost every night, the abnormal heat of that summer in Baie-Trinité charged the sky with electrical storms. France hadn't gotten changed. She was still wearing her high-rise jeans and her T-shirt from St. Mary's, which had burned to the ground and had not been rebuilt. For the school, it was better that way. After her daughters had come and gone, France had lost interest in the principal's job. Few people in the village knew it, but she no longer had the strength to dish out the discipline to the little Gaudreau monster that would have extinguished his pyromaniac impulses. She had watched the school burn from the presbytery balcony. She had poured herself a glass of wine and drunk it with Neronian pleasure. After the fire, she refused to be transferred to another school. The spectrum of things into which she allowed herself to stick her nose then narrowed considerably.

France's T-shirt soon got soaked on the beach. She had a grey sports bra on underneath, which showed when the lightning flashed. She placed the urchins on a big rock the same colour as her bra, in an octagon. They were green, and they had to be destroyed. She smashed them one by one. The orangey entrails spread over the rock. France was going at it too hard and the vibration of the hammer was travelling straight to the nerve in her elbow. The kindly thunder urged her to pound her heart out. With every strike of the hammer, she released a loud cry: "The fucker..." *wham!*, "do that to my daughter..." *bam!* "not right in the head, the Japanese shit..." *splat!*

The beach in Baie-Trinité was the same as always. But only now did Laurie realize that it was in fact a little part of the perimeter of an entire continent. For her, this was the summer of Kundera and of heat. Although all that was before Saturn opened his restaurant.

Laurie would set out early in the morning, with a veggie-paté and pickle sandwich. She would read all day through her big Ray-Bans, in a cove or on a rock. She would apply her creams. Over her black bikini top, she would wear a loose cover-up knit from chunky beige lace and, over her bikini bottoms, not a thing. She would often stop to ponder, daydream, gaze out over the water—letting Kundera sink in. She was used to the uncontrollable sexual flushes that ran through her reading. With Kundera, they were becoming more sudden and, especially, more unfathomable. Reading gave rise to ontological meditations, which went the way of disgrace in the conscience of a moist crotch. Laurie would pull her bikini bottoms to one side to pleasure herself, believing it was for purely cerebral reasons. Twice in short succession, sometimes.

When Mori, combing the beach, came across her, either he would go well out of his way, or he would close his eyes.

"Welcome to Chez Saturne!"

Saturn was standing to attention in front of Laurie, glued to his maître d's lectern. He was dressed in his Tokyo clothes. Florence had brought two silk Burberry dresses back from Montreal for the occasion. Laurie's—it was green—suited her perfectly.

"So glam!" Florence gushed.

"Why did you call the place Chez Saturne?" Laurie asked, with a look of disinterest.

"It seems quite obvious to me," Saturn replied, with grammar.

"Well ... 'Chez' sounds very posh and French. Saturn's your nickname. And it sounds even classier in French: *Saturne*. I can't imagine many other reasons."

The minister responsible for the North Shore, the MNA for the far-from-local Beauce-Nord riding, was waiting behind Laurie. She was starting to lose patience. Florence cupped a hand around her sister's elbow. Saturn was clueless.

"It's both my nickname and the name of the Roman god of the sea," he explained, with language.

"No, that's Neptune."

Saturn's face turned, as if he had taken a trident to the chest. It started in his eyes, then the life briefly left his jaw. A shock wave spread through his stallion's mane of hair. All this time, then, people had been laughing at him. Laurie commandeered her sister's phone and told Saturn she'd show him.

"Saturn eats babies," she announced, as an image appeared on the screen of Saturn devouring one of his sons, courtesy of Rubens, followed by Goya's version.

Saturn, though he let none of it show, had struggled to embrace his nickname. He had taken ownership of it in rehab. In it he had seen a mythological predestination, necessarily a nautical one. The mythology was crumbling. No one had said a word to him before the grand opening of his restaurant. That was how much they loved to make fun of his ignorance. Florence yanked hard on Laurie's elbow.

"Fuck," is what Saturn would have said in any other circumstances, before disappearing to later be found sobbing and sniffing in a corner.

"Good evening, Madam Minister," he said with recovered dignity. "Welcome to Chez Saturne. May we offer you a glass of champagne or the house cocktail?"

Things were not exactly off to a great start.

Corpulent, tattooed, hairy in the mop, and extravagant in the moustache, the chef was shaking hands. He had practised his lines and his smiles. About the Arctic surfclams, about Baie-Trinité, and about the restaurant, he said the same thing: he wanted to put them on the map. He didn't say which map. When he spoke to Florence, Robert kept watch from the corner of his eye.

France had told Laurie she could stay for the drinks before dinner. That part was outside, on the big patio with built-in hemlock furniture where you could nibble appetizers and feast your eyes on the catches sailing in. Tourists drawn by that sort of thing could see for themselves just how fresh their meal would be. When the action moved inside, though, and the allergenic vapours would no longer have the sky to escape into, Laurie, that much was clear, would have to take that Burberry dress of hers somewhere else.

She was in the middle of reading *The Joke*, and the novel was stirring a sticky bitterness in the pit of her stomach.

The crowd on the patio fell into one of seventeen categories: waitresses Laurie knew from school, intelligentsia, people Laurie had never seen, French tourists, foodies, show-offs, well-off folk from Baie-Comeau, deckhands-turned-busboys, Lelarge family members, others included in that category by extension, political types, urban hipsters, people who looked tiny from a great distance, bartenders, high-ups from the Fisheries plant, people who may or may not have been allergic to seafood, and everyone else. Over by the balustrade, Mori was discussing Shintoism with Suzanne. He was drinking Southern Comfort out of politeness toward Robert, wincing inwardly with every sip.

Inside, there were round maple tables and transparent moulded plastic chairs. The servers had ironed the tablecloths. Saturn invited everyone to take their seats. The Ministry of Culture had allowed big bay windows to be cut out of the facade looking over the water. There were some leftovers in the fridge, France said: Laurie could make herself a hot chicken sandwich.

The sun was setting on the presbytery veranda when she finished *The Joke* on an empty stomach. She didn't want to take off her dress. In front of the upstairs bathroom mirror, she told herself the silk made her look as beautiful as a butterfly. But that heaviness was still stuck in her stomach. "*Live!*" every book implored her. Enough was enough.

After the clam étouffée (stewed in smoked seaweed) and urchin sabayon with caviared mussels, between the lobstered crab course (with tart local berry jus) and the crabbed lobster course (with lichen and Labrador tea), the mayor of Baie-Comeau felt a Rabelaisian rumbling between his buttocks that plunged him into perplexity. A former football quarterback and now-wearer of delicate metal-rimmed frames, he was rather robust and accustomed to good food and the proverbial letting-rip; heavy in the eyebrow, he could not help but raise one in a squelch of surprise.

Some misfortunes offer a chance consolation to those first afflicted. When a slipperiness in the hair-down-there answered his sole preoccupying question (Did I just fart or shart?), the mayor was able to go park his monopoly on one of the too-few seats in the lavatories. There, he discovered that the three states of matter were abundantly represented in his ejections.

Thus ensued a most dishonourable of processions: gentlemen in tuxedos sprinted to the restrooms, both hands clutching both cheeks, floodgates well and truly opened; ladies stumbled in their dresses and gentlemen stumbled over ladies. Seated comfortably on the throne, the mayor realized his luck on hearing the inimitable sound of diarrhea (to call it by its name) in a urinal. Next in line were the sinks, and then the floor. The doors to the jammed restrooms no longer in any state to open, people started spewing out the emergency exit. Some stormed the kitchen. Disadvantaged by dresses that could not, like pants, act as a filter, ladies left trails across the floor.

The Lelarges were among the last to fall. At their VIP table, the Premier of Quebec succumbed before they did. In one fell swoop, the contents of his bowels emptied into the depths of his chair. Only when he stood up did he realize the stuff was streaming down to his ankles. He cast a glare of betrayal on the still dry and unsullied family that would later be impossible to speak of in front of Robert ("What happened that night doesn't amount to even one percent of the harm a referendum can do," he would counter in response to anyone who considered broaching the topic, before lavishing the man with praise).

The Premier's wife, in her elegance, all freshness and botox, had every intention of going along to the quiet place where their bodyguards were hoping to usher him, but was forced to think again as the spasm in her guts made her bend over double. They quickly went into extraction mode, as one of the cops reported to the mike in his headset. Meanwhile, Mori Ishikawa took advantage of the chaos to excuse himself without offering any compliments. No one noticed that he seemed to have been spared.

At this unfortunate juncture, Saturn came up to the table after smoking his special victory joint, albeit in defeat. Rogatien's house stank of shite.

"You're holding up all right?"

"At this point, Réginald, I hope it's going to hit us too. Otherwise, people are going to think you're poisoning them," Suzanne insinuated, always prepared to wish the worst (after the darkness comes the light, and all that).

"You don't understand. I've *already* poisoned them. It's *already* done. And it's hitting the fan *right now* ... holy fucking shit."

"If Laurie were here, she would say there's no better way to put it," Florence observed.

Suddenly, feeling it coming and knowing her G-string wouldn't hold a thing in, she regretted not having chosen the green dress for herself: hers was a muted pink that would really show the muck. Gripping the table, Robert was making quite the face. He had just felt a pinching in his stomach the likes of which he hadn't experienced since his last colonoscopy.

"Where's the chef?" he roared.

A passing waiter, addressing Saturn, found himself answering Robert:

"The chef has just fucked off on a floatplane."

"On a floatplane? The fucker!"

"OK, Saturn, get everyone out onto the beach. The area in front of the wharf is already highly contaminated anyway," Robert said in the calm but firm voice it is customary to adopt in an emergency.

Heroically, holding his phone in his left hand while making a valiant retentive effort with his right, Robert got through to the administration people at the wharf and had them turn off the floodlights to ensure some semblance of privacy. Then he let it all go on the sand, really quite audibly, but the sound he released faded into the noise of all the others. Saturn had found a whistle to blow and was gesticulating wildly. The bay of the Trinity River was becoming an open-air cesspit where designer underwear was best worn around the ankles. A sliver of moon was reflecting in the little channels that were beginning to run down the slope of the beach.

"Are whelks any good?"

"Some say periwinkles are better," replied Sar'h, "but don't you believe a word of it. Winkles are all right as an appetizer, but whelks, the real thing, are nice and meaty."

"Meaty?"

"Yup. Here. Have a taste," said Sar'h, extracting the mollusc from a shell he'd found lying around on his boat with his slightly rusty pocket knife.

Laurie grimaced, not without congratulating him on his ability to do this one-handed as he kept smoking with the other. In the shadows of the night where the harsh lighting of the wharf made everything monochrome, her dress wasn't quite as green.

"Er ... no thanks."

The edge of the wharf, where she was sitting, had rumpled the dress up her thighs, but Laurie hadn't noticed. The air was getting cool. She jiggled her bare legs. Sar'h, aboard his moored-up boat, tried not to look.

"Why aren't you at the restaurant opening? Hercules is there."

"Hercules, he's in lobster fishing. Have you ever seen a whelk fisherman all dressed up?"

Sar'h sure liked to cough and splutter his aitches. Florence, since she'd been back, had started pretending not to understand the fishermen. Laurie had a hard time accepting how anyone could lose an ear for something like that. She had no trouble understanding every word they said.

"I wasn't even allowed to have a glass of champagne. I came away hungry."

"Don't tell me, girl, you're still going off and eating shrimp in secret."

"Er ... yes. Who's got some I can buy?"

"Don't you feel like a bit of variety?"

"I will try those whelks of yours, one day," Laurie stalled. "Shrimp are just so good."

There were some cooked shrimp lying around on Josèphat's sons' boat. Laurie got a full grocery bag of them—one from a midscale store, this time. For her, they were free.

She went through the village instead of going along the beach, so no one would see her from the restaurant. The casbah had an end-of-season ease about it: those who were sticking around for the last few weeks, those who'd been there the longest, were smoking and talking on their cellphones. Laurie made her way to her usual hideout. In times like these, the fog inside her head condensed and came down to cover everything around her, as if it were cloaking the background and taking on its contours. At the precise moment she was swallowing the first shrimp, the floodlights on the wharf went dark. The sound of muffled cries made her wonder if there had been a short circuit or if someone had organized a mass skinny-dip.

She heard a rustling in the eelgrass. It was Mori, in his work clothes: cardigan, pale shirt, fisherman's hat. He jumped at the sight of Laurie. Laurie thought he had mistaken her for an animal.

"Oh. Miss Lelarge. Good evening."

"What's happening at the restaurant?"

"Unfortunately things are going very badly for your uncle."

Mori didn't go into detail, so Laurie didn't ask.

"Are you eating shrimp?" Mori was surprised.

"Yes ... I'm supposed to be allergic, but that's not true, not anymore, not for a long time."

"Yes. I know. It would be wise to tell your mother, Miss Lelarge."

Laurie thought that only taking a dump would get rid of the heavy feeling in her stomach. That, or she'd have to wait for her next period. But no: as he rolled her name so formally, yet so gently on his tongue, she felt it dissolve with a little tingle here and there.

"Well, you must do me the honour of tasting urchin," Mori continued.

He stepped toward her. He was wearing work gloves. In one hand, he held two choice urchins; in the other, a lemon and some scissors. He said that, back home, he would use yuzu.

10

Imovane and aquavit

Buried deep in the brains of vertebrates, including the brains of biologists like Frédéric Goyette, is the pineal gland, a bit of a nerve with the slightest sensitivity to light, not so different from an invertebrate's eye. It is the seed of sleeping and waking.

On sleepless summer nights, it was not uncommon for Goyette to suspect his invertebrate's eye was too sensitive. By dint of rubbing shoulders with shellfish, he had remarked some curious resemblances. This was for him the best explanation for the surges of summer tension that always followed his winters of withdrawal.

The second sleepless night would always lead to the same thing: Goyette believed he would find some enlightenment about the ways of the universe. A shower and four espressos at sunrise would make it clear that his too many, too idiosyncratic intuitions weren't going to be illuminating any mysteries. In the winter, they might even have sent him straight to sleep. Still, he was thrilled to have had them.

In the bedroom, his wife Myriam was fast asleep—to the point of drooling—in their Svelvik bed. Frédéric wasn't sure whether to pick up his guitar or down some aquavit. With the guitar, he'd have to go to the basement so as not to wake Myriam. With the aquavit, he'd have to pop an Imovane since it was his fourth sleepless night in a row. Knocking himself out would just be for form: he had never lacked energy on summer days, even if sleep never came.

When his work phone rang, he spat out the pill he'd just popped in his mouth. Ten years he'd been raking in his standby bonus under the Canadian Shellfish Sanitation Program, and never before had his phone rung outside office hours. It was the hospital in Baie-Comeau.

"Yes. Yes, doctor. Well, there are three types of toxins: those that cause paralytic shellfish poisoning, amnesic shellfish poisoning, and diarrhetic shellfish poisoning ... no ... well, all three of them will give you diarrhea, in the beginning."

In the career of a regional director of food inspections, mass poisonings are a rare occurrence. Frédéric Goyette had never been driven by ambition, rather by a concern for the methodical and a job well done. He began by reviewing his notes on the 1987 Prince Edward Island mussels crisis, a comparable case that often came up in inter-ministry exercises and training. This looked like being just as severe, and he didn't yet know the

Premier's wife was in the ICU. For a second he felt dizzy. It was because he hadn't slept, he told himself, then he took a little sip from his flask of espresso.

As he strode over to his Agency pickup, Goyette's eye was drawn to the orange flashing light on top: it had been fitted to the vehicle for emergencies like this. If he didn't turn it on that morning, he probably never would. And so, the equipment remained unused: the orange light, the siren, the hi-vis vest with its fluorescent "Food Inspection" letters, the first-aid kit stuffed with pouches of solution past their use-by date: all part of a view of his career that was not his own.

The 138 to Baie-Trinité was saturated with sea spray in places, the last remnants of the cool night. It was a sunny day, and one of uncertain heat. Goyette had thought about putting on some Tord Gustavsen, but since it wasn't raining and he wanted to crank himself up, he had fished a CD by Mats Gustafsson's The Thing trio from the depths of the glove compartment instead. When he parked at the head of the wharf, he waited for the music to finish before taking the key out of the ignition. Outside, he felt cold on his left side, and hot on his right. That often happened in Baie-Trinité. There were two Moroccans harvesting clams in the distance and a little old lady sat smoking in her rocking chair, staring at him. Otherwise, all was quiet.

He figured he'd mix business with pleasure and go sink a big bottle of Laurentide at Ti-Claude's bar. Perching on a barstool, not saying a word to anyone, and listening with a superhumanly selective ear to a ragtag of conversations, in the past he'd uncovered more than one breach of industrial hygiene and a fair few equipment failures and missing links in the cold chain. For this reason, his bosses tended to rarely bother him; it had also led to Ti-Claude and the regulars at the bar nicknaming him The Snob. Ti-Claude put up with him because he double-tipped, a toonie for every drink, and the Fisheries workers were all right with him being there because it meant bad news for the boss.

Ti-Claude's bar was one of those places that had tinted windows so as not to upset a night-shift worker's pineal gland. Not that this bothered Goyette. The place smelled like the fish no one could smell anymore. He sat at the bar in his windbreaker with his untended beard. Ti-Claude slid a big bottle of Laurentide in front of him right away. Goyette recognized Sar'h at the far end of the bar. He figured he was talking to three guys from Lelarge Fisheries who'd had the time to get drunk after their night shift. Sar'h was the least inebriated of the bunch.

"I went out for my smoke break about half past eleven. I could hear people shouting. I went back inside. But him, yeah. He got lucky."

"I've never seen so many snatches in my life," beamed the worker who was sporting a cap with the Baie-Comeau Drakkar hockey team logo on it.

"No!"

"I'm telling you. I went out for a smoke too. And I saw it was one helluva shit show on the beach. All those pretty ladies with their dresses hiked up! There I was, going around asking them if I could help, but I was getting a real fucking eyeful."

"No!"

"It was dark out last night. I heard the boss had the lights on the wharf turned off."

"There was a little sliver of a moon. I'm tellin' you, I got to lay eyes on 'em by the dozen."

"So that's why you spent the rest of your shift in the shitter. You were jerkin' off, you fucker."

Sar'h, who hadn't said much since Goyette came in, made a curious sound, a cross between a cough, a sigh, an expectoration, a nasal vowel, and a throat-clearing. Its effect was to express a strong sense of disapproval.

"I don't get how anyone would think it's a turn-on to ogle a woman's bush when she has the runs out the back end. Seems to me, one cancels the other out," he argued.

A strange silence came down over them. Ti-Claude scratched at his eye socket a few times. Many a swig was drunk in silence. Two horseflies kept headbutting the fluorescent tube illuminating the bottles of strong stuff behind the bar. Only the lukewarm dregs were left in the bottom of Goyette's Laurentide. He had a flash of sorts.

"What about the chef? Do you know where he lives?" he piped up, with perhaps a little too much enthusiasm.

Ti-Claude was startled.

"You, you just mind your own, all right," came the retort from the far end of the bar.

Sar'h walked out without a glance at Goyette. The Drakkar fan nodded off on the bar after two shots of Jack. The two others gave the belt loops of their jeans a good tug to adjust their package and sloped off to the video poker room. Goyette forced himself to down his dregs to avoid living up to his reputation. Now he knew where to start.

The tide had time enough to wash up the beach before dawn. It was on its way out now, as if the moon had flushed everything away. While he was waiting to speak to the chef, Goyette would go out and take some water and sand samples, gather shellfish from the adjacent areas, forbid the offloading of whelks and winkles, and verify the watertightness and drainage of the purification system that he had always thought of as "Robert's doodad." But first, he had to go back to his pickup and get his little kit of test tubes and reactants.

A headwind was still blowing. As he took his samples, Frédéric thought he was alone on the beach until he spied a small man in the distance who seemed to be doing precisely the same thing: digging, sieving, gathering, dissecting, and testing like he was, with a troubling symmetry. He picked up his binoculars to look at the man observing him through binoculars. It was Mori Ishikawa, carrying the same kit as he was, but with instructions in Japanese on all the bottles. That was easily explained because the kit was made by the Mitsubishi company.

"Good day, sir. My respects. I see we have the same equipment!" Mori said when the approaching Goyette arrived within speaking distance. He spoke in the wary tone of a fisherman protective of his spot when he happens upon another guy on a salmon river, but with a whole lot more bowing.

"Er ... yes. I'm Frédéric Goyette, regional director of inspections for the Canadian Food Inspection Agency. And you are?"

Mori Ishikawa said who he was and what he was doing. Neither he nor Frédéric said why they were doing what they were doing. They each figured the other must be well aware. They had a tiptoeing kind of conversation as they each tried to work out whether they were dealing with a friend or foe. After a while Mori excused himself, saying he had someplace to be.

And he did: the previous evening, he had spent a good hour and a half knocking back raw urchins with Laurie and a squeeze of lemon. She had been dressed in an evening gown and couldn't get enough of the stuff, but the tide was rising in the cove and they'd had to call it a night. Mori had had no intention of proposing that they see one another again. It had just happened that way. Laurie had promised to meet him in the same spot the next day, in the early afternoon, that is, if she wasn't sick or dead, she had said, only half joking.

She was already there when he arrived. She was wearing what had become her uniform that summer (a loose-knit cover-up over her black bikini top, nothing over the bottoms, big Ray-Bans, that cream from Italy) and was reading the opening pages of *The Unbearable Lightness of Being* while she waited for him. Leaning with her back against a rock, she had shaped a little cushion for her hips in the sand. She was sitting in a clump of eelgrass, flattening it with her legs and bum. There were some denser clumps of the stuff growing in front of her, screening her from sight. She was in the habit of paying no attention to her posture. When Mori arrived, she was startled, unsure what he might have seen of her body.

"Ah. Hi."

Mori had a bag filled with a dozen urchins. He had picked a hundred or so and chosen them carefully, following the same quality standards used by Japanese businesses. They were all Category One, or better. They talked as they tasted them. At one point, Laurie spoke of her sense—not a wish, she underscored, a sense—that she would not move to Quebec City at the end of the summer, that something would happen, that she didn't know who or what would prevent her. That was the way it was, that was all. Mori listened to her as he opened the urchins. Amid such firm certainty about such a dense vagueness, Laurie's fog was spreading, soft, smooth, palpable. He delighted in it.

The water began to encroach upon the cove, now an hourglass. In the eelgrass, Laurie and Mori were lying side by side, feet splayed out. Any more and their toes would have been touching. Neither had considered wrenching the other out of the formality that bound them. Mr. Ishikawa asked Miss Lelarge if she'd like to see his sperm. She raised her eyebrows. He clarified that it wasn't his ejaculation he wanted to show her, but his sperm, and only his sperm; he had a little vial of it here, in his sample kit, that he could empty out right there, onto the sand. The thing was, he could sense a curiosity for fluids in her. He could have lied and said that it wasn't a sexual thing or that it was commonplace in Japan to show one's sperm. He didn't do that. He simply assured Laurie he would do nothing she didn't want him to. Then he grinned, which was unusual for him, and looked to the ground. Laurie wondered if the smile was heavy or light. She said yes.

Mori opened his Mitsubishi case. Among the test tubes of mud and mollusc juice was one filled with sperm, the equivalent of an unsatisfying ejaculation. He poured the contents onto the sand, handed an urchin to Laurie, and took one for himself. They consumed them slowly, not saying a thing. The half-warm, half-cold sea breeze and the still-penetrating August sun parched the sample and contracted it slowly. For a long time they looked at the sperm in silence, lying flat on their stomachs, propped up on their forearms. Then the water came in all of a sudden. Mori managed to get up in time. Laurie, in her swimsuit, stayed a moment longer on the sand to see. In the saltwater, curled back on itself, the sperm looked like a gob of spit or a mollusc without its shell.

Laurie couldn't stand the rush of the cold tide on her skin for long. She got up and Mori stood and watched her reaction. It had been a long time since she had experienced the physical sensation of her existence. Feeling it, she imagined a breach in a huge dam, cracking the concrete irremediably as soon as it became apparent. This was an outpouring she could not contain. The universe was going to change.

"I'd like to see you again," she articulated.

Farther along the beach he persisted in patrolling, Frédéric Goyette heard a piercing lament. He turned around. It was Saturn, standing there, well, staggering. He had nodded off somewhere and the rising tide had just flushed him out. He had emerged without his jacket. His white shirt was soaked, the knot in his tie was no more. His hair and face were covered in a fine coating of dust. His arm was a bluey grey, in the first stage of gangrene. Frédéric strode toward him. He knew what was happening: Saturn had forgotten to undo his tourniquet. He helped him to pull it off.

"Thanks, man! Fuck, does that ever feel better. Ooh. Talk about pins and needles."

"Look at me, Saturn."

"Yes. What?"

"Where's the chef?"

"He fucked off. On a floatplane. The fucker."

Then off Saturn went, on his merry way. Later, he would come across Mori.

Goyette was taking a gold digger's interest in the shorebreak. The sediment suspended in it carried a promise of fecal matter particles he could sample and test. He had seen some intriguing ones, small as a big grain of sand, with a peculiar sparkle to them. At first there were just three or four in every wave, but now there were more and more of them. He was sitting where the waves washed in to watch the particles and their singular dance. Their behaviour was more like an animal's than a mineral's. It was easy to imagine them willing themselves on: unfurling their strange shimmers, long trails of the stuff, as far as could be. Goyette stood his ground, caught up in the phenomenon. The tide flowed into his shoes, inside his pants, into his crack. It was cold, and more and more magnificent. He forgot all about the toxicity hazards, the possible fecal origins of the particles, even his federal mission.

At four seventeen that afternoon, laden down with those same particles, a wave to defy all waves broke. There were no more after that one. There was something surreal about the wave, something akin to a hallucination. There was an iridescence of engine oil to it, but it seemed more luminous, somehow incandescent. Goyette saw it coming and ran, swearing as he went. He fell trying to extract his shoes from the mud; he was stuck in his socks.

The roller had left a grain or two for the rising tide to flush away, but between two ripples and for as far as the eye could see, it was impossible to look at the beach without feeling a dizzying sensation of strangeness. Goyette trained his binoculars on the ground because he had no magnifying glass. Immediately he pulled his eyes away, as if they'd just been burned. They didn't hurt, but he kept them closed so he could pull himself together. The image he had seen in the binoculars had not imprinted itself on his brain. Try as he might to remember it, it would provoke a reaction in his whole body: a stiffening chaos had taken hold of him. His eyes were not burning; the pain was existential.

Fourth intermission

the urchin

With its spines, the urchin is the prototype of an introvert. Its flesh is red or yellow on the inside, like the sea.

The etymology of the word *urchin* is a prickly subject. Some say it stems from the same root as the hedgehog (from the Latin, *ēricius*); others, the bear, *ursus*. One might be tempted to settle the debate by considering the creature in its natural habitat. One might observe it in a spherical, armoured state not unlike that of a startled hedgehog, but one might also see it bite into the rock and make a home for itself there with bearlike nonchalance.

In Laurie's shell collection, the most delicate of all were little white or pale green globes, studded with white pearls. She found them on the beach, rarely intact, most often perforated by the distinctive mark of a gull's beak. She had learned early on to love their regularity—always ten double rows of pearls: five of larger ones and five of smaller ones, alternating; always the same globular form; always the same toothy opening at one end, and another, smaller and rounder, at the opposite end. These were not shells, but urchin skeletons. The skeleton of a sea urchin is also known as the "test."

Long before Laurie, Aristotle had harboured an interest in urchin anatomy. Thanks to him, we know that the Greeks had already learned to tell its head from its butt: "Singularly enough, the urchin has what we may call its head and mouth down below, and a place for the issue of the residuum up above." Aristotle had also remarked that everything about an urchin came in fives: five compartments, five teeth, five stomachs. Five gonads too. Not knowing any better, he did what everyone else did and called them eggs: "Underneath the stomach, in another membrane, are the so-called eggs, identical in number in all cases, and that number is always an odd number, to wit five." The gonads are eaten. They excrete the semen of the males or the eggs of the females through a single pore in the test, one pore per gonad, five pores in all.

Aristotle viewed semen, sperm, and men's too, as a principal of order that gives shape to menstrual blood to form the embryo: "In like manner, in the male of those animals which emit semen, Nature uses the semen as a tool and as possessing motion in actuality, just as tools are used in the products of any art, for in them lies in a certain sense the motion of the art." Aristotle was familiar with the philosophy of the

Pythagoreans, namely Alcmaeon of Croton, one of the first philosophers to conceive of the brain as the seat of thought. For Alcmaeon, semen was a part of the brain. Other Pythagoreans argued that sperm was a drop of the brain, in the literal sense.

One day while out scuba diving, a thirty-something Laurie would see a starfish eaten up by five sea urchins, each making a meal of one of the arms. She would float above the doomed starfish for the longest time, fluttering her flippers just enough to counter the current, captivated by the means Nature would employ to reveal herself. It would remind her of the first urchins prepared for her by Mori the summer she was seventeen: their gonads all porous and colourful, arranged in a star shape at the bottom of the shells.

Mori elegantly explained that these were urchin tongues, as they liked to call them in fashionable restaurants. Laurie didn't bat an eye: they did look like little tongues. They had the same roughness, but not the toughness. She was the first of the Lelarges to taste the green urchin. Until then, she had known it only by its spines. France would warn her to be careful when she swam in case she got one stuck in her foot. Laurie had never seen a live one, except once, perhaps, on the submerged part of a rock from where she liked to dive. For her, and for Florence, urchins were straight out of a fairy tale. "Watch out! It's full of urchins down there!"

they would shout to freak each other out when the water got too cold to swim in and they were trying to find somewhere they could touch the bottom.

In the mouth, it was another thing entirely: Laurie's tongue crushed the urchin's tongue on her palate. It made a thick, flavourful juice. The salt, the iodine, the dead-fish pungency: it tasted like the smell of the sea on a foggy day when the water stank. "The urchins are devoid of flesh, and this is a character peculiar to them," wrote Aristotle. Yet of all seafood, urchins taste the fleshiest.

With their five teeth, urchins will eat anything, even rock. Unlike molluscs, they are not filters, but hunter-gatherers. They are particularly partial to laminaria, a green algae that gives them their colour. The Japanese will also eat pretty much anything. Nevertheless, they are particularly partial to urchins. Robert had no real concept of their value while negotiating his contract with Mr. Utsumi of the Isumi Conglomerate of Tones, Colours, Pigments, Molluscs, and Crustaceans. This was a grave strategic error: in his eyes, anyone who ate green urchin was either crazy or fooling around. He'd chuckled when they asked him whether he could deliver urchin gonads in a can. Then they had named a price. Saturn had nearly choked. They'd had to give him a sip of tea. Robert had managed to nudge the figure higher and make some implausible delivery promises.

He had no concept of the process of urchin fishing: underwater, by hand, laborious. When they flew home, he had attempted to suit up a few Moroccans as frogmen, but hadn't even given them proper gloves.

The thought that Mori might be a member of the Japanese police force tasked with incriminating him in the murder of a Tokyo hooker had not completely left Robert's mind. But the more time went by, the more he came around to the idea that Mori was in Baie-Trinité first and foremost to make sure the urchins were delivered. On Laurie's birthday, when Mori had placed the crate on the table, Robert had felt threatened: "See how easy it is to pluck urchins out of that water," the crate had berated him. "Like getting eggs from a rooster. Better not count your chickens before they're hatched."

11

After the wave at four seventeen

In Baie-Trinité, when the river's in a rage, people say the wave's rolling. The wave, as in, a singular collective noun. No one had ever seen a tsunami. That a wave could, by way of its brilliance or its power, detach itself from "the wave" to become "a wave," well, no one had ever seen that either. The wave was a phenomenon of numbers, like a flock of Canada geese or the wrinkles on a face. To notice the wrinkle that isn't a wrinkle, but instead the scar of an old injury, or to notice the flagging goose that's going to get left behind, you have to stop and look. The fishermen didn't have the perspective; the dockers didn't have the time. The folk in the village, Frédéric Goyette would discover, all had something else to focus on: a road, a screen, a baby, the hammering of a nail, a bikini, a tree, a speedometer. Goyette could not believe that he had been the sole witness to the wave at four seventeen. Mori Ishikawa must have seen it: he'd been on the beach too, but it would be very difficult, Goyette was already sure of it, to tackle the question with him head-on.

Moreover, the recollection of the wave was receding in Goyette's mind. How could such a striking image evaporate so quickly from his memory? He had no idea. He put it down, somewhat half-heartedly, to the insomnia.

At four seventeen, in the presbytery, Laurie had noticed, while taking off her bikini to change into a pair of panties, that she was even wetter than she'd thought. She had picked up her book again to read and touch herself some more, as if engaging in both acts at the same time would satisfy two equally compelling appetites. She wasn't very far into *The Unbearable Lightness of Being*: Tereza was recounting her pool dream. Laurie applied her concentration quite entirely to reading; when the time came to turn the page, she endured the mounting pleasure. At one binary moment, reading had become impossible. She closed her eyes and came right then, hard.

Shortly after that, she went out onto the veranda in jeans and a camisole. She wanted to keep reading, but knew Florence would be home soon. France and Robert had gone to pick her up from the hospital in Baie-Comeau, where it had taken the day to rehydrate her. The corridors were overflowing with gurneys where Saturn's victims were recovering, drip by drip.

Laurie picked up the book. She didn't read. She didn't want to read "in the meantime." Her gaze was drawn to the beach, which no longer seemed unusual, then to the Saint Lawrence and its rippling. She started to think about Mori's sperm swept away by the tide: a big drop or a small mass, a ball, endowed with its own transparency in the transparency of the water, spreading its rays as it drifted, shedding its stringiness. The three hundred million spermatozoa from biology class were all there: twice as many little swimmers in Mori's ejaculate as there were Japanese in Japan. The sperm—the little swimmers, and their nourishing liquid habitat—became one with the sea like the rest of the plankton. There came a gust of wind and the sounding of a boat's horn. In a eureka moment lessened by the embarrassment of not having had it earlier, Laurie started to see the sperm for what they were: the material proof of one of Mori's orgasms. Even though it clarified things, she wasn't so sure that was the only thing that had left her all worked up.

Before Robert gave France a Jaguar convertible for her birthday in May, Laurie had never heard an engine throb at such a high pitch. The shrillness, as she had taken to calling it, got in the way of her long little-old-lady chats with Florence. It gave them both goosebumps. Florence said all that mechanical power was an assault on the body, and what sprang to mind was the wild yet clichéd beast the brand suggested. Laurie said it made her think of the dentist's drill. The difference brought them out in gales of laughter.

France didn't drive her Bimmer anymore, not since she got the Jag. Laurie figured she was hanging on to it for the winter, but now that Florence had been in hospital, it was becoming increasingly obvious that their parents would feel guilty and end up giving it to her. As it happened, seeing Florence come home at the beginning of the summer, France had muttered to Robert under her breath that she looked a bit pathetic in that Mazda of hers. And so the Mazda would not end up with Laurie's hands on the wheel. Perhaps a distant cousin's instead. For the sake of fairness, they would give Laurie a Bimmer, a new one, but a small one, for when school started. Laurie had her licence, but she had never really driven. She knew how absent-minded she could be and, with a steering wheel in her hands, she knew she could only be a danger to the public. This only strengthened her conviction that she wouldn't be going to Quebec City and wouldn't be going to college. And she went back to thinking about Mori.

The sound of dentistry curtailed Laurie's daydreaming about how exactly the Japanese guy's sperm might have become plankton. She went to greet them in the hallway. It was France who'd been driving. Robert had let Florence have the front seat. He managed to extract himself and struggled to stretch his legs. Right away Laurie noticed there was no gel in his hair. She wondered if he was sick too. If he was, he was hiding it well. His mouth and eyebrows arched abnormally. It looked more like he was fit to be tied.

Robert went straight up to his office. France went off to fret in the kitchen, looking out at the beach through the slats in the blind. She saw Mori. As usual, he was going about his sampling, his census-taking. He disgusted her: he'd wanted to give seafood to Laurie, he'd been cold at the restaurant before disappearing when everyone started shitting their pants, and Robert behaved like a puppy in front of him. She uttered out loud, but between her teeth, a strange string of words imbued with all the foresight a mother can have but that so often passes for coincidence.

"The Man Who Comes! There he goes again, pacing up and down the beach..."

The nickname would stick.

Florence was happy to have some tea waiting for her. A cuppa's always nice after twenty hours or so of drinking through your veins. Laurie asked her if she would prefer it iced. Yes. The two sisters took their usual seats in the rocking chairs.

"It's not sitting well with me, all this. Everyone saw me shit myself, apparently. Someone might have put it up on Insta," Florence synopsized when they cut to the chase.

"Whaddya mean, 'apparently'?"

"That's just what I've heard, I can't really remember. Listen ... I was looking forward to seeing you, you're the only one I'd dare ask about this. It's just that, at the hospital, I realized I didn't have my G-string on anymore."

"If you shat yourself to the point of ending up in Emergency, that's only natural," Laurie adjudicated.

"No, I mean, I remember I was making eyes at the chef. I'm wondering if I ditched my panties *before* it all hit the fan, if you know what I mean."

"I can't help you. I wasn't there."

"Yes, you were. You told Uncle Réginald he'd had the wrong nickname for at least the last thirty years. Then you took my phone and showed him some freaky paintings."

"I left after the drinks, when you all went inside the restaurant, because of my 'allergies.' Don't you remember?"

Laurie could do air quotes like nobody's business. Her face almost took on the shape of two fingers flexing their rabbit ears.

"No..." Florence replied.

A rising consternation filled her olive-toned face, hollow cheeks, glassy eyes and all.

"Holy fuck," she carried on, "the chef must've slipped some gee-aitch in my glass!"

The GHB, or maybe some other date-rape drug, theory was not implausible. Laurie and Florence looked into it seriously for three days straight: they researched it online, they started grilling the kitchen staff. After those three days, Goyette would put himself out there in his very first televised press conference and announce the more or less reassuring conclusions from his own investigation.

Laurie and Florence were not the only ones to be hatching hypotheses. For three days, in the absence of a media-sanctioned scientific explanation, the fanciful mechanisms of fiction sparked to life, the very same mechanisms behind all the legends and more than a few things that pass for the truth. Everyone drew on their suspicions and added what went without saying. Those who called a spade a spade said it was food poisoning because seafood, everyone knows, gives you food poisoning. How? It was the way it was cooked (Montreal style, so not enough), the way the Moroccans harvested the clams, the way those boats from the Gaspé leaked oil. "Science will reveal all!" no one held out. Word in the village had it that as soon as the restaurant ran out of toilet paper, the boss, Robert Lelarge, had been handing out fifty-dollar bills for folk to wipe their cracks with. The fishermen went on about avenging sea creatures—giant lobsters, three-headed monsters, and all—though never within earshot of anyone not in the business.

The Premier's wife's psychoanalyst went on to give talk after talk about it. He changed the names, but that fooled no one in the know. That theory, like many others, including the most outlandish, kept doing the rounds long after Goyette's press conferences. The thing was, the Premier's wife, once she came out of her coma, had not, like Florence, forgotten what she'd done with her underwear. She had forgotten what she'd done with her life. It was like the plot line of one of those novels from the subgenre that might be called amnesic suspense. The psychoanalyst's first mission was to hypnotize her into thinking that she loved her husband. The Premier figured that would be easy because his spin doctors had done the very same thing with everyone else who lived in Quebec. He was wrong.

The journalists weren't letting anyone at the Canadian Food Inspection Agency off the hook, and Frédéric Goyette, still all at sea long after the wave at four seventeen, would have to come around to that idea, and fast. From his truck, he called the mayor of Baie-Comeau, the government minister responsible for the region, and Myriam, to let her know he wouldn't be home for dinner. Too bad, he'd promised her gravlax. He phoned the chef's restaurant in Montreal. The chef had told the owners he wouldn't be back before Chrimbo. That was the kind of quirky language he used sometimes. How the heck could a guy like that have chartered a floatplane? No one seemed to know.

After a phone call or two to France, Goyette tracked down the *Michelin Guide* inspectors who had made an incognito visit.

"It was certainly going to be one, perhaps two stars, until I had..." the inspector began to whisper, "an upset."

"An upset?"

"Yes. You know ... an upset ... a stirring!"

"A stirring?"

"The shits, for goodness' sake!"

"Ah! All right. Well, actually, that's what I was hoping to shoot the shit with you about, so to speak."

Then he spoke to a few hipster types. He thought they were snobs. Which just went to show, everyone's someone else's snob. When Goyette asked them the very question that would allow him to confirm or rule out the hypothesis according to which the wave at four seventeen had been carrying particles of fecal origin—"Can you describe your stools to me, tell me, at least, what colour they were?"—he invariably ran up against one of these three unhelpful answers:

1. "It was too dark for me to see."

2. "I wish I could help, but I can't really remember. It wasn't just the alcohol, you know."

3. "With all due respect, I have better things to do than examine my excrement."

Robert clung tight to the armrests of his big office chair with four screens in his face. In one corner, the Nikkei was taking a little dive; in another, the yen was feeling the effects; in a third, High Liner had just bought a flash-freezing plant in Iceland. He didn't react. The stiffness wasn't letting up, and he couldn't blame it all on the cramped quarters in the back of the Jag. His body was tense, his colon was still growling despite him knocking back the Imodium like there was no tomorrow. At the hospital in Baie-Comeau, where they'd had to declare a code orange, many of Chez Saturne's victims had recognized him. Few words had been exchanged, but he had detected a feverish disappointment in their eyes. He had felt relieved to have a pale Florence clutching his arm. But now that relief had put him to shame.

Word in the village was, if Robert Lelarge didn't have gel in his hair, he must be running one hell of a fever. Robert knew that, and he'd done it on purpose. Neglecting his hair was all the damage control he was capable of. He would have to hire a firm. He would also have to speak with the shareholders, bring them on board: one was on the brink of an overdose, the other floating between two mantras. He had an urge to take the lead and call Tokyo, call the Isumi Conglomerate of Tones, Colours, Pigments, Molluscs, and Crustaceans. Someone would answer the phone. He would explain what had happened. He resisted the urge: the yen were still piling up in the company's coffers. There was no need for him to do anything right away. If they stopped piling up, Robert knew lawyers who had a way with international lawyering. Mori Ishikawa, if he did actually work for them, must have already contacted the Conglomerate anyway. If they didn't show up in a few days' time with a cease-and-desist and a compensation claim, then Ishikawa was a cop and that was a whole other kettle of fish. There was Goyette too. He or Mori wouldn't be long. The enemy would come from the beach.

On no account whatsoever were Florence and Laurie to enter the office. France had the go-ahead to knock on the door if it was work-related. Contrary to what the sisters had believed throughout their childhood, she and Robert never made love in there. Although Robert had been known to play with himself.

France knocked. Speak of the devil, it was Goyette. He was at the door, downstairs.

From the veranda, Laurie and Florence had seen him arrive, his Mitsubishi kit in hand, but he hadn't looked up—on purpose, they told themselves. Goyette had disappeared beneath the decking, just below them; they couldn't see him through the boards, the gaps were too narrow, but they could hear him all right. Robert's irate strides shook the wood of their rocking chairs—and the whole house—when he stormed down to open the door. He flung it back so hard it rattled the blind.

You can't see bacteria or toxins with the naked eye, but Goyette was holding something all right. Robert's eye was drawn to the sample—a centimetre of a white powder at the bottom of a test tube—but when he looked at it, his whole head turned away, as though instinctively. It seized Robert by the neck, like a crick on top of the stiffness. He wanted to look, but his muscles wouldn't let him. The merest glance was like a fistful of sand to the face, but without the pain. All the reflexes of an irritation were there, except for the pain. The irritation caught in the mucous membranes of the eyes, but neither caustic nor burning, it came from someplace else: from a world between the inside and outside of the body, between perception and reaction, a place where nausea, dizziness, and bedazzlement existed too.

"What the heck is that stuff?"

"I was about to ask you the same question," Goyette replied, proud of his retort.

"Put that thing away, will you!"

Goyette complied. He put the test tube in his Mitsubishi case, inside a black plastic sleeve. Robert resumed his typical tone.

"To what do I owe the pleasure, Goyette?"

"You know."

"If it's about the restaurant, Saturn's the one you should go see."

"I've seen him already. Let's just say that what you saw in the test tube, something tells me it came from the guests' ejections at the restaurant yesterday."

"Ejections ... such big words, Goyette."

"All right, Robert, let me put my cards on the table: I'm trying to find a reason not to shut down your entire plant tomorrow. Give me a hand, will you?"

"How? I don't know what that powder of yours is. I've never seen anything like it. Powder, as you know, that's more Saturn's side of things."

"I want to speak with Florence."

"Want to screw her, do you, Goyette? You wanna screw my daughter?!"

Florence started flailing her arms around up on the veranda. Laurie calmed her down.

Robert was seething. The setting sun and the blood in his face made his acne scars blush. Goyette knew it was more than just lingering resentment.

"I don't want to *screw* her. I want to talk to her about what happened yesterday."

"She doesn't remember a thing. Not a thing. She's forgotten it all."

"Right ... so she has amnesia."

"I'll give you amnesia," Robert white-knuckled.

"And what about you, Robert?"

"Me?"

"Yes. Can you just—now this is important—tell me what colour your feces were?"

"That's none of your fucking business. My shite is mine, and mine alone. Now give the Queen a wave for me," he door-slammed.

Goyette was more than slightly taken aback. He took a deep breath. He saw the Canadian Food Inspection Agency decal with the little maple leaf when he got back to his work truck, and he began to laugh. That had always been his reaction to the truly big questions in life: a little chuckle followed by a serious dose of the blues.

His wife saw nothing in the face where everything, save for one deep desire, came to lose itself. That was the only emotion she knew how to read, and that was enough. They made love without tiredness and without inhibitions. Afterwards, Goyette prepared the gravlax. Insomnia, at times like this, was no bad thing.

12

Until the sea shall free them

You're never more alone than while aboard a forty-two-foot lobster trawler between Natashquan and Anticosti Island, but a long way from both, when a storm no meteorologist saw coming blows up and a mild sore throat seizes and lays up in bed the deckhand you hired because he's a good kid really, but when all's said and done, he's just a lazy little shit.

That'd happened to Serge Cabana aka Hercules, the guy who used to scare the crap out of Laurie, long before Goyette showed up with his powder in a test tube. Until then, Hercules had enjoyed telling people how three times in his life he'd thought he was going to die, but never once aboard his boat: there was the time his beard caught fire, the time he got stabbed at an all-inclusive resort, and the time he had his hunting accident. He never said a word about it again.

When it happened, he had just emptied his traps. It had been a mediocre catch and he'd had no trouble bringing it in without the lazy little shit's help. The name of his boat, the *Mare of Diomedes*, was a testament to his forward thinking. Before that, he had skippered the *Irreplaceable III*, a name forever associated with the incredible hauls of four generations of Cabanas. The *Irreplaceable IV* would have been a bit of a contradiction in terms, he figured. The tradition had to end there.

There wasn't much to say about the storm. "You had to be there," he would always explain. "I would say it was a bastard of a storm, but I've seen some bastard storms before and none of them ever scared me. This one scared me shitless." The sky had turned black. Hercules hadn't even had a chance to realize the wind was starting to howl before waves eight storeys high were pitching the *Mare* this way and that. The fibreglass hull had slammed into the gulf at the bottom of every trough, the impact rattling his bones, his balls, and his jaw. He had been paralyzed, his breath taken away. The bilge pump sure had its work cut out for it. Cresting a wave, he had seen a tornado whirling right for his boat, a tornado full of water, made entirely of water, a waterspout. He swore to anyone who would listen that the tornado was full of lobsters too, and many must have been twenty pounds or more, by the looks of them. People laughed at him: in a whirlwind like that, who was he to eyeball the size of a lobster? They didn't know what kind of eye he had.

What Hercules didn't say to just anyone, though, was that after seeing that tornado made of water and lobsters, he hadn't reached for his foghorn, his lifebuoy, or his packet of cigarettes. He'd reached for his rosary beads. Things had turned out all right. At one point, a ray of light had parted the sky to tell him what he needed to know.

Yes. Hercules believed in God—in Jesus, rather—in that kind of way, in mystical puffs, when he suddenly found himself in need of an intercession. He believed in a particular Jesus who, if you asked him, rejoiced in being worshipped that way: the Jesus of sailors, the same one who walked upon the water.

Among the fishermen who docked at Baie-Trinité, there were a few English-speakers from the Lower North Shore: all quite fervent Protestants, except one Jew who kept that quiet. The others were Catholic to varying degrees, from the churchwardenly to the renegades. A few bohemians had converted to Buddhism as they had to fishing, late in the game. No one proclaimed to be atheist, but plenty didn't really give a shit. In spite of everything, all of them, without exception, carried the odd religious knickknack on board, for emergencies. It wasn't hard to understand: anyone who's ever had a noseful of water has had a fleeting encounter with the Absolute.

It was Suzanne who best understood the fishermen's religious convictions. They all had the same fears, the same desires. So many lovers within such a small group required the downiest discretion to welcome them into. They knew they could confide in her.

"Oh Hercules, you know you're always welcome at the tradesman's entrance," Suzanne giggled as she parted her generous buttocks to flash him her anus and a glimpse of her vulva. Her other hand was busy dribbling lube down her crack. They did have their little habits. He'd had his way with her for the first time on the beach, one very hot May afternoon, after offloading a generous catch had put him in a triumphalist state of mind. He'd been unable to resist the flimsy dress that made her look like a generously endowed gypsy.

Since then, he had relished the secrecy in which they cloaked their Monday afternoons. She would invite him over to her place, into her hobbit house, ("It's a cave," she'd still had to explain, "but with lights and it's nicely decorated."). He knew she slept with a lot of fishermen, but the way she made herself his every time left him reeling. He didn't talk about that. The contact of their bodies was vast and full of lumps and bumps. Afterwards, she would feed him tea or oranges. Such was the smelly score of their secrecy: incense, damp rock, musky obese buttocks, sweat, tea, oranges.

Sometimes, even if his flesh was asking for more, Hercules felt uncomfortable doing it with a big woman. To ease his mind, he would tell himself he was showing solidarity among fishermen. Suzanne sweetly let him kid himself.

Suzanne came back naked, carrying tea, after "freshening up" (her preferred euphemism). She was smoking a Du Maurier. Hercules had draped himself in a sheet on the bed, Roman style. He had turned the TV on. Such a thing might ordinarily have been enough to banish him forever from the select few of Suzanne's fisherman lovers, but it was the news—the serious stuff, not the local fluff. Goyette was performing for a pack of microphones.

"What do you think happened, then?" Suzanne asked, snuggling up to him.

"What happens when you cook a two-pound lobster for seven minutes."

Of all the hypotheses Hercules had entertained, this was the most palatable.

Robert had bought a TV set again to watch Goyette on the news. One hadn't been seen in the presbytery since the *My Girl* ordeal. Florence wasn't there often enough anymore to complain, and Laurie was lost in her books.

It was four days after the "events in Baie-Trinité" (that was the media's preferred euphemism). Goyette was embarking on his hundredth straight waking hour. There was nothing even remotely fun about the sleeplessness anymore. He got the shivers when he stopped drinking coffee and had taken refuge in the lunar soundscape of Edward Vesala's music. His brain was increasingly incapable of distinguishing instincts from ideas doomed for the depths. To make sure he didn't slip up, with a trembling hand he had written a list of things he could say in a press conference—and another of things he had to steer well clear of. He was numb to the nerves he should have been feeling. He should have known that he would seek refuge in silence much more than in dithering.

Things he could say: no one was dead (a good start); some had a certain degree of amnesia about the events prior to the poisoning; a great many samples had been sent to laboratories across Canada; Lelarge Fisheries had agreed to a plant inspection and were cooperating with retailers, but since no one had had symptoms after consuming seafood destined for the supermarket shelves, there was no reason to warrant a recall.

Goyette could not say that the chef from the restaurant had fled on a floatplane, the owner of which had ties to organized crime, nor could he say that he had called his own mother to tell her to stop eating Lelarge shrimp. He could not talk about the wave at four seventeen either, or the irregardable powder he had extracted from it. Chemically, the powder contained only water and some mineral impurities, like snow that had forgotten how to melt. He knew he couldn't say in public what crossed his mind at night: whatever was happening went beyond biology. He was looking for a neurotoxin, like the toxin that caused amnesic shellfish poisoning, but whereas a neurotoxin targeted nerve functioning, he was dealing here, perhaps, with a toxin that targeted the very basis of existence. At night, he called it an *ontotoxin*, a toxin that targeted the being as such. Being *qua* being.

Yes, that was where he was at. Whenever Myriam heard Vesala playing, she knew her Frédéric's thoughts were becoming abstruse and terrifying. She would go out to pick the red seeds for the jam she made to go with his meatballs. She would encourage him to play his guitar. Usually that would be enough to ground him. Not this time.

In the summer, the world slows down and there's no place in the news for anything other than a headline or two that the interns jump on. There was a buzz surrounding Goyette and Goyette hated it. The first sentence he uttered to the barrage of camera flashes began with: "There are others better placed than I am..." His hair was unkempt; his eyes, concave. He hadn't shaved, and he was wearing his customary windbreaker over an unwashed T-shirt. He found himself unable to string a full sentence together.

"We've found several known toxins, but in very low quantities, infi—"

"You mean you let people eat toxins?" an intern pounced on his pause with the tone of a rookie out to make an impression.

"Toxins in infinitesimal quantities."

The message wasn't getting across. There were also the interminable silences, the shrugged shoulders, the apparent lack of nerves that came across as a complete lack of empathy, the reluctance to comment. Not having an opinion is often worse than having the wrong opinion. Goyette came across as an enigmatic giant of a man who inspired no confidence. Nearly every day for two weeks straight, he would return to flounder in front of the microphones. The journalists loved hating him, and getting others to hate him too. That summer, anyone keeping any more than half an eye on the news, between two umbrella-adorned cocktails, might have easily assumed from the look on Frédéric Goyette's face that he had personally poisoned the Premier's wife.

"He rubs me the wrong way, that little shitster of a bureaucrat," said Hercules with class consciousness, as the TV news segued to an outbreak of E. coli bacteria in Montreal public swimming pools; it was a summer of contaminations.

"Give it a rest! He doesn't seem so bad to me," Suzanne purred, with that smile of hers that tuned many a fisherman in to her wavelength.

Robert didn't say anything, but just before the report aired, he had nearly seen white before his eyes. He could breathe easier now. Someone from Loblaws or Metro would no doubt be phoning him, bypassing the distributor, but he might at least be able to reassure them more than Goyette had. As for the Japanese, they would have to wait for The Man Who Comes to come knocking.

Moroccans continued to fill crates with urchins and shellfish. Workers continued to can and flash-freeze.

Stacks of boxes continued to pack refrigerated trucks bound for Dorval. From there, planes continued to take off for Tokyo.

At the far end of the living room, Laurie and Florence were watching Goyette on the flat screen too. They were giggling over his roguish charm. Robert could feel those giggles bouncing around inside his chest. They didn't give a shit, and he knew it was because of him. Their complicity jabbed him in the ribs. For the first time, he thought perhaps it was too late. "How much do you reckon the losses will add up to, girls? And what would you do to get the company back on its feet?" he imagined himself saying across a big table to his preoccupied daughters dressed in business suits, in a different version of his story, as minimalist as the Tokyo premises of the Isumi Conglomerate of Tones, Colours, Pigments, Molluscs, and Crustaceans. He turned off the TV, unplugged it, and moved it into his office on a whim. Florence grumbled a bit. Laurie said nothing.

At Cécile's greasy spoon one evening, Mori Ishikawa tried the shrimp rice. It came in a white sauce. He ate only the shrimp. He had brought a rice cooker in his luggage, but when he'd tried to plug it into the wall in his motel room, it had blown a fuse. He ate a lot of urchins, with Laurie and lemon, or alone, plain. At Cécile's he preferred to order hamburgers or poutine. He liked the rubbery texture of the cheese curds, but that kind of food soon loses its appeal.

The first time Goyette went on the TV news, Mori had just moved in to Louis Berthelot's: Sar'h's brother and night foreman for the freezing line at the plant. Mori had seen a classified ad in the local paper. Berthelot had just been cheated on, divorced, and decided he'd rather hole up at his hunting cabin—until winter, at least, while the cobwebs cleared—and rent out his house.

Mori had taken all the pictures off the walls and piled all the furniture in the basement. He wanted nothing to do with it. He had spent a good week painting the whole place white. To attune his ear to the Quebec accent and alleviate his painter's loneliness, he would leave the TV on all day, on the floor. Goyette came on screen. Mori recognized the guy. He sat down on the hardwood floor to watch him in the empty house.

13

The mosquito impact

Saturn had always enjoyed going to the cash machine. Throughout his life, he'd toyed with the experience under the influence of various psychotropic substances. Ketamine had made him think the machine was a voracious beast, munching his card like a hippo when it's feeding time at the zoo. The super powerful varieties of oleaginous cannabis tended to amplify the sucking sound when he inserted his card: breezy, mechanical, like a magic carpet ride. His PIN was a teenage boy's: 6969, and he shared it with everyone.

To get to his place on Cléophas Lake, it was a good trek by quad or Ski-Doo. In winter, snowshoes were non-negotiable. It was far enough out of the way that no one would venture there without knowing Saturn, or at least his reputation. He wasn't insured for fire, or theft. Not giving a shit about the risks that held back a financial man, letting anyone who wanted to stay for as long as they liked, and tapping into cash machines like fire hydrants: for Saturn, that was pretty much the sum of being rich.

His hunting cabin had been done up some years earlier, using nothing but the finest materials. It was luxurious, but filthy, and everything about it screamed: filthy rich. Saturn was walking around buck naked on the rug that morning. He wasn't really sure if there was anyone else upstairs. One time he didn't care to brag about, a bear had spent a few days at his place because he'd mistaken it for a particularly hungry house guest just passing through.

There were four girls and three guys upstairs: employees headhunted from fashionable restaurants in Montreal, now out of a job and in love with the North Shore. They were watching *Caillou* on TV, eating cereal out of single-serving boxes.

"For fuck's sake! It's like a trashy daycare," Saturn thought he said.

The first pastry chef saw her boss's mouth form an approximate shape of the vowels, but not a sound came out. Réginald's presence was acknowledged all the same with a half-hearted "Hey, Sa-turn."

In the kitchen, Saturn caught a glimpse of his reflection in the polished metal of a commercial percolator. He had never paddled out to ride the espresso wave. At their increasingly infrequent family parties, he was an exasperation to everyone, insisting on a filter coffee with the tone of someone who's not quite become a snob yet. Suzanne or France would plunk a big mug and the full coffee pot beside him. Then they would put another pot on to brew for when he demanded a refill.

He lingered over the skinny image of himself reflected by the lens effect. In the percolator, he looked a bit like a Giacometti sculpture with a little steel wool wig perched on his head. The beard he could put up with, but he hadn't shaved his pubes in ages and he thought that made him ugly.

"Is there coffee in there?"

He knew it was the kind of item in which coffee could typically be found, but he had no idea how the percolator had wound up there.

"Yeah, it's full," said the dishwasher (the dude who washed the dishes, not the appliance, although stranger things had happened).

The percolator held fifteen litres. More than was strictly necessary. Saturn went into the bathroom to get his quetiapine pills (the mildest of antipsychotics, he would explain when asked, aware of the oxymoron) and made himself comfortable at the anthracite quartz counter. With a single flourish of his left hand, he filled his cup with ease. He was taking the quetiapine twenty-five milligrams at a time. That was how he liked to detox these days.

Drugs, for him, were like the colours on a painter's palette. He liked to blend his own kind of buzz. It was a complex art that required knowing the substances and their effects, but more than anything, knowing yourself. After a few days, it was high time for a change of canvas. The coffee and the quetiapine would unfog his mind. Every cup and every pill would snatch a memory. The way he told it, it was like recording a TV show so he wouldn't miss it while he was at a party, only his life was the TV show. Sitting in the nude at the kitchen counter as the crew idly contemplated tossing a frisbee around, he was about to hit the play button.

Owing to a little itch in his sternum, he recalled the Rubens painting on the screen of Florence's phone.

"What say you start calling me Neptune?"

"Neptune? Why? Saturn suits you so well," a sommelier shot him down.

All his life, he'd be the punchline of a running gag.

Round about the fifth litre of coffee, after three hundred milligrams of quetiapine, some choppy images from the beach surfaced in his mind. He could feel the blood flowing back into one arm, ah yes, Goyette had undone his tourniquet. After that, everything had happened all at once.

"Ito sends his regards."

"Who is Ito, and who the fuck are you?" Saturn articulated painfully in his memory, where the monosyllables of English let him stand a chance.

"Réginald Lelarge, you know very well who Ito is."

"What's going on? Who the fuck are you?"

"That's disheartening. Disheartening. Despicable. You don't jump ship like that. You must have put some time into building that restaurant, and plenty of your family's money. Some even say it's your father's house, where you grew up. Now you're leaving it like that, full of shit, first chance you get. And here you are, on this beach, in this village where everyone knows you, lying on your needles."

"Whoa there! Are you judging me?"

"It's not my place to judge you. I think it's my duty to help you do that."

"Hey, listen. You're not very nice."

"ソープランド!"

It was in remembering that word that it dawned on Saturn: this must be the Japanese guy he had spoken to at the restaurant opening.

"Sopo-what?"

"You know what I'm talking about."

"I don't."

"Nothing disappears, Mr. Lelarge. Does this mean anything to you? Nothing is lost, nothing is created. Everything is transformed."

Neither the sixth litre of coffee nor the four hundredth milligram of quetiapine could help Saturn determine with any certainty what had happened next. All he could recall was a vague pain after Mori's admonitions. He figured the Japanese guy had given him a kick in the ribs. The heroin, which had been incredibly pure, could have dulled the pain. And since he'd added a bit of ketamine to his syringe for a bit more orange, and popped half a methamphetamine to fire it all up, a kick in the ribs would have had about as much effect as a mosquito bite. Although sometimes, on seeing the swelling, we're reminded of the impact of the mosquito that went unnoticed. Perhaps Mori had gone on his way, whistling as he went. Perhaps he had beaten him up with the cruelty of someone who knows not to leave a mark.

Not long before or not long after the hypothetical kick, there had been a wave. Saturn was lying on the beach and the wave, immense, had surged into his body by way of his nostrils, his mouth, his eyes, his eardrums, his anus, and even through the meatus of his penis. He had felt it flowing thick and luminous inside him, warming like alcohol. It had persisted like a presence. He could remember having evanescent ideas of pregnancy, envying with great heavings of the soul a woman's capacity to feel two lives inside the same body. Stroboscopic images of interlocked objects, of nesting geometries, had flashed through his brain.

Had he opened his eyes? Had he seen the beach after the wave? He took four more quetiapine pills. He didn't know. Images were coming back to him that could not be true. He saw himself in a sand of many colours. Sand is always multicoloured when you look at it close up, but on that beach there was indigo sand atop sienna sand, and sand in every shade of green too.

Saturn's memory contained several seconds of that far too multicoloured sand where all the colours of the visible spectrum were breaking down, save for a few. Without those omissions, everything would have merged together and turned to white. It was a hell of a buzz, raptured Saturn, still naked on his teak barstool, swept away to the point of worrying his guests, but he didn't know if the buzz was his alone. Another litre of coffee and two hundred milligrams of quetiapine later, he nodded off right there, in his seat. His sleep was calm and filled with dreams. At the zenith of his slumber, the combined potency of his snoring and his erection made everyone feel a bit awkward.

Laurie, who was reading in her room while she awaited her next appearance in the story, had never believed it meant nothing to be in someone's dream. She had often dreamed about boys from school or from the wharf, about big naked women, about her family in monstrous incarnations. Every time, she told herself a pinch would alert them. A pinch, because a pinch was what connected dreams to not-dreams. "Pinch yourself and you'll know if you're asleep," she was told when she was little. You can't pinch yourself in a dream and feel that pinch. In the logic of reality, action leads to feeling. The logic of dreams works the opposite way: feeling leads to action. Laurie knew her whole life was slowly becoming just that. She no longer dared to pinch herself. Her sensations no longer depended on events;

events increasingly depended on her sensations. In the fog, something had been turned upside down, or inside out, or back to front.

It wasn't a pinch, though, that alerted her when Mori dreamed of her. Little electric shocks would fizz at her nipples and wake her in the middle of the night. They would spread down to her belly and sensitize her vulva. She would smile for a second, sure he was dreaming of her, and go back to sleep. She barely questioned her role in Mori's dreams.

They were seeing each other more and more often. Laurie dreaded the day when Mori would confess that he had emptied the Saint Lawrence of all its urchins for her. She knew he had moved in someplace in the village, but they would meet on the beach, when the weather was nice. They spoke little. They were content to name the things around them and sustain the eroticism of formality in their words. In conversations essentially constituted of carefully crafted silence, they avoided each other's gaze less and less.

Laurie was sure Mori's sperm was still swimming in the Saint Lawrence, shrinking as it went; she was sure the subtle shifting of layers that afternoon would continue to unfold, but on a microscopic level—and everywhere at once. They didn't talk about that. She would have sex with him, she told her heart in a tone of inevitability. She would make a note on the calendar of the dates her period started and ended. Sometimes she would catch herself with her index, middle, and ring fingers together in her mouth, practising for Mori's length and finding herself ridiculous.

For weeks, nothing happened.

Then, one day, they spoke about clouds.

"Nimbostratus instill fear in all animals," Mori argued. "They give rise to something primitive in us. They are clouds we can feel."

"Have you ever experienced a very hot day with lots of cirrostratus?" Laurie asked, failing to notice her fractionally more frequent blinking.

"Rarely."

"It is quite rare. It happens here maybe once every three years. The sky is all white. The sun is nowhere to be seen, but the sky is brighter than blue. It's as if the cirrostratus are spreading the light of the sun all around ... it hurts the eyes."

Mori smiled his unusual smile and bowed with his eyes. He reached into his Mitsubishi case for a mussel shell that was a deep shade of blue and purple, likely picked from a thousand. He gave it to Laurie. Then he left.

At first Laurie thought the shell was alive, the two sides were stuck so tightly together. With a bit of effort, she discovered the inside was filled with sperm. She rolled it between her fingers at length, to explore its texture, trying to catch it when it dribbled onto the sand. She brought it to her nose. She was expecting the smell that rose up from the boys' locker room at the high school every time the door swung open. It was nothing like that. The scent was delicate and embracing, not unlike a tropical fruit, but without the hint of sweetness. It smelled of the sea too, but she wondered if that wasn't because of the shell. It was not a masculine odour, but it was the most masculine of odours: it came from the bottom of the balls.

It wasn't until later that evening that Laurie considered the other question: how had Mori managed to clean a mussel shell so meticulously, ejaculate into it, and close it again?

Myriam, Frédéric Goyette's wife, was pretty much at the end of her rope. On top of working all day at the daycare, when evening came she had to put up with the disconnected rambling of her other half. When it wasn't that, it was his silence or his agonizing fears. She had managed to get him to talk one time, figuring he'd pour his heart out and it would do him good, but instead it had been more like pulling the plug out of a bathtub filled with acid. He had cried as he put the devastation into words. She hadn't understood a thing. Neither his guitar nor the *smörgåsbord* it had taken her a weekend to put together could calm him or lull him to sleep. Not the Imovane. Nor the aquavit either. He had the Dostoyevskian look of the misunderstood in movies. His features were sagging. Every day, he got the shakes as he made his way to a motel in town, where the journalists would break him. In the evenings, in a burst of strength and anger, he would yell at Myriam to leave the TV on when he came on screen.

On the third day, he nodded off as he watched himself sputter, as full of tics on TV as he was in his chair. Myriam couldn't believe it. He'd been sitting at the table; his eyes had closed by themselves.

He had only the one dream. Not a fully formed, scripted dream, the kind that comes after a few hours of sleep. His dream was a rough draft of a few powerful images, a few hints at atmosphere. It was a dream about guilt. He flashed back to Laurie in her swimsuit on the beach when she was eight or nine years old. In the dream, Laurie's face was eight or nine years old, but she had the body she had now. Goyette stopped her, asked her what game she was playing. He gave her the shell of an Iceland scallop and desired her. The shell had no colour, but it caused a peculiar bewilderment, since everything must have a colour. Goyette's mind was gauging the extent of that bewilderment, but in one and the same movement, the bewilderment turned and seized his mind completely. That opposition, turned to dissonance, severed the dream, and set the mechanisms of waking in motion. Goyette's eyes opened. Myriam was two inches from his face.

"You nodded off, my love. Let me take you up to bed. Come on, now. Sleep."

"No. I have to find the shell I gave to Laurie."

"Who's Laurie?"

At home, Laurie felt no pinch, no shock, no tickle, no nothing.

Goyette filled his flask with coffee. He went off with his flashlight, even though it was still light out.

Fifth intermission

the mussel

"Now mussels, Réginald, you'd be wise to steer well clear of them."

There was something in the atmosphere of a hospital room that was conducive to taking a word of advice seriously. Rogatien Lelarge had just seen his cancer in the light box. Species by species, he was sharing his projections with Saturn for the business in the medium term. He himself wouldn't even make it to the short term.

"I've not had good experiences with mussels," he went on with an indecipherable grimace.

Saturn responded with a nervous laugh.

More than money, Rogatien had loved people all his life. The narrow-minded folk who thought it impossible that a businessman might harbour such a true and overarching devotion to humanity would often find themselves in the bar with him one night. The next morning, they would shut their hungover mouth: the man was a helluva good guy. At his funeral, people said he'd rather make a friend than a million. It wasn't funeral bullshit.

Saturn knew that for his brother Robert there were no mysteries a calculator couldn't solve, and for his sister there were none beyond the power of a trance. How we go about solving mysteries determines the mysteries we choose to solve. Between buzzes or whenever the drugs began to get out of hand, the words of his dying father sometimes came to mind, not that he wanted them to. That ambiguous remark had led him to question whether Rogatien had loved women too. What was the story behind those whims of a travelling salesman? And those bad experiences with mussels?

"Who really gives a shit?!" he would resolve out loud, even when he was alone with the mystery.

Families, and the dead, were entitled to their secrets.

Suzanne understood her father in karmic terms: he had profited too much from shrimp to profit from mussels too. She saw this as an invitation to restore balance through meditation. As for Robert, he saw nothing untoward: his father had lived through the mussel crisis (which he insisted, like Frédéric Goyette, on calling the "Prince Edward Island mussels crisis"). That's what the old man had against mussels, he would belabour. Nothing more than that.

In 1987 during the crisis, Goyette, who would go on to study all this later, was jazz guitaring at university in Montreal and came close to playing the opening act for

UZEB. He was young and the principal danger lurking in the back alleys after his shows was AIDS.

After the winter semester at Laval University, Robert had helped Rogatien's employees set up some bouchot poles on the mudflats. These were something the old man had seen in France, big poles strung with nets filled with young mussels to be farmed. Mussels cultured in this way would grow three times bigger than the wild mussels Rogatien struggled to market.

That November, mostly in Montreal, at least two hundred people had fallen seriously ill eating mussels from P.E.I.: vomiting, diarrhea, fever, confusion, amnesia. Three had died. They were dead for real, so even in a work of fiction, they couldn't go unnamed: Albert Pomeroy, age 71, from Pointe-Claire, died December 10; David McLaughlan, age 82, from Toronto, died December 16; and Bernadette Gagné, age 84, from Saint-Jean-Chrysostome, died December 17.

Goyette's predecessors had come to take samples of everything Rogatien had. Mice injected with extracts from P.E.I. mussels were dying after scratching at their ears in a frenzy. The newspapers went on and on every day about the "mystery toxin" that no one could get to the bottom of. The cartoonists, the columnists, everyone had put it down to acid rain. If people were dying after eating mussels, other people had to be to blame.

On December 11, the Minister of National Health and Welfare, Jake Epp, stood up in Canada's House of Commons and issued a ban on shellfish from the

Atlantic and the Gulf of St. Lawrence. The definition of the English word "shellfish" extends to both molluscs and crustaceans. When questioned by francophone journalists, a spokesperson for the ministry had declared that yes, the ban applied to shrimp and lobster too. That was when Rogatien had started to take it personally. Not even thirty minutes later, the Department of Fisheries rectified the error: the ban applied only to molluscs. But for Rogatien and many others, the damage had been done.

Rogatien, being a helluva good guy, held only one real grudge, but it was a helluva grudge: he loathed Brian Mulroney, at that time the local MP for the riding of Manicouagan and Prime Minister of Canada. He had seen him sail in from Nova Scotia in 1984 and beat his buddy Maltais, the incumbent Liberal MP he'd gone door to door with in Baie-Trinité. Rogatien had worn himself out with the arm-twisting and the spaghetti suppers, trying to prevent the inevitable. Until people started dying, he had suspected the whole mystery toxin business was a Conservative plot against him. History would go on to show Mulroney was more than capable of it. In any case, for the seafood business, 1987 had been a year of slim pickings. Rogatien had resolved to rent an incinerator. For a couple of days, there had been a curious odour hanging over Baie-Trinité, a not unpleasant whiff of crustacean. Everyone knew it was the smell of millions going up in smoke, and maybe their paycheque with it.

In the end, it had nothing to do with acid rain. The toxin was identified on December 17 by two federal laboratories. It was domoic acid, a substance secreted by a kind of plankton that thrives when the weather is hot and dry, as was the case during the summer of 1987. The substance had been known for a while, especially in Japan where the microscopic algae that produce it are used as a remedy for intestinal worms. But it was the first documented case of mass intoxication. At very high dosages, domoic acid deregulates and paralyzes the neurons in the hippocampus, a structure in the brain that records memory. By feeding—that is, by filtering the water and retaining only the plankton—the P.E.I. mussels had accumulated megadoses of domoic acid in their organisms.

Before 1987, Health Canada had classified shellfish toxins into two main groups: those that caused diarrhetic shellfish poisoning and those that caused paralytic shellfish poisoning. Domoic acid became a toxin group all its own: one that caused amnesic shellfish poisoning. Measures were taken, the harvesting of molluscs was outlawed in many areas, filtration systems were installed. There had been no amnesic shellfish poisoning after 1987. Until the "events in Baie-Trinité," seafood had largely lost the associated aura of danger that was so prized by early connoisseurs.

In March 1988, when no one was talking about it anymore, Rogatien had received a big cheque from the government, for several hundred thousand dollars, that said "Special Universal Compensation for Mollusc Exporters (SUCME)" on it. The cheque had been signed by the Prime Minister. Rogatien had waved it in everyone's faces at family seafood party number one. As the old man drew the cheque toward the flame of his lighter, Robert had begged him to reconsider.

"You're right, it's not worth burning."

That evening, Rogatien had paid a visit to the bathroom. There he had wiped his ass with the cheque, quite literally, and then returned it to the sender. For the rest of his life, he had laughed out loud every time he pictured the face of Mulroney's secretary when she opened the envelope, but he never told a soul what he'd done.

14

Colours that don't exist

"Laurie! Laurie! You know what?"

Laurie had just woken up. She had dreamed all night of clouds, layers of white. She had her period and felt heavy. A pesky pimple had erupted on her chin during her sleep. Florence was standing right there, wriggling and writhing in a short dress like she was in a music video.

"They gave you the Bimmer?"

"Yes!"

The fluttering of excitement in Florence's eyelids was threatening to enucleate her.

"What are they going to do with your Mazda?"

"I dunno ... melt it down? That's so not my problem!"

Florence flapped her arms and kept on prancing.

"When are you leaving again?" Laurie yawned after a while.

"Classes start next Monday. I think I'll head back this Thursday. We could set off together, but I think

Mom will want to go with you to get you settled in Quebec City. And they've probably got a car for you too!"

Laurie went for a walk on the beach in a fleece. Fall was all around: the sand was no longer warm and, swollen with cold water, it could stay brown from one tide to the next; at the wharf, the last measly catches had been two weeks ago; the deciduous trees in the forest surrounding the village were subtly losing their green at the ends of each leaf's stressed veins, one little gangrenous blotch at a time. Every time the topic of junior college or Quebec City came up, Laurie couldn't help it: dense fog would cloud her chest and float up to her head and she would start thinking very hard about something else, hard enough to lose all notion of time and space around her. Monosyllables would emerge from her mouth. Florence didn't push it. Laurie had felt something click that time, an astringency of sorts out of which poured the fog that cut her off from the rest of the world. That initial sensation, she reconnected to it now as she remembered, was conjuring up images of handcuffs and prison bars in her mind. A stratum of clouds bleached the sky. Laurie saw Canada geese take flight, only four, in a lopsided V formation. She sat down. The sand channelled its chill to her kidneys. In a deeply dense fog, everything could well turn white. She started to cry.

When Goyette noticed her, Laurie was still crying. All night, he had walked with his flashlight or drunk coffee in his pickup with his phone. He hadn't found a thing and was smart enough to know that was because he didn't know what he was looking for. He had seen Laurie's shoulders hiccupping from a distance. For a long time, he had stood rooted to the spot, hesitant. He had never been good at consoling girls. In any case, he didn't feel he had the strength. The Premier's wife wasn't doing any better. In the depths of the night and his paranoia, Goyette had convinced himself, based on a few emails from his superiors, that the Premier of Quebec had spoken to the Prime Minister of Canada, who had spoken to the Minister of Fisheries and Oceans (Minister of Fisheries, that was all right, but Minister of Oceans, Goyette had always thought, was going a bit too far.). His superiors were demanding results, and by results they meant closing a plant or two.

He had really wanted to wait for Laurie to stop crying, but she was sobbing a river. He had to speak with her anyway, and she was right there, captive in her sadness. He wouldn't even have to challenge Robert by knocking at his door.

"Er ... Laurie?"

She turned around. It had been a long time since she had seen him for real, not on TV. The waxy skin of his face was a surprise. She thought the slightest gust of wind might blow away the loosely anchored follicles of his beard. The salt from the tears and the breeze was still stinging Laurie's eyes, but she didn't feel ugly compared to him.

"I need to talk to you," Goyette went on with adolescent discomfort.

"Yes. OK. Yes. Yes. What about?"

"You might think this is weird ... when you were young, one day I gave you a shell. We both thought there was something different about it, maybe even a little strange. I think it was an Iceland scallop shell..."

Laurie took a deep breath in. Her shoulders rose once more.

"Are you all right?" asked Goyette, still standing, cautious.

"Yes. Yes. I remember. But I don't collect shells anymore. Not for a while ... I don't know what's happened to it. I think my dad might have it. Why?"

"I can't really tell you why."

"Come on, Frédéric. You work for the Canadian Food Inspection Agency. It's the CFIA, not the CIA," Laurie relativized, proud as Punch.

Goyette turned to look at the river. Another little flock of geese flew by, even in number, asymmetrical.

"Ah. Fuck it. You're the only one in the family who can understand."

Without sitting, still looking out to the horizon, he began to set out his conflicting reasoning. He started with the wave at four seventeen, which he described as dazzling, even though the word was lacking, all the words were lacking.

"Blinding?" Laurie suggested.

"Yes, but not blindingly bright. After the wave, the sand took on a tint ... no, not a tint, a quality ... I don't know ... you just couldn't look at it anymore."

"How so?"

"It's like it hurt, but it didn't sting your eyes."

Goyette set about sharing more bizarre details. It occurred to him that Laurie was listening without disbelief. At one point, she asked an immense question.

"What's happened with the river?"

"With the river? I don't know. That's what I'm trying to find out."

"And that's why you're interested in that shell, because when you looked at it up close, there were these weird coloured dots you don't often see on a shell. So much so, it would give you a bit of a buzz."

Goyette was dumbfounded. He would never have believed that looking at the shell would have given Laurie the same little buzz that he got. Laurie knew exactly where he was going with this, he thought, and that caused a worry to well inside him.

"Actually, when people lose their memory like your sister did after eating seafood, it's often because of a toxin called domoic acid. And I haven't found any trace of that anywhere. So I'm looking somewhere else, for another toxin. Wait a sec..."

Goyette walked to his truck. He hadn't run since the beginning of his investigation, but never had he walked so quickly. Laurie watched him return carrying a case. She saw the Mitsubishi logo.

"What are you doing with that!?!"

"This is my sampling kit."

"Yours?"

"Yes, mine. Why?"

"I thought Mitsubishi only made cars," Laurie backpedalled.

"No, no. They make a whole bunch of scientific equipment too."

Watching Goyette dig through his case, Laurie had no doubt: he was going to show her some sperm. The limit of her curiosity lay with whose it was. At first that's what she thought it was. It was white. Goyette was holding the test tube at arm's length and contorting his neck to avoid looking at the contents: a white powder, about two centimetres in depth.

"What is it?" Laurie downplayed.

"You've got to be kidding me!"

"What?"

"You can look at the powder?"

"OK. If this is like a solar eclipse, then give me a heads-up, would you? Because I don't want to wake up blind tomorrow."

"Well, you'd better not look too hard, then."

Laurie let out a long breath that puffed her cheeks. She turned back to the horizon.

"Because I can't look at that powder for three seconds without my face turning away by itself,"

Goyette continued. "I think that's it, the toxin. And I'm not the only one who isn't able to look at it: your dad can't, either."

So that was what he had shown him when Robert went all paranoid and accused him of wanting to get into Florence's pants.

"So why don't I have a problem looking at it, then? Don't tell me it's like Cinderella's slippers—or unicorns."

"Honestly, I'd not thought about that."

It suddenly dawned on Goyette that his irregardable powder was perhaps not so irregardable to everyone. Testing it only on himself and Robert was not the most scientific of methods.

"What's in your powder, chemically speaking?"

"The chromatograph says it's water. Just water."

"You're talking like a guy who believes a chromatograph," Laurie stood up.

That very evening, stopping by the lab after another humiliating press conference, Goyette showed the powder to the two technicians. They shivered and begged him to take the stuff out of their field of vision. He used pliers to set the test tube down in the middle of a cage of mice. They turned their backs and scurried off to squeak in a corner.

Laurie felt even worse after her conversation with Goyette. She thought about gathering some shells to revive her collection. As a child, she had spent long hours staring at the shell Goyette was now looking for, using it, she only just realized, to find her way to a strangeness as pure as it was familiar, yet too welcoming to be magic or mysticism. Robert had confiscated it from her forever. A bitter wind had risen with the advancing tide to shoo Laurie off the beach. She went to the wharf to buy some shrimp, but there weren't any. Goyette had been right when he'd said she was the only one in her family who could understand, but he himself didn't understand what he was saying. She didn't want to help him: not to protect the company—she didn't give a shit about that, she was beginning to realize as she allowed herself to curse in her mind—but because she intended to remain impervious to the ruse.

The doorbell of the empty house was the kind that didn't ring, but buzzed. It was the first time Mori had heard that sound. Doorbells in Japan didn't crackle like that. No furniture was there to deaden the echo. It made him jump. With obvious difficulty, he opened up to Laurie. He was wearing a heavy white shirt tucked into his cargo pants. His hair was swept to the side.

"What are you doing here?" he welcomed her.

Laurie had never been inside Louis Berthelot's place. She knew the man because everyone knew him. Seventeen is a good age to have strange feelings because it's routine at seventeen to be feeling things for the first time. Entering Mori's house, which used to be Louis' house, Laurie felt a fog surging. The place seemed to be both familiar and out of whack. She had a sense of what Louis might have felt if he had returned, the way it sometimes feels to visit somewhere you used to live: a feeling of returning to how you used to be, a place now occupied by others. The fog was thickening like desire. It was making her want to go on. She wondered all the same what was going on with Louis.

Laurie managed to say she was cold. Mori made some *sencha* green tea. On the floor was a barely begun bowl of rice, topped with an egg sunny side up and cucumber slices, all in a brown drizzle of soy sauce. He motioned for her to put on slippers that were too big for her and went to switch off the TV without the remote.

"Have you eaten? There's rice in the cooker. I have urchins."

"No thanks. Just tea. I've already eaten," Laurie lied and that surprised her.

She went to the bathroom. The toilet bowl was gleaming. Her urine was very dark. She changed her tampon. For a while, she was captivated by the release of red strings into the bowl of yellow fluid. The swirling randomness of colours intermingled orange here and there, but not with any homogeneity. The kettle was boiling in the kitchen.

"You know, Goyette the food inspector, he has the same case as you."

She wondered if calling him that was giving him too much respect.

Mori steeped the *sencha* in a ceramic teapot no larger than a small cup that was stuffed with leaves. He prepared short infusions and poured the lukewarm liquid without holding the handle, perpendicular to the spout. A serious look came over his face, but he managed to recover until he looked circumspect again.

"Yes. I know. Have you spoken to him?"

There was a faint flicker in the ascending tone he took to pronounce the question mark. At first Laurie thought he was jealous. He listened, his face neutral, as she recounted her conversation with Goyette without sipping the tea or touching the rice. Sitting on the floor, he appeared to be supremely intelligent. When Laurie had finished, he asked three precise questions, of which two were about the powder, and he seemed relieved by the answers. He breathed and looked Laurie in the eye for four seconds, which was long for him.

"I have a gift for you. I was keeping it until later in our story, but there's no point waiting any longer."

He disappeared for a moment, down to the basement. Laurie liked that he had said the word *story*. She heard him shifting some furniture. He returned with a black box made of corrugated cardboard with a matte surface. He offered it to her with both hands. Laurie opened the box and removed two layers of grey tissue paper. Inside were a bra and panties of a colour she had never seen. At first she was afraid, yes, well and truly afraid. She couldn't help but give a little yelp and avert her eyes. Mori, standing by her side, wore a vague smile.

"Don't be afraid. It won't take more than ten seconds or so to get used to it."

It was not a new shade, or a new nuance, of any colour Laurie knew. The colour was like no other and as primary as red, blue, or yellow. And, as if by natural order, the eye took to it quickly. Once the initial shock had passed, the colour imposed itself, as though perfectly obvious. Laurie was even beginning to feel soothed by it. Nature, the physical world, had nothing of this colour to show. It was an invention, a synthetic colour. Laurie's eyes were now completely acclimatized. She tried to close them. Yes, the new colour was part of the universe. It was possible. Laurie could imagine a fire hydrant that colour, a Smurf, a dog, a sunflower, a fruit, a fir tree. She reopened her eyes.

"Wow."

That was all she could say. *Wow. Wow. Wow.*

"Do you like it?"

"Yes. I have no words. What's it called?"

"I heard it on the TV. Here, you say panties, right?"

Laurie laughed a lot. She lifted out the bra and panties. She untucked the label to check the size: 34C, hers. She also saw the brand: Fruit of the Loom.

"Does Fruit of the Loom even make underwear that colour?"

"Is that a good brand?"

"No."

"There will only be good brands doing this. I dyed this set."

"Dyed?"

"Yes, dyed."

He must have bought them at the Walmart in Baie-Comeau.

"But what's the name of the colour, I mean?"

"I don't know yet," Mori ventured. "I have some ideas. I'll tell you when I've come to my decision."

Laurie brought the panties close to her eyes so the colour would fill her whole field of vision.

"Will you wear them?" Mori asked, suddenly shy.

"Yes. For sure."

"When you do, don't tell me. You mustn't."

They talked all afternoon, sitting or lying on the hardwood floor. Laurie proposed, somewhat insistently, that she put the underwear on there and then, for Mori. She wanted him to see her wearing it. "When you do, don't tell me. You mustn't," he repeated. At one point, she told him she was starting to dread the next few days. The fog within her was overflowing. It was seeping out of her eyes, her mouth. When she moved, it would try to escape between her purple jeans and the skin of her stomach.

It started with Red Lobster, cheekily enough:

> *As the Canadian Food Inspection Agency draws its conclusions, our customers rightly remain mindful of premium quality products. Since food safety is our No. 1 priority, we have decided to immediately suspend orders of Atlantic and St. Lawrence seafood until further notice.*

Then came Loblaws and Sobeys, the same day, as if everyone had been spreading the word. In his captain's chair on the second floor of the presbytery, Robert was opening emails with his jugulars popping out. A call came in from Émilien, the manager of the Baie-Trinité credit union. Émilien was panicking.

"If you go under, Robert, we're going with you. The Federation will bail out the coffers, but for feck's sake, spare a thought for me, will you?!"

Soon Robert would be supplying no more than two or three eateries in Baie-Comeau, Cécile's greasy spoon, and Japan. He thought back to what his father had told him about eggs and baskets. He took another call, this time from Covington Investment Partners of Boston, an investment bank he had been engaged in secret talks with about getting into the fish market by buying a frozen food company in Maine. When he hung up, Robert started to see white. France inched the door ajar and coughed. She had her binoculars around her neck.

"Laurie's been at Louis Berthelot's for the last two hours," she deadpanned.

"What's she doing there?"

"Don't you remember who's living at Louis Berthelot's these days? The Man Who Comes!"

Robert remembered quick enough. He felt a part of himself die.

"The filthy little—!"

"Robert Lelarge! Don't you say that about your daughter. *He's* the filthy one."

15

Affairs in absentia

Before his divorce, Louis Berthelot, master of overtime and night foreman on the freezing line at the Fisheries, had held the plant's all-time attendance record: six thousand eight hundred and sixty-two days on the job and not a sick day to be seen. To mark the three thousandth, Rogatien Lelarge, a proponent of Tayloristic statistics, had awarded him a commemorative plaque. Berthelot took only two weeks of vacation a year, to go hunting, and he got paid double time on statutory holidays.

At the plant, try as he might to get all the rookies to call him Mr. Freeze, everyone called him Dishrag. Being a stickler for safety and hygiene, he had a thing for mopping up spills from the concrete floor. He was on the short side and wore a net to tame a thick head of hair loaded with an excessive amount of gel—Linda, his wife, was a hairdresser. People in the village called him Louis. There was a dignity to him that stopped his nickname from ever completely sticking. Dishrag, that was usually only on the job.

The freezing process was simple. It involved spreading crab claws, lobster parts, shrimp, whelks, scallops, and urchins on the conveyor without any clumps or clusters. Individuated, each item would lend itself more readily to inspection. A vibrating machine would rid the seafood of impurities and jiggle them around as they passed the first visual inspection station. A trip to the deep freeze for prefreezing would then prevent them from clumping when bagged or canned. On the way out of the deep freeze, there was a second inspection station, brought in during the mid-nineties when the plant earned its certificate of compliance with the ISO 9001 standard. There, careful attention would be paid to any frost on the product. The process was essentially the same for Arctic surfclams, frozen and pressed into ten-kilo blocks with a silicone mould. After that, it was simply a matter of weighing, bagging, canning, packing cases, stacking pallets, and storing them in freezing rooms.

It took some fifteen pairs of hands to feed everything through the chain, not counting the woman who operated the forklift. Dishrag would supervise the steps, calibrate the machines, put in time at the inspection stations, and more often than not, stand in for a couple of employees who were off sick or too stoned to work. The others would rotate stations every thirty minutes, except when urchins were on the line. Only Louis Berthelot and two women, both named Solange, could inspect those because they'd done the Japanese quality grading training.

Before renting out his house to the first Japanese guy who came knocking, Louis Berthelot had caught his wife Linda in flagrante one fine midday in the shampoo closet of her salon with a head between her thighs. The head belonged to Cécile, she of the greasy spoon. Cécile was slurping on her hairdresser's lips. She had a silicone colour cap on her head, and the precision of her movements suggested this wasn't the first time they'd waited for the dye to set like this. For several weeks, Dishrag had showed up on time for work, mostly to help spread a rumour that it was a guy from Baie-Comeau who had cuckolded him. He said it didn't bother him, but with his mind elsewhere, he had been letting Category Two urchins creep into Category One crates and, twice even, into crates of Deluxe Grade. The two Solanges were far too bashful to tell him and it had taken an accident on his watch for everyone to realize the foreman was no longer on top of things, and dangerously so. Bobby Daigneault, the youngest of all the workers (he had been in Florence's class until halfway through high school) had slipped in a puddle of crab juice. In trying to steady himself, he had caught his right hand in the conveyor belt, but he'd still split the back of his head open on the concrete floor. He'd lost his middle finger, ring finger, and the distal phalange of his index finger. He'd also sustained a serious concussion. He'd lost so much blood from his head he had needed a transfusion.

Normally, who would have mopped up that crab juice spill? Yes, Dishrag. That was when he moved out to his hunting cabin, where he started calling moose and calling in sick. A while went by before folk realized they'd stopped hearing from him. They scoured the plant in search of out-of-the-way pipes he might have hung himself from. They took care lifting pallets in the freezing room, just in case he'd opted for a more painful way out. Eventually, they figured he must have done it at home, and they brought in Solange Blanchet to replace him.

It was a good twelve days or so before Serge Berthelot, Sar'h, went to the police to report his brother Louis missing. That was because Sar'h had always believed in the healing power of the woods and some time alone. Plus, he had been going out to sea a lot to try and make up for the disappointing hauls of whelks that year. Since no one could ever say no to Sar'h, the police scrambled a helicopter, three frogmen, and a diver, but from the start they were sure that Louis had taken the suicide route. The North Shore was, after all, a place where that kind of thing happened a lot. "Took his own life," they said at the beginning, then "brought about his own death," after two weeks, then "died by suicide," then "pulled the trigger in the woods, far enough away to get eaten by bears and for no one to ever find him." They told Sar'h his brother wouldn't be dead for seven years, not officially. Until then, he would have to manage Louis' affairs.

Robert used the conference room at the Fisheries plant so little, he asked the building custodians not to bother with it. It was filthy, full of functional furniture and cobwebs. There was a white plastic table with metal legs, ten black plastic stacking chairs, a whiteboard, a projector and its tangle of cables, a roll-up screen rendered stiff and squeaky with neglect. On the floor was a rough, grey, washable carpet. On the ceiling, one of the fluorescent tubes blinked and buzzed.

A picture window far wider than it was tall had been cut into the far wall. It looked down onto the freezing line, two floors below.

France was now reminding Robert daily that The Man Who Comes was circling around his daughter. She had made it clear to Laurie that she didn't want her seeing him anymore; it wasn't good for business. Laurie peered at her mother through the fog and denied everything. France started screaming and threatened to call the police if she saw her with him again.

"Do something, Robert. Do something," she stamped her feet in his office. "Go talk to the Japanese guy. I can't stand this any longer. He's a grown man. We don't know what he's capable of. Or what he's after ... what he wants from her. She doesn't know herself!"

Robert was on the phone. He said he'd call back in ten minutes.

"The rage you're feeling, darling, I feel it too. But don't mix everything up..."

"If you could feel my rage, you'd go talk to the guy. No, you wouldn't. If you could feel my rage, you'd kill him. You'd kill him, Robert. You're the one who started it. With that crazy idea of yours, inviting a perverted businessman to your daughter's birthday!"

France slammed the door behind her. She went to have a cry in bed.

Robert got another call. A mail clerk had just opened a curious letter, carefully written by hand, on paper with a letterhead in Japanese. Robert insisted it be brought to him immediately. He recognized the logo of the Isumi Conglomerate of Tones, Colours, Pigments, Molluscs, and Crustaceans. Mori was requesting a meeting, at the earliest convenience of "Mr. Chief Executive Officer." He did not specify a motive. The postmark showed that the letter had been posted in Baie-Trinité. Robert began to get diarrhea twice a day. He had to concentrate to avoid inhaling too deeply: every breath of air threatened to leave him seeing white.

He wouldn't entertain the thought of inviting The Man Who Comes into his home again. More than anything, he was scared of how France might react. None of that would be good for business. He asked for the cobwebs to be dusted in the conference room. He didn't have the fluorescent light replaced because he'd never noticed it.

Robert and Mori were sitting face to face under the epilepsy-inducing lighting, each wearing a black suit. Mori had not anticipated such inhospitable surroundings. He had thought Robert would choose a place more to his advantage, not a room where the acne scars on his face showed so crudely, like little stains. Mori opened by reminding him of the Japanese people's exacting food safety standards, citing several fictitious examples. Robert's attention flickered like a faulty fluorescent light. Mori went on, telling him the Conglomerate believed in him, in his family, in his company. Robert responded with a goofy smile. After a while, he understood that the contract still stood, that there might be some inspections, a closer eye on things perhaps, but that he was off the hook, at least this time. Mori noticed the slackening of the jaw and face, the relaxing of the cervical spine, the slight quiver of comfort returning to the limbs, the early signs of numbing in Robert Lelarge's mind. The Man Who Comes began to speak of Quebec's vast open spaces, of the winter that would be coming, of the cold he had heard stories about. Robert didn't understand this turn to the trivial. The white was encroaching again at the extremities of his field of vision.

"I believe I am in a position to make an interesting proposal to you, Mr. Chief Executive Officer. May I call you Mr. Lelarge?"

"Yes. Yes. Certainly," Robert replied, not entirely sure if he was consenting to being called Mr. Lelarge or to hearing the proposal.

"Ever since I came here, I have been struck by the vivacious spirit of your daughter Laurie, and by the extreme depth of her thought. To say that she is an important asset to you would not be sufficient. She alone will ensure the prosperous future of your company."

"Well, my money's on Florence. She's got a head for business. Laurie's always got her head in a book."

Robert felt good about himself, confident. It wasn't every day he got to tell the truth.

"Not to take anything away from Florence, who will be an exceptional businesswoman, your youngest daughter, Laurie, is both perceptive and methodical. Frankly, that does not come naturally to everyone."

"It's true, Laurie is like that."

"Mr. Lelarge, here is what I respectfully propose to you, with my apologies for not having waited for your permission before speaking to Mr. Utsumi, whom you met in Tokyo: As early as next year, Laurie might study finance at Keiō University, in Tokyo, where Mr. Utsumi has connections. She might then go on to obtain an MBA from a prestigious school, the likes of Harvard, the London School of Economics, ENA, all doors are open, believe me. There would be a place for her in the Conglomerate, with a commensurate salary and the possibility of significant share ownership. The classes at Keiō will be in English, but she must speak and understand the basics of Japanese. I am a qualified Japanese language instructor and I could teach her everything she needs to know to pass the exacting entrance examination. I propose that I give her private lessons all year, so that she is ready next August."

Robert said nothing. His mind had snagged on ENA; he had no idea what that was. Only intermittently did he seem to be aware of what was happening to him.

"Think what this could do to bring our companies closer together," Mori continued. "By constituting the Conglomerate's base for the penetration of the American market, Lelarge Fisheries could become number one for seafood in North America, not to mention other ventures."

Mori saw the fleeting furrow of Robert's eyebrows when he said *penetration*. The only other things behind the acne scars were idleness and greed.

"What other ventures?" said Robert, who was actually trying very hard to think.

"Look at this."

Mori opened a briefcase. Inside was a box of brushed aluminum equipped with two eyepieces and handles on the sides. Robert had seen similar devices on Dufferin Terrace in Quebec City, but with a slot for coins as well. It was a spyglass. He brought his face to the eyepieces. Mori told him it would take ten seconds or so for his eyes to acclimatize. After that, Robert managed to ask two zigzagging questions. He looked like a child, a child who's just been told he has to repeat second grade.

"For Laurie, I have to talk to France," he eventually shirked.

"The Conglomerate is making her an offer. Let me tell her that. I think Laurie should be the one who decides," Mori went for it. "By the way, I will have to train more employees on urchin quality standards. The Conglomerate received a complaint from a retailer."

"Just the one?"

"Yes. But a complaint is a complaint, Mr. Lelarge."

While Mori was talking to Robert, just next door in the offices, Florence's coworkers had organized a little get-together to mark the end of her summer internship. Florence thanked them, told them they shouldn't have. They gave her a gift. "It's a little something from all of us," they stressed. The box was grey, dolled up with a big red ribbon. It was a miniature convertible car, for Barbies.

"What the hell!" Florence took offence.

"Well, this last week, you were so happy with your new Bimmer, we all figured you'd need one for your Barbie as well," Sabrina Côté, a girl her age replied on everyone's behalf. "Come on, we're going out for a drink in Baie-Comeau."

And out they went in Baie-Comeau: to the Blues, then to the Factory Finish. Florence did not join them.

16

A Japanese lesson in cold weather

The memory of a colour is the memory of light, multiplied to infinity. Laurie often wore her Fruit of the Loom bra and panties in front of the mirror in the big white bathroom at the presbytery. In every hour of sunshine that slipped in through the net curtain, in the evening fluorescence of the vanity's neon, and in the glow of the candles she lit beside the bathtub, she deepened her understanding of their colour. The light was teaching her in shades. Her mind was soaking it all up.

She thought she looked pretty in the mirror, pretty as a weird idea. The new colour marked out across her a territory of self she enjoyed stepping beyond. Sometimes she felt its silky aggression on her, all the while knowing it was just in her head. The skin, she grasped, has a predilection for novelty. The unexplored kindles its flame. She would take the panties off before she got too wet. She didn't want to have to wash them: it would be complicated to find somewhere she could stash them to dry and she was afraid they might fade. She kept the bra on. Orgasm was never far away. It would come almost by itself. Inhaling deeply before she climaxed, Laurie would close her eyes and the colour would seep into her consciousness like the time she had shone a flashlight through the panties onto the white of her bedroom wall in the dark. It had made her think about the northern lights, but the northern lights had none of that colour.

Mori still dreamed about her at night, Laurie could tell from the little electric shocks in her breasts, which were less sharp than the cerebral sensations of this colour whose name was still a mystery to her. She didn't think that mattered much at first, but Mori had told her that the Japanese language hadn't distinguished blue from green until midway through the twentieth century. The meanings of the modern words for blue (青, *ao*) and green (緑, *midori*) remain very fluid: the first may refer to the green of vegetables and traffic lights; and the second, to the colour of the sea. In the dictionary, Laurie had read that the word *blue*, rather than coming from Latin like the other colours in her native French, came from the Frankish word *blao*, meaning pale or pure, in reference to the sky. In the texts of ancient Greek and Latin, blue rarely gets a mention. The eyes see a spectrum of colours; the brain distinguishes them through language. Other definitions of colours followed in form: "Red: a colour bordering the extremity of the solar spectrum, a colour for which nature offers numerous examples (blood, poppy, ruby, etc.)." Every time, the dictionary told Laurie that nature offered numerous examples and arbitrarily cited a few. The whole thing wouldn't have been much help to a blind person, she thought.

If she'd had to choose a name, Laurie would have called it *obvious*. She marvelled that her mind had rallied so rapidly around such a radical statement. The colour stood up and spoke for itself. Sometimes, Laurie had the sense she could see it in the iridescent reflection of a pale stone or a conifer's resinous scars. She saw it in the water of the Saint Lawrence, but since she also saw it so easily when she closed her eyes, she doubted the reality of what she saw with her eyes open. A part of this was taking place inside her. With her mind, she could render anything in this strange and beautiful colour.

Robert Lelarge had much more on his mind. There was little free space for this colour, the prototype of which he had seen in the grey box. Yet it would surge forth, carcinogenically, whenever he closed his eyes. He didn't want to believe it. All that had been said in the conference room, beneath the blinking of the ailing fluorescent light, had been heavy. He felt like a man bound to perform the unacceptable.

He typed the name of Keiō University into the Google rectangle. It seemed to be a highly prestigious school. Before he spoke to France about Mori's offer, he had the second worst diarrhea of his life.

She was drinking coffee on the veranda. His back was sweating. He could see little through the veil of white. All of a sudden, at the very moment when France turned toward him, the veil was no longer white. Robert was no longer seeing white; he was seeing the colour of The Man Who Comes.

"I'm a simple guy. The only thing I know how to do is what my father did: molluscs and crustaceans."

France listened in silence. As soon as Robert said that, she knew he had sacrificed Laurie. She had never seen him humble, and he wasn't. He was measuring and remeasuring the flow of every word, all the time. He could have collapsed; she would have found that less frightening. Robert's humility was rational. Logic, and nothing else, had left him all stooped over. He had lost and it showed.

"It's the only way to keep living the life we live," was his final argument.

Mori's colour now almost entirely blanketed Robert's field of vision. He had to sit down, he was so short of breath. The sky was grey on the other side of the partition. France was sucking in small sips and clinking the cup against its matching saucer. Going on would be excruciating. Everything on the veranda had lost its shine.

Mori had already begun teaching Laurie Japanese. He had started with the short vowels. The pace of his student's progress astonished him. When they were together, there was still the thick silence in which Laurie could think and feel free.

"If you like, we can continue a little. You won't be going to Quebec City. I'm going to teach you Japanese."

Laurie didn't ask what would continue. Beneath her clothes, she was wearing the bra and panties. She didn't tell him; she mustn't.

At the presbytery, no one really spoke to one another anymore.

"What Mr. Ishikawa is proposing, is that really what you want?" she was asked over roast beef that was hard to swallow.

On the last warm morning, France announced to Laurie that even though she'd decided not to go to junior college, she'd still have to learn to be independent. She could live with them, but she'd better not expect them to cook for her and do her laundry and all that. She would have to stand on her own two feet, like any woman, because that's what she was, it seemed. And she'd better wash her own dishes.

With Robert, it was worse. Their eyes never met. In fact, the two times it happened, Laurie noticed a strange reciprocating movement in her father's eyes. It started with the flicker of a metallic glimmer somewhere between pity and reproach. Laurie knew that first twitch: her father usually reserved it for anyone who mentioned junkies or whores with anything approaching empathy. But, rather than filling his gaze, the glimmer gave way under the weight of itself; it left a brief vacuum in his pupils and a panic began to swell, quickly taking over, threatening to upend everything. The iris even started to disappear beneath the upper eyelid, then, in a snap, the momentum stopped and the initial hardness reappeared as if the eyes were controlled by a pendular mechanism. It was swinging between the threatening and the psychotic.

折, Mori drew on the beach with a long twisted length of driftwood that might have been mistaken for the sceptre of a deranged emperor. The symbol covered a square metre of sand. Laurie watched him draw it from a rock, trying to hide her shivering. September had hit hard, with three frigid days in a row. It was too cold to be on the beach now. They did not see each other elsewhere. She had not invited herself over to his place again.

The casbah had been dismantled. The workers who stayed behind settled into shacks that were better insulated with every passing year. Florence had gone back to Montreal. The radio was broadcasting a ground frost advisory.

She and Mori didn't talk about it, but Laurie understood that their paths were crossing. Surely Mori had a plan. Since he'd come, things weren't what they used to be. She had the impression he was accelerating everything, shaking everything up. Even the coastline seemed more eroded. Laurie didn't have a plan. Now, what would happen in her life would influence Mori's movements. These movements were opening infinitely. Everything was vaporous, like fog and freedom. Thrillingly, she was quite sure that, in her story, she was the reader and the main character all at once. It hadn't crossed her mind that she might be the paper, that the story might be written on her.

Mori went on etching Japanese symbols on the beach in Baie-Trinité with his driftwood. And she watched him, sitting on her rock. Her butt cheeks were freezing. The cold passed right through her fleece and the wool of her sweater, nipped at her nipples, made her mindful of her bones, forced her to fold her arms. The beach belonged to them. Laurie wondered why they were still the only ones to realize that. Seeing him inscribe a complex symbol in the sand with short, sharp strokes of his driftwood, she established that Mori was an epicentre.

澱, he completed.

"What does that mean?"

"Wait a moment."

Japanese is written with three alphabets. Mori had taught Laurie the phonetic ones—hiragana and katakana—simple characters representing a sound. The symbols he was drawing on the beach, kanji, represented a meaning. Laurie would have two thousand one hundred and thirty-six of them to learn. The orange sun broke between the clouds on its descent. Off in the distance, the streetlamps lining the 138 added to the orange. It wasn't getting any warmer. Mori finished his line:

折 澱 折り 檻

Laurie recognized the り symbol, the sound *ri* in the hiragana alphabet.

"The first symbol means *chance*, *occasion*, or *opportunity*," Mori set about explaining. His tone, always a little scholarly, was becoming even more so.

"And so, the third word, that's like the symbol for *opportunity*," Laurie deciphered, "but the word ends in *ri*."

"Exactly! It's the symbol for *fold*. And you're right, there is the syllable *ri*."

"Like in origami."

"Yes. That's it. Exactly."

"Strange," Laurie envisioned out loud. As if, from the paper's perspective, the fold was an opportunity.

Mori tended to incline his torso more spontaneously when he was teaching Laurie Japanese. He seldom smiled.

"The second symbol is less usual. It means *sediment* or *lees*. And the fourth means *prison cell*, *enclosure,* or *cage*," he continued.

Laurie didn't see where he was going with all this. The lesson struck her as complex for her level.

"You are quite doubtful," Mori remarked.

"I get the *cage* thing. It's like a lobster pot. I get the *opportunity* thing. But why would I need to know *sediment* or *fold* at this point?"

"It's not really a lesson in Japanese. Or barely. The lesson is that many words can be pronounced exactly the same way. Much more than in French. If I read the line, it goes: ori, ori, ori, ori."

"Wait..." said Laurie softly.

"Yes," Mori acquiesced, knowing she knew, "yes, that's it."

"Ori?"

"Red, blue, yellow ... Ori."

Laurie liked the sound of that. It sounded like her name.

"And how is that written, in Japanese?"

"Like I told you, you have to write it in katakana."

Mori traced オリ.

He hurried home, back to the house of the man who had disappeared. He must have been cold too. Sar'h had told him he could stay as long as he kept quiet, and that he couldn't get a dog. He was so insistent about no dogs, and repeated so often that it was just to keep the place clean, that Mori figured he was concealing a profound phobia.

Laurie told him not to erase a thing. *Opportunity, chance, cage, sediment, fold.* All of that must speak to the way the colour was made, perhaps also to what it could do. *Ori.* The sound was in her name. As she considered that, Laurie realized she and Mori were no more than a single neighbouring consonant apart. It had never occurred to her. In her first Japanese lesson, Mori had told her that katakana was reserved for foreign words, technical terms, and trademarks.

The tide would erase everything. It was nearly dark. Laurie started walking toward the presbytery. As all these things swirled around in her mind, she really couldn't have cared less about making her own meals and enduring her parents' screwed-up faces.

On the beach, she found a stray phone. Touching it to life to identify the owner, she saw the lock screen was in Japanese. Mori must have dropped it. There was no passcode. She swiped her finger. A video player appeared. The screen was filled with a tender, mottled pink, with some more purplish or noticeably blue bits. There were also some luminous streaks in overexposed areas. In the middle, behind the play icon, was a blacker circle. She touched the end of a finger to the icon. The pink surface was seized with an organic movement, but everything remained flat, two-dimensional. The video lasted seventeen seconds. In the third second, the hole in the middle closed in a spasm and opened wider to reveal the channel of which it was the meatus. In the seventh, a drop of transparent liquid pearled at the centre. In the thirteenth second, everything went white. In the fifteenth, everything darkened.

Laurie had to watch the video again several times to understand that it was an extreme close-up, distorted by the wide angle. She did it in pyjamas. She covered the shade of her bedside lamp with her ori panties. The lighting was ori and soft in the bedroom.

Up on the second floor, Robert was doing business with lots of thumps of his fist on his desk. Down below in the kitchen, France was eating mille-feuille pastries from the grocery store and staring at a knife. That's how things were now.

Sixth intermission

the lobster

Few things separate this creature from a scorpion that was eager to get to the bottom of things. It is one of those edibles—cherries, strawberries, apples, maple taffy—that are seasons too, with an annual flavour that makes a memory to savour. Its business is lucrative, dangerous, virile, like a mercenary's. It is the king of the sea: the lobster.

Its swimming stroke is a propulsive reflex that resembles the action of an accordion. It prefers to walk on the bottom, where it finds shelter in rocky crevices. It emerges only to feed, mostly on dead flesh. The first scavenger on the scene, it will be right there waiting for a plaice or an anglerfish to breathe its last. With its mismatched claws—one large one, less serrated, is for crushing; the other, more delicate and pointed, is for cutting—the lobster is also armed to hunt. It feasts on mussels, urchins, whelks, and crab. A reclusive seafood aficionado, it takes its prey back home to dine, like I do.

It has only one true predator: the human being, represented here by Serge "Hercules" Cabana, and frankly, no one would want to be hunted by Hercules. But the lobster has moments of vulnerability in which it might fall prey to a codfish, or get a taste of a ray's medicine: every summer, until it dies a natural death in its fifties, it moults. It takes two or three weeks for it to grow a new shell. The female becomes more accessible when moulting. The male will drag her to his lair and flip her on her back. With his two sex organs, he will insert his sperm directly into her abdomen. Then he will play the paranoid, protective partner until her shell hardens and closes. She will keep his sperm inside her for a good year.

Hercules had plenty of lobster stories, not just the one about the tornado full of lobsters, which was not so much a story as a founding myth. He had always insisted he had caught three canary-yellow lobsters, four indigo lobsters, and even lobsters that were white all over. With a photo to prove it, he said he had trapped a yellow lobster with brown spots like a leopard's, but the lighting was iffy. They had all turned an orangey-red in cooking, like ordinary lobsters, except the white ones, which had remained albino.

One day, when Florence was seven years old, Laurie was three and Hercules had sailed up to the wharf happy as a clam, boasting he'd just caught a yard-long lobster that must weigh a good fifty pounds. The dockers said he was full of shit, that his lobster pots were way too small for that. Hercules explained that the giant lobster wasn't in his traps, that he must have been just passing through, perhaps he was the prince of lobsters, some sort of superhero or righter of wrongs, the claws behind the empty traps he often pulled up that had been torn to shreds. In fact, Hercules had noticed it when he was working the winch: an enormous, convulsive prisoner to his ropes. He had thrown himself into the water to stop the lobster from escaping. "I wrestled it back on board," he triumphed, as if he was on coke. The dockers demanded to see the beast. And they saw it. They gave Hercules a lot of potty-mouthed congratulations and high fives, and gave Rogatien a call.

The timing was grand because seafood party number two was coming up fast. Rogatien forked out two thousand five hundred bucks for the trophy. At the party, besides the family, there was Émilien the credit union manager, as well as executives from the plant, two or three grocery guys from Provigo and their wives, plus the mayors of Baie-Trinité and Baie-Comeau. There were also journalists and two *Guinness Book of Records* inspectors who were wasting their time because, firstly, they didn't like seafood and, secondly, the lobster ended up being only eighty-nine and a half centimetres long and eighteen kilos six hundred and twenty-two grams. They'd seen bigger in the States. Still, it was the society event of the year until the shit show over at Chez Saturne. Mingling on the new patio, cocktail in hand, many could remember the commotion over the forty-pound lobster before it all hit the fan that fateful night.

They poached the monster over three propane burners, in an old bathtub they'd scraped the rust off. Hercules had the honour of cracking its claws with a sledgehammer and extracting its flesh with a spear. At a certain point in the afternoon, everyone was three sheets to the wind and Hercules had insisted on being left alone with the carcass and his circular saw. Florence and Laurie couldn't have been expected to move the swing where they were playing, though. They were the only witnesses to the scene. Hercules made an incision down the length of the creature's body. Plunging his bare hand into the half-bodies, he filled an empty ice cream tub with a greenish substance. Florence came over.

"Yuck! Are those its eggs?"

"Nah, 'course not, it's a male. Look, that's where the eggs would be. Plus, cooked like this, they'd be red," Hercules clarified, with a sweep of his dirty hand to a hypothetical space in the carcass, as if it were obvious.

"What is it? It's all green."

"That, little girl, is the best bit. It's the tomalley. Do you want a taste?"

"No."

Laurie, whom a budding awareness of death was keeping at a distance, was listening to it all. The word *tomalley*, which she would not hear again for a long time, was inscribed in her memory, in the sluice of consciousness where strange words bide their time until they are heard once more and enter the realm of vocabulary. Years later, when she first tasted the substance she had written off as *stuffing* or *green goo*, she had a hunch there must be a better word for it. She dipped the tip of a fork into it. It held all the flavours of the watery part of the world.

It is no ordinary word. It is a remnant of the Carib language, of a Caribbean people wiped out by colonization who largely survived on a broth made with crab innards. They called that broth, and the crab innards too, *tomali*. The word made its first appearance in French in Rochefort's *Histoire naturelle et morale des îles Antilles de l'Amérique* in 1658, with the spelling *taumaly*. An English translation in 1666 kept the same spelling. This book, and other Caribbean travel stories, proved so popular that the word elicited an entry in Diderot and d'Alembert's *Encyclopédie* a century later, which may or may not have read something like this in English:

> TAUMALIN or TAOMALI, substantive, masculine Word in the Carib language meaning sauce, largely constituted of crab fat in its natural state; also commonly called crab taumalin; such substance being cooked, is not so tiresome as other ordinary fats: it is a kind of stuffing composed by nature in the bodies of animals in the crustacean family; it needs no seasoning; its delicacy surpasses that of finer sauces; its taste is exquisite and has no comparison.

The word found its way into the dictionary archives but fell out of use in French in the nineteenth century. It has remained alive in the United States, however, with first the spelling *tom-alley*, then *tomalley*. Lobster words—business words—are American words. So it's the American spelling that Health Canada uses in its press releases to "remind Canadians who are consuming tomalley from lobsters that there may be natural toxins present in this organ."

The scientific name for the lobster is *Homarus americanus*. Messy, loud, oozing, demanding, and delicious, it's hard to find a more American kind of meal. The Lelarges sold lobsters of all sizes, live and frozen. The carcasses went to a handful of environmentally conscious fertilizer manufacturers, tomalley and all.

17

Definition of a dog

That close—the distance between the curved ends of her index finger and her thumb—was as close as Myriam was to getting in the Volvo and, as much as she loved him, driving her husband to the hospital to have him admitted to the psych ward. Frédéric had black eyes from the insomnia. He was always cold. He was switching himself on with coffee and trying to switch himself off with aquavit. It was not working. It could not last. He was stretching himself too thin, Myriam kept trying to remind him.

At the end of the summer, the journalists went off to cover a bigger story; Myriam made a variation on *smørrebrød* and put on a short dress thinking she might finally get her Fred back. He ate little and quickly. He looked scared: all the more troubling, his eyes were widening almost imperceptibly. He never talked about anything.

"Seriously, what is wrong with you?" she cried as she opened the door to the room he had started retreating to after dinner, sitting in front of his computer with impossible-to-listen-to jazz turned up full blast, his bottle of aquavit and flask of coffee at the ready.

She liked it when he neglected his beard a bit, let his hair go a bit greasy, had a bit of a natural odour to him. But now he was flirting with uncleanliness.

"Wait," he replied amid his grumbling, making the same face as usual.

He was sitting with his back to her, eyes glued to his laptop screen. He had his guitars sitting in the corner. Their strings must have lost any tension they once had. A long brass lament blared from the speakers.

"No, I won't wait. Look!"

She hiked up her dress. She wasn't wearing any panties. She had waxed her pubes into a rectangle because he'd liked that when she did it before. Without turning around, Frédéric brandished a test tube of powder above his head.

"No, *you* look."

Myriam's face turned away of its own accord, repelled as though by a magnet. With a twist of her neck, she tugged her dress down again. She moved two steps closer to Frédéric, tried to look up, but the substance at the bottom of the test tube made her face pucker and overwhelmed her senses. She couldn't look at it.

"As if your breath wasn't enough to push me away, you had to fart around and make a powder just to be sure," harrumphed an angry Myriam.

A pest, that's what she felt like.

"No. That's the toxin. I've spent the summer isolating it. My bosses don't think it's that, but I do. I'm working. I'm making myself useful," Goyette chirped.

"That's it, just go and bring toxins home with you, Fred. Knock yourself out. Toxins, for fuck's sake."

"It's not very toxic. It's just water. I've been carting it around for a while."

"A toxin is a toxin! Just look at yourself..."

"It's true. I gave it to some mice ... dead mice, now."

"You disgust me."

Frédéric placed the test tube back in its opaque sleeve. He turned around with a spin of his chair. He had their IKEA oyster knife in his left hand.

"Sometimes the toxin makes me want to gouge my eyes out."

Myriam clenched the Volvo key in her fist. That close, she came. That close.

Instead, she persuaded Frédéric to go to bed. She lay down next to him. He felt the urge to finger her when he noticed her wax job, but he fell asleep before he really got anywhere. She couldn't help but imagine the eye-gouging with the oyster knife: the sound of the shell when the socket split, the plop, the ball hanging by a thread of muscles. At the time when he usually headed over to the motel across town for his press conference, the alarm clock sounded. He didn't have to do that anymore. He tossed it out the open window and slept another thirty-six hours.

Things went better after that. Goyette's superior called him in to his office, in Mont-Joli. Goyette thought he was going to be fired. He had come around to the idea, figuring that being freed from the ministry would give him greater latitude to investigate. He could get the Lelarges to pay him, or find a way to extort money from them. Instead, he was handed a document entitled *Investigation into the Events in Baie-Trinité and a New Potential Phycotoxin*. He was being put on it full time, with a budget of forty thousand dollars for expenses—bankrolled, yes, once more, by heavily taxed Canadians. He would be left in peace, unless he found nothing.

The insomnia returned, although he did more or less bring it on himself by chugging litres of coffee long past midnight. The thing was, he couldn't give up his nighttime thinking, so different was it from his daytime thinking. He was becoming less and less sure that the test tube of powder contained the toxin he was looking for, especially since he had seen Laurie look at it, as if she were staring at the sun without so much as shedding a tear. The powder was made up of water and mineral impurities, but this water stayed solid, even under a soldering iron. The powder was not the toxin, but the product of the toxin's action on water, Goyette was growing more certain by the day. The nature of that action depended on when he looked at it. By day, he believed the toxin acted directly on atoms. By night, when caffeine and alcohol pooled their efforts, he was starting to suspect it twisted the nature of things into another plane. He could picture a toxin in two parts. One, of food-borne origin, defecated on the beach, then activated by the other, of provenance unknown, dispersed in the wave at four seventeen. Assembled, the toxin then changed the beach at a fundamental level. Some water molecules had solidified, but that was not the most significant of the changes. The sand was an *other* sand. The water was an *other* water. Life was dancing to a different tune. *Ontotoxin*—toxin of the being—that was the only word his nighttime thinking could find for the phenomenon.

Since he wasn't sleeping, since he'd sobered up enough to drive and the autumn dawns in Baie-Trinité were of a dated spectrum that went from brown to burnt orange with a hint of pinkish grey along the way, he went to his work truck, pulled on his windbreaker, and roared off to the strains of the Esbjörn Svensson Trio live in Hamburg, without shaving.

He passed no more than a couple of eighteen-wheelers in the damp of the rising day, the kind of morning that shows a man he's stretched himself a little thin. Goyette realized it had been too long since he last set foot in Baie-Trinité. Ever since the food poisoning at Chez Saturne, he had made a habit of being there every two to three days. Two weeks at least had gone by this time. He'd been taking fewer and fewer samples when he was there, and it had been a long time since he'd taken a seat at the bar tended by Ti-Claude. His thoughts had become more accommodating; the coffee would warm him up. The simple pleasure of the search was taking hold in him.

At Ti-Claude's bar, the talk was all about Dishrag Berthelot again. His widow wouldn't leave Cécile's greasy spoon and Cécile was cooing at her curiously. Folk wondered if that was normal. Folk weren't used to seeing Cécile like that. Besides, things hadn't been the same on the freezing line since Dishrag stopped running the show. A lot of workers were hankering after a transfer to the canning line instead, where at least you knew what to expect.

"Don't you think the dogs have all turned into scaredy-cats?" someone changed the subject.

"Scaredy-cats?"

"I was talking to Maurice about it the other day. His dog won't go out anymore. Mine just stays in the yard. Wasn't like that before."

"Before what?"

"Couple of weeks ago, I'd say. Don't you guys think that's weird?"

"Nothing wrong with Steeven," Bobby Daigneault wanted to make it known. He was back on his feet but his fingers wouldn't be growing back.

"Who's Steeven?"

"That dog of mine."

"That's no name for a dog, for fuck's sake, that's what my nephew's called. That 'dog' of yours is a poodle, anyway."

Goyette wasn't paying much attention to the conversation. Getting out of his truck, by the end of the wharf, he had seen a white or grey dog, beige in the light of dawn. The motionless dog had given him a long stare. After, Goyette saw the Japanese symbols as he walked. Mori's grooves on the beach were drawn deep and the powerless tide had not washed them away. Goyette had taken photos of the kanjis with his camera, then with his phone. Discreetly, below the bar, he was trying to run the image through a translation app. When he realized he was drawing attention to himself, he left.

He stuck a Post-it on his bulletin board with the words *cell (cage)*, *sediment*, *chance*, *fold*. He spoke to a Japanese biologist colleague to be sure of the translations and ask him if they meant anything to him. Nothing rang a bell, but the words were all pronounced the same: *oli*. On another Post-it, Goyette wrote "Talk to Mori Ishikawa" but that would not be so easy: Mori hadn't had a phone connected, he didn't answer the door and, the rare times he did go out, he was with Laurie and their body language was elusive.

There ensued some treading of water, some sending of fruitless emails to Japan.

Goyette didn't go all that often anymore to his office at the Canadian Food Inspection Agency in the Baie-Comeau strip mall that was also home to a bowling alley and a Chinese buffet. Already, the other employees didn't have much to say to him (among themselves, they called him "Mr. Mollusc"); now he was on his special mission, they avoided him. Once a week, he went in to get his phone messages. There was one from Florence. *Florence who?* he didn't ask himself for long, but was still left scratching his head. He called back.

"This is Frédéric Goyette, from the Canadian Shellfish Sanitation Program."

"Ooh ... aren't you formal on the phone, Goyette?"

"Why did you call me?"

"The chef. I've got his number. He told me it'd be no problem for him to talk to you."

"You spoke to him?"

"Yep. I ran into him in a bar. He started going on about all kinds of stuff I couldn't give a shit about, but I figured you would."

"Er ... thank you, Florence, I don't really know what to say. I'll call him."

Florence was about to hang up. Goyette figured he had nothing to lose.

"What's going on between your sister and Mori Ishikawa?"

"Well ... the short answer is, it's none of your business. The long answer is, Laurie's living her life and it's not my life and it's not your life."

"What do you mean?"

"Laurie is Laurie. And your investigation isn't my investigation. Bye."

Goyette was on an under-upholstered metal chair covered with a rough grey fabric pilling from thirty years of use. On the pale blue wall in front of him, a clock gave him all the time he needed, a notice ordered him not to smoke despite the fact no one would have dared to in years, and a character on a poster outlawed clam harvesting in cursive letters: "Shellfish harvesting: when it's closed, it's closed." Goyette was no stranger to the font, the same one they used at the turn of the nineties to spread the word that drinking and driving was a crime. He considered the phrasing for a moment: "Laurie is Laurie," and "when it's closed, it's closed." He recalled Myriam yelling at him that a toxin was a toxin. The repetition of the same word underscored that it was not the same word, that something more had to be considered, a profound difference between the word and its repetition. Maybe that was how the toxin worked: by seeking within a thing what makes it a thing.

It happened fast. Two days later, Goyette was in Montreal in a wall-to-wall Molson bar near the Crémazie metro station, where the chef liked to hang out and had said to meet him. "It's near my place and I don't have to get dressed up to have a drink," the semi-repentant chef explained in a pink T-shirt. He had a Super Mario moustache and was even fatter than Goyette remembered.

Goyette had not been to Montreal in ages. He was keen for evening to come so he could park his Volvo near someplace he could hear some jazz, but he had gone by metro to meet the chef. On the platform at Crémazie, he was surprised to find a passing pleasure in something and nothing. It was the colour of the ceramic tiles: their place on the dated end of the spectrum.

The chef was a straight-talker with the gift of the gab and a case of the shakes he was keeping a hold on with bourbon. Goyette asked him if he could record their meeting. The chef said no. He breezed on with the look of a man trying to make peace with his past.

He had met Saturn in rehab, a good guy with an unhealthy appetite for trouble. The treatment centre would never dream of using their story in one of its brochures, maybe that was the best way to put it. Regardless, Saturn was a born host, a gift from God to the profession of maître d', the chef had always been able to see that. Many a time he had been to his place on Cléophas Lake, in every imaginable state, and he had never been treated to anything other than a hearty welcome. "Saturn has hospitality running through his veins, you know?" *Among other things, yes,* Goyette thought, suppressing a smile as he did so well. On the chef went: not to brag, but in the kitchen, he could generally hold his own pretty well, though when it came to seafood he thought he had a real talent, and fuck, he'd never tasted any better than what he made himself, even at Le Bernardin in New York, and that was saying something! So, they'd started up a restaurant together and set their sights on Michelin stars, a big deal, you know, and holy crap, they might just have gotten one, a star, that is. What had to be said, was that the two of them (Saturn and him), they both had the baggage of another life to carry and the restaurant business (if Goyette were naive and lived in a land of milk and honey and gingerbread houses, he might as well have walked away there and then) could be a rough kinda game. Their venture grew out of easy access to first-rate seafood, the prospect of lending a hand to friends who had some money to explain, and a North Shore sort of patriotism dear to Saturn since his father had died.

"When you say 'explain,' you mean 'launder,' right?"

"Well, look at you, Einstein! Got it in fuckin' one. Who do you think is going to come and check if there are ten or a hundred and ten customers at our restaurant with a tasting menu for two hundred and twenty-five bucks a head?!"

The blend of detachment and aggression, the ready yet more or less put-on indignation at any supposed slight to his intelligence: Goyette had never heard anyone other than Saturn speak like that.

The chef had relocated to Cléophas Lake in the middle of March to craft his recipes. Before long he was plating up some incredible dishes with boreal herbs, frozen crab, molluscs, some crazy-ass reductions, and butter, but not too much. It was something to shout about, a triumph, to venture in search of unreal flavours that would plunge the palate into a state of perplexity and stir the senses above and below the belt, if you caught his drift. When it came to cooking urchins, though, they were harder to handle.

"Jeez Louise! You're bent double. What's so funny?"

"Well, urchins ... harder to handle..."

"Do I strike you as the kind of guy to dabble in cheesy wordplay just to amuse you?"

"No, just forget about it, carry on."

The urchins belonged to the Isumi Conglomerate of Tones, Colours, Pigments, Molluscs, and Crustaceans. Saturn hadn't said a word about it to his brother. As it happened, in the beginning, Robert used to let workers put a few urchins aside, but the Conglomerate had sent a delegate or something of the sort to Baie-Trinité and everyone had gone a bit anal-retentive. They'd had to purchase all restaurant supplies through the Conglomerate. For the biggest lobsters, the biggest crabs, the price was out of all proportion. They could command forty dollars a mussel, nope, not a pound, forty dollars *a mussel*, provided it was symmetrical and checked all the right colour boxes.

Mori Ishikawa negotiated the prices. He couldn't grasp that no matter what the shell looked like, the critter inside tasted pretty much the same. He always dressed the same way, all the better to conceal his weapon—the chef could see in him the sweeping yet hurried movements of someone who was carrying; once the Japanese guy's cardigan rode up and he could have sworn he had seen the butt of a Glock.

Those intending to use the restaurant to explain away their money did not appreciate prices being fixed like this. And he personally, the chef, well it really fucked him off. Anyhow, some bikers showed up, on a floatplane, not long before the grand opening, to try and get everyone to see sense and, hey, when in Rome, enjoy the party while they were at it.

"They came back to see us, Saturn and me, and you know what they said? 'We don't mess with those dudes.'"

"So they spoke to Mori?" Goyette didn't believe a word of it.

"I dunno. I think so. They got so freaked, they stayed on the floatplane the whole night of the opening. That worked out well for me. I reckon I'd have been lynched otherwise..."

The chef finished his sixth bourbon. Goyette finished his Laurentide. He was the first to leave. The chef said he was working a lot with meat substitutes these days, that there was a market for it and it wasn't as cutthroat as seafood.

Too bad because there was no two ways about it: no one in Quebec, perhaps the world, had quite the same raw, carnal grasp of the flavours of molluscs and crustaceans as the big guy with the moustache.

18

Love (a chance)

Turns out, it was manouche jazz at the bar. The guitarist wasn't reinventing the wheel, as far as Goyette was concerned, but you could never go wrong with a bit of manouche. Goyette wasn't tired. He hit the road for Baie-Comeau as night was setting in, after a stop at the gas station to fill up on coffee. Taming the familiar raging bull of the 138 immersed him in thought. The guests of honour had been deliberately poisoned, and the seafood likely had nothing to do with it. By the time he reached Les Escoumins, he still couldn't figure out if it had been a biker hit on the Japanese, or a Japanese hit on the bikers. He sped past a Fisheries semitrailer at a hundred and fifty kilometres an hour. Exports hadn't declined, though the prices had probably dropped a bit. Saturn never did open his restaurant. The Isumi Conglomerate of Tones, Colours, Pigments, Molluscs, and Crustaceans had benefited from the poisoning, but crime doesn't always pay the perpetrator. Either it was a brilliant crime by the Japanese, or a bungled crime by the bikers. Both possibilities seemed equally plausible to him. For the first time, Goyette gave some real thought to the word "crime." Now he could hear himself think—generalizing about crimes and investigations, pondering the merits of Japanese organized crime (and its presumable efficiency) along with those of biker organized crime (and its presumable crudeness)—he could picture himself as a detective in a Nordic Noir novel. Then—bam!—there it came, the first snowfall, not long after the fork in the road at Les Îlets–Jérémie. Falling sparkles, freezing in his headlights. It was early and would not settle. At the wheel of his Volvo, Goyette stared blankly ahead.

Laurie didn't know why, but one of the three memories she had left of her grandfather Rogatien featured a much more innocuous episode than the two others. She had stayed overnight at his place on Christmas Eve, the winter he died. In the morning, he had asked if she'd had sweet dreams.

"Yes! I dreamed about my presents. You gave me an orange dinosaur and green and pink candies."

"How do you know the dinosaur was orange?"

"Dunno. It was just orange."

Laurie sure remembered Rogatien's reaction: a full-face puckering the family only got to see when there was talk of big money. "Well, I dream in black and white. I thought everyone did."

Seeking her endorsement, Rogatien had lifted his gaze to France, who was walking across the room.

"Don't look at me to back you up. I don't dream," France had exited.

Because of this, Laurie always thought of her grandfather every time she watched a black-and-white movie. It seemed only fitting to her that, for him, monochrome would be the medium of extraordinary stories and illusions. She could just picture him, at night, setting sail for Casablanca or riding off to the Wild West.

It occurred to her as she grew older that he must not have often dreamed about real people, that he must have been the kind of man whose dreams were filled with strangers. His erotic dreams, if he had any, must have been old-school. But that wasn't something that crossed her mind a lot: no one likes to imagine their grandparents' erotic dreams.

Insidiously, Laurie started to dream in ori. In the beginning, only her panties were ori in her dreams, the sole place where ori was present in her real life. Then the first things to become ori were those with vague boundaries: sheets, curtains, reflections. Next came surroundings, natural and otherwise: walls, grass, sand, and foliage were adorned in every shade of the colour. A few days later, cars, metal things, animals, and even the skin of certain faces turned ori. The clarity with which Laurie could recall these dreams made her head spin. The birds, she realized, were ori verging on yellow; her leggings were a redder tinge of ori: vibrant and warm. Although faded by a few secret washes, the Fruit of the

Loom panties she often wore and looked at every day were a primary shade of ori.

Four or five nights went by without ori. Laurie figured those dreams were behind her, they had showed her what she needed to know.

The following night, a naked Mori was lit up, his back to an equally naked plywood wall. Everything else was black. Laurie was jerking him off. She could feel her hand in the dream, tube-like and extremely sensitive. She was sliding it all the way up and down Mori's length. The penis was generating heat. She could feel the blood pumping. At the end, the meatus was opening and closing. She lifted her gaze to see the pucker of pleasure on Mori's face. He was urging her on with his groans, his cries of "keep going, I'm nearly there." When Laurie woke, the feeling of wetness in her crotch had her thinking about the hazy ending to her dream. It was all a blur, except for the jets of ori sperm Mori spurted from the depths of his being, belly-deep moans suggesting he was in pain.

After that, ori appeared only in a very particular kind of dream. They weren't black and white, but monochrome, like those German expressionist movies with the tinted film that showed the lit-up areas in different colours to give a sense of brightness or emotion. Three or four times a week, Laurie dreamed in black and ori.

Laurie wasn't a late riser. She would get up and go into the kitchen in the morning to make herself some tea and toast. France would just stay in the living room. Robert liked to get an early start in his office. The presbytery was spacious enough for none of them to run into one another, and that was no bad thing. Laurie's dreams unsettled her. She was worried they'd be visible when people looked at her.

There was a sticky sort of silence about the wooden building. It seemed to ooze from every cupboard whose door was opened. In the slots of the toaster, it coated the slices so the bread wouldn't toast as quickly.

UPS showed up with a package. Someone had to sign for it. Laurie opened the door, but France made a beeline from the other end of the house to take charge. Laurie saw her open the package. It was a Cartier necklace—grey pearls a whole centimetre in diameter, fastened with a diamond-encrusted hook and loop. France put the necklace on. She had a look at herself in the hallway mirror. She gave a smile that engaged nothing but her mouth. There was a little card, all black and glossy, inside the necklace box. France read it. She and her necklace retired to the living room to read a book about a strong woman in the darkest depths of the Duplessis era. The card was left half-open on the hallway table. Laurie was able to read it by pressing her temple to the wood.

To help you through these difficult times.
Love.
Robert

Not "I love you," no: "Love." Laurie felt the stirrings of a shiver at the nape of her neck, but the shiver stayed there and swelled without running down her spine. She tried to shake it all off by rolling her shoulders. It didn't work. The shiver ballooned and started to make her arms shake. The *genmaicha* did nothing to warm her up. Worse, the surface of the tea rippled when she lifted the cup.

"Say something, Laurie," France implored, interrupting her family saga on the other side of the wall.

"What?"

"Do you think my necklace is nice?"

"Yes, it's lovely."

It was magnificent. Laurie wasn't lying.

Like clams and mussels, oysters lack the complex nervous system it takes to distinguish a stabbing pain from a simple defensive reflex. Still, they can spend a lifetime smoothing a grain of sand so it won't scrape their flesh. For Laurie, this only added to the beauty of the jewel.

"One day, a man's going to give you gifts like this. You just have to think, when he does, about what we do to deserve them, and what they want from us."

Things like that: the clipped turns of phrase, the little notes left on tables, the evasive behaviour, the spring-loaded glances from her father; so many little things at the presbytery seemed fated to make Laurie feel the shame of a prostitute. She pulled on a chunky wool sweater, mitts, and a toque with big pompoms that dangled at her ears. On the beach, the wind stirred the sand and its fine coat of snow into an overlap of swirls, one far lighter than the other. Laurie managed a shiver at last. It did her good.

By the mini-mart, there was Mori's Lincoln, with the rental company sticker on the bumper. That sticker meant he'd be leaving. Laurie waited for him in the parking lot. He came out with a brown bag: eggs, rice, two frozen trout, a clear container of sesame seeds, green onions, soy sauce, and ketchup and mayonnaise too. He was wearing a chic-looking black overcoat, with crummy clothes underneath. He noticed something imploring in Laurie's gaze. He told her he was doing some work on his place and wasn't planning to stop. He wasn't expecting her to lend a hand, but she was welcome to come by.

"Can I offer you some *genmaicha*? I had it sent over from Japan. It's brown rice tea."

"I know. I've just had some. I wouldn't say no to some *sencha*."

Laurie was surprised by her own abruptness. She smiled to redeem herself.

"I have something better for you."

On a sheet of paper, Mori wrote 玉露 with a felt-tip pen.

"*Gyokuro*," he pronounced. "The second sign is quite unusual; you'll learn it later this year. It means 'dew' and it's pronounced 'ro' in compound words."

(Mori pronounced the consonant the Japanese way, between an *l* and an *r*.)

"Yes. At the top, there's the prefix for rain, 雨," Laurie traced with the same pen.

"Your progress is astonishing."

"I've learned the first thousand signs or so. The first one, that's the one for sphere or ball, and you can say *gyoku* or *tama*."

"Yes. Exactly. But the same word also refers to many other spherical objects: a bowl, a lens, a gemstone, a pearl, or even a pretty girl," Mori explained, choking on the last few syllables.

Mori poured boiling water into a *yuzamashi* to let it cool for several minutes. They said nothing. They watched the water stagnate. When Mori deemed it ready, he poured it into two tiny china cups and heaped far more tea leaves than seemed reasonable to Laurie into a sculpted ceramic *hohin*. He poured the water from the cups directly over the tea. The leaves, rolled into long needles, were a deep blue shade of green. Together, Laurie and Mori watched the substance and colour of them soften. The tea was ready when the leaves began to unroll by themselves. Mori placed one of the cups in front of Laurie. She drank the sole short sip of it. It was lukewarm, concentrated, full, syrupy. It wasn't a flavour, rather a thick veil that coated the mouth with its gentle presence. She'd never tasted that, except, perhaps, yes, it was coming back to her, in the urchin, in the first sensation it delivers before its shot of iodine.

"And *gyokuro*," Mori continued, "is *sench*a tea that is grown in the shade. It's the finest of them all. Like a girl whose delicate skin would burn under too much sun. I had some delivered from Japan too, but this one with you in mind."

Laurie felt herself blush. She wondered what Mori would have said if she had accepted his initial offer of *genmaicha*.

"Do you like it?"

"Yes. It's very good."

"They say it tastes of seaweed."

"I've never eaten seaweed."

Mori snapped his chin to his chest. In his kitchen, an empty crate of Arctic surfclams was full of seaweed he was drying.

"But ... it's everywhere around here!"

They didn't speak much. Laurie's heart had started to beat faster when Mori mentioned her skin, and it wasn't slowing down. He told her to follow him to the basement because that was where he was working.

It was a painting project. There was a metal paint shaker in the corner of the room. Laurie had only seen one before at the hardware store. Mori said he'd bought one especially. There was already a gallon in the paint can holder. Mori switched the shaker on. The noise made them plug their ears. In that one too-loud minute, Laurie noticed the room had been cleared and Mori had already covered one of the walls in a coat of primer.

"Where's the furniture you were storing down here?" Laurie asked once the silence had returned.

Mori made several attempts to open the can with a screwdriver.

"Sal-hi came to get it."

"Who?"

"Sal-hi, the brother of the man who disappeared."

"Ah! Sar'h."

"Yes. Sal-hi. I too have some things to learn," Mori smiled.

The lid popped free. The paint was ori.

Laurie asked him why he wasn't painting the one wall that was bathed in light from the window. Mori replied that he found the people of Baie-Trinité rather curious. She sat down on the floor. He'd found himself some painting duds—an old beer T-shirt, dirty jeans, and a cap from the Atlanta Olympics. Where the heck from, she had no idea. He was going at it with the roller, straight and fast. Great bands of ori were overlapping as he went. Louis Berthelot's basement was becoming Mori Ishikawa's basement, an exceptional elsewhere.

"I can help you," Laurie offered.

Help him she could, but painting is a dirty job. The slightest splash would stain her clothes and someone on the beach or at the presbytery would see an ori they weren't supposed to see. She went barefoot and stripped down to her underwear: pink bra, black panties. She tied her hair up in a bun and covered it in a plastic bag from the hardware store. With a small brush, she applied herself to the delicate work.

Mori reminded her of one of the meanings of the word ori: *chance*, in the sense of the opportune moment, the way we say, "Go for it, this is your chance." He told her how chance had been on his side in life, that ori had been the most fortunate of all chances, that he was alive thanks to this colour and that, without it, he might be dead. He told Laurie she hadn't grasped it yet, but there was a lot of her in this colour. Specifically, he said: "You're in there immensely." He was looking at her without too much embarrassment and, even bending over or crouching down to reach into the hollows of a moulding, she was moving with no excessive modesty.

It was almost dark when they were done. Mori took care to draw the blackout blind before turning on the ceiling light. They watched the paint dry on the wall. Laurie explained what was funny about that. She undid her bun. She sensed Mori was nervous. She hadn't had that impression since their very first encounters in the eelgrass. She placed a hand on his shoulder. They were about the same height. She wanted to kiss him, but he moved his mouth out of the way at the last moment saying no, no, just no, no, with no word of explanation.

19

A daybed on Cléophas Lake

"Talk to Mori Ishikawa," the Post-it on the bulletin board insisted in its jaundice. The more Goyette was sure Mori knew everything, the less he could see himself approaching the guy. They would run into one another in the village, and each would acknowledge the other with a slight tip of the chin. Goyette had gone by Louis Berthelot's house a few times. There were no lights on in the evenings. Mori must go to bed early, he figured, or like the dark. Returning in the daytime, Goyette had noticed in the basement window the blackout blind of someone with something to hide. He'd even rapped a knuckle or two on the door: Mori had not answered. That was before he spoke to the chef. Now that Goyette couldn't play the innocent anymore, no, he couldn't imagine himself talking to the guy. "So, it seems that in Japan, you have crime, how should I put it, of the organized kind..." he failed to see himself stammering. Instead, he pictured himself arriving with his proof, backing Mori up against the wall triumphantly, and making him confess to everything—filling in the two or three remaining blanks.

And so, a rivalry sprouted, even with no affront to warrant it. There were still far too many unknowns. Winter was setting in, and that'd do nothing to help.

Best-case scenario, Laurie was in on it; worst-case, she was in love. Goyette knew this was ratcheting up the rivalry too. He wasn't too keen on the whole thing. His sparks of desire for Myriam were returning. They made love often, passionately. Goyette realized there was an engine inside him, and it was best not to dwell on what kind of fuel it burned.

As for Robert, there was no point talking to him. Word in the village was, he was bitter and routed. He would curse at people for no reason and preferred to be left alone, more so than usual—as an innocent victim would, Goyette reckoned. He was convinced that Robert knew even less than he himself did about what was going on. And that this was torture for him.

That left Saturn.

At Cécile's greasy spoon, Cécile and Linda, Louis Berthelot's widow, were holding back less and less. Linda often went behind the counter. Hands would wander, looks would linger. People were coming around to it. Every now and then, someone would clear their throat and call for a bit of respect for the departed, but once they were back at the plant, they would question their reasoning: was it consideration for Dishrag's memory, or latent homophobia? People weren't used to that sort of thing, but they reminded themselves they were in the year two thousand-whatever-it-was. A vague sense of unease hovered over the deep fryer and the hotplate. Now there was a nip in the air, the heat from the hash browns and the bacon was condensing on the windows. You couldn't see outside. It was easier to grant Cécile a free hand in those more closed-off confines. They didn't call her the boss lady for nothing.

"What'll it be for you, then, Frédéric?" she ducked behind her counter, acknowledging him from the far end.

"An Italian poutine, and a Michigan with mustard. Nah, scratch that. I'll just have a spaghetti."

"Feeling saucy, are we?"

"Can't say I'm not."

"I'll give you an extra spoonful, then. On the house. Want a knife with your spag?"

"No."

"I knew it. You're a twirler."

Goyette wasn't expecting to run into Saturn, but he'd heard the old lady who did the cleaning at his hunting cabin often came by on a Tuesday lunchtime for a big Seven-Up. Very thin and with terrible hair, that's how she'd been described to him. He had a hard time picking her out in the jam-packed snack bar. She was skinny and solo in a seat by the window. A relentless little chill kept running through her and she pursed her lips with every breath since her lungs had seen better days.

Yup, Saturn was out at his place on Cléophas Lake. He'd rounded up a right little gang of druggies there. She often had to pick up the condoms.

"*Used* condoms, you know," the emphysemic disapproved.

"Um. Yes. I figured."

"You'll want to stick some chains on your quad if you go out there, that track's getting slippery as all hell. I've got some on mine, anyway."

"Thanks for the advice. How prudent of you."

"I'll give you *prudent*!"

In the bed of his work truck, Goyette loaded an ATV he'd borrowed from the Ministry of Indigenous Affairs following an afternoon of form-filling. He'd put chains on the tires. He thanked himself later, on the frozen dirt and black ice of the track out to Cléophas Lake.

Wearing his green bathrobe, Saturn greeted him with an enthusiastic "Go-yette!". He flung his arms wide and drew the bureaucrat into a unilateral embrace. That crazy-ass beard of his was prickly. He'd tied his perm in a ponytail. In spite of Goyette's request that they speak one on one, Saturn insisted on introducing him to the others. One of the sommelières had upped and left. She'd been replaced by a couple of cooks. The others had been there since the summer. The dishwasher had gained some weight. The crew were sitting or slouching in the generously fenestrated living space on the main floor. The remaining sommelière and the sauce chef, who were sharing a daybed with half-closed eyes, were the only ones who noticed Goyette. The big entremetier and a young dog took up most of the heated concrete floor.

Saturn handed Goyette a coffee. He took it from a commercial percolator. They sat not far from the coffee machine, and both helped themselves to plenty of refills. A joint was offered and refused. Goyette wanted to put Saturn at ease by explaining that he wasn't working for the police, that there had been some interesting developments in the investigation surrounding the toxin. He wasn't there to put anyone in jail. He just wanted to get to the bottom of things.

Apparently, Saturn hadn't had a lucid person to talk to for a while. He seemed to like it. He went on about anything and everything, from ranting about his restaurant and blaming his misadventure on his name: "I should've fuckin' called it Chez Réginald, or Chez Neptune, but my name's not Neptune," to supernaturalizing: "That house's haunted, I'm telling you. The old man's still there making a laughing stock of us," and soothsaying: "I'm no Suzanne, but heck, she's right when she goes on about karma and all that stuff," as well as pointing the finger at Goyette: "You and your agency should've poked your noses in a while back, that would've stopped us dicking around." He took on board lessons from existentialism: "I'm gonna be a changed man, Goyette, a changed man. I'm like that guy rolling his rock," from psychoanalysis: "Murdering the father, yeah, murdering the father. I mean, he's dead already, but sometimes you gotta kill the dead," and from anthropology: "You know, if the Old Testament says not to eat shellfish, that's why, that's exactly why. It's dangerous, a matter of public health." It wasn't the first time that Saturn had thought these things, that much was clear, but he was voicing them for the first time, in one big outburst. He drew on the proverbs: "Out of bad comes good," and he got stuck into Queen's repertoire, screeching out of tune, but with feeling, about another one biting the dust. Approaching the limits of his composure, Goyette tried to steer him a different way.

"I saw the chef two weeks ago."

"What chef?"

"*The* chef. The one from your restaurant."

"Did you stick your fist in his face for me?"

"Is that what I should have done?"

"Yes."

"Why?"

"Let me guess what he told you: bikers, money laundering, blah-di-blah."

"That was the kind of thing we discussed, yes."

Goyette felt condescending, saying that. He didn't want to be condescending. That wouldn't get him anywhere. The thing was, over in the living room, a girl who was sleeping had rolled over, her blanket had ridden up, and her butt cheeks were exposed. Saturn didn't budge. Goyette wanted to go cover her up, but that wouldn't get him anywhere, either.

"Open that drawer," Saturn pointed.

Goyette opened it. Inside there were gold bars stamped by Crédit Suisse and the Royal Canadian Mint. About sixteen, in all.

"Maybe you should keep those under lock and key?" Goyette suggested.

"Nah, I don't fucking care. You want one?"

Goyette was dumbfounded. For a second, he thought maybe Saturn was trying to corrupt him, but the look on the guy's face led him to believe he simply wanted to show precisely how much he didn't fucking care.

"What I'm getting at, is that I don't need to cut any deals with the bikers, Goyette. I own a quarter of the Fisheries, you know. I wanted the best seafood restaurant in the world, so I partnered with the best seafood chef in the world. Unfortunately, he came with the bikers in tow."

"So, what about you and the bikers?"

Saturn sighed. He went into the next room and Goyette heard a sniffing sound. He came back less dispirited.

"Where were we?"

"You, and the bikers?"

"They must have bled a million and a half off me. Then they left me the fuck alone," Saturn replied flatly, gravely, with a blank stare. "The chef told me it was Mori Ishikawa who was asking batshit crazy prices for the urchins and all, but it's obvious, all that went straight to the bikers."

"But ... I mean ... you must have had words with Mori once or twice about that..."

"No, Saturn was just pumping out the cash," Saturn revealed in the third person. "Mori ... I spoke to him once, or I never did."

A twist of the hips and the blanket slid aside to reveal the sleeping girl's bush. Goyette averted his eyes. "Léa, Léa," the sauce chef stirred her. She soon covered herself up.

"Once, or you never did?"

"I can't be sure. I was as stoned as a wall after the restaurant opening. The next morning, on the beach. He might have hit me."

"Huh?" was all Goyette could say, his head was spinning that fast.

"Yeah. Man. I remember. That was the time you undid my tourniquet. That could've cost me my arm. For real. Gangrene, y'know. Thanks, man. I'll never forget that," Saturn softened, with a few little bro-taps of his fist to his heart.

Something clicked in Goyette's mind, as if the mechanism had just set a pendulum swinging: that was the day of the wave at four seventeen. Mori had seen it. And he might well have reacted by thumping Saturn.

Goyette told Saturn he was going to show him something. He removed the test tube of powder from its black sleeve in front of him. The sauce chef risked a glance, then clamped his hands over his eyes, moaning and groaning that he'd never had a headache like that in his life.

"What is it?"

Saturn's neck jerked away of its own accord. He wanted to look, but it was physically impossible. His body was protecting his eyes.

"That day, the day when Mori might have hit you, there was a wave, at seventeen minutes past four, that did something fundamental to the sand. It changed everything. What you see is water. It's solid water, but it doesn't melt. It was stuck in the sand."

"Wow," Saturn marvelled. "I've seen some weird shit in my life, but ho-ly! Why's it so hard to look at?"

"That's what I'm trying to find out."

"Can you leave me some?"

"Er ... why?" Goyette asked with a hint of apprehension and more than a hint of distaste. "We've got problems with a bear. He comes sniffing around the window every day at a quarter past four to scare Léa's pants off. If we show that stuff to him, I reckon he won't come back."

"Yes!" approved the entremetier, who'd just been roused by the young dog's tongue.

Seeing the powder, the entremetier stayed face down on the floor. The dog whimpered and scarpered.

"A bear?" Goyette repeated.

"Yes. A bear. No shortage of them around these parts."

Back home, sipping his midnight coffee, it occurred to Goyette he should have asked for clarification: was it a quarter past four in the morning, or the afternoon? He regretted having left a bit of powder out at Cléophas Lake. They'd be shooting that up, for sure. Bears are creatures of habit; it's not like he didn't know that. On a work trip to Aguanish before the road went that far, he had learned the routine of a family of bears. Everyone knew it. It was even in *Goldilocks*—those three bears were set in their ways, right down to the temperature of the porridge. He had presumed that the bear came by every day at four seventeen, had believed it had had something to do with the wave. He chased the coffee with a swig of aquavit. *Talk to Mori Ishikawa*, one Post-it insisted. *Cell (cage), sediment, chance, fold*, obfuscated another. He had a clear inkling that he'd been fooled. By whom, he would spend the night trying and failing to figure out.

But he had not been completely fooled: there really was a bear. And he really did run away when they showed him the powder, only to come back stronger the next day. Léa, terrified, had turned around to the home cinema system and its illuminated display.

16:14

She'd boasted to the rest of the crew that the bear-repellant powder was the trip of her life. She was bummed there was none of it left. She needed more of that stuff. There had ensued a lot of nodding, and a promise to get more from Goyette. No matter the cost, Saturn had added.

Yes, it was the day after a big night. There had been champagne and a case of Échezeaux 2005, a moose calf liver poached by the dishwasher, a loin from its mother, French fries and Tomme cheese, espagnole sauce, an immense hydroponic chicory salad, a maple St. Honoré. The bear had just scarpered from the powder. Theories were teeming down about what made it irregardable. The powdery nature of the substance was an invitation to get high on it and no one had suggested anything else: it was obvious to everyone they'd be doing it. But Saturn had wanted to be careful so that no one would overdose. They had rolled a joint of pale hash and sprinkled a bit of Goyette's crystallized water in there. The sommelière had been the first to take two short drags.

"Yeah," she'd confirmed after seven seconds, "yeah, it's a bit like ecstasy, but mellower."

So then they had sniffed a tenth of a gram, and that didn't do anything. They had to take it to the next level.

Saturn put together a few microdoses in one-millilitre syringes. No mean feat because he had to do it all behind his back. But the memory of the movement was ingrained in his hands. Then the time had come to find veins with their eyes closed, to go by feeling. There had been accidents. A cook had planted the needle right in her ulnar nerve and got the tingles all the way to her little finger.

"Why don't we wrap some electrical tape around the doses?" the roast cook had suggested, with admirable pragmatism.

The irregardable powder had entered their veins. The sommelière wasn't wrong: the elation in the body was like being on ecstasy, as was the desire to reach out and touch other people's skin, but the soul was filled with a nirvana-like serenity reminiscent of the finest heroin. The voices of others softened, even for platitudes, and became more beautiful, something approaching Truth, from one second to the next. Time expanded and grew warm.

Ecstasy is an empty promise, more often than not preventing desire from making it all the way down from the chest to below the belt. Goyette's powder was a diving board over a pool of carnal triumph. The guys got hard, real hard. The girls got wet, just like that. It wasn't the first time, up at the hunting cabin on Cléophas Lake, that bodies got in a tangle, caught up in the all-encompassing kind of caress where no one knew who the other mouth belonged to. This caress fell apart when the sauce chef felt he was close to coming. Saturn was on the daybed, getting blown by the sommelière and rimmed by the entremetier—to whom she was also giving a hand job. A sudden desire, one he couldn't hold back, rose up inside him: a desire to be seen.

"Hey, out of my way," he shoved off the entremetier.

"What? Oh, come on, man."

"I want to jizz in front of everyone."

That's not the kind of thing you hear every day, not even at Cléophas Lake. There was a commotion, a gathering around. Saturn stood there, masturbating with zeal and sharp thrusts of his hips. He ejaculated onto the concrete floor, and they all instantly turned away. The sight of the sperm all but made their eyes explode.

Seventh intermission

the Arctic surfclam

During his business studies at Laval University, Robert would often pay a visit to the Quebec City office of the Ministry of Fisheries and Oceans to request a bibliography of new publications. And whenever a promising monograph caught his eye, he would order a copy of the handout. Specialized to the extreme, the subjects never failed to amuse France. Back in the day, she used to laugh with abandon, at anything and nothing.

Now and then, the pen-pushers would conduct studies of clam species with strong market potential—Canadian waters were coming down with them and there was money to be made by exporting to Japan, and maybe on home soil too, if only people would deign to eat the damn things the way they did over there. In 1986, Robert managed to get his hands on a document listing the untapped Arctic surfclam populations in the Gulf of St. Lawrence. He didn't sleep for three nights.

The Arctic surfclam also goes by the name of Stimpson's surfclam. For long before Robert's discovery, a malacologist in Massachusetts, William Stimpson, observed that the foot of certain surfclams in the Atlantic, when cooked, would take on the orangey hue of cooked lobster. It wasn't just the odd clam here and there that had this peculiarity; fishermen were hauling them in as if there were entire deposits of them on the seabed. Nothing made Stimpson happier than discovering a species, and this really did seem to be a new one. That was in 1860. Stimpson named his discovery *Mactromeris polynyma*—surfclam of many names—for the various ways in which the fishermen referred to them. Who was he to decide, anyway?

Many things have many names. In any language, the name of many an everyday object may vary by region and social stratum. A given name not only designates an object, but also says something about its user. Rogatien had a gamut of old names for things, with a tangle of allegiances behind each.

"Have a ganders outside at that shin-tangle that needs pullin' up," he had tried to change the subject. "Stick your mackinaw on and muck in wi' me, will ya?"

"*Mactromeris polynyma...*" Robert had wielded the monograph and scratched his head.

"Ha! Surfclam of many names ... get with it!" Rogatien had understood, thanks to his years at the seminary in Baie-Comeau.

"It's called a Stimpson's surfclam."

Stimpson should have known, or maybe he did: Latin and science had a greater tolerance for paradox than everyday speech and Rogatien. The thing became known as the Arctic surfclam (a.k.a. Stimpson's surfclam, because discovering a species lets you put your name to it) even though it's typically harvested nowhere near the Arctic.

Six years later, Robert had bought some on a romantic getaway in Nova Scotia. France had been the first to taste it, and she was deadly serious about it. For them, molluscs were no longer a laughing matter. Nothing much was, by that point, to be honest. Back in Baie-Trinité, Robert had steamed the things. Then he'd taken them out of their shells and put them on the counter in front of Rogatien. It didn't look like much: an orangey protuberance a bit like a cooked lobster claw caught in a viscous trap, surrounded by superfluous flaps, more or less muscular bands, and inexplicably fleshy bulges.

"Ugh, if I showed that to a priest, he'd swear the Creator didn't exist," the patriarch had hyperbolized.

"Just taste it," the son had insisted.

Something in his tone carried the promise of a taste to redeem all ugliness.

"Stimpson: what's that all about? I hope it's not some guy's name. I wouldn't want my name to go down in posterity for a glob of snot in a shell."

Stimpson died of tuberculosis at forty, leaving his colleagues at the Smithsonian Institute's Department of Invertebrate Zoology and millions of anonymous echinoderms to mourn his passing. When Rogatien said what he said, the malacologist turned in his grave.

"Just taste it before you make up your mind," Robert had suggested, keen to give the mollusc a chance. Rogatien had closed his eyes, then opened his mouth and put the clam's foot in it all at once. Then chewed it. Churned it around in his mouth. And taken his time. He had gone to the fridge to crack open a beer and take a swig between two swallows.

"It's not bad, but it's bloody ugly," he had concluded. "It's going to take a boatload of marketing. Only the Japanese'll eat that. That's your business," he had added, after a brief silence.

They had looked at one another. Something had just happened. Flabbergasted, Robert had looked into his father's eyes, feeling like a little kid, but not wanting to show it. Did his father mean it was up to him to figure it out, or, literally, his *business*?

It turned out to be his *business*. The first cans rolled out of the processing plant in 1990. "Since there has to be a boss," that's what Rogatien's will had said. Robert had not become that boss by default, just because he was the least eccentric of his siblings and the most presentable to an investment banker. Before Rogatien had died, Robert had managed to quadruple sales of Arctic surfclams year after year. He was the one who had the idea of separating the foot from the rest of the clam, promoting it as an alternative to lobster while selling the scraps to the deep fryers. When the contract with the Isumi Conglomerate of Tones, Colours, Pigments, Molluscs, and Crustaceans was signed, it was he, the boss, who decided to deep freeze and export the surf-clam feet in ten-kilo blocks.

But that day, sitting in his office, he was reading and rereading a formal letter of complaint from the Conglomerate. The quality of the Arctic surfclam feet was deteriorating, it seemed. Their orange lacked lustre, and fingers were being pointed at the deep-freezing process. A proposal was made to return both tonnes of the most recent delivery if Robert so wished, or to destroy them, but no, there would be no payment for them. At the edges of Robert's field of vision, flashes of ori were dancing like curtains. The flow of yen was done for. Sobs grabbed him by the throat, but he didn't cry. He banged his fist against his desk. Laurie jumped on the floor below. She had just learned the Japanese word for shell: 貝 (*kai*). It was among the most figurative ones, with its tripartite body and two little legs. It was one she would not forget. Robert's table-thumping curtailed her studies. She switched on the lamp in her bedroom, using her Fruit of the Loom panties as a lampshade, then she read *The Lover* by Marguerite Duras in one sitting in the ori light.

A few days later, Mori gave her a Japanese glossary of seafood terms he had compiled, including the Japanese name for the Arctic surfclam: 北寄貝 (*hokkigai*).

The first symbol, Laurie recognized easily: North. Shell of the north?

"Congratulations, Miss Lelarge, your progress is stunning," Mori made her blush.

20

The crab and the monkey

Mori and Laurie spent a lot of time drinking tea in front of the ori wall in Dishrag Berthelot's basement. Mori spoke in Japanese, with more and more complicated words, repeating or miming them until Laurie understood.

He gave her a cardboard box covered with inscriptions by the Japanese postal service. It contained children's books, traditional Japanese folk tales. One of them was the story of Momotarou. An old peasant woman discovers a giant peach while washing her laundry in a river. Inside the giant peach, she finds a child, whom she decides to call "the boy in the peach." The old peasant woman could have been a little more imaginative, Laurie thought, but the name still seemed better than Little Red Riding Hood. Plus, *momo* (桃) was a super cute word for peach. After that, Laurie read *The Lover* for the fourth time.

Laurie was drinking *genmaicha* at the hefty table in the presbytery. The gloopy silence still coated and weighed everything down. Now the slots in the toaster were completely jammed and Laurie preferred to make rice for herself in her dishes marked with a cursive L. She would listen to NHK on her iPod or read one of Mori's books while she ate. That morning, it was *Sarukani*, a disconcerting story in which a monkey bombards a female crab with hard, unripe persimmons from a tree. The shock of being attacked kills the crab and causes her to give birth. Her offspring then plot revenge, finding allies in a bee and some cow dung. Dictionary in hand, Laurie was about to discover that the monkey is crushed to death by a big traditional mortar.

"What the hell is this?" Robert was barely in the room when he rumbled.

Laurie had her back to him, but his every step resonated at the base of her skull. She could hear, and feel, the jabs of his breathing on her. For the first time in her life, she had the physical certainty that she was going to be hit. It was coming. She sank her head into her shoulders and clenched her teeth, driven by a defensive reflex that would fail to protect her. Her father's fist swept toward her like a gust of wind, then stopped right by her left ear and opened. In the same movement, the Fruit of the Loom panties parachuted to the table and landed flat on the dark wood, open to their slightly soiled crotch.

"Do you think I don't know what that colour is, huh? Do you take your father for a complete idiot? Do you just figure, 'There's a new colour in Baie-Trinité and my dad doesn't know about it,' eh? Well, have I got news for you: I know everything that's going on. Everything."

Laurie turned around. Anger dilated Robert's pupils. The flashes of ori that bounced off the black of his eyes could not merely be the reflection of the panties. There seemed to be patches of it in the depths of his acne scars too, but that could also be a reflection in the sebum. Still shaken, Laurie struggled to contain the surge of emotion that was going to come. All she wanted was not to cry.

"Just calm down! It's been a month since we last sp—" she got off to a pretty good start before an impetuous sob got the better of her.

For France, who had abandoned her family saga on hearing Robert's seismic arrival, it was too much. She was in the doorway and her eyes, even after ten seconds, still could not get used to the ori of the panties. Her mind was wearing itself out trying to find valid comparisons in her memory. There were none. Standing in front of her, hair sticky with gel, Robert was waving a hand at the panties on the table, but France could still see only the table.

"You tell your mother, it was Mori Ishikawa who gave you that filth!"

Laurie kept crying. Her mother saw nothing. Her perceptions remained dull. There was no space. France could feel her nostrils, her eye sockets, her mouth, her vagina, her anus dilating in ring-shaped spasms, as if something was trying to enter her, everywhere at once. A stain appeared on the table, scintillating, arising from the pressure she was feeling in her eyes. Then, something touched the back of her throat and she began to vomit. It took a moment for the vomiting to bend her double and, still standing, she projected a good cupful of food in a brown liquid, in silence, in a single great jet, onto the floor.

Once she could bring herself to look at the table again, she saw the ori panties—a colour she had never seen before. In her throat, the irregular beatings of her heart were funnelled into a sharp point that was preventing her from breathing.

"I'm dying," she announced before inhaling loudly and exhaling too quickly.

"You're hyperventilating, France," Robert observed.

Laurie took advantage of the kerfuffle to rescue her panties, then things calmed down. Alone in her room again, she was struggling to learn her kanjis. Her father had come in and she felt embarrassed, intruded on, but it was her fault: she hadn't closed the door. Robert's eye—he was passing by—had been drawn by the colour of the lampshade. Laurie thought she might have even left the lamp on.

The gloopy silence dissipated, blown away by something or other. The wood of the walls, the frames, and the beams, exposed, somehow expressed its pain when she touched it. Above Laurie, the see-ee-oh was speaking on the phone, in the quietest of tones so as not to be heard. He was negotiating a nine-million-dollar loan to cover the company's operating expenses until the new season. Laurie didn't run into him for two days. He remained holed up in his office. Still, she kept an eye on her mother: her sonorous diarrhea resounded throughout the whole presbytery, and she looked ill. They didn't talk to one another. Two days of opaque fog: when she wasn't touching the wood, Laurie could feel absolutely nothing. She did not go to Mori's. She read folk tales or studied kanjis. She dressed warmly and went cross-country skiing on the beach or snowshoeing in the woods. When she got back, she made tea. She ate only two hot meals—the same thing twice: *tamago kake gohan*, which translated to very hot rice mixed with a raw egg and VH soy sauce. That way, she never had to be in the kitchen for more than five minutes at a time. 卵: *tamago*: egg. Easy, Laurie figured. Her dictionary told her that *gohan* was another way to say a word she knew: *mechi*: 飯: cooked rice, meal, or food. To say *gohan* was to show more respect for the rice. It tasted like carbonara, but saltier. In her mouth, the slightly set egg slid against the starch of the rice, which slid across her tongue. She liked that viscous three-way encounter. It lessened the shame.

On the third day of solitude, thirty-five centimetres of snow fell. Laurie went past Mori's house on her way back from the woods at twilight. A little light was coming from the rear, upstairs. He must be in his office. He didn't like her disturbing him. So she didn't.

Skirting around the side of the presbytery to go in around the back, she saw them in the window: her parents. Darkness had fallen and they hadn't closed the curtains. There was a green tablecloth on the kitchen table and two red candles with timid flames. They were eating pasta. Between them, there was a pot from where, from time to time, they would pluck sections of crab and tear them apart with their fingers. On snowshoes, with her pompom hat on, Laurie felt a freefalling sensation she had experienced only in her nightmares.

Without taking off her snowshoes (there was no point), she made her way to the kitchen covered in snow. The snowshoes snagged on the furniture, knocking it over.

"You're having dinner together ... and eating seafood!"

The bowls held plain linguine with mussels. One mouthful at a time, they were putting a bit of crab meat on the pasta, or not.

"Yes. We want nothing more to do with you," said France in a tone of times past.

"What the hell!" Laurie protested, another sob getting the better of her.

"You're part of the problem, not the solution," dropped Robert, sucking on a claw.

They kept on eating the meal that she'd been left out of. She stood there crying in her too-warm clothes.

"Go away, Laurie. You can't stay with us anymore. No means no," France condemned her.

"But ... where am I going to live?"

"Go stay with the Japanese guy. He's the one you belong to. Body and soul, now," France insisted on clarifying.

"You're completely out of your minds! I'm not sleeping with Mori. He's teaching me Japanese so I can go study in Japan next year. That's all," Laurie oversimplified. "Hell-o!" she then tried to bring them back down to earth.

"We're not worried about you. You're a grown woman. You can stand on your own two feet," said Robert without believing it, with a speck of sarcasm.

"A woman who can call the child protection agency, yes!"

"You wouldn't dare!" the old man dared her.

Laurie took two snowshoed steps toward the table. With her mitts, she grabbed a section of crab and drew it swiftly to her mouth. She bit into the open flesh of the shoulder. It *was* pretty tasty. France screamed, then Robert gave her a weird look. Her scream stopped dead and gave way to a sudden stupefaction, as if a circuit breaker had tripped inside her. She turned to her daughter and told her, quite matter-of-factly, to "go die somewhere else."

Robert's face creased with pain.

With the delicate taste of the crab in her mouth and too many torrents of tears backing up in her trachea, Laurie went back to walking through the powder in her snowshoes.

Most cultures view the rock as a symbol of immobility. As she dashed her way on snowshoes toward an ever-changing destination, the snowy rocks that Laurie saw disassociating themselves from the river in the moonlight were the same as they had been since the Bronze Age. There's nothing changeable about rocks. The most active of them crumble only a few times a century.

Suzanne Lelarge saw things differently. For her, there was a soul in the rock. Being a cave dweller herself, she knew it well. She and the rock of her home had two kinds of relationship. One was static, enhanced every time she discovered a new sparkle to a quartz phenocryst in the living room or a speck of feldspar in the orthogneiss of one of her chambers of reverence. The other was dynamic, based on the sole property of the rock that Suzanne could sense any variation in: its temperature. Everything is alive to some degree, she liked to reason. Pressing her bare skin against the rock was all it took to feel the continual vibration.

It was cold in her place. She had said so to Robert the month before. They'd have to make more microperforations in the walls, run some radiant cables through.

Robert had said he'd had it with her dumping millions into the ground, even though the work was only going to cost three hundred thousand dollars. He was not in a good mood. Ten minutes later, he had called her back to apologize a little and tell her she should cut payments to the fishermen by a third, starting that coming year. How was she supposed to get them on board with that? Well, he hated to say it, but that was her problem. As for the cold, she'd just have to wear a sweater. In the winter, lovers were fewer and farther between. She had gotten into the habit of curling up at night with a hot water bottle.

There was no alarm clock in Suzanne's bedroom. She couldn't bear their turquoise—or worse, red—light, since it disrupted your aura, derailed your dreams, and one day you'd end up with depression and wonder why. Gah. She had refilled her hot water bottle three times and still couldn't sleep. Lelarge Fisheries, in recent years, had vanquished the competition. In the Gulf of St. Lawrence, you had to travel to New Brunswick to find a processing plant that didn't belong to the Lelarges. The fishing boats couldn't land their catches anywhere else. Suzanne was still shivering, but it wasn't because of the temperature of the rock. She was thinking about Hercules, caught in a trap like his own lobsters, but he'd come out all right. Poverty would plague the others: those who fished for whelks or surfclams. The shrimp trawlers might just stay afloat on loans. She looked for a god to pray to. When it came to capitalism, she would often find herself turning to Mercury in her personal pantheon. But there was no god for this kind of capitalism.

So, when she heard a snowmobile out front and the chirp of her door chime, she didn't know what time it was. It was the middle of the night.

Laurie was shivering too. Her teeth were chattering, and her lips were blue. Mori was keeping a better handle on himself, but he still couldn't suppress the occasional shoulder shake. Suzanne gave them wool blankets and fleecy bathrobes. She sat them down in the living room and put a cast-iron teapot in front of them. Laurie, comforted at last, started crying again. She felt as though Suzanne knew everything.

"Don't tell me they kicked you out!"

Laurie was crying too hard to talk. Mori looked down at the ground, embarrassed.

"It was Miss Lelarge who asked me to drive her here," he explained himself. "She trusts you." For several minutes, there was no sound other than Laurie's sobbing, separated by sips of tea. Then Suzanne got up and with an "aw, lovie" ran a hand through her niece's still-cold hair and offered to bring out a bite to eat.

"I've got some fall shrimp, the last catch. That should cheer you up."

"Shrimp? There's not been any at the wharf for what, two weeks?"

The events in our lives have no meaning the moment they're happening. A nighttime snack can turn into a suicide attempt and then turn out to just be a nighttime snack. It had taken months of allusions, unspoken words, and good old clairvoyance for Suzanne to understand exactly what had happened that morning two years earlier when she had found Laurie fast asleep in a pile of shrimp shells amid the eelgrass.

"It's the very last catch of shrimp. The shrimp fishermen usually keep them for themselves, but I have my contacts."

Laurie thought about the other meanings of the word *contact*. Mori lost none of his inhibition. Suzanne put the shrimp on the living-room table, beside the teapot, in their brown paper bag. To accompany them, there was a bag of tortilla chips, sour cream, and a bottle of Tabasco. Laurie sucked the eggs after smearing them with Tabasco. Mori, more circumspect, ate them with his fingers. Suzanne didn't eat them. She ended up lighting a Du Maurier, saying it went well with green tea.

"You're not eating the eggs?" Mori couldn't contain his surprise.

Something in Suzanne's expression changed. "You know, for once, I'm going to do what you lot do."

Suzanne ate the eggs, for the first time in her life. It made her think of her father. They tasted good.

Laurie fell asleep on the couch. Mori, with growing unease, watched Suzanne finish the chips and sour cream.

"Come on, lovie," she said to Laurie. "There's a bed here for you. You, stay here," she ordered Mori.

The guest room was warmer. Laurie was weary of thinking, of feeling.

"Thanks, Suzanne," she yawned.

"My pleasure, lovie," Suzanne tucked her in.

Their eyes met for the first time since she'd gotten there.

"I'm always thinking about him. I think I love him."

"You must think a lot of things. You'll find out for yourself what's true."

Suzanne left the room. Laurie took off all her clothes, except the ori panties. She hid the bra in the pillowcase and soon fell asleep.

Mori was still shivering a little. Suzanne came back and sat in front of him. They didn't talk about Laurie, except when Suzanne asked how her Japanese lessons were going.

"Prodigiously. She has a rare intelligence."

They talked about Japan, about wisdom. Suzanne asked him how he had learned to drive a snowmobile.

"We have them too, in Japan. There are some very snowy places, especially in the mountains."

Suzanne insisted on showing him the room upstairs reserved for ancestor worship. She asked him if he believed in past lives, using her chin to suggest that yes was the right answer.

"Yes. Yes. In some forms of past lives. Yes."

"And you, Mr. Ishikawa, what were you in your most recent past life?"

"A bacterium, probably, but I didn't know it."

21

The fucker

Which is worse: being a cripple, or having no one believe you? Bobby Daigneault had fashioned himself around that question, not one many tend to ponder every day. All his life, his missing fingers would elicit as much disgust as respect, and his story, too often repeated, of what he was about to see that day, would make a real mockery of him. Maybe because he couldn't help but mime it all out with his hands as he went. He would come to see what little progress there'd been in four centuries of Cartesian dualism: for many, the mind extends to the ends of the limbs—and too bad for the amputees. Every time he was met with doubt, with all the *ums*, the *ers*, the *really?*, and the *stop your bullshit!*, never again would Bobby be able to raise his right middle finger in annoyance.

It came as a heck of a surprise when he wound up marrying an able-bodied girl from Ragueneau. Turns out, she was more than able to spend too. They had one of those slightly vengeful weddings that drains the newlyweds' retirement savings and has their families take a hit for three generations. Bobby really milked the payout from the worker's comp too: a good two grand per phalanx. Before he met the girl, though, he did go through a bit of a rough patch when he only had Steeven, his poodle, to console him without raising an eyebrow.

It happened one Tuesday morning around half past five, at the end of the night shift. With a broom, Bobby Daigneault was doing the light duties prescribed by his doctor. He was waiting for the next rotation before he took up his position at the inspection station. They were flash-freezing crab meat in blocks. It was a new process. The bosses insisted on there being no shell fragments and that made the forewoman Solange Blanchet noticeably nervous. She'd get tics in her cheek, like half her face was tensing up and trying to smile in spite of the rest of her. They would last two or three seconds and, at the beginning of the shift, no one noticed it much. Now the sky was starting to lighten in the little window by the ceiling and Solange was cramping up once a minute.

She had gloved up more than once that night. Both hands fingering the filaments of the crab meat, she'd been fishing out tough fibres, bits of membrane, shards of shell, and even a big spiky chunk of claw. The sharp parts tore at her purple nitrile gloves and grazed her skin.

She was yelling her orders at the deboners, and they hollered back that she should get her face looked at—that kind of thing wasn't normal, and her tic was happening more and more often.

Then Bobby Daigneault saw what people would only ever partially believe: Louis "Dishrag" Berthelot, on all fours, mopping up a puddle of crab juice, careful as can be, massaging the concrete floor with his fingers, tensing them, applying maximum friction to displace the lumpy stain.

"Woulda bin easier t' ge' rida if she wasn't s' stubborn," he minced a few vowels and consonants.

On all fours, Dishrag went unseen at first. Failing to recognize his voice for a moment, some thought his observation concerned Solange and had come from one of the deboners. But Bobby had seen the whole thing: Louis Berthelot hadn't been there, then, a second later, he was, at the foot of the conveyor, in a posture that conveyed both industrial hygiene and self-abasement. His movements were confident, his breathing was calm. It hadn't taken him a second to appear, not even a tenth of a second. The matter of his body had materialized in an instant. His beard was trimmed. Dishrag wasn't there, then, in a blink of Bobby's eyes, Dishrag was. He was finishing a slow, precise, scouring motion. That motion, yes, had begun elsewhere, on another stain.

Bobby cried out something between an *a* and an *o* with a thrust of the diaphragm.

It was Dishrag, the fucker.

Folk gathered around him. Solange stayed back in the corner, alone with her tic.

The most important thing to do was get hold of Sar'h. When he actually picked up the phone—people knew what he was like—that in itself was a miracle, people said.

"Are you sitting down?"

"Yes. Yes."

"You'll never believe it, Sar'h. It's your brother. Came from out of thin air, he did."

"Thin air?!"

A long silence added to their fears that he might have fainted.

"Yes, yes, out of thin air," they had to repeat.

"When?"

"Last night."

"The fucker!"

Since it was winter and no one had any hunting, fishing, or work around the camp to distract them, since there was no good weather to enjoy, they all knew right away they'd turn to drink. Since celebrating on an empty stomach was out of the question, they went to Cécile's greasy spoon. Someone phoned ahead to say there'd be a few folk coming, you might want to put an extra pot of beans on the stove. It was only then that, on the other end of the line, Cécile wondered if she should tell Linda to make herself scarce, and it occurred to folk that things might go tits-up. Manning the phone, Roger Lazure said as much to Antoine Tremblay, a.k.a. Li'l Tony a.k.a. Blueberry.

"Where else are folk supposed to go?" Blueberry deadpanned.

Cécile's greasy spoon was all but deserted at that time of day. At the end of the counter, Frédéric Goyette was drinking little sips of coffee and reading documents on his phone. Past him, in a booth, Solange Blanchet was eating alone. The warmth of the coffee and the food was soothing her tic. The other Solange showed up with the group. They sat down as one on the swivelling stools lined up at the counter and at a little table, set back a bit from there. Roger Lazure and Blueberry came up beside the revenant and each wrapped an arm around his shoulders.

Louis Berthelot didn't recognize Linda, his ex, right away. She was standing with her back to him, frying spuds on the hotplate, and she'd changed her hair. It was shorter in the back now. When she turned around, she went weak, and if Cécile hadn't had the foresight to hold on to her, she'd have parked her butt right on the hotplate.

"Louis!"

"Speaking!" Berthelot confirmed cheerily, the way he did when he answered the phone.

"Where were you?" Linda demanded, with an ex's phrasing.

No one had asked him yet, but they all turned around to hear the answer. And, as they all turned, Cécile did something she would regret. The word *regret* was a bit strong, but she would have a word with Linda later to see if it had bothered her. No. It hadn't. But it had rattled her a little that Cécile would even ask. Linda loved her woman full-frontal and unbridled. You don't serve a bunch of lard-ass men six eggs fried in bacon grease if you're inclined to feel remorse.

Cécile simply laid her head on Linda's shoulder and hugged her right arm around her. Probably because two guys were already hugging Louis in front of her, probably more out of a sense of protection than in defiance. But it was in defiance, perhaps, that she then planted a kiss on Linda's neck.

"Yup, Louis, your wife's a lesbian now," clarified Roger Lazure, a man who told it like it was.

"I know," Louis replied, as if his voice were coming from someplace else.

"You'll have to get used to it ... or else you'll be off camping for your breakfast," Blueberry butted in, referring to the restaurant at Domaine Ensoleillé 2000, the campsite up the highway, which turned into a Ski-Doo rest stop in the winter.

"Nah, it's all right," Louis resigned himself.

He cast a gentle eye on Cécile and Linda and ordered an omelette with Cheez-Whiz, the same as usual, the same as before. Then he changed his mind, saying it was a special day and all, and asked for a seafood omelette instead, with shrimp, little scallops, and slivers of whelk.

"Do you want white sauce on that?" Cécile asked, back on the job.

"No. Put me some Cheez-Whiz on there instead."

At the end of the counter, Goyette was pretending not to film with his phone.

Sar'h arrived at this juncture. He nearly kissed his brother on the mouth.

"You're alive, you sonofabitch!"

Louis blushed. He would have gladly just tucked in to his omelette. So many people were looking at him.

"I've never been anything else," he said with his mouth full.

"Where were you?"

Now everyone really did turn around. He was going to tell them.

"Well, I was out at my hunting cabin, just minding my own business and reading..."

The embarrassment still showed on his face. It was partly because, in the real story, he wasn't exactly reading Musil, or even, as folk assumed, a hunting and fishing magazine. No, he had his dick out and was leafing through an old *Playboy*, an issue from the eighties, still in mint condition, with Bo Derek on the cover—after that, it had gotten way too vulgar, if you asked him. Dishrag's erotic imagination was filled with the women of his adolescence. They were beautiful, full-figured, all leather and seduction. They had full, hairy bushes between their legs.

"Then I fell asleep," he carried on. "Like a bear. Then when I woke up, well, I was on the job. Only now, I've just realized it's winter. So I reckon I must have slept a fair bit."

"That doesn't make any sense!" Bobby Daigneault argued. "When you fall asleep, you wake up in the same place, don't you?"

"Yes," Louis was forced to admit.

At the end of the counter, Frédéric Goyette was watching the battery charge dwindle on the display. He was gripping his phone tight in his hands, as if he could squeeze more energy into it. He wanted to document everything: the slightest blink of an eye, the faintest wavering of a voice.

"Do you remember your dreams?" Sar'h asked, ready to hear it all.

"Yes. Yes. It was just a dream ... a funny kind of dream ... a dream about nothing."

"A dream about nothing?" Linda couldn't help but prompt, doing a bad job of pretending she wasn't listening.

"Yes. Nothing happened. I was moving forward. I was walking, and everything was white."

"Like you were str'lling in th' sn'w?" Sar'h apostrophed.

"Yeah. You could say that, but not really, because there was no sky and no horizon either."

"But everything was white?" asked Li'l Tony.

Goyette's arms and legs were tingling impatiently. He was envisioning dozens of questions. This was not the time, though.

"Actually, it wasn't really white. No. Like I said, it was a dream about nothing. Stop asking me what was in my dream. There was nothing."

Louis took a mouthful or two of his omelette. Suddenly, he didn't feel like talking anymore.

"Hard to imagine a dream like that," Roger Lazure was let down.

"Yup," Louis clammed up.

"Must've been a long dream..."

"No, no, as long as a dream, y'know."

Mori looked at Laurie without saying anything. She was at his place. She was about to leave. It wasn't late. They had just finished eating vinegared rice with canned Arctic surfclam and ginger, soft-boiled eggs, miso soup, and *gyokuro*. Laurie was slowly wrapping herself up in a very long white scarf. It must have been the tenth evening in a row that she'd done that, more slowly every time. She would start by wrapping it once over her breasts, with a quick flick of her wrist at some point to make the wool dance. Before the scarf rolled its way around her neck, she would free her confined shoulders with one movement. Then to finish, she would release her lips and chin. Sitting on the floor, Mori would watch her abyssally. Then she would put on her coat with a flourish. She would tug her toque down on her head and plunge her hands into her mitts. He would stand up, in a daze. He would not invite her to spend the night. He would not give her a peck on the cheek. Rather, he would bid her farewell with a complicated movement, repetitions of which had established the series—a combination of a bow and a restrained hug so peculiar to him that it no longer seemed awkward. At the end, he would brush her shoulders with both hands and bid her good night.

But that night, as she was about to do one wrap around the nape of her neck, they heard a rumble of drunks drawing near and clear. Laurie continued with her wrapping as if it was nothing, but she could see all sorts of emergency plans taking shape in the corner of Mori's eye.

They banged on the door and bellowed. Laurie felt the shock wave in the bones of her feet and Mori, still seated, felt it in his pelvis, right to the tip of his coccyx, and in his prostate.

"Please, go downstairs. And stay there," Mori stood up.

Laurie didn't move. She could clearly hear what five or six men were saying on the other side of the door.

"Come on, slanty-eyes. Open the fuck up!"

Mori went into the kitchen. Laurie thought he was opening the knife drawer. He returned with a handgun tucked behind his back. The glistening butt was sticking out of his pants.

"What the!" was all Laurie could say, on the verge of tears and close to hyperventilation.

"Have no fear. It's not loaded. Quick. Go downstairs. They shouldn't see you here, should they? Whatever you do, don't turn on the light."

Laurie did as Mori said, since she didn't know what else to do. She thought she had heard Sar'h. She was very afraid for everyone.

Mori stood in the doorway so they couldn't come in. He soon felt the cold. All he had for Louis Berthelot was a brief nod. "That's not how it works," he reminded them. For starters, he had signed a lease for a year...

"You snooze, you lose, but then you take when you wake," Roger Lazure legislated.

"I'm not familiar with that expression," Mori half-truthed.

All Laurie could hear was him. At that moment, in the darkness, she told herself a revolver was no good whatsoever if it wasn't loaded.

"Scram, you Jap," Li'l Tony got carried away in the background.

Louis Berthelot himself gave Blueberry a pacifying glance that Mori decoded in an instant.

"Gentlemen, I suggest you let your drunkenness pass. Then tomorrow, hire a lawyer if you like. They'll tell you the house is already mine. I'm going to be very firm in my position."

Mori slammed the door and let the locks do the rest of the talking.

In front of the closed door, Bobby Daigneault didn't think twice about using his left hand to make the gesture his right would not permit. They ambled away and turned what had just been said into a slew of filthy jokes. That was how they saved face when someone slighted them.

"Hey, Li'l Tony, that's what you should say to your woman: 'Oh, honeybun, I'm going to be very firm in my position tonight.' Ha!" said Sar'h before he caught himself with a sly sneer. "Oops, I forgot, you've no one to get stiff with, have you?"

"Shut your trap, Sar'h. And you do?"

"All right, all right. Come over to mine. I've got a couple of two-fours knocking around."

22

The unflabbergasting (a cell)

Hair a little dirty, one eye staring hard and the other lost in the void, mouth set in a straight line across his square jaw, Frédéric Goyette was showing signs of a good mood only Myriam could decode. They had sex and, still naked, Frédéric found the six tubes of *smörgåskaviar* that had been slipped through the mail slot during their lovemaking. They hadn't eaten any since they met over there, in Scandinavia. Goyette had bought it online and he'd been keeping an eye out for the mail carrier for a good three weeks.

They made open-face sandwiches laden with slices of hard-boiled egg, over which they drizzled vast quantities of the substance. Its packaging—a tube rarely used in Quebec except for toothpaste—delighted Frédéric. He went on and on about how well it worked. They ate and gazed into each other's eyes, with the unbridled pleasure of a couple plunged into a Proustian moment by a paste made from cod and hake roe, potato flakes, salt, sugar, and canola oil.

Frédéric drank two big flasks of coffee while he played the video from Cécile's over and over again on his computer screen. Amid the bustle, the banter, and the sizzling of bacon and radio static, he was trying to isolate a brief moment of *sotto voce* conversation between Bobby Daigneault and the boss of the greasy spoon. He seemed to be telling her how the reappearance had come about, before the group's triumphant arrival at the snack bar. Goyette had software for that kind of thing. All the sounds merged into a green line he was doing his best to adjust.

"Just like that. Boom. No. [indistinct sounds] … didn't turn around to see. He appeared all of a sudden, right in front of me."

There was also the reference to the white dream that wasn't white. Louis Berthelot was soon at a loss for words, trying to explain himself. Goyette could see from the workers' faces that they didn't believe him. Still, Dishrag didn't appear to be lying. And why would he have any reason to?

"Maybe he was dreaming, but where was his body?" Goyette couldn't help but wonder out loud.

The Post-it urging him to talk to Mori had fallen down and he had not replaced it. The other one was still holding fast: *Cell (cage), sediment, chance, fold*. Goyette persisted in thinking that he held, in his test tubes sheathed in black plastic, the sediment on that list. In his mind, reasonings were emerging one after another; he was trying to develop them and delve deeper into their ramifications. From each of these reasonings, there arose a certain number of possibles. But his thinking was all backed up: the more he followed one trail, the farther he strayed from the others, to the point of eliminating them from consideration. There were no intersections. He sighed. Even the coffee was failing to deliver the mental endurance he felt he needed. It often struck him that, quite simply, he wasn't smart enough, and that drained him more than anything.

He saw his guitars. He remembered the taste of the *smörgåskaviar*. Yes, he was in a good mood. He tuned his Hagström by ear and dusted off an old twelve-watt tube amp. He set about playing a little blues. In the living room, Myriam was napping. The music worked its way into her sleep to make her smile.

Cell. Sediment. Chance. Fold. And it was *cell* in the sense of a prison cell, an enclosure. Goyette thought about other foursomes: John, Paul, George, Ringo; diamonds, clubs, hearts, spades. He kept on playing. Earth, fire, air, water. He remembered having read that the Japanese Buddhist tradition had the same elements, but added one more: the sky, or the void, depending on the translation—the immaterial. He stopped. All classification was arbitrary. Might it be possible to view the entire universe with only cage, sediment, chance, and fold as a frame of reference? He picked up a test tube. His eyes still couldn't bear the sight of the powder, but the revulsion seemed less acute. It had been a while since he'd looked at it. Something was deactivating inside him, over time. Prepared, for once during daylight hours, to be surprised, he wondered if the effect was wearing off or if he was getting used to it.

Frédéric Goyette had put on his windbreaker, scarf, parka, and furry hat. Outside, there was a bright, cold sun. He wanted to talk to Louis Berthelot, maybe Bobby Daigneault too. It was minus thirty-two degrees and the road was in great shape. He parked his pickup by the Baie-Trinité wharf, where the river was driving great chunks of ice as big as belugas, piling them up and bumping them into one another with a slow, deafening, excessive, and geological cracking sound you could feel in your bones.

In Baie-Trinité, this was January proper, the season of seasonal unemployment. The Fisheries were ticking over with a winter staff of forty or so. The ones who'd been there the longest, guys like Dishrag, were working. Bobby Daigneault, the youngest permanent employee, was going to lose his spot to the reappearance. He'd be off to join the others, ski-dooing around all day, to nowhere in particular. They'd ask each other along cynically, under no illusions as to what they might find when they got there. "Wanna go burn some gas?" Some would tinker around with wood, others would paint. Four Moroccans would stay holed up in the casbah, in survival mode, waiting until they were needed. For the more romantically inclined, this was the time for tenderness and cozying up. You had to be really in love to stick it out until the spring. When the mercury dropped below minus twenty-five, there weren't many folk who ventured out: just a few brave souls and kids, forced to keep going to school for as long as the buses kept starting. Cases of Molson Ex empties piled up on balconies, in front of houses. There were the American soaps on TV, the good and the bad sides of the internet, and a solid cannabis distribution network. The streets were luminous, slumbering. People were waiting for spring and its arthropods.

Goyette could no longer feel his earlobes. He had to get inside. There was absolutely no one at Cécile's. It was better at Ti-Claude's: there were four Ski-Doos and two Serges out front. Berthelot was smoking while Hercules looked on. Sar'h was demanding the right to smoke indoors when it dropped to thirty below. Hercules was upholding a strict interpretation of the law and claiming it wasn't that cold, anyway.

"Why didn't you bring your beer out with you?" asked Sar'h, nursing a rye.

"You out of your mind? Think I want it to freeze solid?"

They went back in with Goyette. It was just the three of them and Ti-Claude. Between two swigs of Laurentide, the bureaucrat came to realize something.

"Whose is the other Ski-Doo?"

"Huh?" Sar'h furrowed his brow.

"Listen, there's three of you, including Ti-Claude. I'm here in my pickup. So, whose is the other Ski-Doo?"

"It's his brother's," Hercules clarified. "Did you hear?"

"Yeah. I did. I was there yesterday, at Cécile's."

"Well go figure, we went over to Louis' place after, to move him back in. And we show up, five, six guys. His tenant, the Japanese fucker, well he wouldn't fuck off, would he, the fucker," Sar'h flummoxed, before snapping at Hercules: "Why didn't you want to come? Things would've turned out differently."

"I want nothing to do with it. First, I reckon that's for a lawyer to sort out. Second, that Japanese guy, I don't like the look of him."

Third, I've too much to lose if I can't export my lobsters anymore, he didn't add.

"What happened?" Goyette resolved.

"We really should've kicked his ass. Yessiree. But, I don't know, he, like, stiffened. And you never know with folk like that ... they might pull a jiu-jitsu move on you."

"Oh, come on!" Hercules gagged.

"So, what did you guys do?"

"Well, we left," Sar'h sulked.

"Where's your brother now, then?"

"He's staying with us until it blows over. The Japanese guy came here and picked him up in his Lincoln. They've gone off for a chat at his place. At Louis' place, I mean … well ... there, anyway. He looked to be in a better mood," Sar'h hoped.

"But you can never tell with him," Hercules attenuated.

After a while, Goyette asked if Bobby Daigneault still lived on the same street as Louis.

"He does, but watch out if you go by. That poodle of his is vicious. Looks like he wouldn't hurt a fly, but he's a nasty little fucker."

It was one of those bizarre scenes that were becoming more and more commonplace in Baie-Trinité. Without turning off the engine of his rented Lincoln, Mori had gone into Ti-Claude's bar and come out with Louis Berthelot. His teeth were chattering.

"Gentlemen, I implore your clemency. Yesterday, I demonstrated a regrettable intransigence."

Mori bowed his head only just perceptibly. He managed to resist following through with his torso.

"You having something?" the barman enquired.

"Er, yes ... what's the name again ... a Southern Comfort, if you please."

"On ice?"

"No, certainly not," Mori shivered.

Mori took a seat. He was a good sport, and a slew of jokes failed to get a rise out of him. As soon as he finished his drink, he invited Louis to his place with words that acknowledged that his place was Louis' place. He said they could work things out.

When they got there, it was mostly the absence of furniture that took Louis aback.

"Make yourself at home. Would you like some tea?" Mori took his shoes off.

"Jeez. I'm not big on that. Maybe a little cup of coffee."

"I do beg your pardon, I don't have any."

"No sweat. I'll have some hot water. In a glass."

"I have only one thing to ask of you, Mr. Berthelot. I would be honoured if you would refrain from visiting the basement. The untidiness would reflect rather unfavourably on me."

"All right," Dishrag obeyed, taking this to mean that must be where the Japanese guy kept his *Playboys* and his pot. For a moment he envisioned a stack of Japanese *Playboys* with more curiosity than titillation.

Mori went to pour two glasses of water. He had a cardigan over his shirt and a curious limp. When he brought his right leg forward, he would turn his hip inward a little and exaggerate the rotation, like he had cowboy boots on, or Dishrag thought, a dime up his butt.

Louis downed his glass of water and took a seat on the only stool at the kitchen island. Mori said he had things to go fetch from downstairs. He came back with a briefcase. He placed it on the island and remained standing, without moving, with a half-smile, looking a little to the side of Louis.

"Is it just me," said Berthelot in an attempt to dissipate the discomfort, "or we don't see many Deluxe Grade urchins go by anymore. It's mostly Category Two we see. Even Category One are getting rare."

That was the first time they had met, at the urchin classification workshop. Louis had learned plenty of things, but he'd found the Japanese guy somewhat abrasive.

"That's not what I want to talk about, Mr. Berthelot."

"O-kay..."

"I'm going to give you the explanation I owe you."

"Huh?" Dishrag furrowed his brow, in the family way.

"I know why you disappeared. It's my fault," Mori bowed. "Rest assured, you were not targeted personally. It would have been more appropriate for me to ask your permission, but I was not in a position to do so."

"What?" Berthelot threw out there, into the void in front of Mori, who wasn't straightening up.

"You know what, it's all right. It's all right, Mr. ... Mr. ..."

"Ishikawa," Mori eventually straightened up. "Mori Ishikawa. I regret having, in error, put your life on hold. I will explain everything to you."

"No need."

"No need?"

"Nah, I'm not that interested," Dishrag all but yawned. "I know it seemed like a long time for plenty of folk, but for me, it was just a little snooze."

"Just one moment!" Mori stopped him. "You do realize that snooze lasted several months?"

"So it seems."

"I can explain."

"No thanks, it's all right," Louis tried to call it a day.

"Besides the immense respect I have for you, Mr. Berthelot, I am flabbergasted to find myself before a man whose existence was interrupted and who, now that said existence has resumed, is refusing to hear the explanation on offer."

"Well. Unflabbergast yourself. What more do you want me to say? I'm sure it'd be beyond me, that explanation of yours. It'd do me more harm than good, and the shit'd hit the fan. I just want my house back."

"Ah. Yes. I have two things to say to you about your house. You will hate the first, but the second will be a balm."

"Oh, for fuck's sake," Louis couldn't help but mutter. He had the impression he was facing the Riddler from the *Batmans* of his youth.

Mori opened his briefcase in such a way as to shield its contents from Louis' view. From it, he pulled a document bearing a seal.

"I have bought your house. It belongs to me," Mori demonstrated. "This is the agreement of sale."

"What's the balm?" Dishrag barely batted an eye.

"Here's six hundred thousand," Mori pivoted his briefcase. "Take the time to count it if you wish. I'm offering it to you for your house, which is worth an amount five times less. It's because I know the value it has for you, and I wish to apologize for what happened."

The bills were recent, the polymer ones. On one side, a woman was peering through a binocular microscope at a little vial. On the other, a former prime minister was exuding authority with his moustache.

"I think ... I'll take the money," Berthelot ended up saying, like one of the contestants on a TV game show.

"Be my guest," Mori invited him.

"Can I go now?"

Mori sat down on the floor when Louis Berthelot left. He took in the light, the temperature of the floor. At the precise moment when time eluded him, he was rattled by human cries. He went over to the window. Frédéric Goyette was writhing in pain at the feet of a giant. Mori instinctively shifted a hand to the butt of his Glock.

"I don't give a flying fuck how much you have and where it came from. I'm coming to your place for that powder of yours tomorrow, and you're giving me twice as much, is that clear?" Mori couldn't possibly make out from the other side of the double-glazed windowpane.

Since Goyette was taking his sweet time to confirm this was indeed clear, the entremetier served him another kick in the ribs. To get him to stop, Goyette spat out a bloody clam of a glob on the asphalt by way of an opening argument, then coughed up the clincher with a seriously huge hemoptysis.

Eighth intermission

the whelk and the winkle

Once, when the fishing started up, a journalist from Montreal had come and interviewed Sar'h aboard his boat. Two weeks later, he got his hands on the article: his smoking, his swallowed consonants, his colourful vocabulary, his fisherman's parochial nostalgia. It had really effing riled him up. Over at Cécile's and at Ti-Claude's, folk couldn't understand why.

"Well, you do have 'parochial nostalgia,' Sar'h," they laughed at him.

"If you think ... if you think..." he flapped.

"It's only the truth that hurts," folk reminded him.

Plenty ended up figuring out what he was mad about. He didn't quite put it that way, but he came close: he couldn't stand being treated like folklore. He'd rather have been shat on.

Sar'h had slowly found his temper again and, to round out his summer, he'd had the idea of inviting tourists aboard his boat—not many, forty or so, in small groups. He had them taste his catch and he was careful when there were kids around. They'd always ask him the same question: "Mr. Serge, what's the difference between a whelk and a winkle?"

It was a question worth asking because, in terms of taste and texture, the two things were pretty much one and the same. Sar'h thought the tourists were a bit of a pain. As he became more experienced as a tour guide, he came up with three answers:

1. "They're two different creatures, folks: whelks live on the bottom and winkles live in the rocks," he started telling the skeptical little families. That wasn't what they wanted to hear.

2. "What's next? You're gonna ask me the difference between a porcupine and a hedgehog? Who gives a crap?" he had fumed one day at some snobs from France who insisted on calling the whelks and winkles *littorina*. He'd had to apologize after getting a letter from the tourist board and send them a refund in euros. Nothing but trouble.

3. "Some say winkles are better, but don't believe a word of it," he'd ended up blustering. "Winkles are fine as an appetizer, but whelks're the real deal, nice and meaty."

"Meaty?"

"For sure. Go ahead, knock yourself out," he'd shell them for the beaming tourists.

Answer number three landed in the sweet spot between a tourist's interest in all things related to the senses, and everything that whelk and winkle fishing entailed for Sar'h—all the unsaids, the triumphs, and the injuries.

Whelks are like pharaohs: they wind up in a pyramid. Winkles, clinging to their rocks, well, the best thing you can really say about them is that they don't dry out.

Whelks are hunters: they can easily kill a clam. Winkles, well, they're grazers.

Whelks have presence: their shell twists and turns like a Byzantine palace. Algae sprout in there like spruce forests. Winkles, well, they're weeny and have only camouflage for colour.

Sar'h had a boat for fishing whelks, his father's. He would trap them in pyramid pots using dead fish, a technique that called for coastal know-how and a skipper's savvy.

When whelks grew scarce or their price dwindled, he would go out on the rocks with the Moroccans and wither for winkles, which was more like picking than fishing. He'd go out a fair distance so no one would see him. He felt fragile. His life had always oscillated between waves of whelks and waves of winkles. His misfortune dwelled in little grey shells.

Serge was the eldest of the Berthelot brothers; Louis was the youngest. Between the two of them, one had been gunned down in a Montreal pizza joint, and another was shaping up to spend the rest of his days in the clink. Back when they were youngsters, there'd been four of them. And they were always spoiling for a fight.

Long before prison, Alain Berthelot had dabbled in various misdeeds. One summer, he'd managed to get his hands on a power saw, and that season went down in the history books as "Alain's chainsaw summer." A lobster trawler had perished because he'd sawn the buffers off the dock, just for the hell of it. Before school started back, Alain had sawn through a door at the Fisheries and wreaked havoc. After briefly advocating for him to be hanged, Rogatien, wanting to be a man of his time, had seen idle hands at work in the young lad's rage. And so, he'd taken him on at the Fisheries. He did a good job, even though folk knew he hung out with the Hells whenever he was in Montreal.

The young Berthelots would sometimes go hungry. Sar'h had often wondered why they had a fridge because the only thing in there was the beer belonging to their dad, Maurice. Well, beer and the best thing to go with it: jars of pickled whelks.

Maurice often helped a fisherman friend put the whelks in jars. They'd spend days shelling, cleaning, trimming, and drinking. Once out of their shell, the creatures are surprisingly long. A third of their anatomy is deemed edible. The friend would give Maurice a case or two of whelks to thank him. He'd also let him fill his own jars with the other two thirds. They used vinegar, ensuring safety, flavour, and toughness.

The young Berthelot brothers and their mother would eat bread, spuds, carrots, and what they called meat. The whelks were enough for Maurice. He would spend his time making others afraid of him, in the basement or at the bar. From April onward, whenever his balance was up to it, he would go out and gather mussels, clams, and winkles. Especially winkles. He had invented a contraption for picking them without having to bend down. He called it his "winkle pole." He'd sell the shellfish on the wharf, under the table, by the kilo, and to the Lelarges, who had a drop point there.

One day, his canning companion died an early death and left him his boat and his gear. As a new life dawned for him, Maurice explained to his sons how a whelk pot worked, fyke net in one hand, stubby of Labatt 50 in the other.

"This here's where the whelks come in. You stick some dead fish in there to attract 'em, capelin or perch, whatever you'd just chuck away. Then, once they're in: *clack*! They can't get out."

The four sons were stunned to hear their father talk to them at such length. The three youngest jumped when he went *clack*! They didn't know it yet, but two of them were incorrigible criminals.

Sar'h didn't flinch. He was starting to know a thing or two about carapaces.

Louis would still have plenty more of them to mop up.

23

The forgiveness of shiny things

"It all stops here," Laurie said calmly. "I don't want any more of this. Whatever you're doing, you can carry on without me."

Since she'd been staying at Suzanne's, Laurie had grown used to her aunt disappearing for long stretches, when she would stay upstairs and insist on not being disturbed under any circumstances. These would last anywhere between twelve hours and four days. At first, Laurie thought that Suzanne was engaging in intense meditation sessions, along with a little fasting and mortification, but one day she had heard a man talking, then climaxing. There had to be a secret passage somewhere in the rock.

Mori would sometimes come over during these retreats. Laurie was explaining her fear to him. She had read too much not to know that firearms make a tragedy of everything.

"Let me reiterate," Mori reiterated, "it's not like it is in books. A great many people own weapons. A revolver is not intrinsically more dangerous than a fillet knife."

Mori had one of those at his place; its blade was made of thirty-two layers of Japanese Damascus steel. Laurie liked to look at it. She would hold it in her hand. The blade gleamed as if slicing the light. No fish had yet proved worthy of it since Mori had come to the North Shore.

"We're not in the States," Laurie located. "You need a good reason to have those things."

Mori sensed something changing in Laurie's voice. The fear seemed less heavy and the desire to carry on was re-emerging in her. She wouldn't give up. She wouldn't leave him on his own. He was going to be able to justify his gun.

"I have a reason," he said sharply.

"What is it?"

"What I'm working on ... what *we're* working on ... it's ... it's dangerous."

"And what *are* we working on?" Laurie asked, surprised to be included.

"Ori. It's dangerous. Very dangerous. Imagine what would happen if an ill-intentioned person were to discover that it is possible to make paint of a non-existent colour. Those men the other night, Mr. Berthelot's friends, I don't think you quite grasp what could have happened if they'd gone down to the basement."

"Well ... they would have seen the ori wall..."

"And clearly, they would have kept the secret," Mori mocked.

"So killing them would have been justified?"

"No. The gun is not loaded. It never is. I have no ammunition."

Laurie clenched her fists without realizing. "I don't believe it," she called his bluff. "I don't know much about you, but I do know you wouldn't go around threatening people with an unloaded gun."

"Let me remind you, I threatened no one."

"That's what I'm saying. If you were stupid and your gun really wasn't loaded, you would've already threatened someone. But you're not stupid," Laurie syllogized.

Mori didn't reply right away. He gave one of those micro-bows of his head that Laurie had come to recognize. Then, taking two deep breaths while looking at one of Suzanne's houseplants:

"You leave me no choice but to be upfront. My revolver is under lock and key, in this house that is all mine. I bought it from Mr. Berthelot, and we are both very satisfied with our arrangement. The revolver is under lock and key and loaded, but the safety is on."

"!..." Laurie mouthed.

"Let me continue, if I may. I could just walk away. Yes. I could leave Baie-Trinité and never come back again, but that would be a shame because we have come so far already. I want to tell the world about ori and I want to do it with you. But the thing is, it's dangerous. Very dangerous. There is a secret to protect, that's true. But that's not all. In the very fabric of ori, there are human lives, you see."

"Huh?" Laurie choked.

"Shiny things cannot come from nothing, you know that. The principle of ori, and also what makes ori so sublime," Mori professed, "is the principle of human life. When we see the colour, it's like opening a crack that sends lives other than our own rushing through our veins."

"That's so poetic," Laurie knee-jerked, commenting on the form since the depths of Mori's words seemed unfathomable.

"Yes. I know," Mori slowed. "There is a crack in everything, the poet wrote. That's how the light gets in. When I read those words, it helped me see where I was going."

"Don't go anywhere," Laurie commanded.

She went to the washroom. She urinated a little and produced a short, pale stool, not exempt from browner filaments. To gather her thoughts, she watched it disintegrate in the whirlpool. Why was this happening to her? She, too, felt as though she was whirling around inside that very same question, disintegrating. On the periphery of the concentric circles, the movement was slower and she had time to see what was happening, but she sensed herself nearing the centre that would swallow her up. She hadn't really been hungry, these past few days. Her sleep was possessed. All the same, she was relieved to still be producing shit at regular intervals and still be excreting it through her anus. She remained real and the motion of the stool strings in the water of the toilet bowl never failed to remind her of reality.

"So, people are dying," she returned to the room. "Is that it? We kill them, and they become ori?"

"No. No. They're not dying. I'm not cut out for genocide. But that's precisely what's dangerous. In the wrong hands, the ori manufacturing process might cause something resembling death. It all depends on whose hands it's in, the same as a firearm. That's what I've been trying to explain to you for two hours now."

Laurie didn't understand everything, and there was also, most of all, a bewitching feeling when reality loosened its grip. She had just reached the point of fogginess. She started to smile. All of this could go on.

"Just tell me if I've got this right: is there a little bit of Louis Berthelot in the paint on the basement walls?" she half-joked.

"Well ... it's not that simple," Mori spluttered, embarrassed to the extreme. "It's not just him ... it's not an ... individual principle. He was not personally targeted. I told him that. I wanted to explain, but he didn't want an explanation. I assure you, he has been generously compensated."

Before Mori left, together they read 分福茶釜, *Bunbuku Chagama*, a tale in which a *tanuki*—a Japanese animal, Mori explained, kind of a cross between a dog and a raccoon—turns into a teakettle to thank a down-and-out who helped it escape from a trap. When it is hanging over the fire, the *tanuki*-turned-teakettle takes to its heels because its transformation has not prevented it from feeling pain. The man turns his new teakettle on *tanuki* legs into a circus attraction and gets rich.

Mori went home, leaving behind a little box meticulously wrapped in kraft paper with blue ribbon. Laurie went to her room. Either in a trance or with a man, Suzanne, upstairs, far away, was not alone. Laurie removed her polka-dot skirt and tights. She had her ori panties on. She hadn't told him; she mustn't. Earlier, she'd had a funny feeling, thinking she might be wearing Louis Berthelot down there. It had passed. Things are not that simple. There is a difference between life and individuality, between consciousness and what animates it, between shapes and their outlines.

She undid the wrapping. There were two identical glass jars in the box, the kind of jar whelks go in. One was filled with blue-green *gyokuru* leaves gorged with chlorophyll. The other was half full of Mori's sperm. The sperm was heterogenous, a little jellified. This was the first time there'd been so much of it for her. Laurie opened the jar. An odour all its own emanated from it. She got wet, very wet. The lips of her vulva parted and the ori cotton of the Fruit of the Loom panties rubbed against her clitoris. She dipped her fingers in the sperm. It was a little cool; Mori had probably kept it in the fridge. She smeared some on her mouth with the tip of her index finger and licked her lips.

The next day, surprised in Paul Auster's *City of Glass* by the reviviscent rush of the sour taste in her mouth, she would discover the lengths to which a body could be swept off by sexual excitement. She would pour the rest of the jar into the top of her crack. She would rub the sperm into her pubes and over her pussy. Mori's sperm would liquefy once more on contact with her own liquid. It would all intermingle in her vagina. She would feel deeply confused, on the verge of orgasm, and when it came, the black before her closed eyes would be replaced by ori.

In the beginning there was only one movement, an evolution in the space around which everything fell into place. It was faster than someone running, but slower than a moving car. A symmetry at the source of the movement produced thighs where it would take physical form, and where it would come from. Their movement was fluid, periodic, prolonged, like that, since it was winter, of skating. Now it had become skating, the movement needed ice. There it was: vivid, level, grey. It was an expanse of frozen water, a big lake. The thighs and the capacity to perceive the frozen lake composed the subject. In this universe, only the necessary things would appear. The universe was fragile. The merest inconsistency would obliterate it. Driven by an impulse, women appeared ankle deep in the ice, which tightened around them. They were naked and trying to free themselves, their undulation reflecting the initial movement of skating, which could also have come from the cold wind.

In one moment of brilliance, the subject was completely possessed. Originally thighs, perception, and impulse, it had been imbued by the skating movement and a similar occurrence—in fluid, periodic, prolonged surges—of outpourings of revolt. The subject then perceived a change in the colour of the ice. It had never been grey. It was a colour that had never been seen before. The entire dream—subject, desire, revolt, women—was giving way, drawn to and sucked in by this gravitating colour, as though by a black hole.

After two days in a coma, Frédéric Goyette regained consciousness at the hospital in Baie-Comeau. When he came to, he said to Myriam, now he understood why the word *comma* was pretty much the same as *coma*. He had lived through a comma. He had followed its curve. She smiled. He smiled. He was missing two teeth. Between his ribs, a tube was draining his pneumothorax.

Goyette had a gentle convalescence. Myriam coddled him with kisses, fluffed pillows, and applied them to the painful parts of his body. She made him coffee. He had internal bruising and fractured ribs. They'd told him he'd have all his strength back in a few weeks' time. For now, he had to take hydromorphone pills six times a day, otherwise a sharp, jabbing pain would radiate through the entire right side of his rib cage. He was fine as long as he didn't move.

He spent his days thinking about the bikers, about Mori Ishikawa and his likely allies, about Robert,

Suzanne, Saturn, Laurie. He didn't really hear much about the Lelarges, but rumour had it, times were tough. There was talk of layoffs at the plant. He could remember going to Ti-Claude's and running into the two Serges. He could remember wanting to talk to Bobby Daigneault, the key witness to Dishrag's reappearance. He could remember sticking his neck out and going to Mori's for a look-see. After that, he'd taken a beating. That's what he'd been told. Soothed by the pills, Goyette's thinking kept its distance from his recollections. The pain would shoot right to his eyebrows as soon as he even thought about getting close.

"You know that Japanese guy..." Myriam scratched the surface between two spoonfuls of *lapskaus* once she thought he was doing better.

"Ishikawa? Mori Ishikawa?" Frédéric replied in a voice so deep and animated, he had to nurse his ribs.

"Yes, that's it. He came and talked to me at the hospital when you were in intensive care."

"And you waited till now to tell me! Are you out of your mind?"

"I was waiting until you were better," Myriam weaseled. "He said something strange to me."

"I'm all ears," Goyette moaned, still clutching his ribs.

"He said to tell you he would take care of it. To leave it all to him, but it would take him a month or so. He also said you could keep on doing what you're doing. I remember his exact words: 'He will uncover things out of context. He will derive no satisfaction, and it will change nothing about the course of events.'"

Goyette was astonished.

"Did you not think to make yourself useful?" he blew up. "I don't know, to follow him ... take some photos ... worm something out of the bastard? What's to say he wasn't the one who knocked me out?"

"I'm sorry," Myriam sniffed, "I didn't want to—"

"I mean, seriously, make yourself useful, Myriam! Have some guts! Do something! You don't realize how big this is. There's gang feuds, a mass poisoning, and someone, somewhere, who's getting a kick out of fiddling with the fundamentals. And you're staying well clear of it. But it's all right. We're eating *lapskaus*. You really like being a secondary character, don't you?"

"Yes," Myriam settled on. Then she started to cry and took off to her room because that hadn't been very nice.

The next day, after trying like a hypocrite to put it down to the pain and the meds, he apologized. His gap-toothed smile was growing on her.

Before the apology, unrelenting rage earned Goyette his first night of insomnia since the accident. He was glad to reconnect with his nighttime thinking. He was trying to piece it all together. What exactly was Mori planning to take care of while he was out of the picture? Goyette slipped a vial of powder out of its black plastic sleeve. *Sediment.* He gave some more thought to the *enclosure*, the *fold*, and the *opportunity*. Yes, there was no doubt about it. He could see it better than before. As soon as his eyes saw the powder, they were prickled with the same sensation that makes you turn on a bright light when you hear a suspicious sound in the middle of the night, but they weren't getting used to it. He was able to sneak a few extended glances, all the same, like in those Scandinavian saunas when he always hoped that others wouldn't catch him looking at their privates. Showing it to Myriam, though, he would see that the substance was still just as irregardable for her. Something was changing in him.

He knocked back a sip of aquavit with his hydromorphone. Then he put Eivind Aarset on the turntable. After a while, he got up to double the dose.

It came through his thighs. He recalled seeing a colour in a dream, a colour he had never seen before. He couldn't remember the colour, but he remembered skating over it. There had been naked women. That dream, by latching on to the recollection of another dream, jogged his memory about a shell, the curious Iceland scallop shell that had belonged to Laurie. It was coming to him more and more easily, but the teenage redhead was still the only one who could stare at the powder.

In the middle of the night, he figured he'd have to give something with shells a shot. It had a one in a thousand chance of succeeding; it was a weird idea, but it wouldn't cost much and, by adopting a different tack, a more diffuse and curved, non-binary connection between the causes and the consequences, it might make some kind of sense. He diluted the irregardable powder in a little water and heated the mix over the flame of a lighter, the way heroin addicts did in the movies. Then he took a syringe and injected the solution into some fresh mussels he found in the fridge. They were supposed to be for dinner the next night. He put them in a Tupperware container and attached a label with some sticky tape:

⚠ DANGER ⚠
Do not ingest
Trial in progress
Canadian Shellfish Sanitation Program
Canadian Food Inspection Agency

After collapsing on the couch, he started dipping into his stash of hydromorphone, purely for the buzz. He dozed until he was woken by a noise, a scratching sound. It made him jump. It was the sound of a living thing. He got up. It was at the patio door. The scratching continued. Goyette couldn't see a thing, but he didn't turn on the light. His dulled senses were keeping any fear at bay. There it was again, the scratching; something was having a go at the brick of the back wall. The creature growled, then fell silent before resuming its clawing and releasing a long groan.

"Fuck me, it's a bear," Goyette couldn't help but mutter between his teeth.

He stumbled off in search of his .308. As he returned to the patio door, he heard the muffled voice of a man who seemed to be talking to the bear.

"Good job, Grumpy. Good job. Now, go smash the window."

Goyette flicked the switch for the outside light, then he tottered two steps backward into a shooting position. It all became clearer: the entremetier was holding a bear on a leash, at the end of a big studded leather collar. They scampered off when they saw him. Goyette turned to the clock. It was four seventeen in the morning and now he knew who was out to get him.

24

Blood and more sperm

"I'm trying to give her as much space as possible. She's not having an easy time of it, you know. Kicked out of her own home at seventeen!"

"If he wasn't your brother, I'd tell you Robert's a heartless shit."

When Hercules raised his voice at Suzanne's, the rock in the cave was like a barrel around his rib cage. The double resonance made his voice sound tomb-like. He was getting the hang of the echoes a little more with every visit.

Things hadn't been the same since Laurie moved in. Hercules could see that Suzanne wanted to keep him out of the picture. They stopped going downstairs unless Laurie was out. He had to come and go through a tight secret passage, a kind of chimney that made him feel a bit like Santa Claus. He was careful not to show he was afraid of getting stuck.

They heard the distinctive sound of the custom-built door creaking shut into the rock. Laurie had just left.

"Laurie had me try some Japanese tea. It's not bad at all. Would you like some?" Suzanne offered, sounding sophisticated.

She was naked.

"No, I'll just have coffee."

She went downstairs to pull a shot of espresso. Returning to the bedroom, she realized it smelled of their secret: incense, damp rock, musky obese buttocks, sweat, tea, orange. This time, there was the coffee, too, and the slightly resiny smell of a new kind of lube. There was one thing she absolutely had to tell him before he left.

"Speaking of that heartless shit, do you know what he said to me?"

She'd been mulling it over the whole time Hercules had been there. Even in the throes of sodomy, she hadn't been able to really focus. She told him about the third, the one they'd have to dock from the fishermen's pay or else the company would go under. She asked him not to tell the others right away.

"For fuck's sake! I knew this would happen. It's the same old story. You take out the competition, then bleed your suppliers dry!" Hercules climbed the Richter scale.

"I know. I know," Suzanne was sorry in a soft voice, trying to find some modesty with her arms and legs.

Hercules pulled on his plaid jacket and old pilled jeans. He left through the main door before Suzanne could dare suggest the secret passage. On his way out, he turned around.

"This ain't how things are gonna go, Suzanne," he boomed.

The barrelling of his voice in his chest and the rock bumped the needle on the seismograph over in Grosses-Roches across the water. He'd be damned if he wasn't gonna tell the others.

Laurie was halfway through level two of her kanji education. There were more to learn with every stage. None of the symbols looked alike. Every time she thought she'd found some semblance of logic, she realized there was none. Casting a disheartened eye at the Paul Auster book lying on her bedside table, she wondered whether, by masturbating with Mori's sperm, she could have impregnated herself. The thought, frivolous at first, had initially given her a warm smile. But time had made it weigh heavy on her and now there was no avoiding it. She walked to the pharmacy. It was her determined exit that had made the door groan.

"I know you know who I am. If anyone gets wind of this, if my parents find out in any way whatsoever, I'll make sure you lose your licence," Laurie threatened.

She knew that probably wasn't necessary. She also knew the pharmacist knew everyone in the village. The young woman's lower lip quivered ever so slightly and her eyebrows creased. Her gaze lowered automatically before she became aware of the deviation and corrected it with a twitch of the eyes. Feeling a triumphant calm welling within her, Laurie swallowed the pill right there and then, trying to meet the eye of the pharmacist who no longer dared look at her. She smiled. She was used to being right in silence. It was the first time she'd gotten the better of someone using words.

She bled for a month, not a lot, a few drops a day. When she wore her ori panties, she put four pantyliners on so as not to soil them. She would go over to Mori's to chat. When Suzanne was out, she would drink tea with him in the cold living room of the hobbit house. She could now talk about the weather in Japanese and negotiate pretend seafood contracts. Mori had even had her speak on the phone with employees of the Isumi Conglomerate of Tones, Colours, Pigments, Molluscs, and Crustaceans. She had been surprised to understand them.

Mori remained evasive whenever she tried to talk to him about ori. He would say the development process had been slowed down due to a lack of molluscs.

The warmer it was, the more Laurie bled. Her menstrual cycle had been diverted. She often thought she might fall in line with a new biology, different to a teenager's: she might become a woman or a sugar maple. The first day above freezing point, she got a proper period. She was keen to see what would happen after that. Mori had her get into his rented Lincoln. They drove up the 138 and took a few side roads to a spot near Caye du Brick island, far enough away so they could snowshoe on the snowy beach without being seen by binoculars. The snow was melting, revealing its crystalline, cutting edges. Mori fell two or three times and split his forehead, slightly. They laughed a lot. He bled a little.

Frédéric Goyette also ended up bleeding for a month, but on the inside. There were relapses. He started coughing up blood again. On his thorax, a bruise as big as the palm of his hand healed. Black in the beginning, it turned shades of eggplant, cobalt blue, grass green, orpiment. The degradation of his blood showed the colours Goyette was made of.

Myriam got fed up with seeing him spend his days abusing meds, drinking on the sly, and generally doing sweet fuck all. She went off to her mother's in Sept-Îles for spring break. He was doing a bit better when she came back, but he would slide into another bad patch, no doubt about it. Because his work with the government was now fuzzy at best, the insurance didn't want to cover his dental expenses. He was taking that badly. He wasn't playing the guitar anymore. Myriam didn't like knowing he had syringes in his Mitsubishi case.

Every week, he would pull a mussel out of the experimental Tupperware he kept in the fridge and dissect it on their Smååta cutting board with a scalpel. Every time, the smell would get worse. He would take meticulous samples, bang his fist on the counter, and curse between gritted teeth. One time, he cried.

"It's not just science anymore if you're crying over it," Myriam observed.

The last mussel had stunk up the house. Frédéric swore he could rise above it, but at dissection time, Myriam had seen the spasms in his throat and windpipe, had heard him retching. The smell was everywhere: between the paint and walls, between the threads of the curtains, in the stuffing of the furniture, in the pores of their skin. And it'd still be a while before they could open the windows.

"Why don't you go to Baie-Trinité? That usually does you good," she'd suggested softly over meatballs with red berry jelly.

What he wasn't telling her was that every night he was having nightmares about the entremetier setting Grumpy the bear loose on him. He hadn't mentioned that. She'd been sleeping that night, super soundly, and hadn't woken up. He hadn't wanted to scare her. That whole bear business did strike him as being one hell of a bull to take by the horns.

Even though crab season was about to get going, it was twenty-five below the day Goyette, out on his Ski-Doo, finally got his act together. He was going to swing by Cléophas Lake. His turtleneck was doing a bad job of absorbing his sweat. He slung his rifle over the shoulder of his parka. It gave him courage. He looked like a biathlete as he covered the last stretch on his snowshoes.

When he got to the deluxe hunting cabin, he tucked the weapon under the deck. Saturn came and opened up. He had lost weight. His hair was greyer, not as healthy, very long, still as frizzy, brittle, far sparser. There was nothing spongy anymore about the fabric of his green bathrobe, and it was hanging off him. You would have thought he had no body under his robe, were it not for his waist, where—there was no mistaking it—a supersized, almost vertical erection stood to attention.

Saturn greeted him with an enthusiastic but hoarse "Go-yette!".

"I'm not interrupting?" Goyette inquired, making an effort not to point to his host's penis.

"No. Come in. Take your coat off."

It was hot inside. Following Saturn from the hallway to the kitchen, Goyette glanced into the living room to make sure there were no bears around. What he saw was a lot—a hell of a lot—of bare flesh. He turned around before he could make out any shapes.

"I remember you, you old caffeine fiend. Want some?" Saturn offered, guiding him toward the percolator.

"With pleasure."

Saturn, his back turned, suddenly let his robe fall to the floor. He didn't really have buttocks anymore, only vague arches at the tops of his thighs where his femurs peeked out. In the metal of the percolator, he still looked like a Giacometti, only Giacometti wasn't known for sculpting Priapus. Saturn came back with a beer glass full of coffee for Goyette. His glans was smooth and shiny, manifestly close to ejaculation.

"Keep your clothes on if you want. We've not worn any here for a while."

Leaving him in the background to spectate, Saturn stepped into the living room. On the daybed, the dishwasher was vigorously penetrating the first assistant pastry chef. They were both panting. The others were watching, playing with themselves, just four or five little strokes every now and then. The sommelière was having a snooze. The dog wasn't getting any younger, slowly lapping water in his corner. A mound of powder on a coffee table dazzled Goyette only a little now. The entremetier had learned how to prepare hits without looking. From time to time, he would hand syringes to the others, wrapped in black sticky tape. They were shooting themselves up non-stop.

"You, over there," the roast cook hollered, "wanna blow job?"

"Er ... no," Goyette stammered, surprised to find himself on the menu.

"Even if we do it together?" the sommelière eroticized, her eyes half closed.

"No ... no, thank you," Goyette hesitated a little.

Done with his litre of coffee, Saturn announced:

"Saturn is coming."

The first assistant pastry chef turned her butt to the dishwasher. Saturn strutted toward them, in front of his little audience, masturbating more and more vigorously, asking anyone so inclined to finish him off.

"Watch out!" he warned.

He started to grunt. At one point, he had a Christlike air about him. He was going to come. He stopped to lower his hand to the base of his penis and clasped it. Then they all looked away. Goyette figured they must be used to this. Saturn spurted six good jets onto the girl's buttocks and the roast cook's belly, and the roast cook turned his head away too. Saturn's sperm, like the powder, dazzled Goyette a little.

"Hey!" Saturn pulled himself together, "you can look at my jizz!"

"Um. Yes ... yes. You could say that, yeah ... I can see it."

"Hey! Are you judging our way of life?" Réginald Lelarge was about to get carried away.

"No, no. It's just ... I might like to have a word with you in another room."

Saturn wiped his glans with a Kleenex and tossed the box to the dishwasher, who caught it with an agile hand and a word of thanks. So Goyette would change his tune, he put on his green robe again, then ushered him into another, smaller room: the library. There were shelves of books and LPs running all around the room and up to the ceiling, with a clear fondness for Russian novelists and biographies of nineteen-eighties' metal bands. Many of the biographies were in Swedish, Goyette was surprised to note when he glanced at their spines. They sat down in little studious armchairs. A window looked out over snow-laden spruce.

"What's with your teeth?" Saturn cut to the chase.

"You know," Goyette presumed.

"The bear?"

"No."

"Jay-pee?"

"Who's Jay-pee?"

"The big dude lining up hits in the corner."

"Yeah, it was him," Goyette confirmed in a far from accusatory tone.

"Right ... okay," Saturn tried to find something to say.

"No. Don't say anything. Listen, you're all addicted to the irregardable powder."

"We're not addicted, it's just that it makes us fuck like gods. It's turned this place into the Olympus of sex."

No less, Goyette refrained from saying. "And it's the powder that does that to you..."

"Hmm," Saturn opined.

"And you were running low, so you decided to threaten me so I'd give you some."

Saturn was inscrutable: weary, post-orgasmic, embarrassed, vaguely decerebrated. He took a very deep breath. Goyette could see the muscles between his ribs hollow out through the opening in his robe. Saturn was at death's door; he was sure of it.

"Saturn!" he called him back to life.

"Yes. Right. We had a vote. We put Jay-pee in charge of getting your powder, by any means necessary. We didn't think it would come to that. Seriously, Frédéric, I'm sorry. I'd be ashamed if I didn't have a 24/7 hard-on."

Goyette got the impression he hadn't been able to hold back a smile, but as usual nothing showed on his impenetrable face.

"You know this already. I've told you before. I just want to understand. I don't work for the police. I'm not going to press charges, either..."

"You've nothing more to worry about," Saturn tried to reassure him.

Goyette didn't move a muscle. He hadn't really understood because he was trying too hard to figure out what to say.

"I understand," he ventured all the same, "with all the powder the Japanese guy brought you..."

"Well, exactly!" Saturn was fucked.

"When did he come by?"

"About a week ago. He had a case full of the stuff. You've probably tried it, have you?"

"No."

"Honestly, you don't know what you're missing. You should try some with your wife. Let me know how it goes. More coffee?"

"Yes. Have you got anything stronger?"

"For sure. I've got some Louis XIII. If you're more of a scotch man, I've got some Lagavulin 1976 37 Year Old."

"Er ... I don't suppose you have any aquavit?"

"Aquavit? Krogstad and Linie."

Saturn went to get two thermal carafes of coffee, a bottle of Linie, and two tulip glasses. They drank in silence, taking little sips in short succession. Goyette spoke of his passion for aquavit, and Saturn of his own for all types of alcohol.

"Can I ask you a slightly more indiscreet question?" Goyette inebriated.

"Let me guess, this is about my jizz..."

"I'm not a big fan of that word. It's very vulgar."

"What, then? My come?"

"That's not quite as bad. So ... has it been like that for a while?"

"Since the powder. Must be a side effect or something..."

"Still, it can't be very convenient," Goyette chummy-chummyed. "I mean ... the first time ... you must've wondered what the heck."

"Well, I wasn't that surprised. I'd seen it before."

"Where?"

Saturn hesitated, then, after pouring himself a full glass of aquavit and downing it in one, he started talking. It went back to the weird trip he'd taken to Japan with Robert. Just before the Fisheries really took off, before Robert became a prospective member of Quebec, Inc. They were in Tokyo to negotiate the big contract with the Conglomerate. Saturn had soon made friends over there. Good people, though, looking back, a little sketchy. They had started going to soaplands.

One night, by accident, Saturn had seen a guy named Ito ejaculate and his sperm had been like that. When you saw it, your neck would twist away of its own accord, as if someone had switched on the sun right in front of your face. The girls at the soapland were used to it and they'd turn their heads as soon as Ito's moans started sounding different.

"You can't say I'm holding up your investigation," Saturn concluded.

"What's a soapland?"

"A soapland is a sex paradise. A notch below this place."

"And that guy Ito, do you know his first name?"

"No. For all I know, that could *be* his first name."

"Can you describe him?"

"Sure thing."

Goyette tried to build a photofit image in his mind as he listened. It probably wouldn't amount to much.

They kept on drinking. Saturn slipped away for a moment to inject himself with the ontotoxin. He was rock hard again when he came back.

"I won't keep you long," said Goyette with a knowing smile that didn't show. "But maybe word hasn't travelled this far. Do you know what happened to Louis Berthelot?"

"Sar'h's brother?"

"Yeah, him."

"No."

"He disappeared last summer, did you know?"

"Yeah. It's coming back to me. He killed himself because his wife turned lesbian."

"Not so, as it happens. He turned up again at the Fisheries, on the freezing line, one night this winter."

"Wait, what?" Saturn wondered, doing his best to bury his shaft in his robe.

"Do you think that might have something to do with something?"

"You mean ... he turned up again, just like that? Pop!" Saturn popped the end of his index finger like a champagne cork in his heart-shaped mouth.

"I wasn't there, but that's what I'm told."

"Ooh! That rings a bell. You'd better talk to Robert, though."

"Go on!"

"You'd really, really better talk to Robert, Frédéric. I can't tell you."

"Come on! What happened?"

"In Japan. At a soapland. The same thing. With a girl."

"A girl appeared?"

"No, *disappeared*," Saturn clarified. Losing patience, he gave himself a surreptitious rub. "I can't say any more. Ask Robert. He was there."

25

Night of the chainsaws (a sediment)

Since the middle of February, Mori had often said to Laurie that, of all the emotions, hesitation was the one most characteristic of humans. Predators charge; prey flee; humans hesitate. Laurie had repeated that to Suzanne.

"It's so true. Who wrote that?"

"A wise Japanese man."

"One I know?"

Mori also said it was for that reason, and no other, that humans would so eagerly await the springtime. Spring can be cold, but we still want it to come. It's just that it stalls, freezes our whatevers off until we worry it's tricked us, then shows up with birds and blossoms and twelve temperate degrees. In other words, it hesitates. And if we see a source of hope in its midst, that's because it always makes the right decision.

Laurie knew her aunt wasn't well: anything giving her grief expressed itself first in her body. She would stuff her face and pray like she was dancing. She had shown Laurie an Excel spreadsheet printed out on four pages. It showed the maximum prices payable for every species. For snow crab, it was $1.20 a pound, or $1.60 for premium quality. Suzanne was thinking about the welfare cheques, the fishing families who had the right, like everyone else, to eat something besides winkles now and then.

"Your father is a good man. But no matter where he looks, all he sees are numbers. Your mother as well, she's a fair enough person. But she's been seen as nothing more than a number for so long that it's turned her into one."

"Do they know I'm here?"

"What do you think?"

"I think they do, but they don't give a shit," Laurie got lippy.

"Does it ever occur to you that it's because they know you're here that they can not give a shit?"

No one hangs on the whims of spring or eyes its hesitations more sympathetically than a seafood fisherman. On the North Shore, there were several hundred of them. As the president of their association, it came down to Serge "Hercules" Cabana to decide on the opening date of the fishing season. For the last three years, things had been able to get going in the third week of March, but this year the seas and the union meetings had been turbulent. Splinter groups were forming, brought together by promises to wreak havoc. The lobster and shrimp fishermen were keen to negotiate and were reminded, gold miners that they were, that they had to consider the others who were mining shite. It was cold too. The approach to the Baie-Trinité wharf was hazardous; at several other secondary wharves—Baie-Johan-Beetz, Tête-à-la-Baleine, Rivière-aux-Graines—it was impracticable. Crabs, when March is cold, can easily lose their claws, and their value with them.

The last time Hercules had gone to Suzanne's, he'd gone at it harder with his pelvis. He'd been less affable, and in more of a hurry, and he'd had a hard time keeping a lid on his frustration. Suzanne had felt funny inside. He'd squeezed her breasts with the same grip as usual, probably, but that time it had felt too hard. She wouldn't be inviting him back, she'd told him. At least, not until things blew over. And he had understood. He had left, saying he hoped he hadn't gone at it too hard. Suzanne had gentler lovers, but no, not even with them, she really wasn't feeling it.

In Baie-Comeau, Myriam and Frédéric could finally open the windows of their house one day when it was seven degrees out and, just like every year, hoist the Quebec flag out front again, reminiscing just how close the referendum had been in ninety-five. Big patches of snow were melting in their yard overlooking the river. The lawn was emerging, yellow. The stench of putrefying molluscs continued to hang in the air, but people can get used to anything. The kids at the daycare where she worked would often remind Myriam, whose nose had forgotten all about it, that she stank.

They set up the picnic table so they could see the river and treated themselves in shirtsleeves. She had a strong beer; he had a glass of aquavit. Frédéric was good as new again, apart from his teeth. There was only one mussel left to open in the fridge, but he had a lot of hope invested in it.

"There's going to be something. I wouldn't have done it otherwise."

"You know, we do things in life that amount to nothing more often than not," Myriam reminded him. "Just do it outside this time, at least. And put your painting clothes on."

Myriam went to read on the deck. Down below and in overalls, Goyette got to work on the picnic table. With the tip of the scalpel, sparing the hinge where the two halves of the mussel were welded together, he cut along the length of the conchiolin ligament holding them closed. A stench started to swirl in the damp offshore wind. Goyette severed the two adductor muscles, trying to keep a hold on his gag reflex. He opened the mantle, the diaphanous pouch-like thing encasing the animal's body. The gills were pretty much decomposed and had nothing unusual about them. He cut the muscular brown foot, it too almost putrefied away, and dissected the gills. The mussel's entire nervous system was a colour of which until that moment he'd had only a premonition. The ice that had set in around the ankles of the naked women in his dream reappeared in his mind, clear as ever, its colour pure and unprecedented: that colour. He blinked several times. He cried out, a strange sound of despondency and exaltation.

"What is it?" Myriam appeared at the deck railing with a clothespin on her nose.

"Come see."

"Um ... nope," she nasalized.

"Yes, come see, it's worth it."

Amid the semidecomposed fleshy folds there was a clearer web, a shape. Little circles a few millimetres apart, interconnected by narrow, thin lines like an invisible thread. "The mussel's nervous system," Frédéric pointed out with the tip of his dissection forceps. It was a colour she had never seen.

"Wow."

That was all Myriam could say. *Wow. Wow. Wow. Wow.* Then: "It's like ... my eyes hurt."

"Wait a little."

After ten seconds, she was used to it.

"I've never seen this before," he lied.

"What is it?"

"I have absolutely no idea."

They took dozens of photos, but the colour didn't show up on them: the mussel's nervous system appeared indistinct, transparent perhaps.

Still, they soon realized, the colour, rare as it was, filled their imagination. They could effortlessly visualize a stop sign that colour; the sky; a cat; a lobster; the moon; spinach; a field of wheat.

Suzanne had never wanted a cell phone for two reasons. One, they gave you Alzheimer's, and two, there was no coverage in her cave anyway. There was a beige Sanyo telephone from the late eighties on the main floor, with square keys on a brown background that were yellowed and stiffened by time. The kind of phone that's used only to let others know you could care less about phones. A curly cord connected the receiver to the straight lines of its base. It rang in the middle of the night, more than twelve rings. Suzanne heard nothing since she was asleep upstairs. Laurie changed her underwear to go answer it.

"Hello?" she fretted since, as everyone knows, good news can wait until morning.

"Is that Laurie?" asked a female voice after several seconds of silence.

It was a synthesized voice, straight out of a computer's tinny speakers.

"Yes. Who's speaking?"

"Put your aunt on the phone," the cold voice sounded.

"Is this an anonymous call?"

"What do you think?"

"That's not very clever. You'll be easy to track down."

"Who is it?" Suzanne asked, appearing at the top of the stairs in a see-through robe. The many folds of her thighs and belly were on full display, her bush of tight tufts too.

"It's an anonymous call," Laurie yawned, betraying a tiny bit of interest.

Suzanne took the handset.

"Right, is that Suzanne?" the voice robotted again.

"What are you playing at?"

"It's the night of the chainsaws, Suzanne. You just wait and see, tomorrow."

There was a brief electric flash before the dial tone. The machine had hung up.

Someone must have known the shareholders were meeting the next day at the Fisheries offices. Between Île du Tug islet and Trou à Pierrot-Bacon bay, an armada of shrimp and lobster trawlers had assembled, along with a handful of kayaks. Under cover of darkness, one detachment struck out across the calm river and away from the fleet. The commando unit—Robert would later see from the video surveillance—was a rowboat full of balaclava-clad men. Armed with chainsaws, hatchets, and a harpoon, the rowers made short work of the rubber buffers on the wharf. For Robert, the images on the black-and-white monitor would take on an ori tinge, like in the tinted film of those nineteen-twenties movies and the pigmented dreams Laurie continued to have.

Saturn arrived way too late for the meeting, and Suzanne, way too early. They both blamed the switch to daylight saving time. The company lawyer was in a corner checking the sports news on his phone, content to be paid for doing nothing. Suzanne hadn't seen Robert since Laurie had sought refuge at her place. For those two hours or thereabouts while their brother failed to arrive, she had the time to run through Robert Lelarge's full biography, to identify all the defining moments in his life when he'd put his wallet before his heart, which she'd gone on to qualify as shrivelled, stunted, cemented, amorphous. She hoped he was still able to get it up, she said, going so far as to add that she didn't think so, because that heart of his must be past pumping blood to his pecker. Even the lawyer's face puckered.

"It's easy for you, Suzanne," Robert retorted, "you can say whatever you want. I'm the one who makes all the decisions, and you get all the rewards. You wallow in your eccentricities."

"Why can't you ever look a fisherman in the eye?" Suzanne quizzed him when Saturn arrived.

Robert had put so much gel in his hair, it looked like a shiny, brittle helmet. He had countless blackheads. Some had erupted deep in the pits of his acne scars, where they gathered in a multitude of white peaks.

"So this is where the meeting's at?" Saturn trembled. His sickly thinness came as a surprise to the two others. Every outward breath seemed to remove a little of his mass, stretch his skin over his bones, and expose the tendons in his neck.

"Réginald?" Robert had a scare.

"Here!" Saturn responded to the roll call before asking for coffee. "And not just a cup, eh? I want the whole pot."

The secretary who'd come to take the minutes waited for a look of approval from Robert. Since that wasn't forthcoming, Suzanne said she'd take care of it; there had to be a percolator around somewhere. The percolator was in the broom closet, Robert replied, but to the secretary.

Saturn kept nodding off, all the same. Whenever he opened his mouth to speak, they could barely understand him. They returned his mutterings as multiple-choice questions.

"Are you saying that:

a) You want to sell your own shares?

b) You want us to accept the investment bank's offer?

c) You want us to sell shares on the stock market?"

"What was b) again?"

"Shall we come back to this?" the lawyer attempted to adjourn.

"My shares..." Saturn nodded off, "they're mine, I'm keeping 'em!"

"Seriously, Robert, I don't feel much like helping you. I know you're incapable of love," Suzanne rubbed salt in the wound.

"We're not talking about love, here, Suzanne."

"It's because of Dad that the name is Lelarge Fisheries. He'd have thought it ridiculous not to make space for love."

"That's true," Saturn passed out.

Then the lawyer moved on to the next point on the agenda: the wharf had been vandalized overnight. The rubber buffers were wrecked.

"That means no offloading for the next three days, maybe a week, until you can get some more vulcanized."

"To anyone inclined to sympathize with the fishermen, I'll tell you right away that delay's going to cost us two to three million. And it's not like the millions are raining down these days. Do you have any idea of the yen exchange rate?" Robert pre-empted.

"Who says the fishermen did it?" Suzanne called him out.

"Come on! That's a no-brainer."

To the sound of a Band-Aid ripping off, Saturn woke with a start, his mouth rounding in an ouch of surprise. He sashayed off to the washroom.

"You *are* just going for a pee, right?" Suzanne made sure.

Turns out, he'd taped his 24/7 erection to his thigh so it wouldn't show, and it had just come unstuck. Lucky for him, he had a roll of hockey tape in his pocket. When he came back, they were discussing the appropriate response to counter the previous night's affront.

"So they sawed the buffers off?"

"Oh, for fuck's sake, Réginald. Wake up and smell the coffee," Robert extended an invitation to the voyage. "The fishermen sabotaged the wharf last night. We've been talking about it since before."

"There's nothing to say it was the fishermen," Suzanne argued. "There is such a thing as presumption of innocence."

Saturn looked at the lawyer in bewilderment. The guy wasn't going to say anything, but Réginald's eyes were getting too round. "Yeah, there is," he insisted on confirming.

"I've seen the surveillance camera footage," Robert rubbed his eyes. "Won't be long before the police tell us who it was. Balaclavaed bastards! Takes some guts, that does..."

"Not the police," Saturn sat back down.

"What?"

"The coast guard. Crimes you commit on the water without touching land, they're for the coast guard to deal with," Saturn sobered up. "The feds."

"Jesus, that'll take forever," Robert sobered up too.

"We'd best just let it drop. We're in for a week of this, tops. The coast guard's got better things to do," Suzanne supposed.

"Like what?"

The lawyer swiped his plump index finger over the touchscreen of his phone with the haste of someone whose strong suit has never been maritime law.

"Ah, that's too bad, really, because I was about to be very generous with the fishermen," Robert braggadocioed.

"You, generous?" replied you-know-who.

"I don't believe in fixed prices anymore, or in that twentieth-century model where the business owner takes all the risks and the employees and suppliers pocket stable, guaranteed payments," Robert theorized as Saturn drooled and began to snore, his eyes still wide open. "No, I'm all for doing away with the opposition between the Fisheries and the fishermen, and even, in the long term, the opposition between the Fisheries and the guys and gals at the Fisheries. Baie-Trinité is a small place. Can't say it isn't. And the only economic driver in the village, that's the Fisheries. We should be giving something back to the workers. They should all be able to see the plant, from their street or their boat, and say to themselves, 'You know that building that puts food on my table, well, it belongs to me too.'"

"I can see where you're going with this," Suzanne cut in.

"The fishermen agree to lower their prices by thirty percent. Not just for the season, but for the long haul. In return, we each give their association ten percent of our shares."

"So, forty-six percent of the company would belong to Robert, and ten percent to the fishermen's association. Réginald and Suzanne, by ceding ten percent of their own interests to the fishermen, would each keep a twenty-two percent share in the company," lawyered the student of jurisprudence, refreshing the ownership structure of Lelarge Fisheries in the minds of those, like Saturn, who might have forgotten.

"Yeah, all right," Saturn no sooner said than did.

"Yes. That's something the fishermen might agree to. Well done, Robert," said Suzanne with no hint of irony.

"That way, in future, they can't lay waste to our facilities without laying waste to a bit of themselves."

You couldn't exactly call it a honeymoon period, but France and Robert had enjoyed happier times after kicking Laurie out. Liberated, they had spent evenings eating seafood, coming up with a hundred excuses for their behaviour—"No, we didn't abandon her. She's with Suzanne now. It'll do her good." "Every adolescence is a separation, and hers will just have been more sudden than most." "She's wanted us out of her life since she was six years old, anyway." "Burning bridges can be a good thing, and we're still keeping an eye on her, all the same."—and making love. Robert had been spending less time in his office. France liked it when he sat beside her on the couch while she was reading. She had never believed that he might bounce back, but the more he seemed to love her, the less deposed he seemed. He began to want her again, and that had surprised him. He had found her beautiful when she wandered the presbytery hallways wrapped in nothing more than a white towel. Images of her crotch, and the revived sensation of him thrusting into it, had risen up in his mind. It was a big deal. He hadn't had thoughts like those for decades.

That had lasted two, maybe three weeks.

The evening it had come to an end, naked on the couch, Robert had spoken to France about another order that had been turned down by the Isumi Conglomerate of Tones, Colours, Pigments, Molluscs, and Crustaceans because he couldn't get it up and he thought that was why. France had sensed fear stirring inside her, like a big caustic marble between her belly button and the tip of her sternum. The fear had begun to grow. Robert had begun to sob great sonorous tears.

France was reading a book about how hard life used to be when Robert returned from his special meeting that Saturday. On his way in, he took off his nylon Fisheries overcoat. There were oceans of sweat in the armpits of his blue pinstripe shirt.

"I hope you didn't take your windbreaker off in front of Suzanne and the lawyer."

"No, no."

Their eyes met and, to France, it was immediately obvious: he had been beaten again.

"Was it like you said ... the partnership with the fishermen?"

"Yes. Ten percent. Not too bad," Robert figured.

"You've lost again," France snapped at him, peering over her glasses.

"Lost what?"

"You've finally given in and given up the majority vote. Who's your asshole of a lawyer?"

Robert went straight to his office. He didn't yell any numbers into the phone.

Late that evening, he reappeared to help himself to a plate of Chinese macaroni with little scallops.

"My asshole of a lawyer is looking into putting Réginald's shares in trusteeship. You should have seen him today, Saturn ... high as a kite. On what, I don't know. I'm keeping control. I want to make that very clear to you. Because it is to me. It's just that I can't tell you everything."

Robert came closer. He noticed two empty wrappers from grocery store pastries on the kitchen table. France had another in her mouth.

"You can't just go off like that, Robert. Hide out all day long. It's not right. I had to stop myself phoning Suzanne's in case Laurie picked up. This is getting ridiculous," France dissolved into puff pastry crumbs.

"What are you on about, France?"

"You didn't say anything. You weren't making a sound in your office. What were you doing? I thought you were killing yourself. Slipping off like that. I had to stop myself from going and opening the door. Seriously, I was half expecting to find you dead. On the other hand ... this is going to sound terrible ... I hate myself for even thinking it, but I can't be sure that would have been a bad thing."

Ninth intermission

the razor clam

At the onset of April, the river's metallic sparkles are not so blue. The snow melts in order of dirtiness, from the whitest to the sandiest. Heaps of it cushion the sand, merging with every tide. The mudflats get twice as wet, turning almost mahogany. It's still cold out.

It's clam-digging time, and the foreshore is a constellation of their breathing holes, pores in the beach. On an ebbing tide, you can see them popping up like thousands of little hands saying, "Here we are."

People bring out their shovels. They think it'll be easy and, most of the time, it is. A swish of a spade and the clam's out in the open. Eaten.

Sometimes, nothing goes as planned. A dozen holes close together hint at a cluster. The Sunday digger hopes the shovel will yield a triple bounty and doesn't think twice about picturing a quadruple one. But there's nothing. Time to try a different spot. Unless you're a professional, or Moroccan. If you are, then you know what you're dealing with: a rarer prey, tougher too, even on the teeth: the razor clam.

Its scientific name, *Ensis directus*, means "straight blade," and that's a fair description: a shellfish the length and shape of a dagger blade, its surface a khaki enamel with a more ivoried surface layer, like a nail, made to peel away. Even if it's dead, eaten by a gull on the beach, its shell will easily slice an unsuspecting foot.

Razor clams sever continuity. What an intermission does with time, they do with substance.

When the shadow of a clam digger's shovel looms large, the razor clam is saved by its gravedigger instinct. It goes to ground. It digs faster than a human can. But it can be fooled: the Moroccans learned to put a pinch of salt in holes where their shovels came up empty. They had to wait a bit for the salt to sink into the hole. In prosaic terms, it could be said that the salt suffocates the razor clam and forces it to the surface in search of less arid surroundings. Then all the men needed was a heavy work glove to grab the clam with. Using more poetic language, it could be said that the razor clam felt safe, that it took a single pinch of salt to be the great big sea. It wouldn't be the only one.

Cooked, it's a white cylinder, meaty as a whelk, big as the ring finger of any average human—Laurie, for instance. The straight razor clam, an American species, has been invading the European coasts since the seventies, where it's been ousting the local, arched variety: *Ensis magnus*. Overseas demand was next to non-existent (razor clams had literally been exporting themselves), and the Fisheries supplied them to only a handful of restaurants in Quebec. The Moroccans had gotten into the habit of carrying a stash of them home. They were an inexpensive way of making fish couscous more filling. Pan-fried in butter, with a little salt, lemon, and garlic, they were tasty too. Some liked to wash them down with beer.

In Laurie's dreams—in those of France and Robert too, but not in Florence's—one kind of "straight blade" often stood in for the other. Many a dream is built on an association of sorts.

Since the summer, once she'd learned to identify the little shocks that ran through her body whenever Mori was dreaming about her, Laurie had no longer dared to pinch herself, not ever.

Her dreams had changed, especially in colour. Reality, too, had changed. Laurie had a good grasp of the pinching thing: in a dream, feeling leads to action, so there can be no painful pinches, only pain that turns into a pinch. Pinching oneself in a dream twists the logic of the dream. It destroys it.

When Laurie picked up a blade, it was to cut something or eat it. If she picked up a blade in a dream, it meant that something was being cut or something was happening as a result of her eating a razor clam. In the daytime, Laurie's mind existed in a universe where, in a way, the course of time associates cause and effect. Dreams, where all that is inverted, seemed necessary to her to keep the world in order, and for mental balance. The mechanics of the mind, she had explained to Mori, in order to function well, need to function upside down and inside out a few hours a day.

"当たらずといえども遠からずだ."

"Hmm?"

"*Not far from the truth*," Mori translated.

"How so? Is that what you think as well?"

"I don't think it's a matter of belief," Mori clammed up. "Your theory supposes that reality and dreams exist. How can you be sure that when you're not dreaming, you're in reality?"

"The laws of physics apply here."

"All of them?" Mori whispered socratically.

Laurie looked at him with round eyes. Clouds scudded across her irises, then her eyes grew moist. "The laws of physics apply to everything here, except the colour of my underwear," she specified.

"Don't tell me. You mustn't."

Things that don't exist do not have a name. In order to have a name, they have to exist sufficiently, and they must be conceivable for a critical mass of people. The names of things are like inside jokes played by our ancestors. Jokes that we don't really get nowadays, but that our ancestors always did. The razor clam in its shell looks like a blade lying on the beach, but that "straight blade" is a creature, like a human. Its name, too, speaks of the existence they share.

If Laurie no longer dared to pinch herself, it was because she was noticing, more and more often, that there were different parts to reality: bubble-like places where effect led to cause, where the logic of dreams prevailed. In other, more numerous bubbles, cause and effect bounced around, rubbed together, and blended: a little of the effect could be found in the cause, and a little of the cause in the effect. Language was sly like that. Pinching herself was becoming a much too binary action: superfluous at best, dangerous at worst.

Flee, go to ground, hide, fade into the forgotten, take off, leave. That was what those razor-like clams did; that was what Robert sensed people expected him to do, and he couldn't. If someone had told him the Moroccans were hiding "blades" in their work clothes, he would have reached for his .30-06.

Creatures or objects, straight blades—with or without the air quotes—are either in the kitchen or they're hidden away. When they're hidden, that's when they come alive.

So, was the "straight blade" in Robert Lelarge's desk a weapon or a crustacean?

26

Luminous stars, dimmer switches, and rheostats

Sediment: the deposits in the wave at four seventeen had transformed the sand and water into an irregardable ontotoxin. *Cage:* a life spent ejaculating sperm that makes others twist their necks and look away. A man would find that somewhat restrictive.

Is that sperm fertile? Goyette had scribbled with a blunt, stubby HB pencil on a sheet of white paper. He was scrawling large, undecipherable letters, with the uncertain lines of a seismograph. It was dark and when his hand got cramp, he would give it a rest by alternating between sips of coffee and aquavit.

Chance: the colour, he'd underlined three times, telling himself it was probably going to be a hell of a big one.

Fold? The inside of a mussel wasn't short of those.

Mechanically, Goyette slipped a vial of powder out of its black plastic sleeve. It was like looking at a pinch of salt now. To convince himself that something had well and truly changed inside him, he would often show the powder to Myriam. She had developed a Pavlovian reflex: her neck was starting to arch away as soon as she saw the case. Goyette had feared for his own sperm for a while, but no, that was all right.

He had equipped himself with a whiteboard and attached it to the far wall. It was occupied almost entirely by a diagram, with a complicated system of shapes, dotted lines, and space/time cross-references. He spun a more central web in red, the colour of conceivable hypotheses:

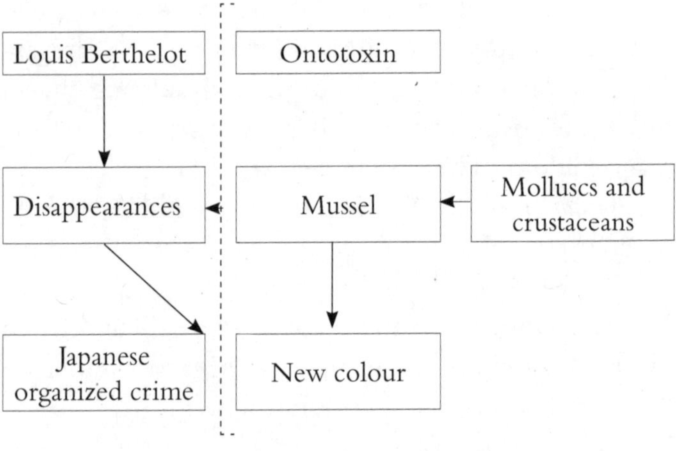

In the depths of the dissected mussel on the picnic table, the colour had persisted for seventeen hours. After that, frankly, you had to imagine it to see it. But imagining it, for Goyette and his wife, was almost too easy. A little of the colour lived on in their brains.

Where do colours exist? Goyette jotted down on his page. It was nighttime and his thinking was naturally drawn to that kind of question.

Mori Ishikawa (石川森)

Goyette still had to redo the part of the diagram around the box representing Mori. Too many connections were converging there. In the nighttime, he detested the diagram he would spend hours drawing in the daytime. He would look at it without trying to puzzle it out, or even reading it, the way he would view abstract paintings. *It's pure thought*, he would marvel. When he got drunk, he would realize his diagram didn't serve much of a purpose—perhaps only to pass the time, instead of going to Baie-Trinité. His rifle was always within reach. No. He would never have a tooth knocked out again.

He drank some coffee. His gaze fell naturally on a smaller box in the diagram, connected only to Mori's sprawling one.

The Conglomerate

He wondered if he should draw a dotted line between that box and the "Japanese organized crime" box, but he pulled himself together and thought better of his daytime instincts.

"What do I know about the Conglomerate?" he caught himself asking out loud.

That didn't happen often to him.

Well, for starters, it was the company that had sent Mori Ishikawa to Baie-Trinité. It had boosted urchin production in the village a thousandfold. It was a company in Japan, in Isumi, and its full name was something like—

"Well, I'll be fucked!"

That was becoming a habit.

No sooner had he wondered what time it was in Tokyo, typed "Isumi Conglomerate of Pigments, Colours and Crustaceans" into Google, been corrected by Google, and dialled 011-81-3-5555-0149, than he was being greeted in Japanese by a voice so high pitched he felt it all through his body, then in professional-sounding English.

"May I speak with someone from the Human Resources department?"

Goyette spoke English with ease, with an accent more American than Québécois. A twinge, however, which was unusual on his constant face, betrayed a real sense of awkwardness. When he spoke English, Myriam said he made a face like he'd been forced to take a dump in public.

They had no knowledge whatsoever of a Mori Ishikawa, came the confirmation after twenty expensive international phone minutes. Robert Lelarge they knew, but no Conglomerate employee had been sent to Canada, let alone Baie-Trinité. They would make inquiries. They would return his call in due course.

Right. Okay. This really wasn't funny anymore. A Japanese guy had arrived out of the blue and had been prowling around Baie-Trinité for the last nine months. An impostor, he was redefining the essence of the world as only impostors can. And he was prowling around Laurie too. A pointed, precise anger suddenly surged through Goyette's body, starting from his testicles and going on to draw little concentric circles around his eyes. The sun had risen. Upstairs, the sound of the shower indicated that Myriam was awake and in the nude. The vaguely criminal urge to stop running away from things sprouted in Goyette and made its way to his face. A robin was singing outside as it finished pecking at the dissected mussel on the picnic table. Goyette was staring—well, squinting—at the whiteboard. The squinting part was involuntary, guided by some unconscious will. Subjecting his eye muscles to that senseless squeezing was something he recognized: back in the mid-nineties, that was how he'd uncovered the image in those once highly popular and since-forgotten Magic Eye pictures. Suddenly on the lookout for anamorphosis, his gaze began to explore the diagram. A flash of real emerged. Goyette had never felt it before, but all this time, he'd been right at the exact point where world history was about to go off the rails. And there was a seventeen-year-old girl to protect too. Yes, he was feeling chivalrous. He went upstairs. Myriam was wrapped in a coral towel.

Goyette dressed in spy-black after stashing a crowbar and his rifle in the trunk of his black Volvo. No one would recognize his own car in Baie-Trinité; he wouldn't park it at the wharf. Normally, by the time he got to Godbout, he would have heard the Laws ranting and raving at him from the dawn of time: "Tell me, Goyette, what have you in mind to do? Are you not intending by this thing you are trying to do, to destroy us, the Laws, and the entire State, so far as in you lies?" But not this time. His Volvo's powerful speakers—louder and more faithful than his pickup's—plunged him into "Three Falling Free, Part II," the carnal, posthumous piece by Esbjörn Svensson. In the distance, a lone ray shone through the opaque sky. A stellar twinkling on the near-black river.

He went straight to Mori's place. Well, not really Mori's place—Louis Berthelot's, he sided. And not really there, either, but to a parallel street, higher up, where he could sit in his parked car and keep watch on the Japanese guy's door and windows. Mori came out after an hour. He went off in his rented Lincoln.

Then everything happened fast. Goyette ran up from behind the house. From the beach, he made it into Mori's still-damp grassy yard, checking the neighbours' windows all the while with his binoculars to make sure no one showed up. Crouching down, he forced the weatherstripping on the back door with his crowbar, then gave the latch a nudge. He searched the drawers upstairs, for a passport most of all. There was nothing. The house was empty. So empty that his plan—to swipe something and make it look like a burglary—was coming apart at the seams. Cupboards full of rice and tea, fish on the fridge's sparse shelves, eggs in their egg compartments, a case of soy sauce bottles covered in used Japanese postage stamps. There was a worthless TV on the wood floor. Under the sink, he eventually found a little strongbox to tuck under his arm. Then he went down to the basement.

Wow. Wow, that was all he could think. *Wow.* There in front of him was a wall the colour of the molluscs. It had taken hold of his imagination ever since he'd seen it, but here, before his eyes, full, pure, primary, and vivid, harnessed, it made him an eyewitness to its existence. Goyette couldn't help but go give the curtains a tug, just a little, so the weak light of day would strike the foot of the wall. That had eased his burglar's adrenalin, but not for long: a noise sent him scarpering with the strongbox back the way he'd broken in. It was just the wind.

He didn't play any music on the way home. He drove either too fast or too slow. He had given the strongbox a shake with one hand. Judging by the sound it made, he guessed it contained a fairly heavy metal object as well as some smaller metal ones, some paper too. He kept having to give his head a shake too so he'd see the asphalt as the colour of asphalt.

He killed the ignition in front of his house on Champlain Street in Baie-Comeau. The rented Lincoln came from Laval Street and pulled up behind his Volvo. Recognizing the car, Goyette shoved the strongbox under a blanket in the backseat, then he got out. Mori approached with an outstretched hand and a bow of the torso.

"Mr. Goyette!"

"Mr. Ishikawa."

"I am sorry to arrive here in such an impromptu fashion. I assure you, it is solely joy that justified my haste," Mori ventured a smile.

"Uh, all right..."

Goyette tried to position himself between Mori and the backseat of his Volvo. His posture was stiff and awkward, but his features betrayed nothing. He still had his spy clothes on.

"I trust you will do me the honour of receiving me for several minutes for a discussion."

"You mean inside, do you?"

"Yes, that's what I mean," Mori articulated slowly.

"Ah. It's not a good time. We're having dinner soon. Sometimes we say there's enough for three when there's food for two, but not tonight," Goyette pretexted, shifting his position in a way he intended to be subtle. "And to what do you owe such joy?" he elevated his grammar.

"You have been the victim of acts of inexcusable violence. As you are a highly observant investigator, you will have deduced that I am partially responsible. I have come to inform you that Réginald Lelarge and his drug addicts will inconvenience you no more."

"And that's what warrants you coming here to tell me in person?"

Mori was standing straight, a jacket open over his black cardigan, the cardigan open over the extra stiff collar of a white shirt. Goyette's attention was captured for a moment by these multiple layers. Myriam appeared at the window and then stepped away so she wouldn't be seen.

"This is good, big news. I thought it only right to let you know in person."

"What do you want?" Goyette snapped.

"I've told you already. I want you to do me the honour of a discussion."

"You can start by telling me how you solved the problem!"

Mori looked to the sky in the hope that it might start to rain, but it was one of those days when the sky was too dark for rain.

"You should be happy to no longer be living under threat. All I will say is that drug addicts sometimes make strange decisions. Their desire becomes their master."

"What do you want from me?" Goyette clouded over. "I won't stop investigating. That's out of the question. Never!"

"No. I am aware of the desperate curiosity that drives you. Pursue it. Continue. You'll see: I have never been, am not, and never will be a drug dealer."

There were more imploring notes to Mori's tone. After a few seconds of confusion, Goyette guessed what he must have been thinking.

"And I'm not a cop."

"So, if I cannot enter your home, please come into my car. I can give you a brief look at the essentials. Then you may go back to investigating. But I will say nothing more."

Goyette waited for Mori to turn around and followed him cautiously into the Lincoln. Myriam scurried off to the basement for Goyette's rifle, but it was in the Volvo. She returned to hyperventilate by the window and feel her heart beating in her throat.

She saw them sit side by side in the backseat. From a briefcase, Mori took a device that was some sort of cross between a pair of binoculars and a metal attaché case. He motioned for Frédéric to stick his eyes in there. While her husband was having a look inside, she saw the Japanese guy say something to him. Then Mori's expectant face betrayed a sliver of disappointment. He regained his composure before Goyette turned to him. Slowly, Goyette returned the device and opened the car door. He got out and walked away with a smile. His toothless grin was bright and deeply unusual, and it unsettled Myriam. It was like he was turning into gold. The Lincoln headed off toward the 138.

"Ori!" Goyette cried on his way in.

"What's that?"

"It's the colour of the molluscs. I'm going back out in my pickup!"

He went to put his windbreaker on. He got into his work truck. Same CD. No flashing lights, though his finger did get close to the button. Most of all, he wanted to check if Saturn was still alive. He was, but even thinner and more disjointed, he was snivelling between two hits, saying he'd really messed up. His crew had a thousand ways to console him.

Goyette went to the end of the wharf to get a breath of air and see if it was true they'd sawed off the buffers. It was true. The sun was setting behind the opaque cloud cover; dusk was gradually dwindling away. Goyette felt good, certain he held an overwhelming intellectual advantage over Mori Ishikawa.

There was a distant rumbling. It could only be coming from Ti-Claude's, and if it was coming from there, that meant something was going on. Still a ways away, over by the mini-mart, Goyette could feel from the vibrating bodywork of his pickup truck that something was going on at the bar, and that the bar was struggling to contain it.

He went inside. It was mostly fishermen in there. Lots of guys from the Fisheries, too, the guys who were closest to the fishermen. The two Serges were there, some Anglos from the Lower North Shore they didn't see often. In all, there were a hundred and fifty or two hundred of them. Folk had come from as far away as Pabos.

"The Snob's here," someone called out.

"Goyette!" someone else recognized him.

He had to elbow his way through. Goyette managed to climb onto a stool; he wasn't the only one. In one corner, there were three strippers sporting G-strings and breast implants. The floor was littered with hundred-dollar bills. The bottles of hard liquor weren't behind the bar anymore, but all around the room. Dockers well below the legal drinking age were knocking back shots, their faces wet with Jägermeister. Ti-Claude was worn-out, going up and down his stepladder to fetch cases from the cellar. People were lending a hand, taking a few swigs with every trip.

"Haven't seen it like this since 'Dammit' Dallaire won the jackpot," Goyette yelled in Roger Lazure's ear.

"You're not wrong," Lazure mimed, knowing he couldn't say much more.

Snatching snippets here and there from the crowd, Goyette was able to piece together that in one day ten percent of the Fisheries had been transferred to the fishermen then sold on for twenty million dollars. Some were saying thirty-two.

"Who to?"

"The Japanese."

"The Japanese in general, or the Japanese guy?"

"What?"

"Forget it. Is it official?"

"Official? Yeah. Check out the lawyer," the guy waved a finger.

In the corner, Mr. Bellavance of Baie-Comeau had a handful of silicone in one hand and was projectile vomiting into the other.

In the pleasantly silent passenger compartment of his Lincoln, Mori Ishikawa was listening to *Death and the Maiden* by the Alban Berg Quartett. He glanced as little as possible at the Saint Lawrence River, a mystery to him that threatened, every time he dwelled on it, to divert him from his course. He enjoyed these rare moments in the car when he could listen to music. He felt good, certain at last that he held an overwhelming intellectual advantage over Frédéric Goyette. He could push on.

He went straight to Suzanne's. Laurie came and opened up, his surprise visit flushing her scarlet. She hushed him in the door, whispering that her aunt was there. Laurie wanted him to give her a peck on the cheek hello—it had taken him months to agree to that—or at least shake her hand, which he did sometimes without dragging it out. Mori avoided all physical contact. His hair was a little dishevelled. She sensed he was troubled.

"These are fateful hours," he said at last. "I wish to see your aunt."

"Why?"

"Miss Lelarge, please, I ask that you go get your aunt. I promise you, everything is proceeding exactly as planned."

Something heavy made itself heard at the top of the stairs and Suzanne appeared. Her expression was appropriately grave.

"I must speak with you."

They went into the upstairs alcove devoted to the Scandinavian deities. There, Mori explained the situation to her frankly, apologizing for not having informed her earlier, telling her extremely delicately that it was extremely delicate.

"So, there you have it," he spilled the beans. "The Fisheries are now thirty-two percent mine. I can assure you, I paid the fishermen, and your brother Réginald, a very fair price. Your brother Robert, for whom I maintain a profound respect, retains a forty-six percent share. The rest belongs to you. And so, you have a decision to make. Either Robert continues to manage the company, which would be disastrous for your entire family. Or I do. And if I do, well, you do too. And most of all, so does Laurie."

"The Conglomerate, or you?"

"Me. I sold my shares in the Conglomerate in order to proceed with this transaction."

Suzanne's gaze flitted between a statuette of Loki and a saintly image of Frigg.

"Well, I see," she had sensed all this was coming.

27

Since there has to be a boss

There was a spring, but there was no fishing, and that was unbearable for Robert Lelarge. Lukewarm rays gilded the beach and the last of the snow lingered only at the feet of the shadiest conifers. He was walking on the sand. Everything was ori, as if, jarred by a whack on the head, he had woken in a monochromatic state approaching blindness. He was sweating in his nylon outer layer. Underneath, he was bare-bellied. He had the tightrope walker's gait of a man not yet used to owning only forty-six percent of himself.

He had holed himself up for three days in his presbytery. France wasn't talking to him. Each only knew the other was alive by the creaking of the floorboards. And the floorboards often creaked by themselves.

Now Robert had just had to get outside. In the beginning, rumour had it, the fishermen had gone off to spend their windfall in Cayo Coco. That was largely untrue. The wharf had been repaired, extended, equipped with new berths, then promptly closed off.

The fishermen were docking elsewhere and then the seafood was being trucked to the plant. There was less of it because the new majority shareholder's first decision had been to close the canning line. He continued to pay all the employees to do nothing and let it be known that he would reassign them once the equipment had been modernized. They were expecting an ocean-going container ship in Baie-Trinité. That would be a first. No one, except perhaps Mori Ishikawa, was keener for it to arrive than Robert.

The container ship was shiny ori. At its stern flew a pale ori flag, with a bold ori circle at the centre. It was slowly making its way along the ori river, casting a dark ori shadow on the shimmering ori sand. By the way the dockers were going about their business, far away and through his binoculars, Robert realized he was the only one to see things like that.

The wharf shook when the ship bumped against it. There was a moment when people weren't sure it was going to hold. The buffers were crushed in a seismic rumble. Some of the dockers were tempted to go back and finish high school when they heard the noise, more with their bones than their ears.

Robert sat down on the sand in a clump of eelgrass. He was warm, but he didn't unzip his windbreaker. Sweat was sticking in the coarse and curly, albeit sparse, hairs on his belly. He was nervous enough to pop a pimple that proved more purulent than he thought. The pus on his fingers was too bright an ori to not be real.

They offloaded an entire plant from the ship. Robert recognized some of the machinery right away: a purification system four times bigger and fifty times newer than his, a Mitsubishi-brand automated tank as big as a half Olympic swimming pool, four versions of a model of electronically controlled mollusc incubator he'd thought was still in the prototype phase. The other units had him suspecting Mori's intentions: computer servers as big as small cars, big-valved pipes of all diameters, rotary presses, antennae, and crate after crate of vacuum tubes.

Wearing a hard hat and sitting at the wheel of a forklift, The Man Who Comes personally handled the handling of four immense secret crates. They were fastened with bolts and stamped with carefully calligraphed Japanese characters among which Robert recognized only the exclamation marks. Mori had spotted him shivering and turning pale in the eelgrass, but he had waited to be done with the containers before sauntering over to him. Robert took a ridiculous amount of time to lower his binoculars, trained at point-blank range. He was observing the pores of the Japanese guy's skin: ori, but darker than his own.

"It's a beautiful day for a fresh start, isn't it, Mr. Lelarge, dear partner?"

Mori stayed standing. Robert crouched down.

"I don't want to see you anymore," Robert weakened.

"I'm not leaving."

"You can't understand," Robert moaned as if his guts were being ripped apart. "When I was little, when the sun was like this, when the beach was like this, I would go with my dad to help unload the first lobster catches. He would be smiling like a millionaire. I'm made of memories like that."

"Business is business," replied Mori.

A long tautological silence ensued. The sun had an ori to it that jogged Robert's memory of yellow. It was setting. It was getting cooler. The clouds appeared as streaks in the sky, ori on ori.

"I don't want to see you anymore," Robert repeated.

"So leave, Mr. Lelarge. Be reasonable. My offer is generous and it still stands. You will have a life of comfort. No one will hold it against you."

Presenting Robert's lawyer with the foregone conclusion (he had taken ownership of the fishermen's shares, as well as Saturn's and Suzanne's), Mori had made it known that he was prepared to pay Robert sixteen billion yen to no longer have him under his feet. Robert hadn't said anything to France because he didn't want to be called a sore loser.

Laurie was aware of everything. She liked that Mori, in triumph, was all the gentler for it. When Suzanne had agreed to sell her all to him—she would later come up with rational reasons to justify a decision that had been based on no more than a feeling—Mori had invited Laurie over to his place. They had drunk tea in the empty house. He had not pumped his fist like a vulgar sports player. He had not hollered any virile monosyllabics. His face's features, fine as they were already, had simply softened. He spoke sparsely, deliberately, and more and more tenderly. His was a calm conquest.

What scant scraps of sympathy Laurie might still have harboured for her father came to her in the form of a punchline to a joke he would tell when she was little. "Don't be shellfish!" he slurred, as if from beyond the grave.

She worked it out in her head: there are few things in the world one can fully master while managing only fifty-four percent of them. The example of a dog sled sprang to mind. She knew Mori wanted everything. Everything is almost always too much.

"I have something for you that I can't allow you to take away right now," Mori had said to her in Japanese.

She had not immediately understood. He'd had to repeat himself.

He had gone to the basement and returned with an oblong object in the palm of his hand. It was made of black plastic. Looking closer, Laurie saw that it had two parts, one inserted into the other. One of them was a cap. Mori removed it. It was a felt pen. Its black tip had fine ori highlights to it. They doodled on sheets of mulberry paper. Mori drew complicated kanjis. Laurie tried to draw a lobster.

"I could draw a symbol on your back, perhaps?" Mori had offered.

He did: 霧. Without taking it off, Laurie had unhooked her bra to give him her whole back. She had closed her eyes to concentrate on the varying pressure of the ink tip. For a long time.

Then she had gone to look in the mirror. The well-defined strokes whirled together in a dance of densities.

"What does it mean?"

"It's a word you know well: *kiri*."

"Fog?"

"Yes," Mori smiled.

"Why such a complicated symbol for fog?"

"I knew you would ask me that," Mori murmured. "For you, fog is simplicity."

Laurie blushed.

"Would you like me to draw another symbol?"

"Of course," she closed her eyes.

Her breathing was getting loud. This was it.

"Where?"

"Here," she parted her thighs a little.

Mori's pupils dilated, then he promptly closed his eyes. His exhale bordered on a sigh as he inclined his face to the bare floorboards.

"But ... that would be most unseemly."

Given his old-fashioned turns of phrase, Laurie sometimes wondered if Mori had learned how to speak the language by reading nineteenth-century novels.

How to live, too.

Baie-Trinité (in raptures) and Robert (in his windbreaker) continued to watch Mori unload. After the crates came fifteen or so Japanese guys who didn't look the seafaring type. They were skinny and, for the most part, far from thirty and far from having good teeth. Without so much as a glance at the light of day, they donned white polyethylene coveralls equipped with laces to cinch the hood. They tugged hard on those laces.

"Who are those men?" Laurie asked as Mori was giving her the grand tour of the plant. "They are Fisheries employees," Mori did not lie.

"You went a long way to find them."

"They are experts. You can see by their eagerness and concentration levels that they have been waiting a long time for the opportunity to connect this type of circuit on such a large scale."

"Why are they dressed like that?"

"This is the new standard of hygiene at the plant. White coveralls must be worn in this zone," Mori explained with, yes, a little touch of pride.

The freezing line was moving across its usual third of the plant's floor space. Even though his shift wasn't starting for another half-hour, Louis Berthelot watched it do its thing with a paternal eye while from time to time allowing himself to cast a defiant one in the other direction. On the rest of the floor, where the canning line had been, frosted glass partitions, variously coloured LEDs that looked like signs, spring-mounted rubber floors, and all sorts of dangerous pipes and tubes were being installed. Keys, PINs, and retinal scanners granted Mori access to the gangway. He had set up his office in the barely spruced-up conference room. From the room's window, Laurie could see how it all slotted together. Chance seemed to determine the colour of the electric arcs that would periodically surge to life between two metal cylinders that looked like telephone poles. To the left, Louis Berthelot was mopping up a spill while whistling a progressive rock tune. That was the Fisheries. To the right, that was something else. Something straight out of Google or *Frankenstein*.

Of all the assembly, Laurie saw only one thing, a zone measuring three metres by three, at the very centre of the new installations. Standing there was a cube with blurred edges. That cube contained, on a smaller scale, Laurie's entire field of vision, and was itself contained in an infinite nesting of ever-smaller infinities. Inside the cube, everything was ori. The contents would change whenever Laurie shifted her gaze. And so, she could see the shades of ori change according to the emotions, of which there were many, that passed through her. When she took a step back and analyzed, venturing more and more into abstraction, trying to find out what purpose all this might serve, the images in the cube followed the same movement as her thoughts. They blurred. Their lines became less precise. They stopped being figurative.

"What the heck is that?" she eventually asked, sending ripples through the cube like those of a rock thrown into water.

A dizziness was rising up inside her.

"That is the invisible zone," Mori matter-of-factly replied before turning to Laurie and adding, with surprise and satisfaction, "but I see that for you, it is not."

In the same brightly lit three-by-three metre space, Mori saw only the lighting—no floor, no ceiling, no colour. A completely unoccupied space. A gaping hole into nothingness. Pure invisibility.

"No."

"That's normal. We will be covering all this up again soon."

That was planned for the following day. Mori and Laurie would be the only ones to see that space before it was screened off by the new Japanese workers.

The dizziness had quickly become intolerable and Laurie was eager to go into another room. Mori acquiesced with a glance.

They went into a smaller and somewhat luxurious office. Mori slid a glossy print of ori letters and characters traced on basswood across the brushed aluminum table: オリ (*ori*). The handwriting was Mori's. He must have taken the photo himself. Laurie understood that this was enormous progress. In order to take a photograph of ori, enough ori had to exist. There was enough red, blue, and yellow in the universe. The colour of things persisted in photographs. One day—Mori hoped it was soon—ori would no longer be in doubt, but in order to be photographed, it first had to exist in abundance.

"Why keep the freezing line? And what's all that for, on the other side?"

Laurie was trying to rein in her senses.

"To have it exist."

Shells show off their knowledge of colours in mother-of-pearl. The premise of ori is that shells know more than we do.

"You, Miss Laurie Lelarge, do you exist?" Mori mused after a minute or two.

An even denser fog embellished Laurie's face. She couldn't be certain.

"I don't think we *exist*. We exist *somewhere*," Laurie had to sit down.

The place where she existed—Baie-Trinité—was perhaps not exactly Baie-Trinité. The world was full of circumstances so unique, ample, and sweet they could only be hers. All that gave her the continuous sense of being Laurie Lelarge. Out of that sense, she gained awareness of the world, but things had a reality all their own. Even though she had the impression she'd lived through multitudes of them, she had an equally strong impression she would never truly know what a spring day was in Baie-Trinité.

"So you understand," Mori marvelled, "that nacre—mother-of-pearl—has more colours than it shows."

"Yes."

"What do you think it is missing in order to make it known?"

"A consciousness of its own?"

"That's really not necessary."

There was a flash of astonishment in Laurie's eyes. As several layers of fog shifted, all the cracks aligned: her thinking had never been so shrewd.

"The shell is alive, and it makes the mother-of-pearl, which is not—but which has, if I am to believe you—every colour. The shell would need to have an idea of what we see."

All this new equipment at the plant would be used to render human existence soluble—perceptive, critical consciousness to be filtered by molluscs.

"There you have it. And this is precisely what we'll give it," Mori articulated imperiously, with a nod of the chin to the photographed ori.

Astute though Mori appeared, he still didn't understand why the process worked equally well—if not more so—with urchins, which don't make mother-of-pearl. Still, ori—Laurie could now be certain of it—was the colour of human existence, of human will felt and expressed by a mollusc. Recollections of the cube that had reverberated her vision, and perhaps even a part of her thoughts, continued to fill her consciousness, and the dizziness wouldn't let go. She felt as though she'd gone too far. Something behind her eyes wanted to take flight, but held back by the skull, it was making her sick to the stomach. She'd already had that feeling when she still didn't know how to swim very well and ventured just a little too far from shore, just far enough to sense the danger of a new current rising from the deep. Even though she was going to turn eighteen in a few days' time, she was still only seventeen. No, all of a sudden, she really wasn't feeling well. She had to ground herself.

"I'm going," she put it out there. "Don't worry. I'll come back. I'm not afraid."

She left. Along the beach, without realizing it, she walked right along the midline between the out-of-work Moroccans and the manic assemblings of Mori's geek squad. She went to her parents' place, to the presbytery, because that was the only place she could call home.

At the ends of the branches plump buds appeared, full of chlorophyll. All her life, Laurie had taken the overabundance of colours for granted. She wondered if winter wasn't merely a scarcity of green, the effects of which a reservoir, somewhere in the southern hemisphere or at the heart of shells, might mitigate. How might that work? She still had the key to the presbytery in her pocket. She knocked louder and louder, then she used it.

There was nothing left to feel in the presbytery air other than a slight and far from gloopy silence. It smelled of meat, too. In the living room, France was on the couch, lying on her back. She was in a bizarre kind of posture with one elbow in midair bearing all the weight of her forearm and threatening to bend the wrong way. She had leggings on, and her thighs parted shamelessly. Smushed against her face in her slightly clenched right hand was volume three of a trilogy about the secrets and everyday, heart-rending struggles of a working-class family in days gone by: *Alphonse and His Progeny*. Laurie knew her mother was dead even before she saw the sub-heading: *Mornings in Ville-Émard*. Behind the couch was a bottle of antifreeze and some alprazolam pills.

Laurie went weak at the knees, but she didn't fall. She felt like puking, like screaming, like screaming puke. She voiced an acidic vowel and started shaking all over. It still smelled of meat. She tried to persuade herself that the meat was not Robert. She ran on all fours, if that was possible, to her father's office.

Robert had done it at the far end, in the corner, his back to the wall. He'd slit his belly open and slumped over until he was sitting. In the corner, his face was waxen, barely released from a wince of pain. His acne scars didn't show as much; you had to give him that, at least. His somewhat revolted cadaverous gaze met Laurie's, and all she could say, on repeat, was "nono, no, nonono, no, no" and feel herself faltering. In his final moments, Robert had pushed his bloodied hunting knife away. He was bare-bellied, legs extended, in a baggy old pair of pale blood-soaked jeans. Laurie closed the door. She reached for her phone and dialled 9-1-... before having a moment of paranoid clarity, a brief flash of the sheer scale of what would come tumbling down. She was all but suffocating. She sensed that she wasn't seeing clearly anymore, but she wanted more than anything to see clearly. That was rare. And that was perhaps why she called Goyette instead.

Goyette had just smeared a small amount of homemade explosive on Mori's strongbox. He had found a simple recipe online and concocted a volatile paste in the kitchen. He was about to set fire to it with a long wick soaked in aquavit when three calls came storming in to his phone. There was one from Laurie, whose number he had saved in his contacts. There was one from Mori, who probably wanted his strongbox back. And there was a call from Tokyo. He answered that one. It was a woman.

"Am I speaking to Frédéric Goyette?" she strangled herself with a strong Japanese accent.

"Yes. Yes. Who are you?"

There was a long silence interspersed with intercontinental static and sounds of heavy breathing.

"With all my respect, why did you call the Isumi Conglomerate of Tones, Colours, Pigments, Molluscs, and Crustaceans, Mr. Goyette?"

"All right, all right. Are you from the Conglomerate?"

Gathering his thoughts, Goyette wondered if it might be best to blow up the strongbox there and then, while they talked.

"Answer my question," the Japanese woman ordered, more breathless than brusque.

"If you don't know why I contacted the Conglomerate, I don't think you'd be calling me," Goyette distrusted.

"Mori Ishikawa. I want to know what he's doing in Canada."

Goyette usually didn't like to hear that word. On his travels, he always found a way to make it clear that he came from Quebec, not Canada. But now, he was so taken aback, it didn't bother him.

"What the devil! That's what I want to know too," he barely kept it together.

"*The devil?*" the woman panicked.

"What the devil ... it's an expression."

"It's a strange expression."

Goyette used the confusion he'd caused by mentioning the devil and Mori in the same breath and took stock of what he had to lose: nothing. "Right. The thing is, he's just bought a seafood company, Lelarge Fisheries."

The woman said something in Japanese. If he'd had to guess, Goyette would have said she'd cursed, but not hard, no, almost tenderly, as if, sounding relieved, she'd said something a bit like: "That's him all over, the bastard." But that was just a hypothesis.

"I beg your pardon," it sailed over Goyette's head.

"I am his wife. I love him. I am looking for him," the woman started to cry.

Someone at the Conglomerate hadn't kept their mouth shut.

Sitting cross-legged in the hallway, shivering in a cold sweat, Laurie had tried to contact Goyette every ten minutes, six times. Like every time someone didn't pick up the phone, she thought he must be having sex, but time was really getting on now. She had to hold herself back from calling Mori. The guided tour of the plant had sent her whole being into a spin. Before she got to the presbytery, she'd had the impression she was a candle flame and Mori had been blowing on her, for a long time, just softly enough to scatter her without snuffing her out. She never knew why he did that, or even if he was doing it on purpose. Every time she felt more alive. She loved him. But there, on the other side of the door, her father was smelling more and more like meat.

She didn't want to call Suzanne either. Her aunt would panic the kind of panic that could send everything off the rails.

She called Goyette for the seventh time.

"Yes. Yes. Laurie. I'm sorry. I was speaking with someone very important."

"How did you know it was me? My number's private. I've never called you. Do you have me in your contacts?

"Er ... maybe. Why would you call me seven times in an hour?"

Goyette was drunk, Laurie thought.

"My parents are dead. Both of them. I think it was suicide."

"!..." Goyette gasped.

"And I don't know what to do."

Laurie disappointed herself as she felt something crack inside, something Goyette couldn't fail to hear.

Goyette heard Laurie's nine-year-old voice, when he had given her shells for her collection.

"What about you? Are you safe?" Goyette meant to reassure her, with an intonation that inferred "Mori Ishikawa."

"Yes."

"I'm on my way."

He hung up. Laurie didn't want Goyette to discover anything, any message the bodies might be carrying, something he would seize hold of, something that might be damaging to Mori. To make sure, she pushed the door to the office open again.

Robert's body had not moved much. His neck was completely relaxed, but stiffened tendons were showing through the transparent skin. He had close bristles on his chest, in sparse little tufts Laurie wouldn't have wished on anyone. He had disembowelled himself with one deep, broad stroke. Yellow abdominal fat bubbled at the edges of the wound. Thicker than red blood, a black-brown substance was spreading, like the stuff you clean out of an urchin. Unformed stools, it had to be. The increasingly overpowering smell had summoned every fly in the house. They were particularly fond of the liver, a greyish slab to the right. The bowels were severed for the most part, but one pale intestinal loop in the midst of the darker bodily fluids spilled out of the wound, uncoiling waistward, extending like a chapter that, awash with an accumulation of sordid details, went on and on and on.

28

Two-gether

Too shaken up to drive her Bimmer and with no one to pay for her plane ticket, Florence Lelarge came home by bus. After not saying a word for two days, she eventually spat the bitter bit out.

"It had to be expected," she forced a smile. "Still, it's funny he did the *hara-kiri* thing."

"Funny? Funny!" hyperventilated Laurie.

Florence tied her wavy brown hair in a ponytail, then she went to boil some water for tea. The presbytery was too big for the two sisters. They'd been living on only one floor since Florence got there.

"No. You're right. It's really not funny," Florence backpedalled.

Reality was chopping her up and spitting her out.

"And your '*hara-kiri* thing' is borderline insulting," Laurie cringed.

"How so? It's just ironic. He kills himself Japanese style because of some Japanese guy."

"Right. First of all, the Japanese stopped killing themselves that way a good while back. It's a bit like saying the Romans are still going around crucifying people. Second, *hara-kiri* is kind of an insulting way of reading 切腹," Laurie drew on a sheet of squared paper.

"Whoa! You didn't miss a year of college for nothing," Florence said, acting impressed in an effort to calm her sister.

Laurie was still short of breath. She wanted to get angry, smash her plates marked with an L against the wall, bite Florence, even, but her rage was still erupting only in sobs.

"Third, for it to be a proper *seppuku*, someone has to be behind you with a sword to put you out of..."

Laurie tried to swallow, and it turned into a coughing fit. She was crying without bothering to cover her face, sitting up straight. In the kitchen, the water began to boil.

They'd had pizza delivered from Cécile's with white sauce, shrimp, scallops, and little sprigs of broccoli. Florence knew that the seafood allergy thing had been bullshit from beginning to end. Another of those ironies all Laurie's own: like a ripple on the pond of her life or a crease in a page turned too fast in one of her books. Flat on their stomachs in the old games room, they'd devoured the pizza and washed it down with a bottle of Puligny-Montrachet from the cellar. Laurie had never drunk, and Florence doubted she'd be good at it. The older sister was more used to it and kept drunkenness at bay by yawning and stretching a lot.

They didn't feel particularly orphaned. Caught unawares, shaken up, yes; thrilled to be together, sovereign. Their grief was laden with possibilities. The funeral would be the next day. The village had taken care of that.

"More wine?"

"No. No," Laurie blushed. "Tea's fine."

"Are you drunk?"

"Yes. A bit, I think."

"Excellent! So, tell me what's going on with..."

"Mori?"

"Mr. I-shi-ka-wa!" Florence vapidly separated the syllables.

"He blows me away," Laurie replied, with a neutral tone and a Bergmanian expression. "He's taken over my whole world."

There was a silence, shattered after seconds of heaviness by a half-smile from Laurie. They burst out laughing.

"Where does he blow you away to?"

"The unreal."

"So, that's what you call it!" Florence joked, even though her parents were dead.

"There are lots of things to understand," said Laurie, more seriously. "Things that you can't say on Facebook..."

"I'm listening."

"No. I think it's best if you see it. The bra I'm wearing, he gave it to me."

"Ooh! I didn't think it was *that* serious!"

Laurie hesitated at length. Florence could see the pros and cons being weighed in a gaze that seemed unduly troubled.

"Look," she eventually yanked up her sweater.

"Wow!" That was all Florence could say. *Wow. Wow. Wow.*

"See what I mean?"

"It's not ... dangerous, is it? It's, like, hurting my eyes a bit."

"Blink. It takes about ten seconds to get used to it."

By imagining her life all over again, back from the very beginning, sprinkled with this colour, Florence could see ("at last," Laurie would have said) the overriding power of what she didn't know.

"I can't believe it," Florence couldn't believe it.

"Right. Can I pull my sweater down now?"

Florence rubbed her eyelids with her fists. "Do you have anything else that colour?"

Laurie was thinking too much to say something more normal. "Yes. A pair of panties, but they're in the wash."

"Well, change into another bra if you like, just take that one off so I can have a look." Forgetting about the tea, Florence headed downstairs for the spirits. There were a few dregs of Southern Comfort.

She returned with two glasses and as many important questions. Laurie drank.

"Right. OK. What's it made of?"

"Fog," Laurie messed with her at first.

"Stop messing with me."

"You know nacre, mother-of-pearl, the stuff on the inside of shells? Well, that's got all the colours in it. Don't you think it's strange how a creature that knows nothing about colours can show them all off?"

"I don't find that especially strange, no. Seems to me, a rainbow doesn't have any more intelligence," Florence wanted details.

"Well, mother-of-pearl has more colours to show, but for that it takes a touch of human consciousness. Mori is refitting the plant to make human consciousness soluble and give it to the shellfish. I think it even works with some crustaceans. The shellfish filter it and secrete the pigments in their nervous system. At least, that's what I understand."

"And where do you come in? I mean ... how do you know all that?"

"Because Mori told me."

"And why did he tell you?"

Laurie turned to Florence. At seventeen years old, things can still happen so slowly, you can't make out the beginning or the end. They just blend into the rest of life.

"I think he enjoys sharing all that with me," Laurie started to explain before a deeper, alcoholic wave went to her head. "I don't know if he loves me, but I love him."

"You didn't have to tell me..." Florence got the picture, flat on her stomach on the floor again, flowing between yoga postures that made the floorboards creak and her vertebrae crack. "Just let me know one thing, though, and you probably haven't," she sighed, "but have you at least thought about 'business,' like Grandpa would have put it?"

Laurie made a face that meant she hadn't. She went to lie down on the couch.

"I don't think about those kinds of things. Those are your kinds of things."

"What's it called, this colour?"

"Ori," Laurie yawned from the couch.

"The colour's named after you?"

"No. O-R-I," she spelled. "There's no L. Not Laurie: *Ori*."

"Well, fuck me!" Florence was wowed. "I want to talk to Mori. Now."

"Can't it wait until tomorrow?" Laurie nodded off.

"No."

"Go knock on his door if you like. It's where Louis Berthelot used to live. I've got a funeral tomorrow. I'm going to sleep."

Laurie woke very early, alone in the presbytery with her very first hangover. She could sense a fear in her neck like a shiver that didn't spread, a heavy sorrow in her eyelids, and at the exact point in her heart where the electrical impulse of each beat was sparked, she hoped that Florence really had gone to Mori's and not to Ti-Claude's to get hammered with the sailors.

Florence came back whistling a Pet Shop Boys tune: *She had the brains. She had the looks. Time to make some money.* She had the looks, for sure: a white lace dress over skinny jeans, work boots on her feet. She hadn't slept. Her face was classy, grief-stricken, rarely so vulnerable. She reminded Laurie that together, they held forty-six percent of Mori's company, which would continue to bear their name, Robert's name, and Rogatien's name. That didn't mean nothing. Laurie liked that she said "together." The word brought peace to life between her stinging eyes.

You don't live in a presbytery without entertaining a few religious illusions. And so, it was up front in the little church in Baie-Trinité that Robert and France now found their cremated selves, even though France had never been much of a Christian (Robert, he'd had his moments). Laurie, Florence, and Mori weren't there yet.

Saturn's pained sighs rose above the whispers, making for quite the atmosphere. The dishwasher and the entremetier were physically holding him up. He had long since passed the stage when people could say he'd had too much of the finer things in life. He was emaciated, the closest thing to a cadaver there was at the funeral. Standing on tiptoes to see him, Linda told her girlfriend Cécile that the boss and his wife could've waited a bit. Put Saturn up there with them and they'd have a three-for-one. That would've made things easier. All eyes were on Saturn's black flannelette shirt and dirty jeans. He had a bad case of the shakes and an erection that was bigger than he was. He would never be seen again.

When Saturn stopped sighing, Suzanne's over-the-top sobs could be heard reverberating off the wood of the chapel and inside Hercules's rib cage. She had done the inexplicable thing she always did whenever someone died: she'd shaved her head. A few pews behind her, Hercules was trying to keep it together. Hercules, Sar'h, Louis Berthelot, Roger Lazure, Li'l Tony a.k.a. Blueberry, and the guys from Cloridorme all agreed: she was no oil painting. There was a troubling anger in her tears, an anger no one had seen in her before, an anger she wasn't holding back. They hadn't discussed it among themselves, but three of the fishermen had told Suzanne they'd be building a hobbit house as big as hers.

Of all the fishermen, only Roger Lazure, a couple of the men from the Gaspé, and two diehards from Rivière-aux-Graines were rigging up regularly. For the fun of it, they said, although it was really out of habit. They were all bitterly picturing the lobsters getting fat, going about their lobster lives, then waddling off to get caught in the Maggies or over in good ol' NB. Hercules would go out once in a while, telling himself the life of a lobster fisherman was just as good when you had a couple of hundred thousand in the bank. But the call of the gulf could quickly lose out to the call of the golf course. Some were getting closer to their wives, and to Florida too. For others, their absence really had made the heart grow fonder. They would all sometimes wonder what to do with their mornings.

The mayor of Baie-Comeau let one rip down the aisle. He wasn't sure for a second, but it was all gas.

The Lelarges' lawyer was checking the sports news on his phone.

Mr. Utsumi had stayed in Tokyo. No one recognized the vice president of procurement for Red Lobster. She'd had a facelift. The Premier was there, sitting next to the wife who'd never love him again.

On his feet, with eyes like an owl's and the swivelling head to go with it, Frédéric Goyette was carrying on a curious cha-cha, mostly with his thighs. It was enough to make anyone think he was desperate for a piss. He had seen Robert dead. He had given Laurie a hug to console her. He had spoken to Mori's wife. The truth was concentrated in the expression on his face. He knew what was happening. It was contorting his features like those press conferences of his at that midscale motel across town, already ancient history. He kept on thinking, reworking his diagram in his head. It was making him open his mouth and everyone could see the gaps in his teeth, which he showed off as testimony to the heart he put into his work. Inside Mori's strongbox, which he'd eventually blown open, he'd found a gun and some bullets. The chef had been right, back at the Crémazie metro station. Goyette had been carrying the gun around with him ever since. He believed he could save lives. Yes, he took himself that fucking seriously. But the two urns in front of him shot that illusion down with their tacky gilding. He was in pain now and again, but it was a salutary pain. He suddenly became aware of his clenched-up body, of all the knots in every muscle. "Give it a bit more, Goyette!" he was now calling himself by his last name. It would all be over soon enough. He was waiting for Mori. He considered him to be dangerous, as all desperate characters are.

And no, he wasn't the only one. The Man Who Comes—the nickname had caught on—was what most of the whispering was about. He wouldn't be putting in an appearance, that was impossible, unless... What followed that "unless" was inconceivable. It was Mori who had killed Robert, a man who'd never been so popular, not since that time he'd brought high-speed internet to Baie-Trinité. Working for a Japanese guy, for that particular Japanese guy at least, was out of the question. He just rubbed folk the wrong way. Some were calling him a fly-by-night. All that was easy enough to say. Still, from a public relations perspective, a double suicide wasn't the best of starts.

So, Laurie, Florence, and Mori weren't there yet, and one plus one plus one made three when the door swung open on its rusty hinges. There he was, in a black overcoat, the girls on each arm, walking down the aisle with them and taking his dark glasses off as if this were the opposite of a wedding.

The parish priest was delighted to see such a turnout. His homily went on about fish and abundance. Suzanne's cries were shrill. Saturn tried not to nod off. Laurie had a headache and Florence found everyone quite dignified, even though the last time she'd seen the most dignified of all of them had been at Saturn's restaurant opening. It all went by quickly.

Some photos have changed the world, and this one came at a time when people had stopped expecting any such thing from photography. In front of a wall of primary ori, Florence was wearing a pale ori dress. She had stockings on, and they were a much darker ori, almost black; no shoes. She was standing side-on, one foot on a wooden stool, showing a hint of thigh at the top of a stocking, hands on hips, leaning forward with her neck held high, staring provocatively into the camera, in ori lipstick. Beside her, Laurie was gazing into the void, her gaze embracing it in its entirety. She was wearing a more shimmering ori dress, cinched, shorter, that revealed her pale thighs. With a luscious look like that, it seemed as though she'd secreted the dress with her skin, the way arthropods do with their shell. Her paradoxical, abundant red hair was gathered any which way on top of her head, loosely bound by a dark ori headband.

The wall was the one in Mori's basement, in what used to be Louis Berthelot's basement. The Japanese guy had knocked together a photo studio down there with a tripod from the Walmart in Baie-Comeau, his big Nikon, and a few white umbrellas. There was something striking about the untouched image, which couldn't be photoshopped because of the ori.

"Laurie and I have to be indissociable from ori."

"I have no other intentions, you'll see..." Mori had teased the night before the funeral.

"That kind of thing must work like a charm on Laurie. But not on me."

"You will always and forever be indissociable from ori."

"Just to be clear, you said *ori*, not *Laurie*. And *you* means me and Laurie, not just me."

"Yes."

"Yes, *you* does mean *me*, or yes, that's right?"

"That's absolutely right."

"What are those umbrellas for in the corner?"

Mori told her. Florence was on board, so long as, no matter what anachronistic turn things would take, the name would continue to be Lelarge Fisheries.

"Yes," Mori kept his cool, "those are two very fine words."

They had a deal and some makeup from the future.

The photo appeared in the first May issue of *Hanako* magazine. Beneath the two sisters' feet, three trilingual lines said in white characters what people needed to know.

オリ/ ori
by Lelarge Fisheries
Bientôt

Very few of the magazine staff had seen the photo before it went to print and they had known how to keep a secret. The inevitable leak had occurred mere hours before the magazine made it to the news stands. An employee at a Japanese press distributor had posted the photo on Twitter. The ori was fading on screens with every passing second. You could see it growing dimmer, bluer. Sharing stretched it even thinner. Ori did not multiply the way we're used to seeing information multiply. Letting it loose lessened it. The first to see it were left dumbfounded for about ten seconds before their eyes got used to it and they'd say, "Oh, yeah, there's always been that colour, I'd just never seen it before." Twenty minutes later, the bland brightness of the photo already had people thinking it was a hoax.

Almost all the TV networks opted not to cover it: there was nothing to show. Online and newspaper articles featured eyewitness accounts. *Hanako* promised that the print copies would hold up better. That proved to be the case.

In her room at the presbytery, Laurie noticed that her ori panties were fading too. She cried soundlessly, so Florence wouldn't hear. The next day, as if he knew that would happen, Mori slipped her an Iceland scallop shell full of his sperm. Laurie let it drip drop by drop onto her bra and panties. It made the ori a little more vivid again and it made her laugh.

That Friday, news that a Japanese man had in all likelihood invented a new colour—a primary, finite one—made its way around the planet. Word got out, too, that the colour was produced in a Quebec village by the name of Baie-Trinité, at a plant that journalists were now crowding around. Mori had planned ahead: barbed wire, watchtowers, shotguns. Until then, the plan had been Mori's doing. He'd been hatching it for a while. The two Lelarge sisters were responsible for what followed. In Brooklyn, by the Metropolitan Avenue subway station, in Montreal, on Mozart Street, in Tokyo, around Akihabara, and in Paris at Place de la République, women left ori silk scarves behind in cafés. Two days later, the whole world was wondering what would happen next. Ori billboards with white characters popped up in those same places. "ORI," said the one in Akihabara. "オリ," said the others.

Tenth intermission

the scallop

Shellfish are creatures of the shadows, except for the scallop, which loves the light. In France, it's called a *coquille Saint-Jacques*, but for Rogatien, *Coquilles Saint-Jacques* was and always had been the name of a scallop *recipe*: how they were served at the Château Frontenac, in shells imported from Europe. The scallop shells in the gulf weren't as white as that. That was his specialty: well-done scallops in a thin, salty béchamel, a smidge of mashed potato piped through a pastry bag when he wanted to make an impression, all topped with the best cheese he could get his hands on. He would put the shells under the broiler until the cheese bubbled gold and the potatoes browned. Then he'd serve them up with a sprinkle of chives, to his friends who weren't fond of the light.

It's meat, he'd convince them. It's muscle.

Like all shellfish, scallops are born clinging by their fibres to the sea bed or to a rock. In a mussel, the fibres form its beard; in an oyster, they turn to minerals. The scallop just gets rid of them. It uses its powerful muscle to swim, fanning its shells open and closed in a self-propelling chewing motion.

Not keen on being tied down, it can be easily led. Shoals of advancing scallops can be found deep in the gulf, chewing up the water in their path until they encounter a human's dredger, a crab's claw, or a starfish's deadly embrace. Those with their wits about them can live for twenty years. They're the ones that make up the U10 category: ten scallop nuggets to the pound.

Thanks to Botticelli, like all redheaded girls, Laurie had wondered long and hard about scallops. When the little shocks to her skin alerted her to her presence in Mori's dreams, she would sometimes imagine herself as the very picture of femininity, surfing on the open shell, trying to cover her modesty with hair that was much too short.

Most of her questions had gone away when she paid a visit to the freezing line at the Fisheries. The ably handled knives, the swift back and forth of the blade, the moving-on to the next stage. There was no miniature Venus rising up, hair blowing in the wind, a breast out in the open air. Instead a network of tiny viscous tubes curled around bright red roe. The roe gave people the creeps. With its earthy taste of the seabed, of sour seaweedy offal, its extraterrestrial appearance could never catch on in the western world. So, off it went in frozen crates straight to the airport in Montreal, straight to Japan. Ovaries and all.

In the midst of the opened scallop's disgusting parts was the white monolith, the muscle that swam, the meat, the nugget. Rogatien kept that part for himself and the local market.

Unlike the other bivalves in its family, the scallop often opens up. It offers up a chink, a more porous border between inside and out. It is at this juncture that its life takes on meaning.

On the freezing line, with a putty knife and lots of help from their fingers, the deboners were removing a double, ring-like rubbery band. Staring at their hands, Laurie figured that band must be what kept the shell sealed. The ring was studded with a hundred or so minuscule beads barely bigger than poppy seeds and the same blueish black.

"What are those?"

"Those are their eyes," Dishrag kept an eye on her.

"They can see?"

"I'm sure they can. They've got eyes, in any case."

I wonder what it's like to be a scallop. My sight is the most developed of my senses because I'm human. However, I can close my eyes and silence my sight. If I pinch my nose, my sense of smell is still stimulated from behind, by the air coming in through my mouth. If I plug my ears, I can still hear the sounds inside my body. Even if I remain naked, there's still air on my skin. My mouth has long since gotten used to its own taste, but I can't decide not to taste. My sight is the only sense I can voluntarily switch off. But, even switched off, in my memory of the world, it continues to show itself. When I switch off my sight, I have the impression of being closer to my consciousness; yet a painting is not its canvas, a novel is not the paper it's printed on. Apparently those who are born blind dream without images. Senses other than sight manage to connect them to the world and give them the feeling of existing.

In his 1974 paper "What Is It Like to Be a Bat?," Thomas Nagel asserts that consciousness is a state that can be described as "what it is like to be something." In attempting to represent what it is like to be a bat, that is, to experience the world by means of sonar and echolocation, he intended to show that experience has a subjective quality that an understanding of its physical mechanisms does not bring across. This subjective, fundamental quality is consciousness.

Scallop eyes, miniature concave-mirrored globes equipped with twin-layer retinas, suggest they see only shadow and light, but to them, shadow is not merely the absence of light.[1] The cells of the first retinal layer detect changes in light intensity diffusely and not in a location-specific way. A reflex arc feeds into the second layer and triggers an instant closure of the shell when the shadow of a starfish looms over the scallop. The

1. S.E. Shumway and G.J. Parsons, eds., *Scallops: Biology, Ecology and Aquaculture*, 2nd ed. (Elsevier Science), 2006, c.5.

shadow is a threat. The scallop has everything it needs to situate the threat in its space and swim away. In a field of varying intensity, shifting spots are presumed dangerous. There are no colours in there. When there are no colours, we say things are black and white, but you have to have seen colours in order to recognize black and white. It's not a colour. It's the imprint of the world on the light.

Of all the underwater marvels, shadows, and colours, the scallop sees no more than is absolutely necessary. In a way all its own, it can see.

29

The Man Who Leaves

So that was that, Megumi Ishikawa slowly realized, smoking a peach-flavoured cigarette on the balcony of her apartment in Chiba. He'd pulled it off. A bitterness tinged with sweet pride filled her lungs with every puff. It was overcast, but the temperature was pleasant. Inside, Ren was tapping a palm against the window. He wanted her to see a smiling lion in his cartoon. After appeasing him with a gentle smile, Megumi turned her gaze once more to the horizon. They'd just put up a billboard in front of the train station: a great big ori rectangle. By now, no written qualification was necessary.

For her, nothing was more beautiful than an awareness that things were wearing away. She would spend the following days trying to put Ren to sleep after lunch, rocking him, singing his lullaby. Once that was done, she used the child's nap to go sip the second infusion of tea on the balcony. She stared long and hard at the billboard, trying to compare its ori to her more vivid memory of it the day before. She wouldn't light up. The moment would not lend itself to smoking. She went back inside when Ren woke up in a bad mood. The first cries she heard through the half-open door would bring her back to her solitude and ask yet more impossible questions.

Ori, for her, was both a wound and a promise. Mori left in a hurry when he'd left. She was no longer sure she loved him and she was no longer sure he loved her. Confusion is something that ages well; ever unresolved, patinated, it was making itself at home in Megumi's slender chest. If she hadn't mustered her courage to call Frédéric Goyette, if the incursion of ori into her existence had surprised her, then she wouldn't have been able to connect it to the longstanding confusion she liked to nurture within herself. A new confusion would have replaced it, one that was too vivid, flooded with questions, full of new pains.

One Wednesday evening two weeks earlier, due to an unseasonably cold wind, tired of knitting, books, and cigarettes, hounded by Ren, she had decided to call Ito. His number was on a Post-it stuck to page 405 of *In the Shadow of Young Girls in Flower*, in one of the drawers of Mori's grandmother's paulownia dresser.

"I must be honest with you, Mrs. Ishikawa," Ito had told her on the phone in Japanese, oblivious to the fact that, in a novel, it would come out in English. And good English, at that. "But I must also be blunt."

"Is he all right? Is he still devoting himself to the cause that's greater than humanity, the cause that is all he ever needs?"

"I will tell you this: if he returns to Japan, I will kill him. And if he stays where he is, well, then I might still kill him. Those are orders. I am not necessarily pleased about it."

"?!..." Megumi had been overwhelmed.

"I know. It's horrible," Ito had followed up, frostily. "Since I must be honest with you, since I must be blunt, I must also be courteous. Call Mr. Frédéric Goyette at +1-418-555-0176."

"Who is this Goyette?"

"A civil servant in need of intrigue, a competent malacologist, or the village idiot. Perhaps all three. That is for you to decide. I do know he called the Conglomerate several days ago asking after Mori Ishikawa."

"The village idiot, you say..."

Speaking with Goyette had reimmersed Megumi in a mellower version of her once-corrosive story. Ori for her was the beauty of time passing over that confusion: a wound because joy hurts when one senses it in the life of a lost lover; a promise because, in that colour, Mori would live on. His existence would extend to soon encompass the planet. She knew she could believe that, at least symbolically. *The Song Is You* went the old jazz standard she loved. Perhaps she could take that literally: the colour is you. When he saw the billboard, in any case, Ren wouldn't stop pointing at it.

"オリ," his mother would teach him, separating the syllables. "O-ri."

Goyette had spoken with Megumi when Robert died, but only a little because Laurie had been calling him every ten minutes. Mori, too, had been calling at the same time, but he hadn't picked up. They had spoken again just before the funeral, he and Megumi, then a few times after that: three or four hours in all, but in twenty-minute chunks because Ren kept waking up, and at ridiculous hours owing to the time difference. Goyette liked knowing Megumi. She was into jazz, whereas Mori, Goyette had long since deduced, was clearly into his classical music. She dispensed with all the bowing and honorific floweriness of Mori's English. Also, she had a soft voice when she wasn't worked up and she gave off a sense of vulnerability that Goyette lapped up. Listening to her sometimes gave him a hard-on, he was embarrassed to realize.

Goyette had recorded everything. Relistening to the conversations, he had filled a pad with notes. He liked that this story of his was concertinaing. Between their exchanges, he would look at where the Ishikawas lived in Chiba using Google Street View. It was from that balcony that she was talking to him. He, in Baie-Comeau or at a quiet table in Cécile's greasy spoon, and she, in a Tokyo suburb, were living through similar things, for the same reasons, and were in turn an influence on the other's feelings. He felt dizzied by the conversation but wasn't going to let the facts colour it. He wanted to stretch it to its limit.

Going back over his notes, Goyette realized he always lingered over the same pages—pages of life and pages of the coming-togethers that become life. Condense the everyday and what remains is the truth. Since it seemed like literature, he came up with the idea of calling it *Five Moments in the Life of Megumi Ishikawa*, and that wasn't a bad idea at all.

Five Moments in the Life of Megumi Ishikawa

—

Megumi Hamasaki and Mori Ishikawa had been married for two months. They had met in an advanced French class at Keiō University. Mori had just found a job at the Isumi Conglomerate of Tones, Colours, Pigments, Molluscs, and Crustaceans, right after graduating with his degree in optical engineering.

"Don't you think that's bizarre?"

"What? What's bizarre?"

"For a company: tones, colours, pigments, molluscs, and crustaceans..." Goyette left that hanging, picturing a crate of Benjamin Moore oysters.

"Of course it's bizarre."

She loved his thick, old-fashioned head of hair, his face, and his movements that were older than his years. When the leaves turned red, they would go see the red leaves like couples do. Same with the cherry blossoms. They made love.

"Often?"

"That's indiscreet."

"Please see only an abundance of enthusiasm," gushed Goyette, remembering Mori's manners.

"I'll see what I want to see."

"Yes. Of course. Forgive me."

"What good is modesty now?" Megumi eventually sighed.

Often enough for her to get pregnant, it turned out, which was awkward. Mori was working as a young Japanese salaryman does (he didn't always have time to come home by train between two workdays.) She was finishing her master's on the principles of immanence in traditional Japanese children's stories.

He had a day off during cherry blossom season. She had prepared a picnic. She had been rehearsing the words in front of the mirror, how to announce the news. She had morning sickness, a peach silk skirt on, and white panties he'd seen when she laid out the picnic blanket and sat down. A red circle was spreading across her underwear.

"You have your period, Megumi," he'd soured, pointing an awkward finger.

"What an asshole!" Goyette felt the need to add.

"He didn't know. And that was so long ago..."

二

"Last Thursday, I accused you of being indiscreet. I apologize for having been so abrupt."

Goyette stumbled over Megumi's words before realizing that, for him, it had been last Wednesday. Disconcerted, he felt he lacked the composure to reply.

"I must have deserved it," he automatically accused himself.

"I want to help you, even if that means I must reveal some very intimate things."

Well, that was a good start.

"Help me to do what?"

"To protect Mori. That's all that matters. Even though, there's no hiding it, I wish he would come back to Japan—but it's not safe for him here anymore. I can't ask you to make Japan less dangerous for him," Megumi conceded, exhaling peach-flavoured smoke.

Goyette's hesitation morphed into a dizzying doubt. Circumspect, Megumi set about recounting the difficult months when she would see her husband seldom, drunk, and always at night. They had moved into an apartment in Chiba: a little two-bedroom place, Goyette gathered, ridiculously big for the two of them. Megumi made flower arrangements, continued with her complicated reading and her French classes. Mori went on loving her, but he loved the idea of her more. It was as if he didn't love her in real life. The apartment, meals, his old heirloom furniture, what Megumi did with her days—he had lost interest in all that. He had stopped reading novels, and that wasn't like him either. At the same time, she sensed in him a renewed attachment, profound and unspeakable, that showed in the depth of his longer looks and also very much in sex. Mori no longer had the physiological need to sleep, eat, quench his thirst. And so, it was then that he began to use expressions like "something bigger than me," "a higher function," "a transcendental experience" to refer to the course his life was taking.

"Of course," Megumi elaborated, lowering her voice, "a man does not speak like that while continuing to dry the dishes or give his opinion on what breed of cat to adopt."

"What was happening?" Goyette egged her on from Cécile's greasy spoon, worried he might lose her to the noise of the static and the frying.

"He persuaded me he was becoming a god."

"A god?"

"No. I'm sorry, that's not what I meant. I should have put more emphasis on the 'becoming.' I believed, as did he, that he had just escaped from everyday concerns. He would often talk of the connection between cause and effect. He could feel it inverting."

"Like a god?"

"Let me explain. A part of him was becoming divine. At certain times, it was clear, his existence was expanding. Then the next minute, he'd want to carry on existing like that, but he wasn't able to. All that remained was the possibility of him reaching that second layer of existence. He would rage around, trying to find its beginning, its middle, and its end. Then he would connect with something or other and start to shine again. In other words, he knew exactly why and how to exist."

"When you say he would shine, you mean physically? Would he give off light?"

Goyette hadn't quite grasped what she meant by all that god stuff, but he'd been feeling like that for a while himself. Right then, as he listened to Megumi and her words took on meaning for him, he felt as though he was reaching this higher plane of existence. It struck him, too, that it had been happening little by little. If he hadn't seen the wave at four seventeen, he would never have realized it, but when he'd played in the regional football final and when he'd decided to come back to the North Shore while watching a crappy movie on TV with Myriam, he'd had a similar feeling. The wave at four seventeen had made it all more obvious. Now he'd recreated ori and he'd seen it in the backseat of Mori's rented Lincoln, in that case with the eyepieces. But he still didn't feel like a god.

ME TOO! Goyette had written in all caps with an exclamation mark in the margin of his notes on that conversation with Megumi. Rereading them, he wondered if he should have.

No pornographic detail had been entered into, but back then Mori had had a very powerful orgasm while penetrating Megumi, the kind of orgasm that transfigures and can even make you look like someone else. She hadn't said who.

Claiming she'd left her packet of cigarettes in the kitchen, she had stood up and walked away because she had the strangest sensation between her legs. She hadn't wanted to stay in the bedroom. Walking naked around the apartment, she had felt Mori's sperm dribbling down her thigh. She had stemmed the flow with her hand. She had gone about things quite mechanically in the bathroom, but she couldn't look at her husband's sperm, not even in the mirror. Her head would turn away by itself before she could so much as feel it dazzling her.

A long silence ensued. Goyette heard her crying and lighting up a cigarette.

"I think you're very brave to be telling me this. I promise, I won't say a word to anyone. This is a huge help to me. In fact, if you can keep a secret too, I know several men to whom the same thing has happened, right here on the North Shore."

Megumi had already hung up. That had not been the click of her lighter.

三

"I'm an engineer, self-employed," Mori had replied at the hospital when asked his profession for a form. Ren was nursing for the fourth time. That was how Megumi, worn-out and lactating, had learned that her husband had lost his job at the Conglomerate. The nurse pulled a condescending face as though she'd expected better.

Mori was home a little more in the first two months of Ren's life. He was not a very good father. What kept the love going with Megumi—the heavy glances and gestures, the risky sex, the accordion-playing with time—was no good for a baby. Every time he held his son, she had the impression he found him far too real. He seemed to know that, to be doing his best. And off he went again. Sometimes he'd be gone three, four nights in a row and when he came back he'd tell her he'd just touched something fundamental. She touched their baby, a lot.

He told her they were going to be very rich. She wondered how he was still paying for the big apartment. Once, he'd gotten a black eye. A microscope accident, he had claimed, then, exhausted, he had conceded that everything was changing and becoming more dangerous. Not dangerous the way she imagined, but dangerous nonetheless. She tried to explain to him that true wealth was peace of mind, that she'd never given a shit about money, anyway. She wouldn't change. He didn't understand. They drifted apart.

One Monday night, around nine o'clock, a guy called Ito showed up at their door. He was wearing a black suit and a narrow blue tie tied very tight. In the lamplight, she could see his fully tattooed torso through his light shirt. He was a gangster and she was alone with Ren and him. He gave her twelve million yen in a metal tea box, saying that it belonged to Mori, that he wouldn't be home for a few weeks, that he wanted to leave her the money. Ito got her to write his cellphone number down on a Post-it. She stuck it in a book and he left.

"He told me to call him if Mori didn't come back. He came back, but he went off again. That was nearly a year ago now. I called. It was Ito who gave me your number. He told me he would kill Mori," she gave a few little coughs, "if he came back to Japan. He also told me he might still kill him if he stayed where he was."

"He's alive," Goyette fell over himself to reassure her.

四

Megumi was nursing Ren, wondering if he wasn't too old for it. It was a sunny day and Mori wasn't there. The wind was rolling out shadows across the wide floorboards. There were no other sounds: if it hadn't been for his ravenous sucking, anyone would have thought Ren was sleeping, his head against the padded arm of the chair, one of his mother's arms curled around his body. Then he disappeared.

Megumi drifted off like a kite Ren was flying with his mouth. The intermittent flow of her milk kept her suspended in half-sleep. When he stopped, she had been about to nod off completely. Her head fell forward, carrying with it her arm and the weight it was no longer supporting. She cried out before she realized: Ren and all the materials he'd been wearing had vanished, just like that, with not the slightest fading. A suspended spurt of milk splashed the arm of the chair.

It doesn't take long to search high and low in a small two-bedroom apartment. No baby. Her iPhone rang. It was Mori.

"Hello," Megumi kept it together.

"My love..."

"Ren! Ren!" gasped mama.

Mori sighed a curse that sounded like a confession.

"What does that word mean?" Goyette wanted to know in the long silence that followed.

"I don't know ... fucking hell? Whatever you like. It's one of the worst swear words in the Japanese language."

Mori came back, but not right away, late, past midnight. He took the time it takes for any parent who loves their child to go crazy. When he opened the door, she hurled a cast-iron teapot at his head, swinging it by the metal handle. He only just got his face out of the way in time. Megumi broke down. She cried all night, curled up into a ball.

"He'll come back ... he'll come back..." Mori would repeat like a speaking clock, trying to stroke her hair.

All she had to do was to sit in the exact same position in the armchair two days later, with her head upright, one breast hanging out, nipple pointed at the window, at four sixteen in the afternoon. One minute later, Ren was back, all smiles. He cooed, latched on, and noisily soiled his diaper.

The worst thing was it happened again. Megumi, used to an absentee husband in spite of herself, became the mother of an intermittent baby. Every time—whether he was napping peacefully, being entertained by a finger puppet, having his diaper changed, busy buzzing his lips to avoid a spoonful of taro—he would dematerialize quicker than the eye could see, fully dressed, then reappear hours later if the conditions in which he had disappeared were recreated.

Goyette, keeled over in front of his diagram, knew he was no Sherlock Holmes. He knew who Ito was. Saturn had told him about the guy. In Tokyo, Saturn had even seen him ejaculate irregardable sperm "by accident." Megumi had told him about that for the first time at least three days ago. When all your eureka moments give you the impression they're late to the party, it's probably because you're not cut out to be a detective, he was discovering, having already jumped in with both feet.

"What you're telling me is vitally important," Goyette showed off all the same. "Right now, I'm investigating disappearances just like that."

To explain himself, Mori had showed up one night with what he would sometimes call an "integrator," or a "beta visualizer," or a "prototype," which looked like a Zero Halliburton with two kaleidoscopes and textured rubber handles.

"I am taking a real risk by bringing this here, but I want you to see because I love you."

Megumi cried when she told Goyette that. Those words are rarely said in Japan. That was only the second time.

"No."

"Look. Once you do, you won't see anything the same way as before."

"No, Mori. No."

Megumi spoke to no one about it (she told her mother and various friends it was a long business trip), but it was then, perhaps, that they ceased to be a couple. Mori packed his bags and his contraption and left in a long raincoat. That was the last Megumi had heard of him until she'd dared to call Ito.

"Ito. Ito. Ito," Goyette lost his shit after he hung up.

He hurled the better part of his office supplies at the diagram, even the ones that leaked easily. Once he calmed down, he realized Myriam was in the doorway.

"Fred. Relax. Relax," she calmed him, a tear in her eye. "I don't want to lose you again."

五

Having grown mistrustful of all technology, and having her style cramped by Ren, Megumi knew nothing of the buzz when her copy of *Hanako* arrived. She'd had a subscription to the magazine since she'd been a teenager. She was reading it in a big brown armchair, in white panties and a violet blouse. Through the open window the wind was refreshing her skin and carrying the scent of spring. Ren was sleeping. She would pause to look at her body in the living-room mirror and admire herself. That was a new thing; she had thought herself irremediably uglified by pregnancy. She didn't leave the apartment much, but she was starting to feel like it again.

"Wow," she happened upon the page. "Wow," she said out loud. "Wow."

It was him. It could only be him, even though she had no proof. A hatred for the two girls in the photo took hold of her, a spontaneous hatred, one she'd never known, whose violence left her lightheaded.

She hated them. Two vulgar white girls. The one who was a darker shade of white seemed a little less hateful, but that redhead! Her thousand-yard stare made her feel queasy. She vomited rice and tea leaves. She thought she saw some ori in her vomit. Standing up, still in her panties, not knowing why, she clenched her teeth and wanted to smash someone's face.

She called Goyette.

"Have you seen it?"

"Yes. Yes. You mean the *Hanako* magazine?"

"How do you know?" she raged.

"It's everywhere. Apparently the colour is more vivid in print."

"It's vivid enough. Who are those girls?"

"All right, all right," she managed to drag it out of Goyette. "They're the Lelarge sisters. Girls from the village. They're well liked around here."

Goyette understood her anger, although she said it had come from out of nowhere.

Then the ori softened. There was nothing more beautiful.

"You know," Goyette stiffened, "that's what was in the aluminum briefcase. When you put your eyes in the eyepieces. You see that colour. Ori."

Megumi fell silent for a long, expensive moment.

"I propose that we no longer speak to one another," she decreed. "You used me. Let us each go our separate ways with the impression of knowing everything."

Workers in polyethylene coveralls installed the ori billboard in front of the train station.

The irregardable powder was made from flickerings of human life, Goyette had concluded, from our moments of absence, coma, amnesia, and disappearance—from the things that put life on hold. Seafood could provoke those flickerings, intoxicate you, but alive it was able to seize those moments and make a surplus of reality out of them, in the form of a colour. They were the source and creation of the ontotoxin.

Goyette went about parking his pickup in Baie-Trinité. The previous day, it had been fifteen degrees. Everyone in the village seemed like they were in a bit of a trance, even Cécile. On the 24-hour news channel at her greasy spoon, she had seen herself passing comment on the matter.

"It beggars belief. It's a sleepy village here. Seems they've installed metal detectors at the doors to the plant. It's not an airport, for frig's sake. And what for? A new colour. As if the world needs that ... let me tell you, red, blue, and yellow have been plenty enough for me all my life. And even yellow, if it weren't for mustard, I could live without that."

The seventh time it looped around, she shut herself up with a tap of the remote.

"At least you didn't swear on TV," someone pointed out.

"Want to see me swear, do you?" Cécile challenged him.

Ding, the timer on the deep fryer held her back.

It was getting harder and harder to talk anyway, now that journalists from all over the world were filling the booths at the snack bar. Cécile took the orders breathlessly. She ran short of ingredients every day and was forced to improvise. Goyette had seen her serving fries and gravy with ground whelks to some Russians and passing that off as a thing.

Goyette was feeling good. He was having plenty of sex. He held all of Mori Ishikawa's weapons: his Glock, for starters, which he had on him right now. He'd been practising in the woods, on *påskmust* cans. And he had a notebook full of confessions from Mori's wife. He also knew how to make ori from the ontotoxin: it had to be metabolized by a mollusc. And molluscs, since he was the local manager for the Canadian Shellfish Sanitation Program, were his domain. Mori was less of a danger than he had believed: all of Japan seemed intent on doing him harm.

At the end of the wharf, Goyette mustered his courage. He had to go looking for Mori. He had to tell Mori that he didn't take shellfish sanitation lightly. He wanted to stop him from making people disappear because you never know who that might happen to. Most of all, he wanted to tell him he knew everything.

He tailed him. Mori parked his rented Lincoln outside the grocery store in Baie-Comeau. In the fancy rice aisle, Goyette figured it was now or never.

"Mr. Ishikawa."

"Are you here to arrest me?" Mori kept his calm in his black cardigan.

"No. No. I told you, I'm not a cop."

"Well? What can I do for you?"

"How's Ren doing?"

Mori's gaze drifted to a bag of basmati. His fists clenched all by themselves, then, as if he'd become aware of it, he relaxed them. He looked up.

"Who have you been talking to?"

"Ito."

Mori sighed in disgust. He turned back to the bags of rice, as if hoping the grains would absorb the sound of his voice.

"No. You've been talking to Megumi. I hope she's well," he winced.

"Has it been a while since you talked to Ito?" pressed Goyette, sticking to his game plan.

"Think about it, Mr. Goyette. If I can be certain that it was not Ito you spoke with, what does that mean?"

Ito was dead. Goyette had a feeling things weren't moving quick enough in his mind.

"I know what you're up to," Goyette changed the subject for the third time in a minute.

"Yes. I'm making ori. It's a new colour. It's made by materializing human consciousness and having it digested by molluscs."

"Er ... what I want to say to you, in my capacity as local manager of the Canadian Shellfish Sanitation Program..."

"Stop right there," Mori cut him short. "Do whatever you want with the shellfish sanitation. But everything else, just stop it. It's pointless. You have been a negligible obstacle in my way," he hesitated a little over the words. "If this has given you a thrill, well, good for you. It's over now."

Goyette wanted to leave. Mori was overwhelming him with a deep and typically Japanese shame that was coiling like a snake around his profound sense of identity.

"I just want to know," Goyette mellowed. "Why here? Baie-Trinité? Why Laurie? You needed a woman?"

"As a man, I need a woman. Laurie is Laurie. All this had to happen to someone."

"And the powder? What does it do when you inject it?"

"It's extraordinary," Mori whispered, "but there is better," he continued in a crescendo, "like inventing a new colour. That is better. I know what you're going to say next, and I don't want to talk to you about that because it would be extremely indiscreet on your part. I'm going to leave," Mori slipped away.

Goyette had to steady himself on something. He knocked over a couple of vacuum packs of arborio.

"I'm OK. I'm OK," he shooed away the bystanders. The only genuine thing about his smile was that it was missing a few teeth.

He had to pass through the fresh produce section. Back at his pickup, he recalled seeing something on the floor: a banana peel. His first thought was that Mori had left it there for him to slip on. There it was, dangerous and ludicrous: a negligible obstacle. And he had sidestepped it.

30

In the unending transparency (a fold)

On the North Shore, someone, somewhere around the fishing and the Fisheries, the fishermen and the fish, occasionally won the 6/49 jackpot. The last time, it had been "Dammit" Dallaire. It never turned out well: Miami, coke, a predictable bullet to the head. Word got around fast and the winner would find out just how many scroungers there were in their family.

Thanks to Mori, the fishermen had collectively won eighteen million dollars. Individually, it was just enough for the older ones to retire and the others to stop fishing for a year or two, the time it'd take for prices to stabilize, Mori knew, and for him to build his factory. The association had doled out the amounts according to a half-assed quota system put together by a hard-drinking accountant. And who got screwed over, again? The whelk fishermen. They each got about forty grand.

With money, you have to be careful not to get your fingers burned, especially when you use it to light a cigar. That was getting harder to do with the new polymer notes. That stuff gives off toxic smoke. That's what the Berthelot brothers learned when Sar'h got his cheque from the association. He was chilling with his brother and a Carling. He'd take a drag of a Player's between two puffs on the cigar.

"The way you're smoking, it won't be long before that forty grand's all mine," Louis joked, betraying the object of his desire.

"Don't even think about it, you fucker," said Sar'h with smoke in every orifice of his face. "Anyway, you got way more than that for your house."

They'd just realized they were both burning through the bounty of the same benefactor.

"Yeah ... well... whatever."

"You don't have a cent left, do you?" Sar'h saw right through the "whatever."

The Berthelot brothers were knocking back the Carling in the semi-basement Sar'h rented out by the highway. Sar'h always said the place was set back a fair way from the 138, and he wasn't wrong: no one likes to live right by the side of that road. Seven hundred and sixty kilometres further down that same ribbon of asphalt, on a hard drive on the twenty-second floor of the Loto-Québec tower, a confidential document listed the bar owners who were pocketing the biggest commissions from their video poker machines. Jean Claude Desrosiers, no hyphen on Jean Claude, was top of the list, way ahead of the competition.

Only too happy to be pocketing his record commission, Ti-Claude had never given it any thought, but part of a fisherman's identity is bound to chance. Fishermen make a living casting their nets out across the huge, black gulf. Shoal by shoal, haul by haul, fishing is a game of chance. Things don't come much more perishable than seafood. You can end up getting your fingers burned with that, too. Accustomed to sporadic hauls of putrescibles, fishermen are naturally inclined to wastefulness.

But that wasn't how Dishrag had first been screwed over. Serge Touré and Kouamé Adie, two Ivorian teenagers, had managed to pass themselves off as a young lady who was head over heels in love with him. Their main talent had been to swiftly identify his sexual preferences and reflect them back to him, in emails full of pornographic promise and a better future.

He'd never wondered what a buxom young African would see in him because he was who he was.

"At least this one won't turn lesbi—" he'd jerk off with apocope.

Émilien, the manager of the Baie-Trinité credit union, hadn't said a word. The employees working the Western Union counter at the Walmart in Baie-Comeau hadn't said anything either.

Serge had wound up lending his brother half of what Mori gave him for his shares: twenty-one thousand dollars. Sometimes, they'd sit side by side with a Carling at the machines, on the dark side of Ti-Claude's bar: Louis because he needed more than twenty grand to rebuild his retirement savings; Sar'h because he knew he'd never see that twenty grand he'd lent his brother again.

Louis preferred to play poker. It gave him the impression that his wits could influence the fate he'd tied to chance.

Sar'h didn't understand the first thing about poker. He mostly played 7s Wild.

"Look who's fuckin' reelin' it in now," he'd say to his brother when lots of the sevens lined up.

Otherwise, he'd be losing at Swinging Bells, a spin that promised a thousand-dollar jackpot; at The Wild Life, a nickel-slot that spun him right into the jungle, rhinoceros, giraffe, zebra, elephant, and all, not forgetting the lion, king of the jungle, whose roar marked a winning line. He felt a world away from shellfish, but closer to the good times of the whelk than the hard times of the winkle. Now and then, he'd splash out on a virtual trip to the Orient with a few spins on Triple Fortune Dragon, but he stayed well clear of Lobstermania. It took him two measly months to empty his pockets.

As for Dishrag, he held on for four, stretching it out with smaller bets. It took his mind off the job on the freezing line, which had never been crummier. They'd built a translucent wall between the two halves of the Fisheries that looked like little white circles projected against a bug screen. It made it seem as though you could pass right through it, but it was completely impenetrable. Through the wall you could see the two iron poles on the other side, a current bursting to life between them, each time a different colour. The electric arc emerged from a network of prisms, spheres, and pyramids, all clad in embossed aluminum. A code determined the colour of the various tubes that ran around the solids: yellow for ventilation, blue for cold water, and so on. On the perimeter, urchins and scallops swarmed in tanks with see-through floors for lids. Now and again, Louis would glimpse a Japanese employee—or maybe a Moroccan, he thought—climbing up to those floors using a ladder on wheels, doing a quick shoulder roll, and slipping out of sight through a trick of the light between the plastic of their coveralls and the patterns on the semitransparent wall. In the centre was a matte metallic hull, peppered with antennae, pumps, pistons, and other tubes whose purpose was beyond Dishrag. It looked like a giant urchin. Most of all, and most disturbing of all, the pipes that were colour-coded orange would sometimes rupture and leak an iridescent liquid. The leak was slow and in big drops. The liquid would pool on the floor without spreading, thick and metallic, in great mirrors of spills that broke down white light. Louis' right hand would clench of its own accord around his dishrag whenever he caught sight of one. It brought out the *Terminator 2* in him. He could almost feel the stain from the future rubbing against the fabric and his fingers, the impossible absorption. It wasn't the kind of spill you mop up, more the kind you scoop up, he caught himself analyzing enviously.

Seated in an armchair she'd moved into the hallway on the top floor of the presbytery, Laurie looked up from her book to see an overdue summer sweeping the beach through the bay window: white sun in the dry sand, desiccated kelp, scattered altocumulus. The wharf was missing the comings and goings of the shrimp trawlers. She was reading. As usual when she was reading, she was unconsciously shifting into nonchalant postures that would hike up her skirt. Her ori panties were starting to show the kinds of stains that show on panties after several months when you love them and wear them a lot. She would turn eighteen the next day.

Florence had moved into Robert's office and would talk like him, loudly and into the phone, all day long. Opportunity was taking her places. She wasn't sleeping. Laurie didn't recognize her. Sapped and supercharged like him, her big sister had also taken the place of Goyette, who no one saw anymore. Her sweetness was slipping, and more than once they had squabbled. As a goodwill gesture, Laurie was reading a book called *The 7 Habits of Highly Effective People*. Florence was between phone calls, updating her in flurries. Silicon Valley hedge funds were vying to buy twenty percent of the company. Florence put a lot of stock in the difference between a billion US and a billion Canadian. Laurie could see that the offers were escaping the Earth's gravity. She could sense she was living through an important moment, in the middle of a financial bubble. The first few lines told her she wouldn't be reading the rest of the book. She was able to read: her eyes would identify words that, placed one after the other, created whole worlds in her mind. That seemed sacred to her. Reading a book like that, if you asked her, was more sacrilegious. The book was just big enough for her to hide another, smaller book inside: *Signals for Seers*.

These words I speak to you
in this language from beyond the sea
that seashells are made of.

Laurie felt herself coming alive in Gilles Hénault's words. Mori had realized that. He'd had that smile she'd learned to detect and he'd said that poetry was all the more powerful when it was clandestine.

Mori made his way to the presbytery every day. Laurie suspected he didn't like being there. There was a contained impatience to his actions. Despite the best efforts of the disaster cleanup team, a hint of death still lingered. Florence was keen to move on, to make everything grow. Laurie avoided the rooms where she had discovered the bodies. She read elsewhere, carrying a heaviness around with her. Mori got straight to the point. To Florence, he spoke in billions. He remained cautious, methodical in the face of her enthusiasm. To

Laurie, with increasing regularity, he gifted his sperm. When she had doubts, when she could no longer find her place in her own story, when she came to believe she was an adjuvant, no more than a catalyst for the capitalist coming together of her sister and Mori, Laurie would dip her fingers into the contents of those carefully packaged little glass jars. The reassuring fog would then rise up inside her.

But one day, it all got too much. Mori closed the door to Robert's old office and was alone in there with Florence for a good hour and a half. Laurie wanted to keep on reading, but the dread she felt kept getting in the way. It was powerful, and mixed with a shameful jealousy. When he left, Mori squirmed toward her in that semi-shy, semi-erect way of his. She knew he had sperm for her. It was viscous and in a small transparent box made like a matchbox. The acrylic had been tinted ori. Outside, it was nearly dark. Laurie hadn't turned on the lamp, even though there wasn't enough light left to read by and Mori had realized as much. Stars were appearing against the purply-blue background on the other side of the wall. Lower down, the contrast lessened between the sky, the Prussian blue river, and the rocks topped with black spruce.

"Don't leave, Mori. Please don't. Don't do the same as usual."

Mori, after leaving his sperm, would always turn swiftly and make a stealthy exit. He stopped, turning first only his face, which showed more kindness than disappointment. Though his words were, his tone was not accusing.

"So, the fog is no longer enough for you," his tight lips observed.

"It's not that."

Mori took a seat on the floor in front of Laurie, his back to the window. Laurie turned the lamp on. The whole scene disappeared. All that remained was Mori, set against a black background that made his conflicted expression more apparent.

"That's not it," she repeated. "The fog is also your ability to turn my life into a state of total astonishment," she'd thought this through. "I love it because we're nurturing it together, it's our story, yours and mine," she fell silent for a second before she resumed. "Now my parents are dead. We're speaking to the whole world with ori, but I don't know how. It's not just you and me anymore, you know? I could care less about the millions and the billions, and you know it. I can't ask the same of you, and that doesn't bother me either. I envy the way Florence can influence things, and how she gets to be with you. Yeah, that's it, I think," she bit her lip.

She sobbed only once, a sob held back like a landslide. The tears streamed down her cheeks. She picked up the little box of sperm and slid the lid back.

"What's all that about?"

She knew he wouldn't like that, that it wouldn't be easy for him: he'd want to look her in the eye. She cried without making a sound. She held up her hands to show him his sperm. What was all that about?

There was a long silence and, behind Mori, imperceptible movements of black on black: bats.

"I have an explanation for you," he pulled himself together, looking away, "but it's not the kind of explanation that makes things simpler. It's going to make them stranger and I risk losing your trust. But I also risk that if I don't give you an explanation. Start by telling me what it's like for you to receive my sperm, what you feel every time. In that, there will be a seed of truth."

Laurie smiled through her tears. She said that in the beginning, she had, like he'd told her back then, "a curiosity for fluids." She liked the thickness of it, the way the sperm stuck to itself, to her fingers. Now, she liked how Mori's sperm could give ori things their shine back when they lost it. She thought it was pretty, and that was another thing she enjoyed about it. She would also think about Mori's ejaculation. She was sure he wasn't with another woman when he stopped to ejaculate into a container. She knew he was masturbating and that was connected to her. More than anything, that turned her on. She masturbated too, and that was connected to him.

"And I know you know, but I want so much to receive it *differently*, the way a woman can receive a man's sperm. Only, you don't want to, and every time I'm confused and so turned on, too, that I relish every second of that confusion."

Sitting up in the armchair, Laurie realized she was getting wet, crying, leaking all over.

Mori took some time to reply.

"Anything can happen," was what he said.

"Yes!" Laurie wasted no time agreeing.

"I came here because there were urchins, molluscs, and crustaceans. Then I met you and I thought there might be the possibility of tending to a world inside of you where ori could materialize. To find out, I showed you my sperm. You saw it and I knew that I wouldn't need to go elsewhere. I knew that I would make ori here and that it would be with you."

"Why?"

"The simple answer is that I accidentally poisoned myself while experimenting with ori a long time ago. That left my sperm irregardable, like the powder at the bottom of Frédéric Goyette's test tube. It's the same thing."

Laurie continued to leak all over the place. Her fog was condensing.

"So, if you put your sperm in a shell..."

"I tried, but it still needed some work. Those times, you couldn't see the ori. Not like that. I had to go about it differently."

"Why don't I have a problem looking at it, then?"

"I don't know, to be honest. Long before I knew you, something happened that gave you the ability to contain everything in your life. Anything can happen to you. As soon as you saw the ori, it became possible to make lots of it. The sperm I give you revives the ori because it fuels the capacity within you to become absolutely anything."

Laurie, her eyes round and streaming, could barely move. Knowing that everything came from her made her head spin and gave her a rush. Her thoughts followed the multiple ramifications, sought all the corollaries of this radical truth. But the strength of her intellect was held back by her belly—she could feel a warmth to it—and by her groin, which she could feel pulsing. She had never wanted anything so badly.

"Mori," she managed to twist his wrist and turn his palm to her, "do you want me? It's my birthday tomorrow, and I really want you."

She could see he was hard. He took a deep breath.

"You are my finish line," he softened, "but I am only the start of things for you. Every day when I wake up, I'm glad that you exist. It fills me with joy, the same joy I have when I breathe in the air, when I look at the sky or the sea. And you are beautiful. But we don't make love with the wind or the waves. You belong to the order of greater things, the ones where I exist, that contain me."

Mori stopped. Laurie's eyes were open even wider and leaking even more tears, without a single sob, just tears flowing in narrow single file, like an ice cube melting in the sun, in April, at noon.

"Also ... before ... in Japan..." Mori decided to go on.

A by-product of the ori manufacturing process could be toxic. Building up in the sexual glands, it could render sperm irregardable, if you had that, or ovaries, if you had those—but ovaries tended not to be visible, so that causes fewer problems. If you had a child, their life, otherwise human and ordinary, would be broken up with intermissions during which they would disappear to become ori. And that Mori knew all too well.

"What's his name?"

"Ren. And she's Megumi. I miss them like crazy sometimes."

"I don't know what to say ... I can't wait to meet them," Laurie smiled tenderly.

This was the smile that would breach the levee and release floods of tears.

The next day, Mori and Florence made the birthday dinner: bowls of sesame rice with stacks of urchin gonads on top, alternating the male gonads, ochre in this season, with the reddish-brown female ones; and seaweed soup. Mori sliced slivers of raw lobster with his fillet knife. They garnished them with yuzu juice and rock salt. With a white miso paste brought in from Japan, they made a compound butter that Florence brushed over the lobster they grilled over maple charcoal. Florence opened a bottle of wine and switched her phone to airplane mode. It was a 2002 Montrachet made by Anne-Claude Leflaive. On the label, Robert had written: "Laurie's 18th birthday."

Florence didn't make the same mistake of giving her cosmetics in front of Mori. Mori did make the same mistake of giving her seafood, but it was no longer a mistake. They talked about what had changed in a year: almost everything. The sky at dusk had shades of neon to it and they wondered if it was the northern lights.

"Florence," the birthday girl sharpened her tone, "Mori and I talked a few things over yesterday. You see ori as a product..."

"... and it cannot last forever," Mori flowed on, catching the cue.

"Yes," Laurie continued. "It's not a product like the others. We've been making it for months now, and—"

"There's no going back! The market can't get enough of it," Florence dug her heels in.

"That's not what's at stake," said Mori, his nose in a wine glass. "As things stand, it's almost infinitely rare. And we control all production. We must be mindful that this will not always be the case."

They had moved on to the grilled lobster. Florence had shelled Laurie's for her. Mori had waited until the last moment to relieve his of its carapace, swiftly, with a short blade, in one fell swoop of every joint in his arm. Things would stay that way for a few years, he explained, as long as it took for a generation of intermittent babies to appear, who would grow up to be intermittent children, then intermittent adults and intermittent old people. Anyone with tanks and purification systems would then be able to produce ori galore.

"That's batshit crazy..." Florence said slowly, gazing into the void, teetering on the brink of being for one brief moment then falling back down on the earth side of the edge. "That means we've got months to cash in!"

"Yes. That's not all we wanted to tell you, but it's part of it. As long as we're looking at the money side of things, that's what has to be done. If we don't, then others will."

"I just don't care. I get that I'll never need to work, one way or another. I don't mind. The rest is your business."

Laurie said it was their business, and it was literally their *business*.

Mori's white plate looked rather like an anatomy chart with the tail, both claws lined up on either side, both knuckles, the meat of the legs, and in the centre, the little mound of tomalley. Laurie smiled. Florence had stopped drinking and was intensely focused. She was doing the math in her head.

"I get that you don't care, Laurie, but can we count on you not to say a word to anyone?"

Mori knew there was no point even asking.

"Of course, of course you can," said Laurie. "There's just one thing bugging me. And it's been bugging me a lot. You'd call it our raw material."

"Seafood?" Florence presumed.

"No. Human consciousness."

Yes, the problem would resolve itself, but by creating a bigger problem instead. The world would already be crying out for ori before production became associated with the emerging phenomenon of *intermittent babies*: the ori babies. Ori would become the leading ethical concern of the next two decades. Groups would lobby for an outright ban, although their position would soften once the Catholic Church came on board. Those demanding that ori be "used responsibly" would be born long after a whole generation had been affected. This would be followed by a liberation movement ready to acknowledge the ori-producing minority, years of struggle culminating in the election of the first ori-producing MP in Vancouver. As she asked her first question in the House of Commons, she would dematerialize to rapturous applause from an emotional Parliament.

It is not possible, when a technology starts to become established, to foresee the somewhat perverse social implications it might have. In ori's case, these implications would be tied to the ontotoxin's use as an injectable drug, a phenomenon that Mori mistakenly predicted would remain marginal at best.

Mori dipped his chopsticks into the little mound of tomalley and reached for some rice. Laurie followed suit. Florence kept to the meat, cooked through by the maple flames. By opening humanity's eyes to its incredible ability to see a colour spawned from its own consciousness and sifted through seafood, the three of them could be certain they were working for the good of humankind. And the first few years of ori would bring joy to the masses, putting people back in touch with their senses.

To create enough of it, people had to be disappeared.

"That's what happened to Louis Berthelot," Laurie told Florence.

Laurie really had a hard time with that.

Florence shrugged.

"So what?" she didn't give a shit. "Mori gave him half a million."

"So you think that's all right, asking people to trade their lives for money?"

"Come on! You call that trading your life for money? I know what I'd call it: work."

Laurie and her sister were on the verge of another argument. Mori tried to stop them, giving them long stares, but always at neck level. Manicured lilac-polished nails dug in to the tablecloth; Laurie turned scarlet.

"I'm very interested in what Mr. Berthelot made of the experience," Mori slipped in, pouncing on a simultaneous sigh from the sisters. "As an interested party, I mean. My own son went through it, though before having the words to tell anyone about it."

"Was that really so bad?" Florence was already shaking her head.

"No. Not at all. He talked about it being a dream. A white dream, he said, where he felt no pain. When he came back to reality, he simply picked up his life where he'd left it. I believe this is a choice that people may take. If someone wants to turn down hundreds of thousands of dollars in return for a few months of hibernation, we won't force them. But it is very important that all three of us be in agreement, and I understand, Laurie, that you want to think it over. But there are not many other possibilities open to us."

Dead and torn apart, the half-eaten lobsters on the table would not be coming back to life. Time had only one direction. Laurie thought she might cry, seeing Mori's half-empty glass on the table, Florence's empty one, and her own full one. The world was crying out for ori, and everything was moving too fast. Her eyes were drawn to the old wooden crucifix they couldn't bring themselves to take down from the wall. Just like in books, some people were going to have to give up their lives.

"Not their whole lives," said Florence.

"And it is doubly temporary: temporary for those who agree to disappear; temporary, too, because this is only an interim stage. This manufacturing procedure will be obsolete in a few months' time."

"Where do people go when they disappear? What becomes of their lives? How do they experience consciousness?" Laurie wanted to know.

"That's not that important," Florence didn't want to go there.

"No. No. It is important," Mori acknowledged. "Important and unknowable."

Between the edges of the high-filtration masks and the cinched hoods of the polyethylene coveralls, it was hard to make out their eyes. Their sentences came from invisible mouths and lost their way. Even though Mori had a man's voice, it was difficult to tell who was saying what. Ahead of them, workers all wearing the same clothes had prepared the way to the disappearing place. The "heart," they'd decided to call it, partly because that was where the red pipes led.

The Berthelot brothers had been spared from wearing sanitary clothing. Instead, they were contractually obliged to wear clothing they deemed representative of their function and personality. Sar'h had put on an old navy-blue polyester toque even though it was warm outside. He was wearing a T-shirt from Ti-Claude's bar with a windbreaker the same shade of navy and a white and blue plaid jacket over the top. He was readying himself for someplace cold and windy, like being out fishing.

"Can I smoke one last one? I'm stressed as fuck," he puffed.

"Yes, no problem," came the reply from the other side of the screen. "Just not too close to the orange pipes."

Louis was trying to reassure his brother.

"It's not that bad, you'll see. Which of the two of us has been there, eh?"

"Well, that'd be you."

"Exactly."

Louis was in his work overalls with a net on his head. The embroidery on his right pec pocket proudly proclaimed *Lelarge Fisheries* in handwritten letters over three mismatched pens. His other pockets were filled with an assortment of rags and cloths.

Sar'h and Louis could see the three masked individuals clearly enough on the other side of the screen. They greeted them by their first names, but they didn't get a reply. They saw one of the characters pull out a tablet, tap in a few passwords, and swipe it in front of their face.

"OK. You can come in."

Nothing had changed, by the look of things, in the semitransparent screen, but they were able to pass through it.

There wasn't much further ado. They drove along in a golf cart, following the red pipes, until there it was.

"Here it is."

A metal wall circled around a central area three metres in diameter. Overhead, Louis Berthelot recognized the giant urchin he'd seen only from a distance. He was going to become its fuel.

Laurie opened the door and said an unsettled and sincere "good luck." There was nothing on the other side; it was invisible the whole way through, and even though the curve of the wall suggested a circular space, there was no wall opposite the door. When she saw the inside of the room, Laurie could give only a dissenting description of it: through the door frame she could see that she'd just opened her whole field of vision, only it was in ori and arranged like a set of Russian dolls, leaving plenty of room for other things. It was as if she was holding a mirror up to another, only no mirror appeared and the space between the images was taken up by refractions and shifting shades of light.

"What about you, Florence, what do you see?" Laurie held back from saying, the moment not allowing for the change of perspective.

"Follow me, Sar'h. There's nothing to be afraid of," Dishrag beckoned with consummate timing.

Louis had crossed the threshold. Nothing in his memory would allow him to find his bearings. Everything had disappeared. There was nothing but light and a sense of horizon; he walked, then ran across it, then he began to have his doubts. He couldn't remember anymore. He had a white, hazy recollection of the first time he disappeared. He began to think he'd put too much stock in that white. His memory had come up with it to fill a void.

Time wasn't passing any differently. He felt the seconds go by like seconds, and they stacked up to make minutes. He had a watch that was still working. Around him, everything stretched on forever, transparent. The light came out of nowhere; it was part of the air, now uniformly luminescent. In front of him, as far as the eye could see, everything was transparent and that transparency only allowed him to see a deeper transparency. He was like an ant in a glass sphere that was perfectly clear and bigger than the Earth.

It took him an hour to get used to it, then another to realize that he was no longer feeling a tiny bit hungry the way he had been when he came in, that he didn't need to take a leak or a dump, that his brother wasn't there, that he was starting to get scared, and that, the first time around, he might well have spent six months, like a dumbass, in the unending transparency. Who can say, inside a dream, how long the dream is lasting?

He lay down on the sense of horizon and tried to sleep. He didn't need to sleep. His watch told him it had been six hours. He'd signed up for four months. He saw what The Man Who Comes was up to: he'd walk out of there feeling like he'd had another long dream, and more folk like him, starved for cash, would agree to disappear too. He wouldn't be able to warn anyone.

He walked, ran, jumped, and didn't get tired. Two days in, he decided to kill himself, not out of sadness or despair, although he was feeling a bit of both; because he didn't know what to do with himself, either. He decided to kill himself just to see what would happen, if it would get him out of there or take him somewhere else. A compulsive gambler through and through, this was a bet he thought he could still win. The movement didn't come naturally: he wanted to jump high enough so he could tip his torso forward, dive headfirst into the sense of horizon, and break his neck. He tried. He stayed on his feet, every step of the way. The sense of horizon was spinning like there was no up, no down, no actual horizon.

He jerked off. He got a real kick out of seeing that it worked.

"At least there's that! Fuck, at least there's that!"

There was no echo. His voice didn't hit a thing.

He came and his sperm disappeared as soon as it pulled away from the meatus. There was no room in the unending transparency for anything other than him.

One month in, there was an impurity, a stain, a spot, a hope. The impurity worked against the rest of it. In this crack, the unending transparency revealed its changing nature. The entirety of Dishrag reached out toward this impurity, perhaps as distant as the stars he had forgotten. He told himself it was his brother, seen from far, far away. Even though it would be harder playing with himself around Sar'h, he reckoned it was still worth going to join him. He kept on walking.

The red pipes pumped out Dishrag's quest, and Sar'h's, too, in perfect symmetry. Scallops, clams, and urchins fed off that will to live on through space and time. They were turning it into a marvel.

MIX
Paper
FSC® C100212

Printed by Imprimerie Gauvin
Gatineau, Québec